SPIES WE KNOW

A NOVEL

LM REYNOLDS

This book is a work of fiction. Names, characters, business organizations, places, and incidents either are the product of the author's imagination or are used fictitiously. The author's use of names of historical or public persons, actual places, events, and characters are incidental to the plot, and are not intended to change the entirely fictional character of the work. Any resemblance to other actual persons, living or dead, or actual events is purely coincidental.

Published in the United States of America by Mirage Books 

ISBN 978-0-9862327-5-6

Cover design by Damonza
Cover photographs: Sunil Purushe, chaoss

For my dad,
Lt. Col. Eugene A. Merrell, USAF (Ret.)

Hence it is that which none in the whole army are more intimate relations to be maintained than with spies. None should be more liberally rewarded. In no other business should greater secrecy be preserved.

—Sun Tzu, The Art of War

Prologue

October, nine months ago
Mt. Carmel, Tennessee

Ken Massery signed the last of the paperwork and climbed into the truck's cab. He switched on the ignition and listened carefully as the engine growled to life and settled into its comfortable rumble. He reached for his logbook and drew a line to indicate the time he had transitioned from on-duty status—while the truck was being loaded—to actually driving. The man on the loading platform tucked his clipboard under his arm and raised his hand in an informal salute. Ken responded in kind before engaging the gears and lifting his foot from the brake. The twenty-six-foot truck eased away from the building and onto the roadway, rolling comfortably despite the thirty-thousand-pound payload in the van at his back.

He'd owned the rig for a month, having shelled out almost $60,000—and another grand for a fresh coat of paint—after his old truck finally gasped its last breath. He had saved enough for the down payment and took a loan for the rest. He figured the loan would be paid off in a year.

After driving a mile through the industrial complex, he braked to a stop at the gate and presented the paperwork to the guard. Satisfied, the guard waved him through, and Ken rolled up to the intersection, where he waited for the green light before turning right onto the busy highway. He did not notice the black Ford van pulling out of the Walgreens on the corner, nor the mud-spattered white Dodge van leaving the McDonalds a half-mile farther down the road. After a few miles of town traffic, he steered onto the entrance ramp for I-26 East, and ten minutes later, merged onto I-81 North. He began to relax, settling in for the six-hour drive.

Traffic was light and the weather clear, always a good omen for a drive through the mountains. He kept to the right lane, the speedometer at 65, and watched as the automobiles raced by on his left. He had always felt that the cars sped up as they passed, although it might have been just an optical illusion. But Ken couldn't really blame people for wanting to put some distance between themselves and his vehicle. It was quite an ordinary truck—with the exception of the orange hazmat placards. *Explosives,* he thought. *It's enough to scare the hell out of anyone, me included.*

Four hours later, Ken swung the rig into the truck stop just outside Greensboro. It was a regular stop on this run—the folks were friendly and not overly nervous about his cargo. He filled the tank and then moved the rig—to a space farther away from the pumps—before locking the doors and walking into the building. With a quick trip to the bathroom, a roast beef sandwich, and a big cup of coffee, he would be good to go for the two-hour leg to Fort Bragg.

Food and beverage in hand, he was whistling a tune he had just heard on the radio, liking its melody, as he walked back across the parking lot. He unlocked the door and climbed up to the seat, never hearing the approaching footsteps and not seeing the man until he was already shoving his way into the cab. Ken was a strong man and he swung his fist around, but the attacker was quicker and more skilled. The arm came up under his chin, pressing hard at the sides of his neck He made one last, futile effort to escape before losing consciousness and collapsing into the passenger seat.

The stranger slapped a precut strip of tape over Ken's eyes, another over his mouth, and yanked a hood over his head, grabbed his arms, and secured them behind his back. Folding Ken's legs, the attacker secured his ankles and taped his thighs to his calves before shoving him down to the floor.

Retrieving the keys from where they had fallen between the seats, the attacker started the engine and put the truck into gear. The hijacking had taken thirty-four seconds.

Pressure on the neck's carotid arteries will render an adult male unconscious in a matter of seconds, but the victim will typically regain consciousness—spontaneously—shortly after the pressure is released. When Ken Massery came to, his initial reaction was panic—he could neither move nor see. The recollection of the attack came flooding back when he realized that he was in a truck—his own truck, judging by the sound of the engine.

His neck and legs were cramping and he tried to shift his weight to a more comfortable position, but the space was so tight that he only made the pain worse. The ride went on for what seemed an eternity, slowing for several turns but never stopping, and otherwise running at a steady speed. He felt the downshift as the truck made another turn, and the crack of gravel hitting the undercarriage as the tires left the paved road. His pulse started racing then, thinking the worst, although his brain kept insisting that if the man wanted him dead, Ken wouldn't be having this conversation with himself.

The truck stopped, and he listened to the driver's door opening and the soft crunch of footsteps on loose gravel. The passenger door of the truck opened roughly, and he felt hands on him, his fear spiking as he imagined a knife or a bullet punching into him. He focused his thoughts on his kids, remembering their visit to the park yesterday, wondering if they would be okay growing up without a dad. He wanted so desperately to see their faces, to hear their giggles, to watch them grow up. He tried to talk ... to plead ... but all that came out was a muffled sob from the base of his throat and a burble of snot running from his nose.

He was quivering as the attacker heaved him out of the truck, and the thought that came to mind was how incredibly *strong* this man was. When the man dragged him across the gravel, then over to a grassy area, Ken's trembling exploded into full-blown shakes.

Ken jerked involuntarily as the hands began to move over his chest and down his back—like an officer frisking a suspect but more gentle ... almost intimate. When he felt the tug on his belt and then the zipper, he pissed himself.

The man grunted loudly and kept working Ken's pants down, oblivious to the sour stink of urine and finally caressing the pocket sewn to the inside of his jeans. He now knew exactly what the man wanted: the security key.

Ken was startled to learn that the hands were wearing gloves—not leather; they felt rubbery, like the ones his wife wore when cleaning. As the attacker fumbled with the pocket, his clothing brushed against Ken's bare arms and legs, and Ken realized that the man was covered in some sort of protective gear—stiff and crinkly.

He heard a vehicle drive up—a truck or a van by the rumble of its engine, heavy-duty—and a few minutes later, another. Doors squeaked in protest as they were opened, and Ken recognized the groan of the door at the back of the truck's box and knew all was lost. Even if he lived, he would never get another call for a government job. He was, in a word, fucked either way.

Squid parked his black van with its butt end close to the back of the truck, and Dancer's van arrived five minutes after that—both having stayed to watch the truck stop for any sign that someone had noticed the assault. By the time they arrived at the farmhouse, the man known as Sandbox had already retrieved the key from the driver's pocket. Squid climbed out of the van and watched as Sandbox inserted the key into the high-security lock and opened the truck's back panel.

The three worked quickly and wordlessly to move the load at the rear of the truck to the ground, making a path deeper inside to the cargo they were seeking. When they found the crates, they formed a bucket brigade—Sandbox lifting the crate and passing it to Dancer, who handed it down to Squid to load into the vans. They completed the transfer in thirty minutes—fifty into Squid's van, fifty into Dancer's, and then five large cardboard boxes into each. They had brought a small load of gardening supplies with them—mostly flats of flowers and peat moss. They covered the crates with sheets of landscaping plastic and topped off the heap with the peat and the plants. The ruse only had to survive a casual glance in the window. If someone actually inspected one of the vans, they were screwed.

Squid and Dancer switched on the vans' engines and turned them around to point back toward the road. Sandbox waited for the signal that they had stripped off the protective gear—coveralls, booties, gloves, and hoods—and stuffed them into the garbage bags before walking over to the shivering bundle that was Ken Massery. He wound a few more strips of tape around the man's head before cutting off his clothes. He laid the shredded fabric on the ground and began spraying. When he was finished, he moved to the truck's cab, wetting the entire interior, then up into the van, where he sprayed the alleyway they had created, and finally the boxes and crates that had been moved outside.

With the stench of bleach heavy in the air, Sandbox turned back to the crumpled man on the ground. He drew out a generic folding knife and pressed it into the terrified man's fingers. He was on the verge of feeling sorry for the guy—naked, cold, alone, incapacitated, and scared shitless—before remembering what had brought them both to this place. The man was lucky to be alive; Dancer had insisted that the truck driver was a witness—hooded or not—and should be eliminated. While Dancer had been outvoted, Sandbox and Squid remained alert to his every movement—never sure what might trigger the man's volatile temper ... or whet his sadistic appetite.

Sandbox sprinted back to Dancer's van and, as they sped away, stripped and added his gear to the bag. He lifted the burner phone from the console and sent an innocuous text to the man they called Tin Man:

Will pick up pizza for dinner.

It was one hour and three minutes since they had left the truck stop.

February, five months ago
Boston, Massachusetts

Farid Mahdavi felt a wave of nausea and signaled the waiter for another bottle of Perrier. The last few bites of pasta had soured on his tongue, and the bile in his stomach was threatening to erupt. According to the planned schedule, there should have been news by now. He glanced around at the other patrons in the restaurant, searching for the first sign of concern that would quickly sweep through the crowd. Instead, the room was filled with the pleasant buzz of conversation as couples and friends enjoyed their meals and each other's company. Something had gone terribly wrong.

The phone's ping alerted him to breaking news. *Finally*, he thought. He opened the alert and nearly vomited upon reading the headline. He stood abruptly and threw three twenties on the table, more than enough to cover the bill and tip, before shouldering through the crowd toward the door. Stepping outside, he looked back and saw that many customers now had their phones in hand.

He was tempted to stop in front of the restaurant, but feared his reaction to the bad news would attract unwanted attention. He walked briskly for half a block before settling next to a lamppost. Thumbing the phone, he willed the alert to change. It didn't. He muttered a stream of obscenities under his breath as he read.

Police Foil Harbor Attack
–by Elaine Lieberman

An unidentified male was shot and killed in Boston Harbor this evening during an apparent attempt to detonate an explosive device at a petroleum tank farm just north of downtown Boston. The northeast corner of the inner harbor is presently closed to all vessels and will remain closed while authorities process the scene.

Initial reports indicate that the suspect was navigating a small dinghy through the harbor while transporting a large quantity of explosives. Witnesses stated that as authorities were attempting to apprehend the suspect, he triggered one of the devices. Police responded with gunfire, killing him. The bomb fell into the water, where it exploded harmlessly. Sources close to the investigation stated that the suspect was carrying no identification.

The tank farms, located along Chelsea Creek and the Mystic River, have long been a source of concern for residents and law enforcement personnel.

> One official, speaking on condition of anonymity, was frank in his assessment. "This incident should be a wake-up call to the citizens of Boston. Having these facilities situated in such a densely populated area is an invitation to catastrophe. We just got lucky tonight."

Farid rubbed his hand across his brow and tried to gather his thoughts. The attack had been meticulously planned. They had been exceptionally careful to avoid raising questions or suspicions about their activities. He considered the young man who had sacrificed himself and wondered how he had been discovered. Surely, he thought, if surveillance had been in place, the authorities would have taken action before the boat entered the harbor proper. And more to the point, once the man was identified, would there be any evidence pointing toward others? Farid's palms were sweating as he browsed for further news.

I should book a flight, he mumbled. He admitted to himself that he would have been elated to hail a cab and go directly to the airport, taking a flight anywhere away from the United States. But he was quite familiar with the reach of American technology, and a sudden departure might raise a flag. The authorities' ability to unravel a seemingly perfectly camouflaged operation was a constant source of irritation—and fear.

He drew a deep breath and let it out slowly, reaching a decision. He would go about his everyday business as if nothing had happened, and in three days, book a flight for the following day. There would be other targets to come.

PART ONE

Menace

July, present day

Wednesday through Monday

Chapter 1

Wednesday afternoon
Washington, DC

I gave my name and fished my passport out of my purse. As much as I cherish my driver's license from the Commonwealth of Massachusetts, the document in my hand, with its distinctive blue cover and gold-stamped Great Seal, conveys greater meaning. It identifies me as an American. In this imposing building on C Street in Washington, DC, it just seems the more appropriate choice. One guard shoved my purse and overnight bag through the X-ray machine, while another reviewed the passport. I managed to step through the metal detector without setting off any alarms, and then retrieved my belongings and walked into the main lobby.

After giving my name at one of the desks positioned on the bustling public side of the lobby, I stepped back to wait for an escort. I'd been here on several occasions, and as always, my eyes were drawn to the plaques on the east and west walls. The inscriptions memorialized those who had lost their lives while in the service of their country. I was always saddened when I found that more names had been added, and today was no exception. The plaques are a grim reminder of the perils faced by our foreign-service personnel, and a bleak commentary about how the nature of those dangers has changed over the years. From the early 1800s until the mid-1960s, most were victims of tropical disease or natural disaster, with murder being a rarity. From the era of the Vietnam conflict until today, however, nearly all of the entries involved war, assassination, and terrorism.

My musings were interrupted by the arrival of my escort, and I turned my thoughts to more pleasant subjects. We exchanged idle banter as he guided me through the electronic gates, into the elevator, and to the door of my destination. He twisted the handle and showed me into the suite.

The woman at the desk gave a nod of recognition as I approached, and spoke briskly into the handset of her desk phone. "Lindsey Carlisle is here." She listened for a moment before rising to guide me to an inner office. "Go ahead and have a seat. He's just finishing an e-mail."

Former Ambassador Paul Marshfield glanced up and waved distractedly before returning to his keyboard. I took the proffered chair in front of his desk, and let my eyes wander while he typed. The office was more barren than I would have expected given his penchant for collecting indigenous artwork and handicrafts from his travels abroad.

I smiled when I spotted the framed photo on the credenza, with Paul, his deceased wife Maggie, my half-sister Cat Powell, her husband Tom, and me. Their arms were draped over each other's shoulders, and one of Cat's hands rested lightly against my cheek. In that picture-perfect moment, the crinkled eyes and wide smiles spoke of some shared amusement. It had been taken on July 3, when I was fourteen and on my first international trip, in the Sea Lounge restaurant at the Taj Hotel in Bombay.

My recollections of the scene in the photo are still vivid: the lush red carpet on the wide stairway rising from the ground floor of the hotel, the slowly rotating ceiling fans gently rippling the air, the view of the harbor and the throngs of people milling about on the waterfront promenade, the crisp white jackets of the waiters hovering over our table, and my first taste of Indian cuisine. I'd been enthralled.

The Ambassador stood suddenly and, wearing a broad smile, walked around the desk. Extending his right hand for a handshake, he embraced my shoulder with his left. "Cat keeps me up-to-date, but it is good to see you in person. You are looking well." He took the seat across from me, folded his hands loosely in his lap, and crossed one leg over the other. "I'm not sure that I ever thanked you properly for your assistance up in Boston."

"I'm just glad we figured it out in time. I'm proud to have played a part."

"Indeed. It was a tense business, and we're quite proud of you as well. Tell me, how are you?"

Tucking a wayward strand of hair behind my ear, I considered my response. "I have a recurring dream that I'm running through the streets of Boston trying to catch a faceless terrorist. I wake up tangled in the sheets, my heart pounding, and sweating like I've just been through an extreme workout. I didn't think about it much at the time, but we had a huge responsibility. And now I'm left wondering what would have happened if we had failed, and worrying about what will happen the next time."

The Ambassador's brow pinched in concern. "I have a couple of names of people you can talk to. They're very good."

"I'll keep it in mind." *Do I need a shrink? God, I hope not.*

I lead a mundane existence. I socialize with friends, travel when I can, and own a small IT company. We build computer applications and websites, and consult on network and security architecture. A few months earlier, I had a brush with an alternate lifestyle when I'd found myself involved in a frenzied effort to prevent a terrorist attack in Boston.

I'd been drawn into the tempest after the FBI came calling late on a Friday night last February. The lead agent had calmly informed me that my older sister, Cat, had been killed in an explosion at her home. They were treating her as a criminal. I was incensed and, over the course of the next week, had focused on discovering what really happened. Layer by intricate layer, the truth had emerged.

My sister had been trying to uncover a suspected terrorist plot, and was instead framed as a participant. She had staged her death, and that of her husband, to buy time and uncover the identity of the person who had fabricated the evidence. Circumstances brought together the unlikely alliance of my IT group, special agents from the FBI, analysts from the NSA, a former international airline director, Ambassador Marshfield, and my sister and her husband.

Together, we uncovered and prevented what could have been a catastrophic attack in Boston. And together we exposed the man who had framed Cat as a traitor. In the course of our efforts to unmask him, two members of her team had been killed. One of the victims was a longtime colleague of Cat, a man I'd met when I was thirteen. It still hurt.

In retrospect, it sounds like spy fiction. It should. My sister, as I learned during the course of those events, is a spy.

Chapter 2

I am generally relaxed when in Ambassador Paul Marshfield's company. He is one of my sister's oldest and dearest friends, and I've known him since I was a child. My experiences in February, however, have somewhat skewed my perceptions. On the one hand, I trust him completely and think of him as family. On the other hand, I'm not sure that I know him at all.

The Ambassador's call had come earlier today, as I was having breakfast with a client, and I'd let it go directly to voice mail. After retrieving the message, I left the office and rushed home to pack a bag. Three hours later I was on a flight to Washington, DC.

At the moment I was wondering why I was here. Several questions lingered with regard to February's events. While I had made a number of deductions, I still wasn't clear about Paul Marshfield's current position. He began his career as an officer in the Foreign Service and rose to become a two-time ambassador. For reasons unknown to me, he had abruptly exited the State Department, but had then been tapped by the president as a special envoy. Most recently, he had been residing in Berlin, and was rumored to be short-listed for a Cabinet post. He was in Germany when I had phoned to tell him of Cat's death.

From the moment I called with the news, Paul was channeled into the investigation about Cat, and ultimately directed our search and discovery of the planned attack in Boston. He was obviously involved with the intelligence community, and at a very high level, but I could not assemble all the pieces of that puzzle. I wanted to know more. I have a reputation for being irreverent and outspoken, and I'm not easily intimidated. In the arena of national security, however, I find myself in unfamiliar territory. I'm still trying to find the balance between wanting to satisfy my inquisitive nature and accepting that possession of certain knowledge can be a heavy burden. As a result, I'm torn between conflicting desires: to know everything, or to know nothing at all.

"I'm sure you're wondering why I invited you here today."

"I am curious, yes." I winced inwardly. *Had he read my thoughts?*

He took a deep breath. "A matter related to the February incident has come up. We would value your participation."

This was unexpected, and I'm sure my facial expression betrayed my surprise. "You've found Conrad27?" While we had been successful in preventing the actual attack, we'd been stymied in our attempts to uncover all of those involved. Of those still out there, the person associated with the e-mail conrad27.barrymore@gmail.com was the one we wanted most.

"Not exactly. But after months of silence on that account, someone sent him an e-mail yesterday. And he responded."

I sat up straighter. "Whoa. Where is he?"

"That's one of the things we'd like you and your team to explore with us. Are you interested?"

I sat pensively for a minute and weighed my answer. I had put my business on hold last February, losing a considerable amount of income as a result. My accounts manager had managed to smooth over relationships with our clients, but their patience had been tested to the breaking point. They wouldn't be nearly as understanding if we ditched them a second time.

Complicating the issue was that my accounts manager had eventually resigned out of frustration. I couldn't blame her. Out of the four full-time people in my company, she was the only one who wasn't involved with the February operation. She knew only that her boss and the two programmers had left town and weren't responding to phone or e-mail. In her shoes, I might have quit on the spot. I give her credit for staying as long as she did.

Now, with two employees, two part-timers, and myself to support, finances were going to be tight if I had to sustain another prolonged period of volunteer work for Uncle Sam. On the other hand, I love my country and am gratified by my role in February's events.

"I'm honored to be asked, and of course I'm interested. But before I commit, I have questions."

"Fire away."

"Who is 'we'?"

Paul leaned back and gently tapped his steepled index fingers against his upper lip. "That is a multifaceted question with a multifaceted answer, so some background is in order." He paused to assemble his thoughts. "While the sharing of intelligence has improved greatly since 9-11, some subjects are so sensitive that the reluctance to reveal them is understandable. It's not a matter of trust; it's a matter of security. When the tiniest misstep or slip of the tongue could cost a life or affect national security, the danger grows in direct proportion to the number of people with access to that sensitive information.

"This closely held information can create gaps and misunderstandings. You encountered some of that yourself, back in February. About a year ago, three of our intelligence leaders found themselves bandying about methods for sharing this high-level information without compromising what we know or those involved. They ultimately envisioned the creation of a very special unit, to be comprised of a select handful of people from each of their three agencies. It was, in my estimation, a rare show of genuine cooperation. They asked Cat to lead the unit's operations, and they asked me to be the intelligence liaison. We accepted."

"Does that mean that Cat no longer works for the CIA?"

"Technically, she is still an employee, but tasked to involvement in what we call 'Special Projects.' It helps keep her actual responsibilities under wraps. She maintains her relationship and connections to the Agency, but most of her effort is with the new unit."

"How do I fit? I'm not a government employee."

"As part of its mandate, the unit is encouraged to bring in talented or knowledgeable civilians as the need arises. The advantage in having external participants is that they offer a different perspective. After Cat's disappearance, you rather invited yourself to the party."

If his words were intended to make me feel chagrined, the tactic failed. I let the comment slide; I carried no regrets about what I had done.

"The others ... they are the same people we worked with in February?"

"They are. When we sequestered you at the safe house in Foxborough, we did so for your safety. But it also introduced you to some members of the unit and gave them an opportunity to evaluate you. It was unanimously agreed that you and your two cohorts would make a formidable addition to our roster of outside consultants."

I sat back and took a deep breath. While the balance in my bank account would scream in agony, the decision required little thought—the need to find Conrad27 was paramount. "I'm in. Foxborough again?"

"Yes, but only for a few days. For the longer term, it's not a reasonable solution, and we're exploring alternatives. And I hope that you will accept this as a gesture of our appreciation for all that you and your team accomplished." He lifted an envelope from the desk and handed it to me.

A coupon for some caffeine-rich beverage? A gift certificate from a pizza joint? Box seats for the Patriots? Ha! Curious, I tore the sealed flap and peeked inside. My jaw dropped; this was a complete surprise. The envelope held a check—a big one—from the US government, made out to my company. "I didn't expect this at all. We didn't do it for the money."

"I know you didn't. But if we want you to continue providing your time and expertise at our request, we cannot expect you to do so without compensation. I trust you find it to be a fair figure."

I hadn't even thought about calculating the hours we'd spent. I was about to inquire how he'd arrived at the number when the subtle buzz of his intercom interrupted our conversation.

"This will be Adrian, I think."

Adrian? Here? Tonight? Adrian Santori is a special agent with the FBI. Specifically, he is the agent who had told me of Cat's death. His role as the bearer of bad news left a sour taste, although we established a friendship during the course of February's events.

"I need for you to return to Boston first thing in the morning. If possible, I'd like you to clear your team to join you the following day. We will, of course, provide the transport."

So much for well-laid plans. I had envisioned a quiet night, with room service as an intimate restaurant and my computer as my dining companion. Tomorrow, I had planned to visit the memorials lining the National Mall, as I tried to do whenever visiting DC. In an age of political partisanship and self-aggrandizement, a visit to the Vietnam Memorial reminded me of the tragic cost of a shoot-first, aim-later, political strategy. After the Wall, the Lincoln Memorial always restored my faith in the power of the human spirit. I had planned a quiet dinner afterward, alone, at a favorite Georgetown restaurant.

"On a different subject, I'll arrange to have your bag delivered to the hotel, because I believe your dinner plans have now changed. Adrian wants to meet with you." He strode over to the door and extended a hand to the man entering the room.

How in the world could he know that? And then, thunderstruck, I realized that Adrian must be a member of Paul's phantom "unit."

Adrian was tall, ruggedly good-looking, and his dark hair was damp—as if he'd just showered. I stood, my palms suddenly clammy, and brushed them over my skirt before offering my hand. The green eyes sparkled in merriment as he reciprocated with a firm shake. "Miss Carlisle, it's a pleasure to see you again."

Chapter 3

Wednesday evening
Georgetown, Washington, DC

Adrian hailed a cab for the fifteen-minute ride into Georgetown, a historic, upscale neighborhood in the northwest quadrant of DC. We exchanged idle chitchat, as if we were strangers randomly paired to endure sitting side by side in a cab. I asked how he was enjoying the summer; he inquired likewise. He asked about my jogging route; I asked if he still drove the BMW. The pedantic conversation continued until the taxi stopped in front of 1789, one of the area's most distinguished restaurants.

Stepping onto the sidewalk, I chuckled inwardly at a memory that suddenly bubbled to the surface. In the basement of the building was the Tombs, a pub frequented by students at Georgetown University. I'd spent several weekends with a former boyfriend attending school here, and we'd consumed our share of burgers and brew downstairs. The Tombs was several worlds apart from the tony 1789 restaurant on the floors above.

The maître d' smiled politely as we approached, then consulted the reservations list. "Yes, Mr. Santori, you'll be dining in the Wickets room this evening." While waiting to be shown to our table, I overheard the maître d' explain to a walk-in couple that they would experience a two-hour wait. I was amazed that Adrian had scored reservations at the last minute.

We were escorted to an intimate table in the corner. Adrian accepted the menu and consulted the wine selection, asking my preference. His last attempt to offer me a glass of wine had not gone well—I had accused him of eavesdropping, and he had ushered me into the local FBI office—so I deferred to his judgment. I studied his face as he interacted with the waiter and, for the second time today, found myself wondering why I was here.

He had asked if I would have dinner with him once my part in the investigation was complete, but had been recalled to Washington before we could schedule. I confess that I was attracted to the man; the air tingled with electricity whenever we were near one another. And I had grown to care about him ... a lot. The ring he wore on his left hand, however, tempered any further development of our relationship.

"It's the Ambassador's table," Adrian confessed. "He has a standing reservation for eight thirty on Wednesday night. If he's not in town, he cancels before five. Tonight, he offered it to me."

Keeping my voice low, I leaned closer. "You've heard about the e-mail?"

"Yes. The originator, we believe, is in Boston. I'm not sure if the Ambassador told you, but I'm flying up with you tomorrow. Once we locate him, or her, I'll be there for the interview."

I absorbed that Adrian was traveling to Boston. "I'll

assume that, um, Mr. P still hasn't been cooperative." I stumbled over the words, unsure of the protocol for using actual names in a public space.

"Mr. P?" Adrian's brows knitted for a moment before relaxing in comprehension. "Ah! Not a word. I can't imagine the mind-set that steered him down that path, and he's presently not inclined to offer us any insight. It's up to us to untangle it."

Roger Pulaski—Mr. P—had been Cat's boss prior to his arrest for treason and murder. Last month, Cat had stormed into a conference room at CIA Headquarters and confronted the man, then watched with barely disguised glee as Adrian placed Roger under arrest. She was still fuming about the man's betrayal of his colleagues and his country.

Adrian deftly steered the conversation away from Roger and into more personal terrain as he began sharing details of his childhood in Texas. I stopped twisting my napkin, a habit I exhibit when I'm nervous, and immersed myself in the narrative. I regaled him with a few stories of my own, and found myself laughing and enjoying his company as if I had known him for years. I'm embarrassed to admit that, aside from my first taste of the delicious roasted squab, I actually remember very little about the food.

We left the restaurant shortly after ten, and Adrian suggested that we walk to my hotel, a scant fifteen minutes away on the opposite side of the Potomac River. We strolled beneath the trees lining Prospect Street, then down the hill on the cobblestones of Thirty-Fifth. Crossing M Street, we were funneled onto Key Bridge.

The night was perfectly clear, and we stopped midway across the bridge to admire the view. Beneath us the Potomac flowed swiftly toward Chesapeake Bay, its water shimmering with the reflected lights from the bridge. Georgetown's bluffs rose behind us, with the spires of the university's Healy Hall dominating the cityscape. To the southeast, the Washington Monument peeked above its surroundings, and the Kennedy Center shone in the foreground. The rumble and roar of the cars beside us, however, was an unwelcome intrusion. When we reached the hotel, I was eager for the quiet of my room.

I stopped short of the entry and faced him. "Thank you for the evening. It was lovely."

His lips formed a half-smile. "Yes, it was. Thank you for the company."

As I moved toward the door, he laid his hand on my arm. I turned back to face him, and he moved his hand up to my face, his fingers lacing into my hair. My heart hammering wildly, I started to protest ... and then his lips found mine. "Let's get you checked into your room," he whispered.

He stood behind me, close, as I handed my credit card to the desk clerk. The heat was rolling off me in tsunami-size waves, and my scribble on the registration was illegible. The clerk eyed me knowingly and asked, "Two keys?"

We retrieved my luggage from the bellman and tried to maintain a normal pace as we headed to the elevator. Taking my hand, he held it for what seemed like an interminable ride to the tenth floor. He pulled the key from my grip and opened the room door, ushering me inside. When the door closed, he leaned back against it and looked at me intently. I found myself holding my breath. I was wildly attracted to this man. But I have an unbreakable rule about becoming involved with married men.

In a voice so quiet that I strained to hear, he said, "My wife died several years ago. It's been a long time since I've been with anyone."

I waited for him to continue. He had held onto this secret for months, and I was afraid of rushing him. I stood mute, unsure what to say or do.

"I want to tell you about her—but some other time. Right now, I just want you."

I stepped toward him, and suddenly he had his arms around me, kissing me in spurts and gulps both passionate and gentle. I lost myself then as we explored and tasted each other. I have never experienced anything so exquisite.

Afterward, he lay on his side with his head propped up on his hand and ran his index finger down my spine. "I have to go," he said. "I need to check my e-mail and pack a bag. I'll pick you up in the morning."

I sat up and saw his eyes drift to my breasts. I felt my cheeks flush and modestly pulled the sheet up. "No need to pick me up," I said. "It's out of your way, and you'll be short on time anyhow. I'll take the Metro." He pulled the sheet away and wrapped his arm around my waist.

An hour later, I watched him dress and gather his keys and his weapon. He leaned over me, brushing his lips against my forehead. "Good night, Lindsey; sleep well." And he was gone.

Chapter 4

Thursday morning
Northern Virginia

My intention was to take the Metro from Rosslyn station to Reagan Airport for the eight thirty flight, so it was just before six when I groggily stopped by the front desk to turn in my key card. On a whim, I asked the clerk about the frequency of trains. She glanced at my wheelie bag and grimaced, explaining that the station was closed for two weeks. *I should have looked it up. Woulda, shoulda.* I was asking about a cab when an older gentleman in line offered a ride. He looked harmless enough; I accepted.

The man had a swarthy complexion and his English bore a slight accent that I interpreted as Eastern European or Russian. We chatted amiably during the ten-minute ride down the GW Parkway until he drove past the airport exit.

"You missed the exit," I said, glancing at him. And in that moment, seeing the butt of a gun peeking out from beneath his jacket, I felt a bolt of terror.

He reached over with his right hand and grabbed my wrist, hard. In a low, hoarse voice he said, "You have no idea what you've stepped into. You're meddling in matters where you don't belong. So now you're going to tell me about your meeting with Paul Marshfield."

The shock that he knew the Ambassador's name—and that he knew of my visit—took my breath away. The adrenaline kicked in, and I wrenched my arm free. "Get the fuck away from me! Stop the car!"

His eyes were cold and unblinking as he rasped, "Tell me about your meeting, Lindsey."

Seeing his hand moving toward the gun, I gasped, and then reacted. In one fluid motion, I swung my legs up and around and kangaroo-kicked him. His head slammed hard into the window. His other hand flew off the wheel, and I frantically reached out, fighting the seat belt and somehow managing to yank the wheel hard to the left. The tires screamed as the car careened into the left lane and into a spin. The car lost its grip on the pavement and started to tumble.

Chapter 5

Thursday morning
Near Reagan National Airport

Adrian parked and set out for the terminal, thumbing his phone to Lindsey's number as he walked. Four rings and voice mail. Two minutes later, he tried again. Still no answer. He strode into the terminal, half expecting to find her near the counter. He scanned the area and smiled to himself, imagining her still curled up in bed. He found the number for the Marriott and asked to be connected to Ms. Carlisle's room.

"Ms. Carlisle has already checked out, sir."

Thinking quickly, he said, "I'm supposed to meet her at the airport, and she isn't here yet. Could you tell me what time she checked out?"

"One moment, sir."

Seconds ticked by, and a new voice finally came on the line. "Sir? I'm the on-duty manager. You're inquiring about Ms. Carlisle? I'm sorry, but we can't give out personal information."

"I can appreciate that. My name is Adrian Santori. I'm a special agent with the FBI. You can call them to verify if you need to; I'll hang on. But Ms. Carlisle and I are scheduled to fly up to Boston on an eight thirty flight. She was staying alone in the hotel, and she's not yet at the airport. I'm concerned. All I want to know is what time she checked out."

The manager made a decision. "At 6:04 a.m., sir. She should be there by now."

"Would the desk clerk know if she took a cab?"

"I'll ask. Can you hold?"

"Yes; any information they have would be helpful."

When the manager came back on, Adrian learned that the desk clerk had overheard Lindsey accepting a ride from a man in line behind her. *What the hell?* He expressed his gratitude to the hotel staff and hung up. He called Lindsey's number again. No answer.

The officer had found the purse fifty feet away from where the car came to rest. Busy with the scene, she had ignored the first two calls. On the third call, however, she opened the bag and glanced at the caller ID. *Santori—FBI.* She walked over to the sergeant and held the phone in front of his face, showing him the phone log.

"Three calls, a few minutes apart. She has him in her contacts as FBI. Next time it rings, maybe you should answer."

The sergeant nodded and took the phone. "It could be the Farming Bureau of Ithaca for all we know. What do you have so far?"

"She was traveling at a good clip, but the witnesses say she wasn't going any faster than anyone else. The two cars behind both said she veered suddenly into the left lane and went into a spin ... rolled over before it hit the guardrail.

The plates don't match, which may suggest it's stolen. Suitcase came out when the trunk popped open during the roll. Driver's license is from Massachusetts. And one more thing."

The sergeant grunted. "There's always one more thing," he said.

"Yes, sir. A man in the northbound lane swears he saw a man crawl out of the car and walk away from the wreck. He says he has video."

"Someone walked away?"

"That's what he says. He gave a pretty good description, too, and he sounds credible. He works at Langley."

The sergeant rolled his eyes upward and laughed. "He probably set the whole thing up and our victim is a Russian spy. Go ahead and get the video." He was going to say more when the phone in his hand rang. The same caller ID. He flicked the icon to answer. "Mr. Santori?"

Adrian's heart skipped a beat on hearing the stranger's voice on Lindsey's phone. "And you are?"

"Sergeant Laski, US Park Police. Could you tell me your relationship to Ms. Carlisle?"

Adrian's pulse was now racing. *Police?* He fought to keep his words calm and deliberate. "I'm a special agent with the FBI. Ms. Carlisle is consulting on a case, and we were supposed to meet at the airport. Is she okay? What's happened?"

"She was southbound on the GW and flipped her car. They've transported her to the hospital."

Paul took in a deep breath, held it, and exhaled slowly. "Sergeant, she didn't have a car. She checked out of her hotel this morning, and one of the guests offered her a ride. I've just spoken with the manager at the Marriott."

It was the sergeant's turn to be surprised. "We're near the next exit south of the airport. Maybe she decided she didn't want to fly. How can you be sure she didn't have a car?"

"I'm positive. She flew in yesterday afternoon, took a cab into the city, and I took her to dinner last night. No car. Talk to the hotel manager ... she was trying to get to the airport. Which hospital, and what's her condition?"

Dinner last night? Four calls? More to that story, the sergeant thought. "They took her to Medstar Washington. She was conscious, but pretty banged up. I don't know any more than that."

"Sergeant, do you have cameras along the parkway?"

The cop thought about it. "There's nothing operational on the parkway, but Reagan has cameras in strategic locations. Don't know if any of them would have a good angle. There are also several cams down in the area of the Marriott."

"Thanks. One more thing."

The sergeant shook his head in resignation. *Always one more thing.* "What's that?"

"Could you send a uniform over to watch her until I can get there? I'm going to bring a team over to you."

The sergeant thought about it for a half-second. This was *Washington* after all. "We'll need a statement when she wakes up, so I think that can be arranged."

"And, sergeant, I can guarantee that whatever happened, it wasn't of her choosing."

Chapter 6

Thursday morning
Georgetown, Washington, DC

Paul Marshfield left the office five minutes after Adrian's call, speed walking down the corridor and through the parking garage, only to end up caught in traffic with no good shortcut. He grappled with the notion that Lindsey might have been abducted, his intuition screaming that he had set the wheels in motion by meeting with her. He phoned her sister Cat who, while seeming to take the news stoically, was almost certainly in a rage inwardly. She would be gunning for bear.

After enduring forty-five minutes of the snail's pace drive, he went straight to the ER. After explaining the situation—that Lindsey was from out of town and like a daughter to him—they guided him to her bedside, amid the chaos of rolling beds and tubes and beeping machines and medical personnel. She was awake and her eyes were open—if you could call it that, mere slits in a face that was puffy and bruised and split with lacerations. The next thing he noticed was the collar around her neck.

Hearing his voice, she tried to sit up, but the nurse restrained her. "Hang on there, ma'am! Let us finish taking care of you. Please try not to move."

Paul saw Lindsey's fingers flutter, and then she stretched her left leg, and he breathed a long sigh of relief. She opened her palm—fingers reaching out—and Paul made eye contact with the nurse. He received a short nod, and Paul moved over to the bed, grasping Lindsey's hand and squeezing it reassuringly.

Another nurse approached, holding a chart in the crook of his arm, and looking at Paul questioningly. "Are you her father?"

He shook his head. "Almost. Close family friend. She lives in Boston."

The nurse pointed his chin toward the door, signaling that he wanted a conversation out of Lindsey's hearing. Paul squeezed Lindsey's hand again, and he and the nurse stepped away and into the path of one of the ER physicians.

"She looks worse than she is," the doctor said. "She's very lucky. There's always a danger of head trauma and internal bleeding with something like this, so we ran a complete CT scan—chest, abdomen, pelvis, neck, and head—all negative. The first responders put her in a cervical collar at the scene, and we'll want to leave that on for a few days. She will probably have ligament strain in her neck—whiplash—and the collar will help.

"Both bones in her left forearm are broken. She'll need surgery; we'll get her in there as soon as practical. This is a trauma center, so urgency dictates timing. She has a concussion and a good-size gash on her head that we'll take care of shortly, and we'll clean up all those small lacerations. She also has the usual seat-belt burns, which is a good sight better than what we would be facing if she'd not been wearing one. Her heart rate and blood pressure are somewhat elevated, which is to be expected given the physical stress to her body. We'll monitor her for any change that would indicate a problem. Questions?"

"Assuming no problems, how long will she be in here?"

"Assuming, as you said, we should be able to repair her arm today. We'll keep her overnight for observation, but make no mistake—she's had a serious jolt to her system. She might go home tomorrow, but she will be feeling the effects for a while."

Adrian arrived at the hospital in midafternoon, hot and sweaty after working the evidence from the crash and interviewing witnesses—and dog-tired after a night with little sleep. He and Paul had exchanged texts and calls throughout the day, Paul keeping him updated on Lindsey's condition. The surgeons had repaired her forearm, they had shaved an oval on the side of her head to stitch the gash, her face was a patchwork of small cuts, and she was bruised all over. The doctor had told Paul she was lucky. Lucky, indeed.

He usurped Paul's place in the room and moved the chair to Lindsey's bedside. She was asleep, her chest rising and falling rhythmically. He laid his hand lightly on hers, leaned his head back, and was asleep within minutes.

I opened my eyes, confused, my brain trying to make some connection with the sights and sounds around me. My eyesight was blurry, but I spotted Adrian in a chair next to my bed, his head crammed against his shoulder and breathing softly. His presence calmed me until the memory of the morning's events flooded back into my consciousness. I shifted position and groaned involuntarily as a hot lick of pain shot through my head.

Adrian sat up, startled, and then gingerly took my hand. I squeezed his fingers and said, "Some way to begin the morning, huh?" My voice was hoarse, and the timbre seemed foreign to me. *Anesthesia,* I thought.

"You had us scared for a bit. What happened? Can you remember?"

"I screwed up,' I rasped, and related every detail I could think of, up until the moment when the car went out of control. "Adrian, I got into a car with him ... a complete stranger. He knew I was staying at the Marriott. He knew my name. How could I have been so stupid? Oh, my God. He was just a nice older man with a suitcase, and then it was like someone flipped a switch. He was so ... so ... cold. Oh, my God."

"You got away; that's what's important. And you'll never get in a car with a stranger again, will you?"

I shook my head. "Never." Unbelievable. I disregarded a rule I'd been taught since I was two.

He screwed up his face and spread his hands. "And what were you thinking, grabbing the steering wheel like that? Are you crazy?"

I shuddered. "No. I was terrified, but I wasn't going to just submit. I'd seen his face; he had a gun. I didn't think I had much of a choice."

Adrian smiled grimly. "You can be quite formidable, I'll give you that."

"I've learned a few moves over the years. I also hurt like hell. Did you find him? The cop told me that when they got there, I was the only one in the car. They thought I was driving."

"Well, you have to admit that you did have the wheel." He grinned and I tried to grin back, but my face felt like it had gone ten rounds with Muhammad Ali.

"No. No trace of him," he continued. "We're processing some footage from cameras at and near the Marriott. And we have some video from the crash. One of the witnesses, who was three cars back, has a dash cam and recorded the whole thing. Another witness, going northbound, has the scene after the crash. Can you believe it? Everybody wants to go viral. It turns out that your driver crawled out of the car, climbed over the guardrail in the median, and limped across to the other side of the highway. He's in the wind."

Chapter 7

Thursday afternoon
Marblehead, Massachusetts

Matt Pierce felt the vibration in his pocket and looked at the screen. *Crap. Not good.* He texted back, 5 min, and walked across the hall to the study. Jason Bigby was hunched over his keyboard, absorbed—as he often was—in some gibberish on his screen.

"I thought I'd whip us up a bite to eat for lunch. Interested?

Jason didn't even look up. "Sounds great," he said. Which is what he answered to almost every question asked of him when he was in the middle of writing software code.

"I'm running to the store. Need anything?"

"Nope; sounds great."

Matt hopped into the car and set out for the small market downtown, or at least what passed for downtown in Marblehead. The entire town occupied a little less than twenty square miles, almost sixteen of which were water. That left only four square miles of land mass, so walking anywhere was hardly an issue. But he wanted privacy, and amid the local abundance of walkers and joggers, it was hard to find. Thus, the car.

He pressed the screen to dial the last number in the log and heard the man they called Dancer say, "We have a problem."

"Which is?"

"The package was damaged en route."

Matt swore, drummed his fingers on the steering wheel, and tried to think of a response that did not involve killing the man. Finally, he said, "Is it recoverable?"

"Doubtful. It wasn't insured originally, but it is now."

He swore again, interpreting the response to mean that the target now had someone with her. He wished he could just ask what the *fuck* was going on, but he didn't dare, not with NSA looking over everyone's shoulder. So the jabbering continued, in some inane on-the-fly coded language that left each trying to interpret the other.

"Do you know where the package is?"

"Affirmative."

"Can you recover it?"

"Negative."

"Well, try to keep your eyes on it while I think about what we should do next.

"I could eliminate the issue entirely."

"Don't even think about it, man. They'll head back up to Boston; I'm sure of it. I'll reach out to Tin Man, but I think you should plan to get your butt up here ASAP."

Jason Bigby watched in admiration as Matt sprinkled the tarragon into the aioli and began separating the lobster from its shell. Matt added the finishing touches to the dish and handed it across the counter with a flourish and a wink, as if to say *gotcha*, which was certainly true enough. Jason's last serious relationship had ended over a year ago, and he liked the comfort of having a partner. The past two months with Matt had been like a dream. That his new partner was also a great cook was the cherry on top of the sundae.

The phone rang, and he looked at the caller ID, mildly surprised at the 202 area code for Washington, DC. As a general rule, he ignored calls from persons unknown, since a legitimate caller would leave a message. But Lindsey was in Washington and had, on more than one occasion, been known to misplace her phone. He picked up, ready to give her a dash of grief, and got his second surprise. The caller was Adrian Santori.

Adrian broke the news gently, aware of Jason's deep friendship with Lindsey. Jason dropped his fork and gestured wildly to Matt, who hurried around the kitchen island and wrapped his arms around his distraught friend.

"But you're sure she's going to be all right?" Jason inquired into the phone. After a pause, he asked, "When will she be coming back?" Another pause, then, "So we're delayed a day. That's fine; I'll be ready." Then, "I will, absolutely." He ended the call and leaned against the counter.

Matt looked at him with concern. "What's happened?"

"Lindsey was in a bad accident this morning. She's in the hospital."

"What? Is she okay?"

"Something happened on her way to the airport ... I don't have the whole story. She was attacked, and the car she was in flipped over. That's all I know. They said she'll be fine, but her arm is broken, she has a concussion, and she's terribly bruised up."

"My God, that's horrible ... but at least she's not badly hurt. Are you traveling down to see her?"

"No. She will probably be back on Saturday. So it looks like you and I will have an extra day before I have to leave. Isn't that grand?"

Matt considered the news in light of what Dancer had told him. Matt and his crew had been watching Lindsey Carlisle for months, going so far as to bug her house and office. At one point, they had even discussed the possibility of having Matt strike up a relationship with her. Certainly he was handsome and charming enough. But in the end they deemed it too risky, believing that there was a strong likelihood that Cat Powell would have eyes on her little sister. Instead, they targeted Jason.

Matt, fully heterosexual, was not pleased or even amused at the idea of establishing an intimate relationship with another man. But they had ultimately persuaded him to take on the role of someone who was unsure of his sexuality. It would help explain his discomfort and, potentially, touch Jason's emotions.

It was clear that Jason cared a great deal for Lindsey. Through him, Matt had learned much about her life ... although the most important detail still eluded them: the whereabouts of Cat Powell. When Lindsey had called yesterday to say that she was going to DC, Jason had told Matt. Thinking that they had finally caught a break, Matt had dispatched Dancer to follow her.

Matt now had a better understanding of the story behind Dancer's phone call. He plastered on a broad smile and said, "I'm so glad to hear she's okay and will be back soon." He breathed a sigh of relief, but not for the reasons Jason thought. Lindsey Carlisle was more valuable alive than dead, and Jason was going to lead him right to her safe house.

Chapter 8

Friday afternoon
Washington, DC

I am not sure that anyone sleeps well in a hospital, but my overnight stay was fraught with demons, the aches and pains from the rollover only adding to the misery. When they released me, I was happy to leave.

Adrian drove me to his town house and assisted me up the stairs and into the large master bedroom. His place was comfortable, tastefully decorated, and masculine—but well short of the man-cave category—and it was clean and tidy without being obsessively so. I lay down carefully on the bed, off-kilter from the pain meds and watchful of the cast on my arm. I had already hit myself a dozen times, adding more bruises to my collection.

He made sure I was comfortable before telling me he would be in the next room catching up on work and that I should give a shout if I needed anything. I eventually drifted into la-la land, awakening four hours later. Turning my head, I saw him on the small sofa by the window, legs stretched out over an ottoman and computer in his lap.

"What's up?" I asked.

He looked up from the screen and smiled. "I guess *you*

are, sleepyhead. Hungry?"

I was starving and admitted it. He helped me downstairs, where I took another pain pill and watched him prepare dinner. He was comfortable in the kitchen, deftly chopping, blending, sautéing, and producing a perfect salmon in a delicate dill sauce. He poured himself a glass of wine and handed me a glass of water.

"You're feeling better."

He said it as a statement, not a question. Considering my present state, I realized just how bad I must have looked in the emergency room. I decided to be diplomatic. "I am. Much better."

"I don't want to push," he said, "but things are developing fast. I have to get up to Boston. I don't want to leave you here alone, and I would feel much better if you were at the safe house. Could you manage an airplane in the morning?"

The absolute last thing I wanted to do was to get on a flight ... or any mode of transport, for that matter. But that was just me being selfish; there were greater issues at stake. "I can make it," I replied, not sure if I really believed it.

He picked up his glass, swirling the wine absently, then stretched out his left hand and covered mine. I blinked hard. He wasn't wearing the ring. His eyes found mine and held them as he spoke. "My wife and I were living in Texas in 2001. That September, we took some vacation time and went to New York City. I had just finished my law degree, and one of my professors was giving a guest lecture at NYU. I wanted to be there, and my wife had never been to the city. So on the morning of September 11, I took a cab to NYU, and my wife took a cab to the World Trade Center.

She wanted to stand on the observation deck and look out over the rest of the world. She was so excited."

He took a deep breath and looked away. "Her name was Elena. We never found her." A tear leaked from his left eye, and he brushed it away. "Two weeks later I submitted my application to the FBI."

My hand had moved involuntarily over my mouth, and I realized that I was holding my breath. *Oh my God.* I sat frozen in my chair.

"It's not something I talk about. For a while, it consumed me. I wore the ring to remind me and to try to keep her close. Over time, it just became part of my skin, and wearing a ring was more convenient than explaining why I wasn't interested in a relationship with Debbie or Sue or Nancy. I was just waiting for someone who felt right. I don't know if you and I would be the perfect couple, but I'd like to find out."

My voice was unsteady. "I'd like that, too," I managed to say.

Chapter 9

Saturday morning
En route to Boston, Massachusetts

We took different paths at the American Airlines ticket counter, as Adrian followed the procedures allowing him to carry a gun aboard a commercial aircraft. I checked in at the kiosk and followed the maze leading to the luggage scanners. A laptop bag I could manage, but there was no way I could carry a suitcase on board. I knew I was attracting a lot of attention—I looked a mess. One helpful airline employee rushed over with a wheelchair, which I politely refused. The kidnapping had terrified me, but I would not allow it to turn me into an invalid.

I reconnected with Adrian on the secure side of the TSA checkpoint and boarded the flight. We were separated by a dozen rows for the flight to Boston, my seat by a window in the rear and his midcabin on the aisle. I am comfortable with airplanes and frequently fall asleep before the wheels leave the tarmac. On this flight, however, I was feeling the residual effects of my encounter and repeatedly glanced at every person within my field of vision. None of my fellow passengers seemed threatening, but I had discovered how easily I could be duped.

Leaning my head against the window, I looked out over the tapestry of the terrain and watched as first Philadelphia, and then New York, silently slid beneath us. I dozed off somewhere over Long Island Sound and woke as the tires bumped the runway on touchdown at Logan Airport.

Adrian pressed his phone to his ear and signaled for me to wait, allowing the other passengers to disembark first. A flight attendant made her way toward us from the rear of the aircraft, curious about our dawdling. Adrian held up his badge and quietly advised the woman that we would be off the airplane momentarily. I watched as she went back to the rear and picked up the handset for the plane's interphone.

Adrian's voice was urgent. "Give me your phone and laptop. You'll get them back later, but we can't have them at the safe house."

Having been through the drill once before, I complied without hesitation. He steered me out of the aircraft, stopping briefly to lean into the cockpit. "Thanks for the ride, Captain. Have a safe flight to Atlanta."

The captain turned in his seat and offered his hand. "Thank you, Agent Santori. You stay safe as well."

Adrian was vigilant, studying the faces and movements of the people around us as we hurried through the terminal. I noticed him give the barest of nods to a face in a sea of travelers, and tried to match his stride as we headed first to baggage claim and then the exit. Crossing the roadway at the front of the terminal, he walked toward a cluster of black SUVs parked at the far end of the drop-off zone. The State Police at Logan are relentless in chasing away private cars attempting to wait in front of the terminal, so the fact that they were parked said a great deal about the credentials of these vehicles.

A nondescript man in a navy jacket stepped out of one SUV and tossed the keys to Adrian. Adrian, in turn, handed him my laptop bag and climbed into the driver's seat. We pulled away from the airport as a convoy of three, our vehicle tucked in the middle, and sped south through the Ted Williams tunnel and out of the city.

Free of the highway chaos downtown, the lead car sped forward, and the other dropped back, until both were indistinguishable in the river of automobiles and trucks streaming down the Southeast Expressway. Adrian's features were taut, his eyes darting left and right as he assessed our position.

"Why didn't we stay together?" I asked.

"We would do that if we anticipated an overt action. But right now, we're more concerned about who might have followed you, and why. We're looking for anyone who appears to be tailing us, or any indication of leapfrog surveillance. In a pack, we're very noticeable. Spreading out a bit gives us a better opportunity to spot anything out of the ordinary."

I nodded sagely, as if I was familiar with these procedures, while deducing his meaning. I'd watched enough television to know that when multiple cars are following a suspect, they try to avoid detection by exchanging positions ... leapfrogging one another.

"Who's in the other cars?"

"Jones is in one. He met up with your team, and they're with him. There's a new player in the other. Her name is Jasmine, but everyone just calls her Jazz. She's been with the Bureau for seven years—two in Memphis, four in Chicago, and a year here in Boston. From everything I've heard, she's a real rock star."

Jones was a close associate of my sister, Cat. I'd first met him when I was thirteen, the result of an unplanned meeting in one of the seediest areas in Boston. I'd been frightened by the neighborhood, and my heart had pounded crazily when Cat rolled down the window and asked for Jones. He was a mountain of a man, and the throng of people had parted as he approached. My fear spiked when he rested his muscled forearms on the window frame and dangled his enormous black hands into the car. I remember being fascinated by the heavy gold rings he wore on all fingers save his thumbs. At that moment, I'd wished desperately to be anywhere but in that place. Then he'd winked and, in an astonishingly gentle voice, wished me a happy birthday.

Back in February, Jones had conspired with Cat to arrange her disappearance, and he had been critically injured in the explosion that took the lives of two other agents from their group. His courage and integrity had earned my respect; his steadfast support of my sister earned my trust.

As we moved farther south, the traffic grew more porous. Approaching the I-95 interchange, I was surprised when we stayed in the center lane instead of taking the exit south. In a dizzying sequence of turns, we left the interstate, turned north on Route 1 into Dedham, looped back east and then south, and picked up I-93 again a few miles east of where we'd exited. This time, we took the ramp for Route 1 southbound, toward Foxborough.

Adrian's mobile chirped. He activated the call on his

headset and, after listening intently for a few minutes, asked, "Just the one car? Where is it now?"

My uneasiness grew as I listened to the one-sided conversation. If my interpretation was correct, we were being followed.

After disconnecting, he broke into a wide grin. "Slick. See the little box in the back window? And the ones mounted just above the passenger windows? Those are cameras, and they've been streaming video to our servers. The software scans the traffic and keeps a running tabulation of every car it finds, along with that vehicle's proximity in relation to ours."

I turned to stare at the small black cubes. "Seriously?"

"Yep. It's pretty cool: facial recognition for cars. The camera idea has been around for a while, but the software application is relatively new."

"So someone *was* following us? Where is he?"

He chuckled. "Stuck at a malfunctioning set of lights in Dedham. It seems that just as we hit every green light going through town, he hit every red."

"You hacked into Dedham's electrical grid?"

His eyes widened in mock horror. "Now who would ever do such a thing?"

My feelings about this were conflicted. We as Americans have enemies who would like nothing better than to destroy our way of life. I get that. And because I'm in the IT business, I understand the nuances of the information grid. My sister's in the spy business; she appreciates the power of that information. Still, I often wonder what we have given up to accomplish this all-seeing capability. While my sister has no such doubt, it makes me exceedingly uncomfortable to realize that there really is a Big Brother watching.

I will admit, however, that recent encounters were confounding my perspective. I wanted the man who had kidnapped me to be found and punished. And I recalled a young man from last February, arms outstretched with a block of C-4 explosive in his palm, just before the police shot him. I shuddered at the memory of how close we had come to a catastrophe a few months ago. I shoveled my skepticism into a corner of the darkest room in my brain and slammed the door.

Chapter 10

Saturday morning
Foxborough, Massachusetts

The rambling house near Lake Cocasset, secluded from neighbors and invisible from the road, stood as I remembered it from my previous visit. While not impenetrable from assault, it was outfitted with the latest in intrusion detection and deterrence devices. I'd been instructed to stay off the grass and, when on the driveway, never to venture beyond the magnificent old elm standing just beyond the garage. The mere idea of what might be buried in the lawn was enough to ensure my obedience.

Aside from the bare refrigerator, I had no way of knowing if the house had been unoccupied for the last several months. The furnishings were immaculate, with no dust to indicate lack of use, and the rooms were missing the musty odor that generally accompanies a closed and unoccupied building. This was a safe house—a place for sequestering certain people who needed government protection. I had fit that description for a couple of weeks last February.

After the early morning and trauma of the last three days, I was in dire need of caffeine and found a bag of French Roast in the freezer. I was also hungry, and voiced my need for sustenance.

Adrian measured the coffee and set the machine to brew. "Jones and Jazz are stopping for supplies; they should be here within the hour. While we wait, let's get on a call with our friends down at Fort Meade to get their take on your driver the other morning. I also want to know what they think about the fact that someone tailed us after we arrived at Logan."

"You think the two are related."

"I do. It seems entirely too coincidental to be otherwise, don't you think?"

"Yep." And you can bet your Ray-Bans that I'll be keeping my eyes on my rearview mirror for the foreseeable future.

Coffee mugs in hand, we stepped into the conference room, which also served as a no-cube office. An exceptionally large monitor occupied most of one wall, and a number of computers sat idle on tables around the room. The wall monitor lit up with the flip of a switch, and Adrian initiated a secure video conference with Fort Meade, the campus of the NSA. The screen flickered to life, revealing the faces of Melodie and Trent—the two NSA-affiliated members of Paul Marshfield's unit.

Trent had an independent streak, as evidenced by the intricate tattoo snaking down his arm. In working with him, I'd discovered that he was an insightful analyst with a gift for data mining, but I knew little of his life outside the grounds of Fort Meade.

Melodie possessed an exceptional talent for distilling a flood of information into consumable portions and identifying the most salient details and promising leads. In the elite and closed community of NSA workers, she had a stellar reputation. She invariably wore a headband to keep her short natural twists away from her face, and seemed to have a collection that paralleled every hue in the color spectrum. Today's choice was a cheery purple that was in sharp contrast to the worried creases lining her forehead.

Dispensing with pleasantries, she jumped immediately to the business at hand. "We lost the car following you. Trent's going over all the video feeds to see if we can pick him up elsewhere, but I wouldn't hold my breath. I think he got suspicious of all the red lights and bailed. What we can tell you is that your tail was a silver Kia ... no decals or other identifying markings. We'll review any video footage from the area around the airport and hope we catch a break."

Adrian balled his fist and rested his chin in the hollow formed by his thumb. "Whoever it was, he—or she—knew what they were doing. Any images of the driver?"

Melodie shook her head. "Nothing so far, but we're continuing to look. The car's windows were heavily tinted ... that's probably why they used it.

"We're a bit luckier with some of the footage from DC. Trent and I already have our own ideas, but have a look and tell me what you think."

A surprisingly high-resolution video filled the screen. Most surveillance footage that I'd seen wasn't actual video, but rather a series of grainy black-and-white images taken at timed intervals. Depending on timing, people would appear to be marionettes moving jerkily across the screen or magically beamed from one position on the screen to another. It was apparent that the Marriott had invested in top-notch equipment.

Viewing it for the first time, Adrian watched intently. I relived the encounter, remembering the initial kindness of the man and, later, the strength of his grip and the malice in his voice. Adrian asked to see the video again, and afterward observed, "He's not as old as he looks."

Melodie's eyes sparkled with interest. "I'd agree, yes. Regardless, he works out. See how agile he is getting into and out of the car? And look at the bulge of his thigh muscle against his blue jeans as he gets into the car. What else do you see?"

I'd noticed something. "He never takes his jacket off. He doesn't even unbutton it. Who does that in the middle of July? Did he wear it to hide the gun?"

"Possibly, but there's another reason. Let's slow it down, and I want you to watch as he leans over and stows your suitcase in the trunk."

I didn't see it, but Adrian noticed immediately.

"He's padded."

"Bingo." She rewound the video for a few seconds and paused on one frame. She pointed, showing us that his shirt had ridden up when he lifted the suitcase. It was not skin beneath the shirt, nor was it an undershirt. What we were seeing was body padding.

I nodded humbly. I could have watched that video all day and would never have noticed those details.

"Could you zoom in on his face?" asked Adrian.

Trent found a frontal image and enlarged it. He took us through the troubling aspects of the man's face, commenting that the cheeks were rounder than he would expect for someone in good shape. He suggested that the man could be wearing cheek pads.

Continuing, Trent said, "We think that the crown of his head is naturally bald, or shaved. It takes hours of preparatory makeup to make a bald cap look natural. It doesn't seem reasonable that he would spend that time. But from there, we're not so sure. Some, all, or none of that horseshoe of hair over his ears and the back of his head could be real. Certainly the color is wrong for a younger guy. If we had to assess the probabilities, we'd say there's an 80 percent chance that he sports a completely bald head in his everyday life.

"Most intriguing, however, are his sunglasses and unibrow. The unibrow isn't natural. The hairs across the nose are far too bushy compared to the remainder of the eyebrow. And look at the sunglasses. They're not only unusually thick, but the section over the bridge of the nose is much wider than a normal pair of glasses. And we can't see his eyes; therefore we can't measure the distance between them or the depth of the eye sockets. We view these inconsistencies as a deliberate attempt to obscure this area of his face."

"He was prepared for cameras," observed Adrian.

"I'd say so, yes," answered Melodie. "We've run him through facial recognition, but there's just not enough data."

"Is there anything that can be done to develop a more accurate rendering of what he might look like?"

"We're working on it. But we also need to determine why he targeted Lindsey."

"You're right. She hasn't been directly involved since mid-March, so what triggered this?" He turned and focused his full attention on me. "Have you done anything or met anyone or had any conversations related to the events in February?"

Without hesitation, I shook my head. "No. We don't talk about any of this at work, and I haven't spoken with Cat for about three weeks. Nothing has occurred that's out of the ordinary." I frowned. "Well, except for the phone call from Paul."

Adrian inclined his head toward Melodie before turning back to me. "We'll need to sweep your office and home. You may have picked up a bug."

My voice went up an octave. "Again?" Back in February, a number of eavesdropping electronics had been found in my home and offices. A security specialist, retained by my lawyer, had removed the intrusive devices and kept me bug-free for a month. We'd canceled his service in March, believing that the danger was past. Overwhelmed by the maelstrom of activity at the time, I had neglected to pursue the question of who had placed the devices in the first place. Now, the idea that someone had again entered my home without my knowledge and was listening to me, was infuriating. "I'll call my guy and have him check it out again."

"Actually, let me get someone," Adrian offered. "I'm sure that your guy is quite capable, but I'll guarantee that my guy is more so."

"Well," Melodie interrupted, "you could do a thorough cleaning and be pest-free. Or, you could do a bit of light dusting that incurs a little breakage ..."

I nodded my head in comprehension. "And hope they come back to investigate why it's not working."

Melodie grinned evilly. "Bingo," she chirped.

"Even better," agreed Adrian. "But I feel that we've

somehow missed something."

They were obsessed with the attack, and so was I, but my only engagement with the team's operations had been five months ago, when we averted the bombing in the harbor and traced the planning back to Roger. Yet the attack on me seemed to be triggered by my visit to the Ambassador. The driver had wanted to know what was said in the meeting. That seemed to indicate that Paul's office was not bugged, nor were the things I carried with me.

Whoever these people were, they were well-informed about my whereabouts and worried about something that I might see or hear. Since I didn't know anything, and the Ambassador rarely knew all the particulars of the group's activities, there was only one intersecting factor: Cat. She carried secrets in her head that none of us would ever know.

Melodie nodded thoughtfully. "Either way, we don't want to spend time and manpower chasing this threat down a rabbit hole, distracting us from our real objective."

"I agree," conceded Adrian. "Conrad27 still has to be our main focus, but this man is connected somehow. Keep that in mind. I can't help but think that it has to be someone who knows Roger and Cat, and knows of Cat's connection to Lindsey. That's a fairly small circle."

"I'll admit that there is a certain beauty in your logic. But now you're asking me to start a deep search for a bald guy who has somehow been associated with Cat and Roger, on enough of a personal level that he knew of Lindsey." Melodie rolled her eyes and, her voice dripping with sarcasm, added, "This ought to be a walk in the park, considering that Cat's life is such an open book."

Adrian winked at her. "When it comes to cracking the

impenetrable, there is nobody better than you and Trent."

He turned to face me, his voice more serious. "I think that something about the Ambassador's phone call touched a nerve. This man," he said, pointing at the picture on the screen, "had a gun on you, and you took steps to neutralize the threat ... crazy, but very gutsy. I want you to see what happened."

He started a slow-motion playback. The parkway came into focus, with light traffic and all the vehicles going the same speed. I was trying to figure out which car I was in when a sedan up ahead suddenly cut to the left, leaving the driver's side exposed for an instant and then facing directly into oncoming traffic. The car continued counterclockwise until the wheels hit the shoulder, slid into the grass, lost traction, and launched the vehicle onto its roof.

I had acted instinctively, the primitive part of my brain commanding me to fight. But watching the crash was horrifying. The man may have been out to kill me, but I could easily have killed myself.

"Rule number one: don't go anywhere alone. The rest of us have some training; you just got lucky."

I swallowed hard and tried to banish the images of the crash from my brain.

Chapter 11

It was just before noon when Jones and Jazz shuffled into the house—arms full of groceries—trailed by Jason and Gabe, the two programmers from my company. While I knew Jones to have talent in the kitchen, my stomach was howling for more immediate gratification, and I was relieved when he pulled a variety of subs from one of the bags.

I watched Jazz as she interacted with the others, and knew that we were going to enjoy each other. She had a soft Southern accent and a lively, irreverent wit, and there seemed to be little that escaped her attention.

We sat in front of the monitor in the conference room, devouring our sandwiches, while Melodie provided the details of what they had learned about the e-mail sent to Conrad27.

"We've pinpointed the location where the e-mail originated. It was sent from a condo building on Mt. Vernon Street in Beacon Hill. The condo is leased to a Deepak Cothary, age twenty-six."

The screen filled with the face of a serious-looking man in his midtwenties. He was clean-shaven, with soft features and the pale countenance of someone who spent most of his time indoors. He wore a pin-striped light blue shirt, open at the neck, with the knot of his tie loosened. The photo appeared to have been taken in a coffee shop, and showed Deepak sitting alone at a table, with a cup of coffee and studying the book resting on his knee."

"What's he reading?" asked Jazz.

Melodie zoomed into the cover: *Employing Informatics to Enhance the Value of Radiologic Imagery*.

Jazz laughed. "There's a real page-turner."

Melodie continued reciting the known facts about Deepak. "He was born in Mumbai, immigrated here at the age of twelve, and is now a US citizen. He's a graduate of MIT, heavily involved in informatics with the MGH radiology department—guess that explains the book. Clean record, no known questionable associations, nothing that would lead us to suspect radicalization."

Adrian canted his eyes toward Jones. "Field trip?"

"Oh yeah, let's go have a chat with this guy."

"Jazz, you've got the more technical background, so you're the better choice to stay here with Lindsey and her crew. Together, maybe you can make some progress on the origin of that e-mail."

If Jazz was offended by missing out on the action of cornering Deepak, she gave no indication. "Got it. We'll see what we can turn up."

Adrian started to turn away, then whirled back to face the monitor. "Melodie, I'm going to snatch the glasses. We'll stream the interview with Mr. Cothary to you."

He opened a cabinet on the far wall, pulled out a pair of glasses and what appeared to be a pen, and lifted a briefcase from the shelf. Intrigued, I walked over for a better look. The glasses were slim and fashionable, and I never would have detected that the nose bridge concealed a tiny camera, the left hinge contained a long-life battery, the designer logo on the right temple held an antenna and transmitter for wireless communications, and two microcomputers were built into the temple arms. The gradient lenses, with the top quarter tinted gray, helped disguise the integrated heads-up, or HUD, display. The glasses could send and receive data, images, voice, and streaming video.

The rollerball pen was equally clever. Its fat grip disguised the same functionality as the glasses, minus the HUD, with the camera mounted in the clip. Pressing the clip to extend the writing tip also activated the camera. Adrian confided that while the pen actually did work, its supply of ink was minimal. The other device was integrated into a sleek leather briefcase, albeit a bit battered to lend authenticity, and held an independent transmitter and receiver with a range of one thousand feet. The final component was a more powerful unit in the trunk of the car.

Adrian explained the setup. "Each of these devices can communicate independently. But signal strength is a big factor. For the glasses, you really want a constant, strong signal—the same as four or five bars on your phone. Having all these devices gives us redundancy, because at least one of them will almost always have a signal. And we can link them together in an ad hoc network so they talk to one another. Because signal strength in a building can be so unpredictable, the glasses can talk to the pen or the briefcase, and the briefcase can talk to the car. Jones will set the briefcase down, because it would look unnatural to carry it everywhere. I can then wander with the glasses, and Jones can walk about with the pen. It works like a charm. And if anything fails in transmission, we'll still have the recordings from each."

I was impressed. "Those glasses would make a nice birthday present," I joked, already envisioning the myriad uses I could find for them.

Adrian shook his head tolerantly and turned on his heel, leaving the rest of us to the relatively bland task of tracking an e-mail. We gave our full attention to Melodie and Trent, who had pulled up a map of India on the screen.

"The e-mail ended up here, somewhere in Mumbai." She zoomed in on a peninsula jutting into the Arabian Sea on the northwestern coast of India. "It's the most populous city in India, and one of the most populous in the world. Look at that little peninsula and imagine that 12 million people live there. In contrast, New York City has about twice as much land and only 8 million people."

"So I suppose no luck in pinpointing his location from the IP address," Jason commented.

I noticed a flicker of uncertainty play across Jazz's face. "Jazz, are you okay?" I asked.

She pursed her lips. "I hate to admit it, but I've heard the term IP address thrown about more times than I can count, and I don't really understand it."

I remembered my first exposure to network terminology and could empathize with her discomfort. "Don't feel like you're alone in the world. Most people throw the term around without actually having a clue about what it is. I'll try to explain.

"An IP, or Internet Protocol, address is a sequence of

numbers—and sometimes letters—that identifies a device on computer networks. Basically, anything that connects to the Internet will have its own address—your smartphone, tablet, and computer. The address is generally assigned by whatever device is actually making the connection to the outside world. My cable modem, for instance, gets an address when it's powered on and connects to the cable company. Then, when I access my home network from my laptop, it gets its address from the modem.

"But at Starbucks or OfficeMax, I get a different address because I'm connecting through their setup. As people come and go, numbers are reused. That means that once I disconnect from Starbucks, the IP address I was just using could be assigned to the next person who walks in the door."

Jason jumped in. "That's why it can be so difficult to track data sent from a public hotspot, unless you have an array of cameras capturing what's on everyone's screen and an accurate date-time stamp on the video."

The interest on Jazz's face dissolved in disappointment. "So having an IP doesn't really help."

Jason shrugged his shoulders. "It depends. Sometimes those public places require you to register, and the system sends a confirmation e-mail; that e-mail account might have clues about who you are, like a credit card receipt from an online purchase. But it's tedious, time-consuming, and not always fruitful."

"But," I interjected, "connections are frequently made in more private locations, like a home or an office. That translates to information."

Jazz's eyes lit up in comprehension. "So we figure out

who the connecting device belongs to. If it turns out that the IP is at Starbucks, forget it. But if it's at someone's home ..."

"Bingo!" exclaimed Melodie. "That's how we found Deepak Cothary. His service provider is here in America. It took a court order for access to his personal information, but we got it, and we've been in his e-mail. To get details about Conrad27, well, that's a different story.

"Conrad's a cautious guy. All of his earlier e-mails were sent from highly trafficked public places, and we tried for months to get a bead on him, with no success. On occasion, he even used a service that effectively hides the sending IP address. Ordinary people don't do that. The more we learn about him, the more he smells. But everybody makes a mistake at some point—we've just been waiting for him to slip up."

Melodie glanced at the printout in her hand as she spoke. "Maybe he suspects that someone might be watching his e-mail account, which of course we are. But for whatever reason, he didn't use Gmail for his reply to Deepak; he used a totally different account. What caught our eye was that he used the moniker *Conrad* in the body of the message. The e-mail is tied to an internet provider—one that doesn't hand out free usage. So either he works there, or he has an account there. Either way ..."

"We've got him," Jazz interrupted, her voice filled with satisfaction.

"If only it could be that easy," Melodie responded, her expression despondent. "Legally, though, we'd have to go through the Indian government. Of late, they've become much more cautious about giving us the keys to their kingdom."

"And not legally?" I asked, feigning innocence.

All eyes turned instantly toward Gabe, whose hacking skills were legendary.

He rubbed his hands together in anticipation and beckoned Jason to join him. "Let's have some fun."

Jazz held up her hand to stop him, pointing her index finger toward a recess in the far wall. "First things first. We need your biometrics so I can show you some of the more interesting features of this house, and then Lindsey and I are gonna have our own brand o' fun."

Chapter 12

Saturday afternoon
Foxborough, Massachusetts

Jazz retrieved a camera and tripod from the storage cabinet, and then stood before a computer terminal mounted into the wall. I heard her speak a series of numbers before she plugged the camera's cable into the USB port. She positioned a chair in the niche and instructed me to keep my eyes wide open while she adjusted the angle. After commanding me to "sit up straight" and "look down a little," she seemed satisfied, and I heard the distinctive snick-snack sounds of the shutter opening and closing.

She studied the monitor, presumably verifying that the images had been successfully captured, before beckoning me toward the computer. She explained that when I was ready, I should touch the screen, speak my full name in a normal voice, and read the numbers as they appeared.

I tapped the screen and said, "Lindsey Morgan Carlisle." The screen blinked, and I spoke the numbers from the display, "1-0-9-2-3-5-7-1-8-8-2-3," followed by another series, "4-6-9-7-3-2-4-5-7-5-0-1." I read several sequences before Jazz gave me the thumbs up.

As my mouth began to form the question, Jason

answered it for me. "Iris scanning. And they would already have facial recognition, of course, so this is mostly iris matching. And a voiceprint for additional security."

Jazz nodded in confirmation. "He's right. The pictures and your voice are being uploaded now, along with your other biometrics.

I wondered if I had misunderstood. "My *other* biometrics?"

"We have your fingerprints from your Global Entry enrollment. We'll take a DNA swab later."

I felt a little like I'd fallen down a rabbit hole. Tired of waiting in security and customs lines at the airport, I'd shelled out a hundred dollars and applied for the Global Entry program three years ago. Now my fingerprints, my voice, and my eyes had been added to the massive amount of data that's being accumulated about me every day. My phone, my credit cards, and the ubiquitous video cameras broadcast where I am, what I'm buying, how much I spend, and who's with me. Privacy hasn't just left the building; it's been thrown out on its ear.

Jazz spoke into the headset again, confirming that the images had uploaded successfully, before repeating the procedure for Jason and Gabe.

Signaling us to follow, Jazz led us into the kitchen. She walked briskly to the island of cabinets dividing the cooking facilities from the living space and positioned her fingers on the four rocker switches in the electrical panel just below the counter. The overhead and undercounter lights blinked on and off as she toggled the switches in what appeared to be random order.

"One-Two, on-off. One-Four, on-off-on."

We gasped in unison as the center section of the island, along with its undermount sink, rose and slid quietly backward. I'd previously wondered why, in this area of the country where nearly every home held a basement, the safe house did not. And now, with no other evidence to indicate the presence of a lower level, a staircase was revealed.

"Amazing, isn't it?" Jazz commented. "Now, hurry!"

She crouched under the cabinet and descended the steps. We followed, close on her heels. Behind us the cabinet repositioned, sealing us off from the upper floors. At nearly the same time, the door in front of us hissed open.

Pointing at two lenses protruding from the walls, she explained that they were iris scanners. "The cabinets close automatically after three seconds of no activity on the scanners. They'll also close automatically if an unauthorized person tries to enter. This door at the bottom won't open until the top is secured and everyone in the stairwell has passed validation." She turned to us with a sly grin. "Looks like your data uploaded successfully."

The bottom door revealed a short hallway with two doors on each side. An alcove to the right housed what appeared to be the door to a vault. The place was eerily silent.

"What's down here?" Gabe asked quietly.

"Ya'll don't need to whisper," she replied. "It's soundproofed like crazy. When it was built, everyone on the team had a say, but it was mostly Cat's design. I swear, I think she thought of everything. Barring an all-out armed assault on the property, it's extremely secure. There are a number of multipurpose rooms, including twenty beds and a month's supply of MREs—that's *Meals Ready to Eat* in military lingo. There are other amenities and I'll give you the complete tour later, but ya'll should scamper back upstairs while I spend some time educating Lindsey on the fundamentals of using a firearm."

She turned back to the door and pointed out an array of monitors to the right of the doorframe. Touching the first panel brought up a video feed from the stairwell. "From inside, the door control is voice activated. Look at the panel by the display and say the numbers."

Gabe stepped toward the door. "1-1-8-9-0." As the bottom door opened, Jason read a different sequence to open the cabinetry at the top.

"When you get upstairs, press all the rocker switches down to reset the system."

After watching Jason and Gabe climb back to the floor above, Jazz strode down the hallway and opened the last door on the left, stepping into a large, open area that I recognized immediately as an indoor shooting range.

She pulled a few paper targets from a cabinet, along with two sets of earplugs, earmuffs, and safety glasses. Pivoting toward a vault-like mechanism on the left, she pressed her fingers onto a glowing red panel. The panel's color changed to green, and she pulled the heavy door open. I felt my jaw drop as I took in the sight of the firearms shelved inside.

"I'm going to acquaint you with a Glock first. It's what most of us carry—except Cat—so it's the logical weapon of choice. We can explore others later, but for now, let's get you comfortable with this one." She pulled a malevolent-looking pistol from a rack.

"Glock? You want me to carry a gun?"

"Hell no, sugah! That would be almost as dangerous as

giving me a recipe and asking me to cook!" She laughed heartily, her shoulders heaving, before her face resumed its serious expression. "But we want you to know how to use one, should it ever become necessary."

I drew in a deep breath, wondering what had caused the earth to shift under my feet. Even during our pursuit of the terrorists back in February, I'd never felt myself to be in real danger. I'd been home, or here at the safe house, through that entire ordeal. The only physical jeopardy I'd been in was on the subway, when some thug had tried to steal my bag. My recurring nightmares were the product of the stress I'd been under while trying to locate the terrorists in time to prevent the attack. This was something entirely different. I bit down hard on my lower lip and submitted to her instruction.

She took her time, drilling into my head the rules for handling guns and explaining the mechanics of loading, unloading, aiming, and firing the weapon. She demonstrated a basic stance, with feet apart and knees slightly bent. Stuffing the earplugs in her ears and looping the muffs over her head, she urged me to follow suit. Finally, she stood behind me, braced my shoulder, gripped my arm, and told me to line up the sight to the target and shoot.

With my right arm in a sling, I was forced to use a one-handed grip. I am primarily left-handed, but my first few shots missed the paper entirely. I gripped the weapon too tightly or too softly, squeezed the trigger too hard or not hard enough, and the gun slipped in my hand and I jerked from noise and the recoil. But as I became accustomed to the touch needed to press the trigger and learned what to expect when the firing pin struck the round, I found that I was hitting the target's body mass with regularity.

I'd fired about fifty rounds, I guessed, when some of the shell casings, which normally ejected out to the right, started hitting my body. One grazed my arm, another flipped down the front of my shirt, and yet another flew behind my safety glasses and burned my face—high on my cheekbone just beneath my eye. I'd heard the term *hot brass* before ... now I understood it. "Is that normal?" I asked.

Jazz signaled an end to the lesson. "No, you're getting tired, and your grip is getting sloppy. No improvement to be gained right now." She passed me a towel in exchange for the gun, and only then did I realize that my eyes were stinging from perspiration and that my shirt was dripping sweat. Before we returned upstairs, she breathed a few final words of advice into my ear. "If you feel the need to point that gun at someone, be ready to pull the trigger and keep pulling until the bastard is dead. Because if you don't, hon, he is sure as hell gonna kill you."

Chapter 13

Saturday afternoon
Boston, Massachusetts

Adrian maneuvered the SUV through the narrow streets of Beacon Hill, silently cursing a neighborhood that reserved most of its limited street parking to residents. Finding even a single space presented a challenge. Locating one in proximity to Deepak Cothary's building was a long shot.

Jones tried to lighten the mood by giving a running narrative about the area that he considered to be the most charming and cherished part of the city. He pointed out the golden dome of the Massachusetts State House, perched majestically at the top of the hill, enumerated the offerings of the quaint shops and cozy restaurants lining Charles Street, and spoke nostalgically of romantic walks along the Esplanade and the Charles River.

"Lindsey lived here for a while, you know."

Adrian shifted his gaze toward the passenger seat, wondering where this turn in the conversation was headed. "I didn't know that."

"Yep, right after she graduated from BU. She spent several months house-sitting for one of Cat's friends." He pointed to a congested intersection ahead. "Enough cruising the neighborhood. Turn left at the stoplight."

Midway up the hill on Mt. Vernon Street, he directed Adrian to pull up next to the fire hydrant. "This is Louisburg Square. Lindsey stayed over there." He pointed to a fastidiously maintained Greek Revival townhome facing the small park. "You should take a walk up here sometime. Evening is good, when the gas lamps are lit. It's a step back in time."

"So why did she move up to Marblehead?"

Jones grimaced and looked at Adrian thoughtfully. "Cat's friends were in the business. They left on an undercover op over on the Indian subcontinent and never came back. There wasn't much to go on ... they were last seen climbing into a taxi at the Oberoi Hotel in Mumbai, and poof, they were gone. No ransom, no note, no nothing. Lindsey came home one day to find the place ransacked—thoroughly and professionally. I scoured the place and came up dry. I still don't know who it was, what they were after, or if they found it. Anyhow, Cat thought it would be best to find Lindsey safer accommodations. So, Marblehead."

"Does Lindsey know?"

"As far as I know, she doesn't have a clue. I think Cat told her that the couple unexpectedly decided to sell and move to the south of France."

Adrian retrieved the FBI placard from under the seat and mounted it on the dash. "I hate using this. Attracts too many curiosity seekers."

"Better than the alternative of being towed, or driving around all day. We've got to have the car in range." He patted the briefcase. "I don't have any idea how all these old buildings will affect transmission."

Adrian slipped the tiny wireless speakers into his ears. Stepping onto the sidewalk, he slipped on the glasses and discreetly turned on the device. As he surveyed the building two doors down, he spoke softly. "Comm check. Do you read?"

Trent's disembodied voice filled his ears. "Loud and clear. Did you hit traffic?"

"In a manner of speaking. It took us twenty minutes to find a parking space, in front of a hydrant, no less. We're headed to his condo now; I'm leaving the camera on."

"Watch your footing," Jones warned. "Beacon Hill may be historical and all that, but the old brick sidewalks are a pain in the ass."

Adrian glanced down, eyeing the bricks that had been displaced by the wandering roots of old elms. The walkway resembled the moguls on a ski run. "Thanks for the heads-up. Everyone get ready—here we go."

They walked to the doorway of the building. Jones, finding the name D. Cothary, pressed the buzzer and waited. His finger was poised over the button to ring again, when a deep voice resonated from the intercom.

"Yes?"

"Mr. Cothary?"

"Yes. You can just leave the package in the foyer. Thank you for buzzing."

"Actually, Mr. Cothary, I'm Special Agent Adrian Santori of the FBI. We'd like a few minutes of your time."

"FBI? What is this about?"

"Please, Mr. Cothary. We need to talk face-to-face. It's important."

"I can't imagine what the FBI would want with me.

Can't you give me some idea what this is about?"

"I understand your concern, sir. This should only take a few minutes."

"I'll be right down. I'll need to see identification first."

"Thank you, sir."

Adrian could appreciate Deepak Cothary's hesitation, having seen the aftermath of a victim opening the door to an imposter. With so many crime dramas on television, however, the prevailing wisdom among the population was to demand identification. Still, the average citizen, including Deepak, wouldn't know how to verify that an ID was legitimate.

When Mr. Cothary opened the door a few minutes later, Adrian instantly reassessed the man's level of naïveté. Phone in hand, he read Adrian's name and badge number aloud and waited for a voice on the other end to confirm the identity.

Adrian waited patiently until the man turned to Jones. "Mr. Jones is with another agency and is here under my authority."

"What does that mean? That I'm not entitled to see his ID? Then he can wait outside."

Adrian kept his face composed, thinking, *My, this guy has guts.*

"Mr. Cothary, while I can empathize with your concern, the sensitive nature of Mr. Jones's work precludes me from divulging that information to you. He is here as an observer and to make sure that I don't inadvertently overlook an important question. This should only take a few minutes of your time, and we would appreciate your cooperation."

Adrian leveled an uncompromising stare at the man, knowing this was the moment that determined the better poker player. Not surprisingly, Deepak Cothary blinked first, motioning them to follow.

In keeping with the neighborhood, the elevator was an antique, with a capacity of only three people. Crammed next to Jones, Deepak seemed almost Lilliputian in comparison, and the overall space seemed unmercifully tight. Adrian found himself questioning the elevator's weight capacity, and he held his breath as the car rose. Jones must have been somewhat worried himself, because when the door opened and he stepped out, the sheen of perspiration on his forehead was evident.

Deepak Cothary led the way into his condo, directing his uninvited guests toward a love seat in the small living room. Adrian and Jones sat shoulder to shoulder, directly across from the smaller Mr. Cothary. Watching the man's eyes as he responded to the interrogation, Adrian looked for any sign of deception or unease. The man's gaze was steady, and he couldn't see any trace of fear.

"Now, what's this about?"

"Mr. Cothary, where were you on Thursday evening?"

"Me? Thursday? I was here."

"Were you alone?"

"No, I had friends over. We were watching Germany play Brazil." He must have detected puzzlement in Adrian's expression, and continued, "Soccer? The World Cup?"

"Oh, right. I don't follow it."

"Few Americans do, unless the US is competing."

"What time did your friends arrive?"

"At about seven, I think. We had a few beers, ordered

in some pizza, watched the match, and they left around eleven or eleven thirty. I'm not completely sure of the time. Why is this important?"

"Did any of your friends have a computer or use yours while they were here?"

Deepak's eyes registered alarm. "Why? Why is that important?"

Adrian said nothing, waiting for the response. Deepak's eyes flitted from Adrian to Jones and back.

"Nobody brought a computer that I remember. Certainly I don't remember anyone actually using one, since nearly everyone carries a smartphone these days. But one of them did ask to use mine to check his e-mail. Has he done something?"

"Why would you ask that, Mr. Cothary?"

"No reason, other than you're asking a lot of questions and not giving me any context by which to respond. I'm trying to fill in the blanks for something I know nothing about."

"This friend ... do you know if he actually checked his e-mail, or are you aware of any websites he might have visited?"

"Now how would I know that? Do you think I stood over his shoulder and monitored his every keystroke? I was watching the match. I've no idea what he did. What do you think he did?"

"How well do you know this friend?"

"We knew each other as children in Mumbai; our parents are close. We socialize occasionally."

"What is your friend's name?"

"Rajeev. Rajeev Malik."

"Does he live here in Boston?"

"Not permanently, no. He occasionally leases an apartment, when he's going to be in town for an extended period. He's a businessman, import-export, but I don't know any of the details ... his work doesn't really interest me."

"Why here? Why not New York?"

"I'm not sure. He took a graduate degree here and knows people in the area; maybe it's just a case of familiarity. I'll ask again, what is this about?"

"What do you talk about when you're together?"

"What do you mean, what do we talk about? That's a ridiculous question. We discuss whatever comes up; it's not limited to a single subject."

"Just tell me in general. Do you discuss sports, the weather, travel, politics, or any one subject more than another?"

"I don't know ... all of the above. I've never tried to quantify our talks."

"How would you characterize his political views?"

Deepak's stare was long and thoughtful, as if he were trying to read Adrian's thoughts. "This isn't about his business at all, is it? This is something else. You think he's involved with something political—that he's a dissident or something. Is that what you think?"

"Do you?"

"You keep answering my questions with more questions. What do you think he has done?"

"Are you worried about what he might have done?"

It was apparent that Deepak was becoming annoyed with the unrelenting stream of questions. His lips compressed into a thin line, and the deep V of a frown appeared between his eyebrows.

"I wasn't before, but apparently I should be now."

"I'd just like to determine how you would characterize him."

"He's politically active, but I wouldn't consider him an extremist. He sometimes sees the US as a bully that abuses its power. This isn't unusual, you know. A lot of people around the globe feel the same way."

Adrian spotted the almost imperceptible microsecond of contempt that played at the corner of the man's mouth.

"We're talking about your friend, Mr. Cothary. Not the global populace."

"Do I need to stay away from him? Should I warn my other friends?"

"Mr. Cothary, I'm going to ask you to go about your usual routine, and to not mention this conversation to anyone. Please, let us handle it. On the one hand, your friend's involvement in our investigation may be purely incidental, and we would not want him wrongly accused of an action in which he had no part. On the other hand, if we discover that his involvement was something other than incidental, we wouldn't want him warned of our interest. Do you understand?"

"I do understand, but in the interest of self-preservation, if he's involved in something, I'd rather steer clear. I'll handle it. We don't see each other that often, anyhow."

Believing that the interview was over, Deepak stood. Adrian and Jones remained seated.

"It's a difficult position to be in," Adrian said, "and I

appreciate your cooperation. I have two more questions."

Deepak tilted his head, surprised, and sat down reluctantly. "Yes?"

"In February, when we uncovered a plot to bomb one of the fuel farms near the harbor, what was Mr. Malik's reaction?"

Deepak paled. "The harbor attack? Oh, my God." He turned his gaze toward the window and stared at the trees for a long moment.

"Mr. Cothary?"

"He asked me ... he asked me what I would do if I thought I knew someone involved. I thought he was playing devil's advocate. It never occurred to me ..."

Adrian swiveled his eyes toward Jones, who was perched to leap from his seat, before settling back on Deepak. "Mr. Cothary, where can we find Rajeev?"

Chapter 14

Saturday afternoon
Foxborough, Massachusetts

While Jazz ran a search for Rajeev in the FBI's database, Melodie and Trent sent deep probes into the mines of NSA data, looking for e-mails, phone calls, postings on social media, and any trace of his presence on the web.

With Gabe and Jason deeply engrossed in trying to find a back door to the server that had sent the e-mail from Conrad27, I decided to use Google Street View to tour the area around Rajeev's apartment. The building was in Somerville, close to Davis Square and only a few blocks south of the Tufts University campus. Cruising the streets, I thought that at one time the neighborhood must have been quite lovely. While it still boasted several large Victorian homes, with their round, cone-topped towers and asymmetrical shape, they appeared to have been converted to condos and apartments. The neighborhood's remaining architecture was plainer and more utilitarian, devoid of any aesthetic appeal. If Rajeev's living accommodations were any indication, his success as a businessman was open to question.

I enabled the speaker on one of the secure phones at the safe house and called Adrian. "It's a one-way street, parking on both sides and one lane for traffic in the middle. I wish you luck in finding a space to park."

Adrian wasn't amused. "Thanks for that news. If there's no open space when I get there, I may be tempted to start a demolition derby."

"I feel your pain. I've looked at the house on Street View. The photos are dated from May this year, so I wouldn't expect any major changes. It's an older building with three stories—a pretty good-size place. Earth View shows an extension at the rear that looks newer, so it was probably an addition. I'd say there could be five or six apartments in the main structure, and maybe two or three more in the back.

"Trent says records show Rajeev at number three; Jazz is working on getting the building plans now. I can tell you that it has two separate entrances at the front, and fire escapes down both sides. We're sending you photos of the building, along with a picture of Rajeev."

Jazz shouted across the room, "I've got the plans," and walked briskly over to the speakerphone. "Number three is on the second floor in the front, on the left as you face the house. Use the front door on the left; it has enclosed access to his apartment. I'll send you the drawings, but if you're just doing a meet and greet, it might be more detail than you need. There's a living area to the left of the entry; the kitchen, bath, and single bedroom are to the right, in that order. There's a fire escape that drops out of the bedroom window. I'm worried about that. Want me to call for backup?"

After a long moment, Jones spoke. "I'm all for cooperation among agencies and all that crap, but if we make an official request for backup, this story instantly goes viral and our asses are in a sling. Do we really want to go there?"

"If we don't, and this goes down badly," Adrian countered, "the repercussions won't be pretty." He took a deep breath and kept his tone measured. "But since our intent is to only interview the guy, let's try to keep this low-key. Do we have any expectation that he's armed? If not, I'll be satisfied with someone who could just tackle the guy if needed."

Melodie, who had been trawling through all the electronic bytes of Rajeev's existence, was quick to respond. "There's no record that he owns a gun, at least not legally. He's had no run-ins with the law, he keeps a low profile, his business appears to be legit, although not terribly profitable, and his online presence is what you'd expect from someone his age. I found a few references to sampling weed and consuming too much alcohol—all very ordinary. As Deepak suggested, Rajeev has opinions that reflect an anti-US government viewpoint on certain hot-button topics like drones and our involvement in Iraq and Afghanistan, but again, not unusual."

Jazz agreed. "The FBI doesn't have a file on him, and he has no known radical associations."

"He doesn't appear to be on anyone's radar. If he is, that info is being tightly held," Melodie added.

I couldn't help but draw the parallel: the brothers responsible for the Boston Marathon bombings hadn't been on the radar, either. "Just because we aren't aware of any extremist tendencies, it doesn't mean that we should ignore the possibility." The room became very quiet as heads swiveled her way. Thinking she had overstepped, she blurted out, "Right?"

Jones was reluctant to concede. "You *are* right, Lindsey, but I still don't want to make an official request. If we need to have feet on the ground, find someone who's out of the official loop."

Adrian came to a decision. "Let's reach out to Arnie Powell. He's in good shape, big, formidable, and dependable. If this goes south, he can just tackle the guy and sit on him."

Arnie Powell, who was related to the husband of my sister Cat, had previously performed contract work for the CIA as a cryptologist and computer systems expert. Like Cat, he'd been victimized by the treachery of the CIA's Roger Pulaski and had lived under a cloud for years. When we'd untangled Roger's web of lies, Arnie had been made righteous again.

"Good choice," agreed Melodie. "I'll call him."

Chapter 15

Adrian called after scouting Rajeev's street to say they were parked at the end of the block, with a good view of the house, and would be back in touch when Arnie arrived.

After disconnecting, I looked up at Melodie and Trent on the display. "Anything else you've discovered about this guy?"

"Nope. He's here on a B-1 visa, and arranges import of Indian goods to the US and export of some US goods to India—mostly the former. He applied for the initial visa within a month of graduating, went through the usual channels, and was approved. This is his eighth visit in the last four years. So far he's made two trips each year, and he's completely predictable, always arriving in late May and departing late July, then coming again mid-September and leaving late October."

"I'll guess that he's not a fan of New England winters. Where does he spend the remainder of his time? Any exotic destinations in his travels?"

"Good question. But remember that Rajeev is an Indian national. If the guy were on a watch list, we'd have more information. If we come up with some evidence suggesting that he's a threat, we can petition the Indians for a deep dive into his movements, but it will take time. And we don't know if he might have used a different identity to travel elsewhere."

Jazz jumped up, excitement written on her face. "I've had a thought. Please call Adrian."

I dialed, and put the call on speaker when Adrian picked up. "Jazz has an idea to share."

"We're all ears."

Jazz's words came out in a rush. "Let's wait. If Rajeev is involved and you approach him, he'll get spooked. Let's explore some options. One is that we could turn Gabe and Jason loose on the Indian systems ..."

I noticed Gabe's head pop up at the mention of another hacking opportunity.

Adrian interrupted. "What you're suggesting is a decision that's above my pay grade; we need Cat or Paul to weigh in before going down that path."

"I understand, but hear me out. Assuming that Gabe gets in, he could search the database and all the passenger manifests at the major international departure points. But there's no telling how many Rajeev Maliks we'd discover, and if he used another identity, we wouldn't even know who to look for. Regardless, we'd need an incredible stroke of good luck to find him. Let's give ourselves an advantage."

"What are you proposing?"

"Let's first find out if he has anything interesting in his apartment or on his computer."

There was silence on the line until Jones finally growled, "Without a warrant? Girl, you got a set on you." He clucked his tongue before continuing. "But it's really not a bad idea."

A long silence ensued as they digested the idea. If I hadn't heard the drum of someone's fingers against some part of the car's interior, I would have thought we'd been disconnected. I used the opportunity to perform a quick search on Google to find out about passports from India.

"You could also look for his passport or any other travel documentation," I interjected. "And here's another thing: India uses RFID in their passports. Gabe doesn't have to search by Rajeev's name; he could use the chip's data to probe the Indian servers."

Radio Frequency Identification, RFID, is a wireless system for exchanging data. Depending on the type of technology used, the readable distance can be anywhere from a few inches to several hundred yards. Quite a few countries, including the United States, embed RFID chips in their passports. The chip contains the same personal information found in the passport, such as date and place of birth and a photo of the bearer.

Officially, the chip is a security measure permitting storage of the passport holder's photo. This allows Immigration and Customs officials to use methods such as facial recognition technology to verify your identity. Once your identity is known, they can access other personal details held in a massive government database. I know that, in theory, this isn't really much different than it was a couple decades ago, when an arriving passenger stopped at a desk in passport control. The officer would access the traveler's information from a mainframe in the bowels of some government building complex and dutifully enter the details of the incoming flight.

What's never been clear to me, however, is who has access to that information, how it's shared, or which other agencies might employ their own tracking of the holder's whereabouts. With an RFID chip in my passport, my presence could be detected by some undercover group lurking behind that door in the shopping mall marked "Authorized Personnel Only." Should I care? It's another one of those internal conflicts that's been raging within me ever since becoming involved with the workings of Paul and Cat's unit. I mentally flipped off the switch for my conspiracy paranoia and focused on the problem at hand.

"If the passport is in the apartment, have Arnie clone it. We can figure out the encryption algorithm later." I knew that Arnie carried an Android phone and that there were apps available to penetrate or clone an RFID chip. It wasn't even that difficult. The encryption, however, might be another story.

Trent was quick to add his two cents. "I'd almost guarantee that we have a copy of the Indian encryption key here. I'll run it by the boss."

Of course, I thought. And I'll bet the NSA already has a back door to their servers, too.

"Now *that* could really prove interesting," Adrian commented. "But I have to tell you that my tradecraft doesn't extend to breaking and entering, though I understand that Jones has some skills. But using Jones in this neighborhood would be risky; some nosy neighbor is likely to call the cops. The last thing we need is for him to be shot."

"There's an easier solution," Jones responded. "Get Cat. She'd be perceived as less of a threat."

Jazz pumped her fist in the air, and when I looked up at Melodie and Trent, they were bobbing their heads vigorously.

"We're all in agreement here," I offered. The thought of seeing Cat again brought a smile to my face. The events earlier this year had burned my sister's carefully crafted cover and forced her to live elsewhere. Previously, she'd lived in Marblehead, and we had seen each other frequently. Now, I didn't know where she and her husband were calling home. I hadn't seen her in weeks, although she could have walked right by me without my recognizing her. I'd learned that her proficiency at disguise was the stuff of legend.

Adrian dialed Cat's number to tie her into the call, and she was on the line almost instantly.

"Good afternoon, Adrian. I heard about the incident at Reagan. I'll assume that you've sequestered Lindsey."

"Lindsey's with Jazz in Foxborough. I'm in Somerville, with Jones. We're all on the call."

"Somerville? Do tell."

Adrian gave a quick summary of the interview with Deepak and relayed Jazz's suggestion to search Rajeev's apartment before making an approach.

"I like the idea," she said after mulling it over. "And I believe there's enough justification to include it in our general warrant, so we'd be technically legal to go in. Who do you have in mind?"

"That's one of the reasons we're calling you."

"My! I don't know whether to be flattered or appalled. None of you knows how to pick a lock?"

Jones's deep laughter rumbled through the speaker. "Now ya'll know better than that. Not to rub it in, but last time I checked, our quick-pick score was 55–43 in my favor."

Cat's retort was quick. "Only because our bet was that I could do one-handed what takes you two. So what's the problem? Neighborhood a little too white for you?"

"Oh yeah. Getting shot by some rookie Somerville badge wouldn't be on my bucket list."

"Then I guess I'll have to save your ass. What do we know about this guy's schedule?"

"As far as we know, he works out of his apartment. Other than that, we know he likes soccer. That's why he was at Deepak's place the other night."

"So are there any World Cup matches tonight? Could we somehow use that to get him out?"

Trent scrambled to pull up the schedule online. "Yes, two: a big match at six and another at nine."

I listened, fascinated, as they hatched a scheme to lure Rajeev into the city for the evening. Deepak would invite Rajeev to join him for dinner at a local sports bar, where they could watch the soccer match on an enormous wide screen. At the time they were supposed to meet, Deepak would call and say he had a critical problem with the radiology software and would be there within thirty to forty-five minutes, then use the same tactic to delay again, before canceling on the third call. All told, Rajeev should be out of the house for at least two hours. But it all hinged on Deepak playing along.

Cat picked at a few details, explaining that someone would be tasked to maintain a visual on Rajeev and let the team know when he started back to Somerville. She also let it be known that she wanted Arnie with her inside the apartment to grab whatever data were on Rajeev's computer, leaving Adrian as the spotter outside.

"We do believe that he'll leave the computer at home, correct? Is there any reason to think he only uses a laptop and would take it with him?" she asked.

Jones fielded the question. "Yes to the first, no to the second. We believe that's why he used Deepak's computer to send the e-mail the other night, because he didn't have his own. And no sane person would take a laptop into a place that's going to be gut-to-butt jammed with drunks."

"Don't you think it's odd that he used Deepak's machine? Nearly everyone, particularly at his age, uses a smartphone for e-mail."

Jason spoke up. "I thought it was strange, too, so when Deepak gave us Rajeev's cell number, I traced the account. He has a minimal data plan. Hard to say if he's just being frugal or if he intentionally avoids using that phone for e-mail and browsing. He works out of his apartment; maybe he just doesn't need it."

"Or maybe he uses a burner. Regardless, it's still unusual, and all the more reason to see what's on his computer. Jones, I want you at the sports bar before he arrives. I'll get two of my Harvard kids to follow Rajeev on the subway. One will tail Rajeev from the Davis Square station; the other will –pre-position at Kendall Square, and they'll do a pass-off. I've been working with them on tradecraft over the last couple of months, so it's a good opportunity to put their training into practice. They'll handle it fine."

"What's your ETA?" asked Adrian.

"Give me thirty minutes."

Chapter 16

Saturday late afternoon
Somerville, Massachusetts

Adrian would have preferred to talk to Deepak Cothary in person but, when weighed against the time it would take to get back to Beacon Hill, quashed the thought. He made a few mental notes of the points he wanted to make and then punched in the number.

Deepak was initially reluctant to participate in the subterfuge, but eventually agreed to invite Rajeev downtown. He dictated one condition—that any actual contact would be by phone only—and chose the Warehouse, a well-known sports bar catering to young professionals who lived or worked in the heart of the city.

After learning the meeting place and disconnecting, Adrian turned to Jones. "You know this bar?"

Jones nodded. "Been there a few times."

"We'll send you a photo when he leaves the house, so you'll know what he's wearing. I don't expect he'll be doing any costume changes for a night of watching soccer, but don't let this guy out of your sight. The last thing we need is for him to come back and surprise us."

"No problem. He won't be able to take a piss without

me holding his dick for him. Speaking metaphorically, that is."

Adrian's nose scrunched up at the image. "That's more than I needed to know."

"Surveillance on this dude isn't going to be an issue; trust me. There's something else I want you to know about."

Jones gave Adrian a web address and a login to access the secure site. The screen displayed a map, with a ticker tape spilling out a steady stream of latitude-longitude coordinates, and a glowing dot in the middle.

"That's me; that's where we are." He went on to explain that a miniature GPS chip was embedded in one of his rings. "When I'm working undercover, the phone is always suspect. It's the first thing, aside from a weapon, that people look for. They'll turn off a phone, take out the battery, dump it in a separate location to pick up later, or flat out smash the thing. But nobody's going to screw with my finger décor unless I'm dead or they cut off my hands, so I have a tracker in one of my rings. If they're really paranoid and use some kind of active detector, I can turn the transmission on and off without anyone being the wiser."

"Who knows about this?"

"Cat, and now you. Smith knew about it, too."

Smith and Jones had teamed up on many projects over the years, until they were targeted for extinction last February. Jones had survived; Smith hadn't.

"You can't share this. When I go dark on some of these ops, I don't want a bunch of desk jockeys thinking they have a license to monitor my whereabouts. I'm only telling you because if something were to happen and you need me, you'll be able to figure out where I am."

Adrian couldn't help but stare at Jones's enormous hands, wondering which of the eight massive rings held the chip. He'd always thought the jewelry a bit over the top, and realized that he'd misjudged him. The bling was merely a functional prop for the role Jones played in his work, rather than the trappings of a man wanting to make a statement.

"Why tell me now?"

"Logistics, I guess. If Rajeev leaves the bar, I'm gonna stick to him like a burr on a sock. I don't want to be screwing around trying to text or call you.

"There's an alert available on this app, so you don't have to keep your eyes focused on the dot. After I settle in at the bar, turn it on. Once it's set, if I walk more than seventy-five feet from my established position, the screen will turn red, and an alarm will sound. If that happens, you should assume he's headed home. You'll only have twenty minutes to pack up and get out of Dodge."

"Got it. Now, get moving. You need to be in place before he shows up."

Jones reached for the door handle and stopped. "This is our only lead."

Adrian blew out a long breath. "I know. It's got legs, though. I can feel it."

"I hope you're right. Later, amigo."

Adrian watched as Jones walked to the next block and turned the corner, disappearing behind a tall hedge. He cast his eyes to the screen, where the reassuring dot was moving at a brisk pace toward the T station at Davis Square.

Sitting alone in the car, he leaned his head back against

the headrest. Trying to imagine what might go wrong once Cat and Arnie entered the apartment, he let his thoughts wander. Was Rajeev sophisticated enough to have booby traps? Did he have a webcam? Did he have self-destruct software on his computer? Without knowing more about the guy's intentions, it was impossible to predict. He was certain of one thing: Cat was a pro. When they exited, there would be no trace of the intrusion.

When a departing car left a space up the street, Adrian opted to move into the spot. It was nearer to the apartment, although it meant that the apartment house was now behind him. He put on the glasses, linked them to the SUV's cameras, and activated the voice communications with the safe house. "Comm check."

Melodie's voice came over the wire. "You're loud and clear, and we've got a room with a view."

"Anything new to report?"

"Arnie says he's ready to rock and roll. He's wandering around Davis Square, waiting for instructions."

"Tell him to hook up with Cat and meet me here; she should be coming out of the station any minute. As a couple, no one will give them a second glance. I want a powwow before they go in."

Several minutes later, he spotted Cat and Arnie behind him, hand in hand—a couple seemingly enjoying a leisurely stroll. The only oddity about the scene was the large square valise that the gentleman was carrying. As they came abreast of the house, Cat bent over to retie her sneakers, taking an opportunity to personally assess the layout. They continued walking, past Adrian and for an additional block, before doubling back. Arnie climbed into the back, while Cat settled into the seat recently vacated by Jones.

Her smile vanished. "Any action?" she asked Adrian.

"No, it's quiet. Jones is en route to the bar." He pointed to the glowing dot on the screen.

Cat raised her eyebrows and gave Adrian an appraising look, but said nothing. In return, Adrian gave her a brief nod of acknowledgment. They'd talk about Jones later, and in a more private setting.

She twisted toward Arnie, all business now, with her expression taut and a crease between her brows. "When we get inside, your first order of business is the computer. I'll look for any other documents. If I find the passport, can you clone it?"

"Shouldn't be a problem."

"I'm hoping that this guy is a doofus. But if he isn't and this all goes to shit, he could be back here in twenty minutes. Doesn't matter if it's T or taxi, that's all the time we'll have."

Arnie calmly laid out the obstacles. "It all depends on the size of his drive. I could just grab the user files and it would be faster, but our best bet is to grab a mirror image. There could be suspect software or hidden files that a quick copy might not capture. I've got the capability to grab 500 gig in about twenty minutes. Anything bigger than that means we need more time."

Cat turned back to face the windshield, engrossed in thought. When she replied, directing her words toward Adrian's glasses, her voice was steely. "Melodie and Trent, if Rajeev bolts from the bar, you need to stall him. I don't care how you do it. Talk to Jones and figure it out."

Adrian handed the communication pen to Arnie and

pointed to the briefcase in the cargo compartment. Explaining how the HUD on the glasses functioned, he demonstrated the linking mechanisms. "Cat will wear the glasses. She'll be doing the primary search, so we'll want to record everything she touches. We can check the video later to see if we missed anything, but it will also help ensure that Cat puts everything back exactly as she found it."

Indicating a sturdy ballistic nylon bag in the rear of the SUV, Adrian told Arnie to open it. "We've got a small stock of supplies that might be useful. I was particularly thinking about the balaclavas."

Arnie rooted around in the bag and pulled out two black hoods. "If he's got a webcam in there, it could be hooked to his phone or some server up in the cloud. So covering our faces would be good. No point in advertising ourselves."

Nodding in agreement, Adrian started to lift the glasses from his nose when the image in the HUD flickered. His posture stiffened, and he lowered his voice to a whisper. "Heads up, everyone. The door's opening. Arnie, slide down to the floor. When he walks by, I don't want him seeing you. Melodie, pull the file and confirm that it's Rajeev."

Adrian held a phone to his ear and, glancing at Cat as she shifted to face away from the sidewalk, began a one-sided conversation with himself. "Harriet talked to Shirley earlier, so we thought she'd be back from the store by now. Betty wanted to stop by and see the new baby." Pause. "Really?" Pause. "That's great news." Pause. "Sure, we can wait." Pause. "Sure." Pause. "When did that happen?"

He continued to babble, knowing that his voice would carry through the car's open windows, and suppressed the urge to look up as a shadow briefly blocked the sunlight streaming into the front seat of the SUV.

"Bingo," Melodie trilled once the man had passed. "That's Rajeev Malik."

"Capture the image and send it to Jones and the kids," Cat directed before picking up her BlackBerry and pressing it to her ear. "He's headed your way. Dark blue polo, khakis, boat shoes, no socks. Shuffles his feet, hands are empty. No hand-carry. Photo's on its way. Text me when you have him."

Cat's gaze followed Rajeev as he approached the next intersection. "I want as much distance between him and us as possible. We'll go in after Jones has eyes on him at the bar." She cocked her face toward Adrian. "Harriet? Shirley?"

"The names just popped out."

"And which am I?"

Adrian winked at her. "You're the spy—figure it out."

Arnie mumbled from the rear, "While you two are bantering, I'm feeling like a pretzel back here."

Cat looked between the seats and couldn't help but chuckle at the sight of Arnie wedged into the space on the floor. "We're clear." Her BlackBerry pinged, and she glanced down at the incoming text: Eyes on subject.

Minutes later, Adrian's phone pinged with a text. "Jones is in position," he told the others. "All we have to do now is wait."

Suddenly remembering Jones's instructions about setting the proximity warning, he moved the cursor over the dot and clicked. A small text box appeared at the bottom right of the screen: Alert configured.

Chapter 17

Saturday late afternoon
Boston, Massachusetts

Jones claimed an open stool nearest to the front door of the sports bar. From his vantage point, he could see the entire room, and anyone entering or exiting the establishment would have to pass directly in front of him. He eyed the crowd and evaluated the likelihood of anyone becoming involved if the plan with Rajeev backfired. His gaze rested on a face in the far corner of the room, moved on, and then slowly pivoted back. *Crap.* He knew that face—DEA ... Wes something. Smart guy, but often a jerk. Jones locked eyes with the narc, who raised his eyebrows in an unspoken question. Jones gave the barest shake of his head and continued eyeballing the other patrons. He spotted another longtime agent nursing a drink at the bar. *WTF*? He suppressed the urge to confront the two players and instead concentrated on staying out of their way. Whatever their op, it didn't involve Rajeev. *Or did it? What were the chances?*

Jones measured the reactions of the DEA crew as Rajeev pushed the door open and stood in the entryway, searching for the friend who would be a no-show tonight.

The narcs didn't blink; there was no tell in their expressions or actions. Smart money said that they had a different target on their radar, but Jones couldn't shake the feeling that something didn't feel quite right. He stretched his neck and, while Rajeev settled into a seat at a vacant high top about twenty feet away, sent the text to Adrian: Sub in place. Wait 4 food. They wanted Rajeev relaxed and comfortable before Cat and Arnie breached the apartment. Having food and drink, and a bill to settle, would ultimately delay his ability to leave quickly.

Pointing his nose toward the wide-screen monitor suspended just above the high top, Jones pretended to watch the end of an extra-innings game at Yankee Stadium while keeping a surreptitious eye on his prey. Rajeev fiddled with his phone, placed it on top of the table, and finally opened the menu. Several minutes passed before he flagged a server and placed an order. Jones thumbed another text to Adrian. Ordering. Must b hungry.

Jones watched the server stop at two additional tables, then rose to intercept her as she returned to the serving station. He leaned slowly into her space, avoiding any sudden or aggressive movements that might startle the woman, and palmed a badge onto the counter. "I'm a federal agent. Please keep working and don't look around. Please tap your finger once if you understand."

The woman, to her credit, tapped her finger once on the counter and continued touching selections on the electronic ordering device. She called out to the bartender, "ginger martini, double Fortaleza rocks, and two Smuttynose." In a low, raspy voice, she asked, "What do you want?"

"You just took an order from an Indian man sitting

alone at a table for two. He has very dark hair and a wart on his left nostril. Please tap your finger once if you know who I'm talking about."

She tapped once on the counter.

"Good. You're not in danger, but I need your help. We're expecting him to stay for about an hour. If he suddenly wants to leave before that, stall as much as you can with the bill. Blame it on a broken computer or spill a drink on him—anything will do. If he tries to leave without paying, raise a ruckus, but don't confront him. And most important, you've got to keep this between us. Can you do that?"

She glanced at her watch and tapped her finger.

Jones noticed that her hand was shaking. "Everything will be fine. This is a surveillance operation. There's no danger." He silently prayed they were right and that Rajeev wasn't carrying a weapon.

She tapped her finger again, reached for two platters of burgers and fries, and turned away without a word. Jones followed her with his eyes, admiring her calm composure, and wondered briefly if he should start frequenting the place ... maybe try to strike up a conversation. *Relationships have begun under stranger circumstances*, he thought, *so why not?*

Returning to his stool, Jones once again feigned interest in the baseball game as a runner slid into home. He saw Rajeev place the phone to his ear and speak a few words, concluding that this was the first of Deepak's "I'm delayed" calls. When the waitress placed Rajeev's platter of food on the high top, he sent the text to Adrian: Food on table. Go.

Chapter 18

Saturday late afternoon
Somerville, Massachusetts

Cat snatched the glasses from Adrian's head and, sliding out of the car, reminded Arnie that the sound of doors slamming could draw unwanted attention. She gently pushed the passenger door closed before briskly walking to the door Rajeev had just used to exit the house. Hefting the briefcase and the valise, Arnie followed.

It took Cat precisely eight seconds to pick the inexpensive lock on the outer door. They stepped inside and closed the door, then slipped the hoods over their heads. Cat confirmed that their communications were operational and waited for a few more seconds, alert to any indication that their entry had been observed, before climbing the stairs.

On the landing outside the apartment, Arnie pulled a flashlight from his valise and, thumbing the switch on, handed it to Cat.

Cat played the light across the floor and over the door, examining the frame for any trips that would alert Rajeev to an intrusion in his apartment. Satisfied, she leaned forward to study the door lock, a run-of-the-mill dead bolt. Working the torsion wrench and pick in the jagged keyhole, she felt the pins separate and steadily rotated the cylinder to release the bolt. She easily defeated the lock in the door handle, and rotated the knob slightly. Raising her eyes to Arnie, she whispered, "Here we go."

Cat gently cracked the door, checked for any triggering devices, and repeated the sequence until the door was fully open. She let her eyes take in the room and lifted her chin toward the desk in the corner of the living room. "You see the computer?"

"Yep." Arnie noted the familiar logo and grimaced. "If that thing has a fingerprint scanner, we're screwed."

"You tackle the machine. I'll do the search."

Cat started for the bedroom, thinking about Rajeev's situation. If he was involved in illegal activities, he might also be concerned about physical safety. It would explain why he'd chosen an apartment with a fire escape outside the bedroom window. Such a person might also have important documents, money, medications, a change of clothes, and other essential items packed and ready. She opened the closet and, spotting a wheelie bag on the floor, lifted it to test the weight. She spoke softly. "He's got a go bag."

In the car, Adrian squinted against the sun's glare and shifted positions to have a better view of the screen. "Be careful when you open it. I don't like ..." He froze as a shrill squeal pierced the conversation. Momentarily confused, he swiveled his head, searching for the source, until his eyes fell on the display of Jones's locator app. To his dismay, the alert box glowed bright red—Jones was on the move. "Cat, we've got a problem."

"What's wrong?"

"Jones is moving. And since he's following ..."

"It means our bogey is moving, too. Damn."

"You've got fifteen minutes to get what you can and get the hell out of there."

"Got it."

Cat walked swiftly into the living room and found Arnie absorbed with the computer. "We're out of time. We have to stage this as a robbery. Grab the laptop and anything else that a thief would think of as valuable. Something triggered this guy to leave the bar. See what you can find."

The incoming text icon winked on Adrian's phone. He read the message and spoke softly to Cat. "Something spooked him. Jones says Rajeev skipped out on the bill, bolted from the bar, and ran for a cab."

"Damn. Can Melodie and Trent do anything?"

"We're on it," Melodie answered. "Your fellow Bostonians aren't going to be happy, but the traffic signal grid is going to experience a major meltdown. Right ... now."

Adrian's text icon blinked again a few seconds later, and he relayed the message to Cat. "You should be good. Jones is two cars behind Rajeev, and all the traffic lights just went out. They're gridlocked."

"Until Rajeev gets out of the cab and heads for the T."

"Are you always such a pessimist?"

"I'm a realist."

Melodie's voice was somber. "If he heads for the subway, we have to let him go. We can fool the locals into thinking the signal mess was a hardware failure, but if we interfere with the T, they'll know they were hacked."

Cat closed her eyes in resignation. "Okay. We're at

fourteen minutes and counting. Let me know if anything changes." She went back to the bedroom and lifted the go bag onto the mattress. Unzipping the bag, she found it fully packed with clothes, shoes, and other typical travel accoutrements. "This is interesting."

"What?"

"He's got a stack of money in here ..." She flipped through the bundles. "Dollars, euros, some Saudi, a few Indian rupees, and Iranian rials."

"Iran? Really? But I don't get it. Why leave cash in such a conspicuous place?"

"My guess? He's got travel plans." Cat focused on a suit hanging from the closet rod—clean, pressed, belt dangling from the hook on the hanger, and separate from the remaining garments, as if everything had been shoved aside to make way for this ensemble. She ran her hands over the jacket and then spread it open, pulling three passports from the inside pocket—two from India and the third from Iran.

Adrian, watching on the HUD, blinked. "Whoa."

Cat pulled the jacket and pants from the hanger and folded them into the suitcase. "Our boy is definitely not on the side of the angels."

She rifled through the remaining garments and found nothing further of interest. The clothes were all well-worn, and a quick inspection found no suspicious seams or pockets. The shoes were equally tame, revealing no removable insole or hidden cache in a heel. As she bent over to replace one of the shoes, a tiny light caught her eye. "He's got a motion detector ... in his freaking closet, of all places. I must have set it off when I lifted the bag."

"A motion detector? For a go bag? Something's not

right, Cat. I mean, the money and passports are important, but ..."

She examined the closet more carefully, tapping on the interior walls. They should have sounded hollow where the drywall covered the space between the studs, but instead she heard the dull thunk of a solid core. She beamed the flashlight over the wall, and finally discovered two small holes punched into the wallboard. Not finger holes—they were considerably smaller and perfectly matched. She thought for a minute, remembering an oddity about the belt that was hung with the suit—a belt with two tongues. Pulling it free from the hanger, she aligned the two tongues with the holes in the wall and found a perfect match. On pushing them in, she heard a click as they snapped into place.

"Uh, Cat ..." began Adrian.

Cat pulled on the belt, and the wall came with it.

Entering the room, Arnie whispered urgently, "There's a wireless app running on the computer. He's got a sensor of some sort, but I can't figure out where it's ... holy shit!"

"I tripped it," responded Cat. "We're gonna need the bomb squad."

Cat and Arnie gaped at the cache behind the wall. The blocks of Mylar-wrapped C-4 were vertically stacked, eight on each row and two deep, floor to ceiling, between four studs. Performing some quick multiplication, she calculated that 576 bricks—720 pounds of high explosive—were crammed into the narrow wall space. She ran the flashlight over the blocks.

"Anything?" asked Adrian.

"I don't see any triggering devices. It doesn't mean that

there couldn't be an initiator in there somewhere, but I'm wagering that this is just a place for storage."

"What do you want to do?"

Her anger surging, Cat hissed to Adrian, "Tell Jones to take down Rajeev, and I mean right fucking now. And get a team over here to secure this place. Invoke federal authority; we can't afford to lose time turf-fighting with the Somerville PD or anyone else. Give me a moment to think of a cover for why you're here."

She machine-gunned orders to Arnie. "Grab the computer and flash drives, backups, CDs, whatever." She pulled an empty nylon tote from the floor of the closet. "Take this, and stuff your valise, too. Five minutes, and we're gone."

Two cars behind Rajeev, Jones answered Adrian's call and listened in disbelief. He'd spent over two decades in the shadowy world of the FBI's counterterrorism division, maintaining a façade that insulated the true nature of his work from the scumbags he monitored. Now, in the middle of what should have been a simple surveillance op, they risked unraveling the carefully woven fabric of his pseudo-identity.

The Jones legend had nearly imploded five years ago, when his profile had been inadvertently captured in the background of a front-page photo in the *Boston Globe.* But that had been containable, before everyone and their dogs and their grandmothers had smartphones and were tethered to social media. Today, in the middle of Boston, with crowds of people, an arrest would pique the curiosity of everyone in the vicinity. Cell phone cameras would point his way and, faster than one could spell T-w-i-t-t-e-r, his face would go viral. And with traffic gridlocked, getting anyone else to the scene was out of the question.

I'm truly fucked, he thought as he tossed a twenty through the taxi's sliding window and flashed his badge at the driver. "FBI," he said in a clipped voice. "Stay in the car and keep crawling with the traffic. I'm going out the passenger side."

Knowing he would have little time to take control and subdue Rajeev—and not scare the hell out of everyone nearby—he heaved his bulk out of the taxi and ran the two car lengths in a low crouch. When he reached Rajeev's cab, he raised himself to full height and aimed the barrel of his gun at the rear window. The backseat was empty.

"FBI," he yelled at the startled driver. "Your passenger—where did he go?"

The driver's heavily accented response was indecipherable, but the man's gestures pointed through the windshield to an eleven o'clock position.

Jones spotted Rajeev then, about seventy or eighty yards ahead on the left and walking fast—toward State Street and the T station there. Jones broke into a run and had gone half a block when a voice called out behind him.

"Mr. Jones?"

Mr.? Jones glanced back over his shoulder and saw a scrawny kid who looked about twelve.

"What did you say?"

"Mr. Jones," he panted, "my name's ... Terry.... I work for ... Cat.... I followed ... that guy ... when he went ... to the bar.... I hung around ... you know ... just in case."

Running and trying to keep his eye on Rajeev, Jones

didn't have time to figure out what the kid wanted. He shook his head and kept going.

The kid was persistent and managed to keep pace. "Should I ... call ... backup?"

And as simple as that, the solution to the dilemma had presented itself. "Yes!" Jones shouted, gasping for breath. "Transit Police! And Farrell ... FBI ... field office!"

"What charge?"

"Conspiring ... to use ... weapons ... mass destruction."

Jones pressed on and left the kid standing in the middle of the sidewalk, bug-eyed and stabbing at his phone.

Cat pulled the dresser away from the wall, yanked open the dresser drawers and searched them roughly, looked behind the hanging mirror, ran the flashlight over the baseboards, flung open the curtains, climbed onto a chair and checked the finials on the rods, then lifted the mattress and box spring, and finally crawled under the bed. Nothing. She tugged the go bag into the kitchen and rummaged through the cabinets, stove, and refrigerator. Still nothing. *Time's up*, she thought. *Gotta go.*

Helping Arnie pack the electronics, she wove the cover story. "Adrian, I think your angle is that you and Jones came to have a chat with Rajeev. You saw him leaving the house, so Jones followed while you stayed to see if there were any other occupants. You saw two people go inside not long after Rajeev left, one carrying a toolbox. When you noticed the curtains being knocked around, you investigated. The intruders heard you and bolted down the fire escape. The place is a mess—just as you found it. You didn't touch anything."

Adrian mulled it over. "It's even almost true."

"Exactly."

"And after I phoned Jones, it took me a few minutes to call it in because ...?"

Returning to the bedroom, Cat invented a plausible explanation. "You ran back downstairs and chased after the intruders, but they were gone. There was no sense of real urgency. But when you went back upstairs and entered the apartment, you cleared the rooms first, and discovered the C-4." She opened the bedroom window and looked down the fire escape. "It should work." She let her eyes wander over the apartment. "I needed more time here; I feel I've missed something. Tell me we have everything on video."

Trent and Melodie spoke at the same time. "We do." Trent continued, "We'll analyze it while you drive back to the safe house. I'm itching to find out what's on that computer."

"Aren't we all? All right, we're coming down."

At the bottom of the stairs, Arnie and Cat pulled off the balaclavas. Arm in arm, they opened the door and wheeled the bags to the sidewalk and down the street, turning the corner toward the T station—just a nice older couple leaving on a trip.

Adrian waited until Arnie and Cat were out of sight before placing the call to the FBI's Boston field office. He reached Leo Farrell, the Special Agent in Charge at the Boston office, and relayed the story that Cat had invented. He kept his recitation simple and brief, knowing that it would be recorded and relayed verbatim to the locals. Later, he'd face more probing questions from his own people. For now, it would have to do.

As Adrian requested a backup team downtown for Jones and deployment of the bomb squad and ATF agents to Somerville, a part of him wished that they could have waited for Rajeev's next move. Aborting an operation was always a tough call, but he couldn't fault Cat's rationale. Several hundred pounds of high explosive C-4, in an apartment in the middle of an urban area, made the decision a no-brainer.

Jones sprinted down the escalator at the station's entrance, bulldozing his way forward and eliciting numerous shouts and curses from the people he shoved aside. He lost sight of Rajeev, who blended into the churning crowd of dark-haired, dark-shirted bodies. Piggybacking behind another rider, he slipped through the electronic gates and raced toward the tracks for the Orange Line.

As he approached the train platform, Jones noticed two transit police uniforms. The men were clearly agitated, with their necks craned and eyes flicking rapidly over the sea of riders. He slowed and thumbed his phone to the MBTA app, learning that the next train would arrive in three minutes. At this time of day, it meant that the last train had departed five minutes ago. Thinking about his run to the station, he estimated that he couldn't have been more than ninety seconds behind Rajeev. And he'd been running; Rajeev hadn't. He concluded that there was no way Rajeev had made the previous train.

Jones found a position with an unobstructed view encompassing most of the platform. Keeping the transit cops in his field of vision, he started scanning the crowd. When he noticed one of the officers jerk his chin toward the far end of the platform, he followed the gesture. Rajeev was standing alone, impatiently tapping his foot as he waited.

The two cops separated and walked briskly toward their quarry, with Rajeev seemingly oblivious to their presence. Jones, who was closer, angled his stride in Rajeev's direction. He was about fifty feet away when Rajeev shifted his stance and, with it, his gaze. Their eyes met, and Rajeev's widened as he recognized Jones from the pub.

In that same moment, Rajeev alerted to the uniforms converging on his position. He was looking about wildly, seeking a path for escape, when he heard an officer call his name. For an instant, Jones thought he detected an expression of sadness on Rajeev's face, before registering that the man had jumped off the edge of the platform.

Jones bolted forward as riders began shouting and screaming at the man navigating his way across the railbed. Rajeev glanced back as a train, its horn blaring in warning, roared into the station on the rails he'd just traversed. He smiled smugly at Jones before pivoting toward the opposite platform and stepping onto the next set of tracks. The train from the opposite direction, arriving nearly simultaneously and its sound masked by that of its counterpart, struck him full-on.

Chapter 19

As Adrian finished his conversation with SAC Farrell, he could already hear sirens wailing above the drone of urban traffic. A loud yelp erupted, disturbingly close. *One or two blocks*, he thought, just as the cruiser's flashing blue lights reflected in the rearview mirror, followed immediately by an unmarked Chevy Impala. Pulling his credentials from his jacket pocket, he stepped out of the SUV.

Two uniforms—one midthirties and the other a fresh-faced kid barely out of puberty—emerged from the patrol car and were joined by a lean, weathered man in a sport coat, who unfolded his long legs from the driver's seat of the Impala. Introducing himself, Adrian learned that the uniforms were just finishing their shift and heading back to the station when the call came in. The wearer of the sport coat, Captain Frank Samms, offered his hand and listened intently as Adrian quickly described the cache of explosives in the building and the circumstances that had led to the discovery.

The older patrol cop digested the information and looked to Samms for guidance, while the younger patrolman kept glancing around the scene and shifting his weight from foot to foot. *A rookie*, Adrian thought, *full of adrenaline, itching for action, and not big on fact gathering.*

The captain calmly directed them to barricade the streets and begin evacuating a four-block area surrounding the apartment. Turning to face Adrian, he raised his eyebrows in an unspoken question: who would be taking the lead, local or federal?

"It's integral to a federal investigation," Adrian offered. "ATF is on the way, and I understand that the State Police will handle the actual disposal. Once the C-4's been removed and the building cleared, my team will handle the evidence in the apartment. I'm going to ask that you respect our need to manage this situation and restrict entry until my people are in place. But it *is* your town, and I'll share with you as much as I can—up to the point that it might jeopardize our case."

Samms glanced over his shoulder and, seeing the two patrolmen moving into the expanding sea of blue and red flashing lights, locked eyes with Adrian and asked bluntly, "Is this related to the harbor bombing?"

Adrian held the man's stare and considered how much to reveal. The resentment of local agencies toward the often heavy-handed authority of the federal government was well-known. He personally felt that the locals had suffered more from the "need to know" rule than was justified, and the communication failures that had come to light after the marathon bombing were still fresh in the Boston-area psyche. They deserved better, he thought, and decided to take the cooperative approach. "Our working theory is that there is a connection between the occupant of this apartment and the harbor incident." He paused and added, "I'd rather keep that out of the media for the time being."

Samms nodded appreciatively. "Thank you for that. I'll do what I can."

"Out of curiosity, what made you choose a four-block perimeter?"

"Seven hundred pounds of C-4 is a helluva bang, and there's no certainty about whether or not there's a timing device or other trigger involved, is there? Or an additional stockpile you didn't find? Considering the concussive impact and the potential for fire spread, a four-block area seems prudent." He rolled his eyes in annoyance. "Assuming that the Staties and ATF don't have some other preference they'd like to assert."

"Speaking of ..." Adrian shifted his eyes toward the black Ford truck threading its way toward them. "I think we'll soon find out."

Turning to watch the approaching vehicle, Samms said acidly, "Hallelujah, we're all safe now."

Adrian cocked his head and, absorbing the captain's obvious hostility, was about to ask for context when a hand gripped his shoulder.

"Agent Santori?" asked a deep voice.

Shrugging out of the hold on his shoulder, Adrian pivoted toward the voice and came face to face with a man geared from the neck down in a green and black bomb suit. "That would be me," he responded.

"I'm Sergeant Wayne Wilson, Massachusetts State Police." He glanced at Samms and acknowledged him tersely before giving Adrian his full attention. "What's the situation?"

Adrian repeated the story about finding the explosives

and mentioned that the total weight was probably over seven hundred pounds.

Sergeant Wilson gave Adrian a hard stare. "I think we'll be the judge of that. Thank you for the report. We'll take it from here." Without another word, he started walking toward the house.

Taking a deep breath, Adrian forced himself to remain calm. Clearly there was tension between the captain and the sergeant, but they would have to table their differences until later. "Sergeant Wilson!" he called. The man stopped walking but didn't turn, forcing Adrian to walk to him.

"I have a tremendous amount of respect for what you do. But let's be very clear here. This is a federal investigation, in which your participation has been requested. I view this as a team effort. Your part is to clear the building, get me samples of the material, and bring to my attention anything that catches your eye as an experienced bomb technician. In matters of securing the explosives, I'll defer to your expertise. For everything else, let's work together to determine the best course of action for disposing of the hazard. Can you work with me?"

Wilson's features hardened for an instant, and then relaxed. He extended his hand. "I'll let you know what we find."

Adrian shook the sergeant's hand and watched the man's back as he strode toward the apartment house, where he was joined by another man with a dog. *Explosive detection canine team*, he realized. The black Labrador retriever and its handler would systematically search for any other explosives on the property. He turned back to reengage with Samms, who had joined a knot of uniforms at the far corner of the lawn.

Feeling his phone vibrate, Adrian glanced at the screen and stopped to take the call.

"Tell me you've got him."

"In about a thousand pieces," Jones responded, explaining how Rajeev had ended up as subway roadkill.

"Christ! He was our only damn lead." He sighed audibly, and finally asked, "Are you clear?"

"Yeah. The cops didn't make the connection, and Farrell sent a team to take over. Weird, though. There were two DEA undercovers at the bar. I can't see how it would be connected, since this op was last minute, but it tweaked my radar, and now they're aware I was in the area. Probably nothing, but I'm going to poke a bit. Afterward, where do you want me?"

"Foxborough. We need to put our heads together and figure out what the hell we've stumbled into, but I'm going to be tied up in Somerville for a while."

"No problem. I'll hook up with Cat. We'll get started on Rajeev's computer, and maybe we'll get lucky."

"Everywhere we turn, we're hitting another dead end. A little luck would be a welcome change."

Chapter 20

Saturday night
Boston, Massachusetts

Jones shouldered his way out of the chaos of the T station and hustled back to the Warehouse. He found the two DEA guys still in their original seats, nursing their drinks. He mashed through the crowd and nudged the arm of the narc at the bar as he signaled the bartender. He eyed the man on the stool to the left, judging him to be oblivious to everyone—save the attractive blonde talking about her work.

He looked up at the screen and—to no one in particular—asked, "Who's winning?"

"Brazil," came the response—from the narc Jones knew as Wes.

No one else seemed particularly interested in following the conversation, so Jones took a step closer and dropped his voice. "Waiting for anyone in particular?"

"I thought you might be back. Let's take a walk."

"Damn." *Coincidence was just too much to hope for.* Jones noticed the bartender approaching and waved him off.

Turning to leave, he nearly collided with the server who had helped him earlier. She broke into a big smile, raising his hopes that there could be potential there. Returning the smile, he said, "Duty calls. Maybe I could come back when it's not so busy?"

Her smile grew wider. "I'd like that," she said. "I'm here Wednesday through Sunday. Mondays and Tuesdays are free." She scribbled a phone number on a napkin and handed it to Jones.

"I'm in the middle of something right now, but I *will* call." He laid his hand over his heart. "Promise."

"I look forward to it," she said.

In a moment of wild fantasy, he imagined settling into a seat, ordering a bite, and waiting until she got off work. The sight of the second narc leaving the pub brought him back to reality. He headed for the door, a bounce in his step that hadn't been there before.

Outside, Jones and the two agents moved down the sidewalk, taking a bench in the narrow plaza leading to the 75 State Street building. Enclosed on three sides, they could easily see anyone approaching or taking an interest in them.

Wes, not bothering with introductions, was the first to speak. "We heard that the subject was meeting someone at the Warehouse this evening. It tickled our interest. Imagine our surprise when you showed up. Imagine our greater surprise when our subject bugged out and you followed him. Where is he now?"

"On a train to the afterlife."

Wes blinked.

Jones looked around before asking, "How exactly did you get turned on to the meeting?"

"Wiretap. We're looking at someone we believe is a real player. Your guy's name came up, so we tagged his phone. We heard him agree to the meet."

"Who's the player?"

"We think his name is Emilio Paredes ... we've heard him called El Bailador. That's *Dancer* in Spanish ... no clue how he came by the moniker. He first popped up on our radar about four months ago. Don't know much about him; it's like he came out of nowhere. What's interesting is that he's not Latino, and he's not talking to Latinos. He's talking to people from South Asia ... mostly India, some Pakistan. Our take is he's operating his own pipeline for smack coming out of Afghanistan."

"His own heroin pipeline? Bypassing the cartels? Ballsy guy."

"Or maybe he has a death wish. Most on the team think he's new to the game. But he's smart, and he knows the ropes. We," he motioned toward his partner, "think he may have been at this for a long time. He's incredibly careful ... we still don't have a handle on his whereabouts or a good photo of his face. The guy is a fucking ghost. The best we've got is a voice on a burn phone."

"If he's using burn phones ..."

"Oh, he's using burn phones all right. The number changes at least twice a day ... that's part of what I mean when I say he's careful. The geeks are pulling phone calls from a ten-mile radius and running them through some voice recognition software. It's all gobbledygook to me, but it seems to be working ... except for the times when he's more than ten miles away. Another thing, he's never on a call for more than fifteen seconds, and the signal disappears as soon as he hangs up. He's either pulling the SIM card and battery, or he's jamming the signal."

"Could you send over copies of whatever you have?

Voice and art? If your guy Paredes used the name of our guy, it can't be coincidence."

"Your turn. What's your interest?"

Jones looked away for a moment, knowing he would need to give Wes a nugget or two, but not wanting to reveal the underlying investigation. He turned back to study Wes. "So, hypothetically, let's say our guy was in possession of a significant quantity of high explosive. You have any thoughts on how that might relate to your drug angle?"

The agents exchanged a look, and Jones caught it. "What?" he asked.

The second agent spoke for the first time. "How much did he have?"

"About seven hundred pounds of C-4 last I heard. The bomb squad's working the scene."

Both agents whistled. The second agent finally spoke. "Indian with C-4, non-Latino with Latino name hustling for a smack pipeline. Usually drugs are exchanged for money. We," he waved his hand to include Wes, "have been tossing around a theory that Paredes is former military or former intelligence. What if our guy traded C-4 for drugs from your guy?"

The agent's words fused all of the questions bouncing around in Jones's head. *Weapons for drugs. Crap,* he thought.

Jones stood and pulled a pen and the napkin with the server's phone number from his pocket. *Trisha,* she'd written. Carefully tearing away part of the napkin, he scribbled a phone number and gave it to Wes. "Call this number; they'll give you a secure link. Send me everything you've got ... I need it yesterday."

Chapter 21

Sunday early morning
Foxborough, Massachusetts

I glanced at the clock when Adrian finally joined us at the safe house: 1:30 a.m. As tired as we all were, the urgency of our discoveries dictated a long night ahead.

Ever since Jones and Cat had hustled into the house a few hours earlier, Jones and Jason had been hunched over a computer in the corner. When Cat asked what they were working on, his only reply had been, "A theory."

Gabe had spent the afternoon penetrating the firewalls on the servers at the Indian Internet company, where his expectations of formidable security were met in spades. His ace in the hole, however, was his personal knowledge of the man who had designed the company's system.

At a conference in Las Vegas a few years ago, a friend had introduced Gabe to the genius who was considered the top computer infrastructure and security expert on the Indian subcontinent. After earning an advanced degree at the University of California at Berkeley, the man had promoted the need for a radical system restructuring to protect India's industrial giants from electronic attack and corporate espionage.

The three geeks had bonded and spent much of their time together at the conference. One evening—following an extended cocktail hour, lengthy dinner, and several nightcaps—the trio were well-lubricated and sharing stories about their exploits in cyberspace. In due course, the man had divulged a method by which he constructed his own back door for remote access to the systems he designed. Seeming to recognize the misstep—particularly given his reputation as a stickler for security—he had dismissed his statements as a joke and abruptly turned the talk to another topic.

The conversation, however, had stuck with Gabe. "That guy was arrogant enough to think that he didn't have to abide by his own rules. What an asshole."

Adrian asked, "Will he know someone tunneled in?"

"It's possible, but if there were trip wires, I didn't see them. Remember, he built this so he could actually use it. He wouldn't want alarms going off."

"Let's assume he discovers the intrusion. Can he trace it back to us?"

"Nearly impossible. If he manages to follow it at all, he'll end up with Astrid Gustafsson."

"Who is Astrid Gustafsson?"

"An eighty-six-year-old widowed great-grandmother living in a nursing home just outside of Stockholm."

"Stockholm, as in Sweden?"

"Yep."

Adrian shook his head in amazement. "I don't know whether to admire you or be afraid of you."

Gabe laughed. "The only people who should be afraid are the bad guys." Continuing, his expression grew somber.

"And I'd say that Conrad is firmly seated in that category."

Gabe went on to explain that he'd located and pulled the profile of Conrad's e-mail account in India. "He opened the account for Internet service back in 1995; the e-mail came with the package. He's kept it all this time, augmenting it with broadband in 2002 and wireless in 2011. That tells us something about his age: he's not a kid.

"He doesn't seem to use the Internet much, but he has a tendency to hang on to old correspondence and has e-mails going back to 1999. What I found interesting was that he uses encryption—first-generation basic off-the-shelf stuff."

Melodie stretched her arms above her head and yawned. "NSA cracked that program years ago. Trent and I have been reading, and there isn't any content that would make us stand up and take notice. But why bother encrypting when the messages are so mundane?"

Gabe agreed enthusiastically. "Exactly. I found it curious, so I started looking further. The first encrypted message appears in 2007. Prior to that, they're all clear text, and all the addresses had regularly appeared in multiple e-mails over the years. But in 2007, within a week, he received messages from two people who had no prior history in that account. And the extension on the e-mail addresses? Dot-P-K and Dot-I-R."

Cat, who had been quietly listening, suddenly sat erect. "Say again?"

Gabe raised an eyebrow. "I thought you'd find that interesting. Pakistan and Iran." He scrolled through a list on the screen. "The first ones came in late October 2007. There's a steady—but not overly frequent—stream of back and forth until early November 2008. Then there's an avalanche. It seems to be all run-of-the-mill crap, but as Trent and Melodie pointed out to me, the timing is extraordinary."

I heard Cat's sharp intake of breath and was trying to recall what had happened in November 2008 when the realization hit me. "Wasn't that …?"

Cat, her fingers pressed hard into her temples, was nodding her head furiously. "The Mumbai bombings. The attacks started on November 26 and lasted for four days."

Adrian sat forward, his fists balled on his knees. "They were Pakistanis."

"Yes. Recruited and trained by a terrorist group called Lashkar-e-Taiba. It's long been held by Western intelligence that they had plenty of help from the ISI." She looked at me and explained, "That's short for Inter-Services Intelligence. It's Pakistan's CIA equivalent."

Adrian let out a low whistle. "And now you're wondering if there's some connection between the LeT and Conrad27?"

"Could it just be coincidence that this guy—who we know to be involved with the harbor bombing attempt—receives a flood of e-mails from Pakistan right around the time of the Mumbai incident? I don't buy it. Some of us in the agency always felt that there were more people involved in the attacks than were identified by our Indian friends. There were even some rumors that the Iranians might have lent a hand."

"But no evidence to back up the talk?"

Cat compressed her lips into a thin slash and said bitterly, "Roger told me to drop it—said it was just a red herring—and put me on another case. All along, that son of a bitch has known about Conrad27. He probably even knew about the plans for the Mumbai attack. Remind me again why he's in a federal prison wasting taxpayer money, instead of rotting six feet under with a bullet in his head?"

"Because we're Americans, and we believe in the rule of law. And because we keep hoping that he'll spill his guts."

Cat threw up her hands in frustration. "He's never going to give us any useful intel ... he's too far over the edge, and we have no leverage to use against him. From the time he joined the agency, Roger insulated himself from any emotional attachment. There's nothing and no one that he cares about, and he actually believes he did the right thing by betraying his colleagues and his country."

"You may be right. But I think he has a network. Not just Conrad27, but also people here—in America, like the guy who kidnapped Lindsey and whoever followed us out of the airport here in Boston. I don't think those were Conrad's people ... I think they were Roger's people."

Melodie, who had been listening intently to the exchange, cleared her throat. "Well, speaking of ..." she began, while setting up a split-screen display on the monitor, "take a look and tell me what you see."

On the left was a frontal photo of a very fit man in his midforties, his well-defined musculature revealed by a tight T shirt emblazoned with the picture of a handgun and a slogan that read *I support gun control ... by gun owners.* He wore a plain black baseball cap that shadowed his face—making his features difficult to distinguish—and was pumping gas into a silver Kia.

The photo on the right captured a man feeding a fare

card into the reader at a subway station turnstile. He wore a navy blue parka and a black watch cap, implying that the image was captured in the winter. He was caught in three-quarter profile with his chin raised, jaw set, and his eyes squinting to focus on something in the distance.

"Is it the same guy in both photos?" I asked.

"Look at his right hand," Melodie directed.

It took me a few seconds to realize that in both photos, the ring finger of the man's left hand was a stub, shorn off at the first knuckle. "He's missing a finger."

"Do you recognize him?"

I was puzzled. *Why would I know this guy?* And then his clothing registered a hit in my memory. I'd been the victim of an attempted purse snatching on the subway last February when I'd been carrying several flash drives with files from Cat's computer. The thief had pulled the emergency cord—yelling about a bomb—and yanked my bag from my shoulder. A marine on home leave had managed to grapple the man and retrieve my purse, but the thug escaped in the chaos. He had been wearing a navy parka and a black watch cap ... and gloves. No way of knowing if he was missing a finger.

"Is he the one from the subway? The one who tried to steal my bag?"

"I think so, yes. Unfortunately, so far, there's no facial match in the system. Trent just tracked down the real owner of the Kia, who parked his automobile in the long-term lot at the airport early this morning ... before catching a 7:00 a.m. flight to Vegas. Interestingly, he's now discovered that his keys are missing."

"Wait ... are you saying that someone actually lifted his

car keys? That's pretty bold."

"Oh yeah ... very gutsy ... and clever. Nobody would suspect a thing until the owner returned to Boston or started looking for his keys—whichever came first. We caught a break with the image from the gas station. Trent's reviewing more video from inside the airport, trying to determine how the keys were stolen and hopefully track the thief's whereabouts earlier. We know the image at the gas station was captured at 6:38 a.m., which had to be right after the car was taken. With a full tank of gas, the guy was prepared to follow you for as long as necessary. He's smart."

Cat's eyes narrowed, and a deep frown creased her forehead. "He's more than smart. He's done this type of op before ... you don't get those skills sitting on your ass in an office all day. He's military, law enforcement, contract security, or, heaven forbid, intelligence."

Jones—still at the desk in the corner—stood, commanding our attention. "I think you've nailed it. Earlier today, we were trying to figure out what triggered the warning to Lindsey and why we had someone following us. I had an interesting conversation with a couple of DEA folks today."

Jones related what he had learned about the heroin connection and went on to explain that he and Jason had been researching the possibility of a drug smuggling network. They had become convinced that the smuggling operation had intersected with the harbor bombing.

"If we consider the possibility that an organized group of military or Agency operatives might have been running an operation at the height of the war ..."

Adrian interrupted. "They would have been using

connections in Pakistan or Afghanistan to deliver the product, and government aircraft for transport. They would have had a real cash cow. Now that we've scaled down and recalled most of our troops, there's no channel for taking delivery or moving the stuff. They've had to find other means."

"And they're worried that our investigation into Conrad27 might expose them," I said.

Cat stood up. "The missing finger is a huge break. This guy is in the system somewhere. Find him."

After the failure in DC, the man they called Tin Man had raged for over a day, worrying about the potential for their entire mission to unravel, until learning that the woman and her coworkers were planning to travel to a safe house in Foxborough. He had convinced Squid and Sandbox to devise a plan for locating and storming the property. Their mission was simple: grab the woman and eliminate anyone who got in the way. His own mission, on the other hand, lay elsewhere.

He had reconnoitered the property late in the afternoon, remaining in the woods and circumnavigating the house. He had found the dirt track, effectively camouflaged by the undergrowth, and judged it to be an attractive avenue of escape. It was certainly the route he would choose, given a choice. The driveway was the only other option for a vehicle, but it would be a kill zone.

After studying the home and its surrounding topography, he had pinpointed a suitable location and saved the GPS coordinates before making his way back to his car a half-mile away.

He returned to the property shortly after midnight and turned his unmarked car onto the long drive, easing off the macadam and into the brush some fifty feet from the main road. Setting off into the woods, he let the GPS guide him to the position he had chosen earlier.

He relaxed, breathing deeply, his heart rate settling into a calm rhythm. If all the occupants of the house were killed tonight, so be it. But there was one person who had become well-acquainted with Squid, and allowing him to live would be sentimental and foolish ... and dangerous. Unlike his compatriots, he never let emotion rule his decisions. If they did not eliminate the witness, he would.

He was satisfied with his field of fire, considering that the occupants of the house could choose any of the four compass points to effect an escape. He could not cover four, but he could reasonably cover a good portion of three.

He assembled the compact sniper rifle, racked the nightscope, and waited.

Chapter 22

Trent put his talents to work in search of the elusive man with the missing finger, while Gabe, Jason, and Melodie busied themselves with tracking down more information about Conrad27. An hour later, an excited whoop sounded from the back of the room.

"Wanna know who Conrad27 is?" asked Jason, a wide grin splitting his face. "I'll feed it to you."

An image materialized on the panel at the front of the room. The grainy black-and-white photo captured a slightly built, jowly, light-skinned man in his early sixties, with dark hair going silver. He was in a wide hallway or anteroom with ornately carved crown molding, standing before a raised desk or platform. His neck craned upward as if he were making an inquiry of an unseen person stationed there.

"Let me introduce you to Ghadir Kharoti—the name on the Internet account—which we were able to pair with the photo in front of you. This image is from archives of video for the main offices of CMCC—the Central Mumbai Communications Company.

"I was rummaging through the files for his account and found a notation that he'd registered a complaint on the ninth of December in 2008, at 1:27 in the afternoon. Leave it to the Indians and their lust for detail to have written down not only the date, but also the time! When I finally realized that he had gone to their offices in person, Gabe tracked down the actual video."

I blurted in amazement, "You found digital security videos from 2008? Seriously?"

"Yep ... they keep everything. Anyhow, according to the file, Mr. Kharoti complained of being overcharged for service. It seems that during the month of November, his account had consumed a considerable chunk of bandwidth, and the company charged accordingly."

"At the time, CMCC billed home Internet service similar to the way cell providers charge for data usage on smartphones," Gabe interjected. "The customer chooses a data plan and pays a premium per megabit for anything over the limit. Mr. Kharoti had exceeded his limit ... by a lot. Can you imagine if they implemented that billing model in the US?"

"Rioting in the streets, for sure," Melodie said, rolling her eyes in disbelief.

Jason brought another image to the screen. "Mr. Kharoti is a very successful businessman in Mumbai. He owns a large export business—carpets and luggage, of all things—with showrooms in Los Angeles, Seattle, New York, and Atlanta. The guy caters to money ... he has a number of celebrities and tech execs on his client list."

"You know, I've actually met this guy. Tom and I bought several carpets from him, back when," Cat said.

Jason continued, "Seriously? Well, here's where it gets interesting. Mr. Kharoti maintained that he never used the

Internet and that the account must have been billed in error. When assured that the bill was correct, he stated that he would verify with his son and a nephew, both of whom were temporarily living at the residence. All of these details were dutifully recorded on paper by the clerk attending to Mr. Kharoti's complaint."

"Two younger men living with the elder Mr. Kharoti. That *is* interesting," Cat observed. "So, what do we know about them?"

A new photo appeared on the panel as Melodie's chin bobbed up and down. "This is the son, Farshad, taken in 2012." The relationship was immediately obvious. The son's face was a clone of the father's.

"I'm still working on fleshing out the bio. Farshad Kharoti graduated with a degree in biochemistry from the University of Michigan in 2006. He initially took a job with a pharmaceutical company in Minneapolis, returning to Mumbai four months later after his mother died. Presently, he lives in Chembur and works for a biotech company in Trombay—both of which are northern suburbs of Mumbai. Of note is that Trombay is home to the Bhabha Atomic Research Center, or BARC.

"He travels to the States about once every eighteen months, and—before you ask—his last known entry into the States was almost a year ago. He was not here during the harbor attack."

"And the elder Mr. Kharoti mentioned a nephew?" asked Cat.

"Yes. Identifying him is trickier, but there are photos and postings all over social media placing young Farshad Kharoti with this person ..."

The next image showed a somber man, in his late twenties or early thirties, staring straight into the camera. Cat observed that his relatively fair skin, narrow nose, dark hair, amber eyes, and bushy eyebrows hinted at origins in the northern region of the Asian subcontinent—notably Pakistan or northeast India.

Cat studied the face and asked, "Who is he?"

Melodie slowly shook her head. "I'm not sure. On social media, he's referred to as Aashif Ahmedani, but I haven't found any active accounts for him. He seems to be a bystander, rather than a participant."

"If this Aashif guy is the nephew, where is he in the family tree?"

"We're trying to piece that together. I've been digging for facts about the elder Mr. Kharoti and his wife, but there is a limit to what is available electronically. The Indians keep detailed records, but until a decade ago, it was all paper."

Adrian, who had been quietly absorbing the discussion, asked, "Just the one son? What about previous marriages?"

Melodie's face went blank for a moment. She squinted in thought and lightly tapped a knuckle against her nose. "Hmm. I was concentrating on Farshad's mother, but I'll keep ..." Her words were cut off by the deafening shriek of an alarm.

Chapter 23

Cat reacted instantly to the sound, pulling a gun from beneath her jacket and shouting, "Safe room! *Now*!"

Jones's booming shout carried above the piercing alarm. "Perimeter breach! I count four bandits. *Go, go, go*!"

Simultaneously, Cat yelled at Melodie's visage on screen, "Code Rubicon!"

A rumbling noise swept through the house as barriers automatically deployed over the windows and doors, effectively sealing us inside. I scrambled toward the door leading to the kitchen and was the first to reach the cabinets hiding the entry to the safe room. I pressed my fingers to the switches and was praying to all the gods of this earth that I'd get the sequence right, when Gabe crouched beside me and spoke calmly in my ear. "One-Two, on-off. One-Four, on-off-on."

The cabinet lifted, and Gabe and I ducked into the stairwell, followed by Jazz, Arnie, and Jones. I yelled over my shoulder at Adrian, who was still at the top of the stairs and waving frantically for me to keep moving. Like frightened mice, we scampered down the steps and into the basement complex, with the doors thumping closed behind us.

My heart rate was skyrocketing and I was near panic when I remembered the monitors. Pressing the panels at the right of the door gave us a room-by-room view of the floors upstairs. We could see Cat, Adrian, and Jason near the cabinets when Jason mouthed something to Cat and bolted back toward the conference room. A wave of surprise washed over Cat's face, and I had no difficulty interpreting the F-bomb that escaped her lips. She moved to follow, but Adrian's reaction was faster. He sprinted after Jason and caught him in a flying tackle just as the door shattered. The room erupted in a spray of flaming shrapnel, clouds of smoke obscuring the image from the camera.

Why had Jason gone back? All I could think was that there was some piece of information he didn't want to leave behind. Praying for some sign that they were okay, I was helplessly watching the monitors when motion in the lower corner of the screen caught my eye. The stairwell door whooshed open, and Cat staggered into the safety of the basement.

Cat gulped air for a few moments before looking up at the monitors. "Any sign of Adrian and Jason?"

"Not yet," responded Jazz. "Where did the smoke come from?"

"We had a system installed. I will say that it worked as advertised ... the smoke seems to have covered our escape.

I touched Cat's forearm. She placed her other hand over mine and guided me away from the door. I couldn't believe she was so calm.

"What now?" I asked.

"Melodie and Trent will have made calls for a special

response team. I issued a Code Rubicon, which disables all the electronics. That means no communications until the house is secure. The only systems still active are the one running the closed circuit cameras and the status light. Everything else is disabled. Short of being hit by a bunker-busting bomb, we should be safe here. But I think our best option is to get out. This place is going to be swarming with cops."

"What about Adrian and Jason?"

"They're on their own for the moment. If they got to the conference room, they might be able to hold off the attack until the cavalry arrives. There's also a hidden hatch that opens to the outside. It's a measure of last resort, because they would be going out blind."

"C'mon, we've gotta move," Jones called.

I turned toward the control panel, the irrational part of my brain thinking that somehow I could bring them into the safety of the basement, when Gabe put his arm over my shoulders and led me away.

Jones herded us through a series of undetectable doors and hidden rooms until we emerged at the entrance to a long tunnel. The opening was about six feet in height—tall enough for me to stand comfortably but requiring Jones and Arnie to stoop—and barely wide enough for a single person.

Panting, Jones said, "There's no power in the tunnel Run your hand along the wall and feel for the bumps to guide you. We've got a truck and a car in a shed about three hundred yards from here."

We moved quickly—half running, half walking—until the burn in my legs told me we were on an incline. I had no idea how far we had traveled—or for how long—when the bumps in the wall began to run closer together, much like the dividing white lines between two merging lanes on a highway become shorter as one lane ends. I slowed down, unsure what lay ahead, and Jones instructed us to stop.

The darkness absolute, I tried to focus my other senses but could not decipher the sounds I was hearing while Jones explored the space. I finally recognized the grind of a garage door rising in its tracks. Jones stumbled ahead and pulled open a truck door. The wash of light provided enough illumination that I could make out the forms of a big dark pickup and a smaller four-door sedan.

Jazz pushed me into the car's backseat and scooted in beside me, while Cat slid behind the wheel. Jones and Gabe climbed into the truck. Finding the keys under the floor mats, Cat and Jones drove the vehicles out of the garage and waited while Arnie pulled the doors closed. As soon as Arnie heaved himself into the car beside Cat, Jones started the truck rolling across the clearing—with Cat right on his tail. The dirt road was overgrown and barely discernible, so we proceeded at a snail's pace until intersecting with a stretch of blacktop. The narrow blacktop ran into a wider road, and another even wider, eventually bumping into the ramp to I-95. We took the lead and turned south—away from Boston.

Ten minutes later, Cat instructed Jazz to slide her seat back and pull the black-coated wire descending from the seat into the chassis. Two sharp tugs lifted a hidden panel beneath the seat, revealing a small cache of weapons and communications gear.

Jazz handed a phone to Cat, who poked the earbud

into her right ear and pressed a preprogrammed number. "Alias authenticating 1-1-2-7-2-4," we heard her say. She listened intently to the voice at the other end of the connection, finally interjecting, "Agreed," followed shortly thereafter by, "Roger that." She didn't share the content of the conversation.

Chapter 24

Adrian's flying tackle of Jason drove them both to the floor and inadvertently saved them from being struck by the shrapnel from the door. Deciding that they would never make it to the safe room, Adrian grabbed Jason by the shoulder and propelled him forward into the conference room as smoke began spewing from the vents.

Jason grabbed Adrian's forearm. "I wrecked my ankle when I hit the floor."

"Can you make it? We have to move."

"Yeah. Give me a hand."

Adrian gripped Jason's outstretched arm. "Ready?"

Jason blew out two breaths and clenched his teeth. "Yes. Where are we going?"

"That far wall."

Hobbling, Jason gripped Adrian's shoulder and leaned into him for support. Under the cover of the smoke, the two men strained to feel their way to the same niche they had used earlier in the day for photos.

The niche was about seven feet wide and five feet deep. Adrian shoved Jason into the space. Adrenaline spiking, he hauled two of the heavy metal desks to the front of the niche. He tipped them on their sides, one nestling into the other, to create a double-walled barricade. Crouching below the lip of the inner desk, he pulled a spare pistol from the holster under his arm and passed it to Jason.

"You've fired a Glock before, right?"

"Sigs, mostly, occasional Glock. I'm rusty, though. I haven't been on a range in a while."

"Rusty is fine, just as long as you're aiming at *them*."

They heard a loud pop and the *thwtt* of a bullet as it smacked into the wall behind them, followed by two more pops and heavy thuds as shots hit the desks.

"They're trying to draw a reaction. Keep down and stay behind the desks. They're not perfect protection, but they're not typical cheap government-issue. Cat ordered them reinforced. We thought she was crazy.

"Keep your eyes open. If you see anything moving, shoot it. We just need to keep them at bay until the cavalry gets here."

A burst of automatic fire tore at the desks, but didn't penetrate into their tiny den. Adrian was a split second from returning fire when they heard the wail of sirens in the distance. Shouts and expletives sounded around the room, along with a distinct, "Fall back!" Boots clattered across the floor.

Adrian jumped to his feet and, facing the back wall, gave a hard kick to the floorboard. This caused the side wall to separate and rotate inward, exposing an oval hatch similar to those used on ships. He pulled the quick-action handle to pop the hatch, which opened into an alcove at the side of the house. Well-concealed by a thick growth of evergreens, he carefully poked his head outside and, finding the area clear, wedged himself through the opening. He pulled Jason out quickly and reclosed the hatch, sealing them outside.

After allowing a few minutes for his eyes to adjust to the darkness, Adrian whispered to Jason that they should try to make it to one of the SUVs, which were about fifty yards away and around the corner at the side of the house. If they were fast, they could get there before the cops arrived. Hooking his arm under Jason's shoulder, Adrian grabbed Jason's shirt, winched him up, and hefted him forward.

They reached the vehicle and separated, Adrian retrieving the key from behind the license plate, punching the button to unlock the doors, and heading for the driver's side, while Jason clambered around to the passenger side.

Adrian stepped on the gas, revving the engine before shoving the gearshift into drive. He peeled away from the house and, halfway down the driveway, turned onto the lawn. The grounds around the house were cleared for a good hundred yards, eventually giving way to tall timber. He headed straight toward a giant elm at the edge of the woods, veering at the last minute onto a rutted dirt track that led into the trees. The SUV bounced over the rough terrain for a short distance before the track took a sharp turn to the right.

Rounding the bend, they encountered two cars blocking the way and a forest of gun muzzles demanding attention. The sudden glare of spotlights was accompanied by a hollow voice from a megaphone. "Massachusetts State Police! Drop your weapons and put your hands outside the windows! Now!"

The only movement Adrian made was pressing the switch to lower the window. "I'm Special Agent Adrian Santori, FBI," he shouted. "If you don't have the code phrase, you're not authorized to stop me."

Jason wriggled in his seat. "Uh, Adrian, these guys look like they're at DEFCON-1," referring to the highest state of US military alert—a term popularized by the spate of nuclear devastation movies produced during the Cold War.

The corner of Adrian's lip twitched as he suppressed a smile. "Let's see who blinks first."

Adrian and Jason sat perfectly still during the long silence that followed, attentive to the slightest noise or movement. Finally, the voice from the megaphone broke the standoff. "I've been instructed to tell you that Julius Caesar and his legions have crossed the Rubicon. And you're supposed to tell me the name of Lindsey's first dog."

"I don't have a clue," Adrian whispered. "Do you?"

"Brewster," Jason said. "The dog's name was Brewster."

Tensions having stepped down from the adrenaline-spiking checkmate, they complied with the demand to hold their hands outside the car's windows. The man with the bullhorn approached, pointing to the ID dangling from his neck. Adrian slowly reached for his own credentials and raised his eyes to the approaching trooper. He felt the hairs rise on the back of his neck and tried to mask his alarm. *No way this is a coincidence.*

"Sergeant Wilson, isn't it? You were in Somerville earlier."

"They always say you FBI boys have good memories. Care to explain your presence here?"

Adrian flashed to the previous afternoon and the

obvious discord between Wilson and the police captain from Somerville. *More to that story*, he thought.

"This *was*"—using the past tense for the damaged building—"a secure government facility. Anything more than that is need to know, Sergeant. Sorry."

Wilson's nostrils flared, and his shoulders rolled back with the rebuff. "If you have information about the safety and security of citizens of the Commonwealth of Massachusetts, you'd be wise to share. Gets embarrassing when you know things and a bunch of folks get hurt because you kept quiet."

He was referring to the bombing at the marathon and that the feds had been stingy with their intelligence. Wilson was right, but now wasn't the time. Adrian shrugged sympathetically. "The current situation is very fluid, and there are still a lot of unanswered questions. When we piece it together, I'll personally brief you. But at this moment, the case is off-limits."

Wilson wrinkled his nose, as if the words had a stink to them—which, Adrian had to admit, they did.

He changed the subject. "Do you have a medical crew? My colleague took a fall and banged up his ankle. You got anyone who could take a quick look?" He hated to bring attention to Jason, although one of the Staties surely had already taken a digital capture of their faces.

Wilson lifted the megaphone and yelled, "Suarez!" A moment later, a dark-haired young woman ran up to the truck, a medical kit slung over her shoulder.

Jason opened the door and dangled his leg over the edge of the seat while Ms. Suarez removed his shoe. She suggested moving him to the ground—where she could elevate his leg and more properly evaluate the injury—but Jason declined. He winced as she palpated the swollen joint.

She finally offered an assessment. "You need a hospital. I think you may have a fracture, likely from a ligament tearing off a bone end when you hyperextended it during your fall. We can transport you, or your boss can take you. But either way, we should immobilize it first."

Jason and Adrian looked at each other and burst into laughter.

"What's so funny?"

Between guffaws, Adrian tried to explain. "Sorry; nothing personal. This man just gritted his way out of a battlefield, and now you want to immobilize him."

She smiled politely and turned away from the truck to gather her equipment. Jason was still laughing when the spray of blood exploded from his chest, followed a microsecond later by the unmistakable sound of a gunshot.

Chapter 25

Sunday morning
I-95 South, near Providence, Rhode Island

I stared out the window and saw nothing but occasional headlights on the interstate and winks of light between the trees as we passed buildings just off the highway. My heart was still racing and my head was pounding like a jackhammer. I breathed in deeply, trying to calm myself. I sensed eyes on me and peeked out from my cocoon to find Cat watching me in the rearview mirror.

"You okay back there?"

"Mostly. If I could get my heart rate back to normal, I'd be fine. What the hell was that about?"

Cat's expression turned dark and her eyes narrowed. "If Jones is right, it's about drugs and explosives. If not, it could be someone who thinks we're a threat. I can't think of anything we've stumbled onto that would warrant this reaction, so I'm leaning toward Jones's theory." She glanced back at Jazz. "How were we even detected at the house?"

Jazz shook her head in frustration. "I don't know. Jones and I did a thorough sweep and were constantly monitoring for transmissions. The house, and everyone in it, was clean."

Cat's mouth formed a perfect *O* as she puffed out her cheeks and blew out a long breath. "Maybe not transmissions."

I had no idea what she was thinking, so went with my own question. "So those men were former military?"

Cat was quiet for several seconds before answering, "One could reasonably conclude that. But I'm also wondering if they're linked to Roger ... or both."

"But what do they hope to accomplish? I don't understand. We had no idea they existed ... now we're aware of them."

Posture rigid, lips compressed in a thin line and nose flared, Cat locked her eyes on mine. "I suspect that they want me. And if they can't get to me, they'll come after you and use you as leverage."

I jerked my head backward, caught off guard by the intensity of her words and the realization that Cat was terribly worried about my involvement.

She ran a palm over her forehead and stared out the windshield, lost in thought.

Jazz leaned forward. "And that brings us to an immediate concern. How do they know about us, and how did they locate us? How did they know Lindsey was in DC? How did they know to tail us from the airport?"

Cat's voice dropped to a whisper. "Are you thinking that we've been compromised?"

Jazz read her face, and her eyes went wide. "This isn't a revelation, is it? You already suspected?"

She shrugged. "Let's just say that I think it's a possibility." Rolling her eyes to the mirror, she focused on me. "You've known Jason most of your life, haven't you?"

I felt the blood drain from my face. *Where was this going?* "Yes," I answered, the tension in my voice evident, "since we were rug rats."

"And you confide in each other. You know just about everything about each other." She said it as a statement—not a question. I nodded.

"So, how many times have you met his new boyfriend?"

Puzzled, I frowned. "What new boyfriend?" I knew everything about Jason's relationships—the good, the bad, and the indifferent—and at the moment, he was unattached.

Cat's eyebrows arched. "Six weeks ago, a man named Matthew Pierce signed up for one of Jason's personal advanced martial arts classes."

"So? That's not unusual." Jason, a tae kwon do black belt, occasionally offered one-on-one personal defense training.

"I'll venture a guess that the nightly home lessons in which Jason and Mr. Pierce are currently participating have nothing to do with tae kwon do—particularly when those sessions are taking place in conjunction with dinner and breakfast.

"I will also tell you that Mr. Pierce doesn't need the training. He was Special Forces and is already quite skilled in hand-to-hand combat. He was, in fact, an instructor. If the two of them were ever to go seriously face-to-face, Jason would be in real trouble."

Unconvinced, I argued with her. "What? No way! He would tell me."

"Mr. Pierce is quite a good manipulator." Deepening

her voice, she mimicked the man. "I know you want me to meet Lindsey, but let's wait until you and I know each other better. She is so important to you ... I want to make sure I put my best foot forward."

Stunned, I glanced back at the pickup behind us, wondering if Gabe was aware of the entanglement.

Cat read my thoughts. "Nobody else knows. Jason has kept the relationship very quiet."

"But you've been *listening*?" I attempted to keep my tone even, but inside I was seething, and my irritation was evident. Her tactics seemed to have no boundaries.

She was unperturbed. "Yes, for about a month. We detected changes in his behavior—fewer evenings with you and other good friends, more charges at the grocery store, more empty wine bottles in the recycle bin, and most telling, no mention of Mr. Pierce in any conversation with you."

Seriously pissed off at the invasion of privacy, I squared my shoulders and opened my mouth in protest. "You have no right!" Even as the words escaped my lips, I realized how defensive and foolish I sounded.

"I call it like I see it, Lindsey. I have to wonder why Mr. Pierce was so adamant about keeping the relationship from you. And with the attack tonight, I'm looking at all the possibilities."

I had no answers and turned my head away. I had known Jason nearly all my life. We had shared strollers and pacifiers and everything else since. I had never known him to keep a relationship from me. It wasn't like him.

We approached downtown Providence just as the sun boiled over the horizon. I was staring vacantly out the window, only vaguely aware of our location, when the Rhode Island State House came into view on the left. Cast in the pink and gold light of dawn, its dome of white marble shimmered with an iridescent glow. The effect should have lifted my spirits. Instead, I sagged against the car door as guilt washed over me. The truth of the matter was that I hadn't been paying attention to my best friend. I leaned my head against the window and drifted into blackness.

Chapter 26

Sunday morning
New London, Connecticut

I awoke with a start, struggling to orient myself before remembering why I was in a car. We were stopped in a small, deserted lot, our two-vehicle convoy parked side by side with engines off and windows closed. Having been lulled to sleep by the car's vibration, the cessation of motion and noise had probably triggered an alarm in my subconscious.

Squinting against the brightness of the morning sun, I spotted Cat, Arnie, Jazz, and Jones standing a few feet away. Cat, cell phone pressed to her ear, wore an irritated scowl as she distractedly clenched and unclenched her free hand. Jazz stood at Cat's elbow, her hands on her hips and her stance aggressive. From all appearances, the conversation was not going well. Looking up at the truck, I realized that the mound in the window was Gabe's shoulder and that he must be fast asleep. Arnie was nowhere to be seen, and I imagined that nature's call had lured him behind a bush somewhere nearby.

When Cat lowered the phone and pressed the button to disconnect, I took that as my cue. After scrambling out of the car, I banged on the truck window to wake up Gabe and walked over to join the rest of the team.

"Where are we?" I croaked.

"New London," Jazz answered. "We've just been discussing the merits of I-95 versus the ferry. Cat's been in touch with Paul."

I assumed she was talking about the ferry across Long Island Sound, from New London, Connecticut, to Orient Point at the eastern tip of Long Island. "Where are we headed?"

"Washington."

I frowned. "Why?"

"Our safe house in Foxborough is blown, Lindsey. We have a couple of other places in the Boston area, but we have to assume—for now—that they may have been compromised. In Washington, there are a number of other highly secure sites operated by various agencies. Given the circumstances, it's prudent to reach outside our normal operational sphere. Paul is making the arrangements."

I bowed my head and bit my lip, attempting to control my building anxiety. This was not what I wanted to hear. It was one thing to collaborate intellectually in finding Conrad27; it was quite another to be running for my life. Admittedly, I was scared. My primal instincts were urging me to flee—to just go home and try to find normalcy again. And yet, as I looked at the others—this group of men and women who put themselves on the line every day—I felt ashamed. *Suck it up, Lindsey. You want to do something with your life? Then do something that has some real importance.*

Raising my head, I caught Cat and Jazz exchanging a silent look. Had they read my thoughts? "What?" I asked.

Cat reached out and took my hand in hers.

"Jason's been hurt. He's in the hospital."

Her words took my breath away. I squeezed her hand tighter and managed to find my voice. "What do you mean, *hurt*? What happened?"

"According to Adrian, he and Jason were intercepted by the State Police after they escaped from the house. Once the boys established who had the biggest dick, the Staties stood down and were supposed to escort them out of the area. Instead, it appears that they came under fire from a sniper. Jason was hit. They airlifted him to Mass General, but he's in bad shape."

So many emotions coursed through my veins at that moment that I was having difficulty gaining control of my senses. Fear, sadness, hope, impotence, love, anger, and hatred swirled around in a toxic, irrational stew. "I need to be there."

"No, Lindsey, you don't. He's got the best of care, and right now, your presence would only be a complication."

I started to argue, "But ..."

Cat raised her hand in a stop gesture, and her voice was hard and unyielding as she interrupted. "You can't go. Until we know more, the risk is simply too great. We have security minding Jason, but we can't cover both of you." She turned away and walked briskly back to the car. Reaching for the door handle, she swiveled her head back toward me. "Are you with us?"

I hesitated and noticed Jazz and Cat exchanging a glance. *Just suck it up and get in the damn car.* I balled my hands into fists. "I'm coming."

Paul pulled strings—or bullied the management—to get us on the sold-out ferry at 7:00 a.m. The tickets came with priority status, guaranteeing that we'd be first off when it docked on the other side. Accommodating the sedan and the big pickup cost three cars their reserved spots on the morning's first departure, with the ferry staff apologizing for an apparent software hiccup. The denied-boarding passengers complained loudly. One woman, fastidiously groomed and wearing an emerald-green, midcalf silk blouson dress—with matching shoes—was in tears. "It's my sister's wedding," she cried. "I'm the maid of honor! I can't be late!"

I was exhausted, irritable, and decidedly unsympathetic. I had an overwhelming urge to get in the woman's face and remind her that one should always prepare for the unexpected. If the wedding was that damn important, she should have gone the night before. Forcing myself to turn away before my mouth got ahead of my brain, I reminded myself to be grateful that no one knew that we had usurped their seats.

We split into couples to more easily blend with the crowd—Jazz and Jones, Cat and Arnie, Gabe and me. I stood on the deck, basking in the warmth of the sun and letting the salt air perform its magic on my mood while the ferry made its way across the sound. An hour later we were back on the road.

Chapter 27

Sunday late afternoon
Southwest of Washington, DC

Taking turns at the wheel, we drove the length of Long Island, over the Verrazano-Narrows Bridge and Staten Island into New Jersey, across the northern tip of Delaware, southwest through Maryland, around the DC Beltway, and west out of the city, eventually leaving the traffic behind and exiting southwest into rural Virginia. On our right, the hazy Blue Ridge Mountains rose out of the lush countryside. Ahead of us, the highway rolled gently through woodlands, fertile farmland, lazy pastures, and empty expanses of green.

I had traveled these roads years ago, spending three weeks on the road with my mom and dad to take in the monuments of DC and the colonial history of Virginia. Back then, it was miles between houses. Although the area was still lightly populated, civilization had made its mark—as evidenced by the McMansions dotting the countryside.

Based on my admittedly limited experience with safe houses, I expected our destination to be a home similar to the one in Foxborough. I was taken aback when we took the turn at the entrance to Montpelier, the home of the fourth US president. Crossing the bridge, I could see James Madison's stately mansion ahead of us. I had read that the house was restored a decade or so ago, after Marion duPont willed it to the National Trust upon her death in the eighties. In an unusual twist, the restoration involved demolishing thousands of square feet added by the duPont family during their ownership. I remember wishing that the Trust could have found a way to embrace the duPont additions, but purists had apparently won the battle of wills and walls.

I wanted to see more, but we turned away from the main house and headed toward a modern glass and brick building some distance away. The parking lot was teeming with busses and cars, but most seemed to be preparing to leave—as one might expect late on a Sunday afternoon.

Cat pulled near to a gate—its red sign reading *Official Use Only*—at the right side of the structure. Amid the precisely trimmed hedges was a subtly landscaped concrete pillar with an embedded electronic card reader. Cat lifted a lanyard from beneath her shirt and swiped the card dangling from its end. The gate slid open and closed swiftly behind us. I reasoned that Jones had his own card, because a moment later the gate reopened and the truck ambled down the drive behind us. The pavement swerved to the left, taking us behind the building, where an extension with a garage blocked our way. Cat and Jones swung the vehicles into unmarked spaces beneath the long adjoining carport. I took a moment to look around and realized that we could only be observed by someone who had wandered well off the walking paths and into a sliver of woods fronting the parking lot.

Following Cat, we unfolded ourselves from the cars

and scurried to the door beside the garage. Cat typed a code into the security panel, and we moved inside to a short hallway. I was intrigued by her apparent familiarity with the place and marveled—not for the first time—at the extent of clandestine operations that seemed to be taking place right under the noses of the general public.

We trailed her to the end of the hall. She tapped lightly on the last door at the right, and I heard someone call out, "Come in." Cat pushed the door open, and we spilled into a comfortably sized—but shabbily furnished—office with two rickety-looking wooden chairs facing an ugly metal desk. The room was otherwise adorned with a few photographs of the Montpelier mansion in various stages of restoration, a bookshelf laden with scholarly works about the estate and early American architecture, and two open boxes of informational pamphlets on a side table. This was not a room that encouraged lingering or social interaction. We ignored the seats and kept our eyes on Cat.

The young man seated behind the desk was dressed in civilian clothes: a button-down shirt and khaki pants, navy sport coat, but no tie. He greeted us perfunctorily and slid an electronic pad across the desk toward Cat. She placed her hand on the pad, which seemed to verify her handprint. He then lifted a camera-like device from a drawer. *Another iris scanner*, I thought, as the man pointed it at Cat's face. Her credentials apparently did not extend to the rest of us, as we were each required to follow the same ritual.

Our verification complete, the man politely intoned, "Good afternoon, Ms. Powell. You and your party are authorized to enter the facility. Bear in mind that access for the members of your party is strictly limited to the white-floor area. Their entry to other areas of the facility is strictly prohibited. Please confirm your understanding of these restrictions."

Whoa, I thought, reading between the lines. *Cat has privileges here; the restrictions are for the rest of us.*

Cat swept her gaze over us, nodding, and acknowledged the conditions. "We confirm our understanding. My guests will confine themselves to the white floor."

"Thank you. Welcome to Timely Manor."

I winced at the name. *Timely Manor? Really?* Not sure what to expect next, my eyes popped wide when an entire section of the back wall—ten inches thick and wide enough for two people—slid almost soundlessly to the right, exposing a narrow, shallow room about half the width of the office. Embedded in the right interior wall was a door that looked as if it should lead to a bank vault—and appeared equally impenetrable. As soon as the panel behind us closed, a young man—clad entirely in black and with an evil-looking weapon hanging across his chest—opened the vault and beckoned us inside.

"Ms. Powell, and guests, please use this elevator." He canted his head to the left. "Press the button for *4*."

As we packed ourselves into the car, I tried to align his words with what I had seen of the building's exterior: *single story,* I thought. *No more.* Cat pushed the button as instructed, and instead of *up*, we were quickly going *down*.

Cat, with her back to us and facing the elevator doors, spoke quietly. "You should assume that, while in this building, you will be under constant surveillance. You will be watched and listened to, in real time by real people. Everything you say, everything you do, will be recorded.

"There is one acoustically shielded room on our floor that guarantees we won't be overheard. It's technically called a *SKIF*, the acronym for a Sensitive Compartmented Information Facility. Paul and I call it a *bubble*. We use it whenever we're discussing highly classified projects. Any recording can only be accomplished if manually triggered from inside the room. The bubble is near our rooms, and we'll use it for our debrief and dinner tonight. Please don't even consider going exploring. I'm sure they are less than overjoyed at our unscheduled visit and would love an excuse to throw us out in the woods. So right now, catch a nap and shower. We'll meet for dinner at seven thirty."

I started to ask what this place was, and who *they* were, but the elevator bumped to a stop. Its doors opened onto a narrow lobby, with doorways straight ahead and to the left and right. The door immediately facing us was red, while the one on the right was white and the door to the left was yellow. The floor, likewise, provided red, yellow, and white paths leading to their respectively colored doors. I was reminded of hospitals, with their colored lines guiding beleaguered visitors to maternity, cardiology, radiology, and the like.

I was instantly curious about the red door, and barely managed to hold my tongue. I reluctantly followed Cat and stepped through the white portal. The hallway beyond was reminiscent of nearly every hotel in the world, albeit not as long, with a set of two doors on each side every fifteen feet or so. But unlike any hotel I'd ever seen, there were no room numbers, and an iris scanner was mounted beside each door.

"We have the last seven rooms in this hall. Choose

one," Cat instructed. "There are no keys; you'll use the iris scanner, which will designate your choice and allow entry." She pointed to an alcove at the end of the hall that one would typically expect to house a soda machine and ice maker. "That leads to the bubble. I'll see you there at seven thirty."

So, no ice maker and no diet soda, I thought. Great. I sure hope they have toothpaste and toilet paper.

I opted for the next-to-last door on the left, subjected myself to the iris scan, and was pleasantly surprised. While smaller than a typical hotel room—and hopelessly devoid of charm—it was squeaky clean and furnished with the essentials, including toothpaste, the usual amenities, and oddly, a spray bottle of Febreze. *Weird.*

As I stripped off my clothes, I again wondered about *they* and what this place might be. Obviously, there were secrets here. And the place had accommodations for overnight visitors. But why was it underground? And why was it hidden beneath a public facility in the middle of nowhere? I set the alarm for six forty-five as random ideas drifted around my brain like dust motes. Exhausted, I couldn't seem to hold onto any single thought. I stumbled to the bed and fell into a dreamless sleep.

Chapter 28

Sunday night
Orange, Virginia

Cat locked herself in her room and pressed her ear to the closed door. She waited for the fragments of conversation outside to drift away before stepping back into the hall. Following the white line, she reached the landing by the elevators and kept walking—straight to the yellow door.

The yellow corridor required a voice match and password in addition to the standard iris scan, and she heard the lock release as both were accepted. She slipped through the entry, the door latching quickly behind. After surrendering her weapon to the two guards on duty, she held her hands high and stepped into the detector. The machine was far more sophisticated than those used at airport terminals across the nation, and there was no expectation of privacy. The soldier looking at the body scan could feel lust or disgust for all Cat cared. Security was security and damn well ought to be thorough.

One of the two armed guards approached. "Who are you here to see today?"

"Foxtrot-Uniform-One-Eight," she responded.

In the phonetic alphabet of airlines and military, *Foxtrot* was the letter *F* and *Uniform* was the letter *U*. The combination *F-U* might have drawn snickers in some quarters, but in this facility, *F-U* occupants were highly regarded and zealously protected. *F-U* stood for *Friendly-Undercover*: men and women who had infiltrated some of the most vicious terrorist organizations in the world. F-U-1-8 was the eighteenth occupant to bear the F-U designation since the underground building's construction.

The occupant's room was comfortably furnished, and the food was superb. But the room was monitored 24-7 with both sound and video, its door could be opened only by an armed guard, and social interaction was generally limited to a handful of medical personnel specializing in psychological trauma. Some F-U designees had come back from their missions severely damaged, and they could be dangerous as hell. Occasionally, certain specially authorized personnel were allowed to visit. Some of those personnel were also authorized to temporarily turn off the recordings. Cat was in both categories.

Cat turned to the other sentry. "Please deactivate all recording."

"Yes, ma'am," he answered. He pressed several icons on a touch screen, one of which started a recording of the deactivation request. "This is Corporal William S. Riley, authorization 9-2-7-Alpha-Kilo-Beta-9-0-3, confirming deactivation of visual and audio recording for Foxtrot-Uniform-One-Eight as directed by Catherine Ames Powell, authorization 1-1-0-Alpha-Beta-Alpha-1-0-2." He pressed his thumb on the pad, and a single green light illuminated.

He passed the device to Cat, who verbally affirmed the

request and recorded her thumbprint. A second light on the device turned green,

"Thank you, ma'am," he said, retrieving the pad from Cat. "The recordings for F-U-1-8 have been deactivated."

The first guard escorted her through another set of reinforced doors. The hall could have been any hotel in America, except that each door was reinforced and had a bulletproof viewing panel. Stopping in front of one such door, the guard verified the position of the man inside and pressed a button to announce the presence of a visitor. The man inside did not respond. The guard unlocked the door, allowing Cat to slip inside, and relocked the door after her.

Cat wasn't overly concerned about her personal safety when she was around F-U-1-8; she was perfectly capable of protecting herself. On the other hand, seriously crazy people could be completely unpredictable.

She stepped over toward the sofa and stood directly across from an overstuffed chair, where F-U-1-8 was seated, his eyes closed.

"Good morning, Trumpeter. Please say your status." The man facing her didn't move a muscle ... didn't give any sign of recognition. *Trumpeter* had been the man's code name.

She tried a different approach. "Good evening, Jalil."

The man's eyes flew open. "Cat. I've been waiting for you to come back. I think I've remembered something. But I can't ... can't quite ..."

Cat used a motherly voice to soothe him. No pressure; just steady encouragement. She needed his memory.

"I was in Iran, and then I was on a boat. A big boat ... a container ship. Could I have been working as part of the crew? I can't be sure. I have recollections of a uniform, but I don't know if I was wearing it or if she was." The expression on his face turned puzzled. "She was on the boat, too. And she was beautiful, just as you said she would be."

What? Cat had never mentioned a beautiful woman to Jalil; she was sure of it. "Who, Jalil? Who was she?"

"The Goreva woman. The one your message told me to go see."

Cat's composure slipped, the shock showing in her eyes.

"You sent me, right? To the Goreva woman?"

"Everything's fine, Jalil," Cat said quickly. "What else do you remember?"

"I think the boat must have docked in Mumbai because, in my mind, I can see the Taj Hotel. That's it. I'm sorry; everything is still a jumble."

Cat reassured him and promised to be back as soon as possible. It had been a long haul with Jalil, but she was seeing a flicker of hope—even if his words made no sense. She had never sent him to see the woman he spoke of. Tanya Goreva had died years ago.

She left the room, and after authorizing the reactivation of the recording devices, made her way back to the white hallway.

Chapter 29

I woke, startled by the sound of people talking in my ear. It took me a moment to realize that the clock was sounding the radio rather than an alarm. Annoyed that I had forgotten to change the settings, I slammed the *Off* button. While some people enjoy being awakened by music or talk shows, I prefer that shrill beep-beep-beep to jump-start my day. Lying back to organize my brain, it took some effort to remember that I was somewhere in the Virginia countryside.Craving a short run, I grimaced at the realization that I was not only confined to the white floor of the underground warren—I had no gear with me. My only clothes, now carelessly tossed on the floor, were those I had pulled from my suitcase yesterday morning. I picked up my sour business suit and blouse and was instantly grateful for the Febreze. I've spent a lot of time in hotels around the world, but I've never seen one supply a spray deodorizer. *What kind of people stay here? Marines fresh out of the desert, or people like me—on the run?*

Thirty minutes later I was showered, blown dry, dressed, and insanely hungry. I walked briskly toward the alcove at the end of the hall, early for dinner but hoping to find quick sustenance before our meeting. Rounding the corner, I spotted yet another iris scanner positioned high on the wall. I must have passed the verification because the two doors blocking my way slid apart with a *whoosh*—as if an airtight seal had been broken.

I found myself the sole occupant of a minimally furnished conference room, with a table against the wall stacked with dinnerware and food warmers. My stomach growled in anguish when I lifted a lid and found the container empty. *The early bird does NOT get the worm in this place.*

I took a seat at one leg of the U-shaped conference table and waited. Several minutes later, a well-concealed door at the back of the room popped open. Cat walked through the doorway, followed by two young men toting food carriers. The men were dressed in camouflage. *Military.*

"Cool camo," Gabe whispered, sneaking up behind me and disrupting my attention on the food. "Look at the design. You could put one of those guys in the woods, and nobody would ever see him."

I nodded absently, more concerned with the mouth-watering scent of food that was wafting its way into my nostrils. I made a halfhearted attempt to remain in my seat until the others arrived, but succumbed to temptation. I found a plate, piled it high, and was stuffing my face as the others trailed in.

When Paul arrived, he responded patiently and reassuringly to the chorus of concern about Jason's injuries. "He is still in critical condition. They tell me the bullet nicked his heart and damaged the upper lobe of his left lung. The surgery went well, but the first twenty-four hours will tell us more. There's always a risk of infection and other complications, but he's young and very fit, and they are optimistic about his recovery."

Jones asked the question that was on everyone's mind. "Do we know who attacked us ... or who shot Jason?"

"Adrian should be here shortly, and I'll let him fill you in on what he's learned today. He flew into Baltimore this morning and spent the day at Ft. Meade with Melodie and Trent. In the interim, Cat has some information to share."

I focused on Cat and realized that the events of the past thirty-six hours had taken a toll ... her face was drawn, her eyes were bloodshot, and she seemed to have lost some of her normal composure. She remained in her seat as she spoke.

"I've been trying to figure out how they found us. The location of the safe house was very closely held and funded from untraceable black money; Roger never even knew of its existence, and I can assure you that no one in our unit let the information slip. Last night, Jones assured me that they'd swept the house and everyone in it and that no transmissions were detected.

"I considered the attackers. These guys had access to some serious hardware—military-grade optics and weaponry that isn't available to the average citizen. It started me wondering. If they were military, or former military, what other tricks might they have packed in their bags? That led me into thinking about nanoparticles."

Gabe raised his eyebrows. "Nanotechnology? Hmm ... impossibly tiny particles that stick to a surface. *That* would explain a lot. But, Cat, it probably wasn't aerial delivery. I believe that the army tried using a spray to track vehicles in Afghanistan, but wind drift made the accuracy unreliable."

"You're right." She nodded. "The army used drones, but they were spraying from some height. The closer the source is to the target, however, the more accurate it will be. I asked Paul to have a team examine our SUVs earlier today. They have confirmed the presence of nanoparticles. Eliminating aerial spray, I began to suspect that it must have happened at the airport. All three vehicles were parked together, and there were throngs of people milling about. Hand delivery would have been entirely feasible."

Gabe's brow wrinkled. "That makes sense. There are some commercial handheld systems available ... about the size of those breath-freshener sprays that people used to carry. You can hide one in the palm of your hand, and nobody would notice. They probably would have used a distinct spectral signature in the spray—something that could be tracked by ultraviolet or infrared scanners—and maybe an aerial drone to perform the search later."

I stared at Gabe in astonishment, wondering where he learned all this information and how he retained it. "Seriously? What are you reading at night?"

His face flushed, and I realized that I had embarrassed him. "No, really, I'm impressed," I blurted quickly. "It's just that you never cease to amaze me."

Cat nodded her head in resignation. "Gabe is exactly right. And if we looked at video footage, I'll bet we'd discover who and how."

"The *how* part is interesting," Adrian interjected as he strode into the room. "But the *who* part will definitely get your attention. Sorry to be late, but it's been a busy afternoon."

Chapter 30

Adrian worked to hook up his laptop to a monitor on the wall and establish a secure communication link to Ft. Meade. He explained that Melodie and Trent had been digging—looking for the person who had sprayed the cars at Logan and for the man with the missing finger. After he had the system up, Melodie opened a file, and the screen lit up with this morning's recording of the inside of Terminal B. We watched the silent footage of Adrian and me emerging from the jet bridge into the building.

"Watch this woman." Adrian pointed at a female I estimated to be in her early thirties. Dark-haired, slim, stylishly dressed, and exceptionally attractive, she was seated in the gate area where we'd arrived, presumably waiting for the next departure. When we started walking down the concourse, the woman stood and walked in the same direction. She pulled a cell phone from a small tote slung over her shoulder and held it to her ear, speaking a few words in apparent response to the person on the other end of the line. She had no other visible baggage.

Melodie accessed another video, this one of the arrivals area at Terminal B. Our SUVs were clearly visible, and the video showed us approaching the vehicles. The woman was directly behind us, not more than fifteen or twenty feet, the cell phone no longer in her hand. We watched as she approached one of the state troopers and engaged him in conversation. Presumably she asked a question, because his head bobbed and he pointed in a generally eastward direction, which is also where we were parked.

The subject then walked directly toward us. As she neared the lead car, she lifted her right arm and gripped the edge of the tote to open it wide. In the same moment, she jammed her left hand inside. She continued walking at a normal pace on a path that took her directly alongside our little convoy. It looked perfectly normal ... a woman trying to find something in the depths of her bag. As soon as she passed the third SUV, she dropped her arms and veered back into the terminal.

Jones was incredulous. "What was that? Did she have some kind of spray canister? And how did she get it through security?"

"Do you have an isolation of the bag?" Jazz asked.

Cat leaned forward, a worried frown on her forehead. "I can do you one better. I've actually seen one of those bags before ... eighteen months ago, when I was running an op in Peshawar. We ... uh ... intercepted it from an ISI agent."

Paul's eyes went wide. "Intercepted?"

"Well, the Pakis are rather protective of their turf. They don't like it when they think we are carrying out covert operations on their soil. On the other hand, we don't like it that the country is a haven for extremists. We regard each other with mutual low esteem."

"Should I ask how you got it away from him?"

"Not *him* ... *her*," Cat corrected. "One of the few females in ISI. She was recruited ... although coerced might be a more accurate description. So we made a trade: give us the bag and the camera, and we'll give you a passport."

Cat explained that the camera in the bag was an adaptation of the pinhole camera idea that people have used for decades. In this case, the bag was specially constructed so that the camera lens on certain mobile phones would easily mount to a grommet in the bag.

The primary difference between the average smartphone and this was the addition of mechanisms for loading and dispersing nanoparticles. As with most cell phones, pressing the shutter would take a picture. On this device, however, pressing and holding the button past the normal detent caused the nanoparticles to spew through the lens. We watched the video again, now understanding what the woman had been doing with her left hand.

Gabe frowned. "And the particles are so small you can't see them. Is it our design?"

Taking a long breath, Cat shook her head. "Russian, actually, which begs the question of how it ended up here. First, though, what do we know about the woman? There's something ... she seems familiar, but I can't place her."

"TSA shows her as a regular on flights between New York and Boston, typically leaving LaGuardia Friday evening and returning from Boston on Sunday night," Adrian answered. "She's a weekender, which suggests some sort of tie to Boston. This time was different, though. Early yesterday morning, she booked a midday flight back to New York. She got to the airport early, went through security, and waited for us. After spraying the cars, she went back into the terminal, through security again, and boarded the flight. We have it all on video."

Cat spread her hands in exasperation. "So who the hell is she?"

"Her name is Sophia Capreze ..."

Paul suddenly frowned. He looked over at Cat and, catching her eye, raised his eyebrows. "Capreze?"

Adrian continued, "Although records indicate that she has applied for a legal name change ... to Natalya Goreva."

A long crease of uncertainty spread across Cat's brow. She whipped toward Adrian and repeated the name. "Did you say Goreva? As in the daughter of Anatoly Gorev?"

Adrian glanced down at the screen of his laptop. "I don't have that information. We would have to retrieve the official documents to find out about parentage—if that was the reason given." He sat back and swung his gaze between Paul and Cat. "Who is Anatoly Gorev?"

"What else do you know about the woman?" Paul asked, deflecting Adrian's question with one of his own.

Visibly annoyed, Adrian remained silent for several long moments. Reluctantly accepting that no further details about Anatoly Gorev would be forthcoming, he gestured at Melodie to continue.

According to their findings, Sophia Cabreze grew up in Nyack, New York, and graduated at the top of her high school class. She applied to Princeton and was accepted, but dropped out after her freshman year to pursue a modeling career. Represented by a top New York modeling agency, she enjoyed a lucrative career for several years before returning to Princeton to complete a degree in political science. She then spent a summer in India on a paid internship for one of their largest conglomerates. Law school at Columbia came next, followed by employment at a prestigious law firm in Manhattan.

"She's never been in any trouble; there's nothing to indicate any *personal* connection to Russia or the Soviet Union other than her new name," Melodie reported. "Three years ago, however, she represented a purported member of the Russian mob in a contract dispute. She won the case. Since then, she's been the attorney of record in several cases involving former citizens of the USSR, but only one with known mob connections and none were high-profile. If she was one of their go-to attorneys, there would be more—a lot more.

"We staged an intrusion into the firm's servers to find more information and learned that Monday morning, the day following the early-morning attack at the safe house, Ms. Capreze requested a two-month, unpaid, personal leave of absence. We were initially concerned that she might have fled the country, but there is no record of her passport being processed. Unless she's using another identity or has access to a private jet, we believe she's still in the country."

"Any trips to India since the internship? And has she ever gone to Russia?" asked Cat.

I had been keeping my eyes on Cat and Paul, looking for any reaction to Melodie's words. Both faces had displayed bland, neutral expressions until the internship in India was mentioned. Cat's eyes widened ever so slightly, and Paul sat a little straighter. Cat and Paul kept secrets, and they were certainly holding back now. I stole a look at Adrian and saw that the corners of his mouth were downturned, his irritation evident. I offered him a small shrug of empathy. I understood the requirement of keeping sensitive information compartmentalized, but it was still hard to swallow.

"None that we have found," Melodie admitted, scowling. "But I have more news." She loaded a man's image to the screen. "Trent's been reviewing Sophia's Facebook account. She isn't big into social media, but does post occasionally. Meet Randall Forsythe, aka Missing Finger. He has no address currently recorded, but posts have popped up enough in the area of Boston's North Shore to make us almost certain that he has some sort of living accommodation there. More to the point, our mysterious Sophia Capreze appears to be in a relationship with him."

Chapter 31

We stared at the picture on the screen, comparing it to the images captured from the gas station earlier yesterday and the T a few months ago.

"Who is he?" Cat asked.

Trent spat out the bullet points of Missing Finger's life: born in 1978 in York, Pennsylvania, outstanding student and athlete, graduated from U-Penn with a degree in history, enlisted in the army shortly after 9-11, applied for Special Forces. He had made it through the program, but all mission-specific details have been redacted from the file. Forsythe had a sheaf of commendations, including a Purple Heart, Bronze Star, and Silver Star.

Adrian whistled. "Not your everyday grunt. How did he go from army rock star to terrorist-abetting scumbag?"

Trent went on, "He separated from the army in 2011. That was during the big drawdown from Iraq, when the army no longer needed the numbers. No mention anywhere of him losing a finger, so it probably happened after his discharge.

"He took a job with a private security firm after that and has been there ever since. I haven't been able to access their personnel records, but his passport shows travel to

Eastern Europe, Russia, the Middle East, and South Asia. Whatever he's been doing, they've kept him busy with it."

"So, what are you thinking?" I asked. "He was part of a rogue army group smuggling drugs out of Iraq or Afghanistan or wherever, and now he's running drugs into the States on his own? And his girlfriend arranges delivery to the Russian mob?"

Adrian looked at me appraisingly. "Something like that, maybe." He broke his stare and turned toward Jones. "But it's probably a bit more complicated, I would think."

Jones's huge head bobbed slowly. "First, if we're assuming that this guy is leading a drug operation today, his product would most likely arrive by air or sea. In New England, water transport is more likely—except in winter. But he still has to retrieve the product from the vessel and get it to shore without being detected, and then get it into the distribution channels. A lot of it comes through in containers or hidden compartments—some underwater—on large freighters. The dogs catch some of it, and we'll send divers down if we have suspicions, but the shippers are clever.

"Second, if he was smuggling drugs out of Iraq or Afghanistan while on active duty, he had help. He had support from someone in his unit and from personnel loading the aircraft."

"And you believe that some of those people have continued to participate?" asked Adrian.

Jones considered the question before replying. "I think it's almost a certainty. This isn't a one-man job. And where else would he find people he trusted?"

"Where's the product originating? I mean, what's the routing?" Cat asked.

Jones wrinkled his nose. "If this guy is involved? It's most likely coming out of Afghanistan. From there, through Pakistan. Americans probably would not want to deal with the Pakis directly; they're not in anyone's little black book of trustworthy associates. So through Pakistan to India. My guess? Mumbai. A huge port, a zillion people, wantonly corrupt—a drug smuggler's utopia."

Paul faced Jones. "How do you think we should proceed?"

"The way I see it? Find Missing Finger and follow him—physically, electronically, every which way. You said that the DEA has a ten-mile radius on calls. Let's make it thirty. There's a needle in the haystack, and we need to find it; otherwise we're just twiddling our thumbs until he screws up. We need to get ahead of him, because I'd bet the bank that—if we can apprehend him—he'll make a deal and lead us to whoever's organizing the bomb attacks."

"Thoughts on including DEA? This is really their turf."

"Tough call. If we include Wes and his partner, we gain expertise and feet on the ground. On the other hand, they work with people who will ask questions, and that organization has more leaks than Swiss cheese has holes."

"But you trust Wes?"

Jones did not immediately answer. Finally, he replied, "I suppose as much as I trust any narc. I've worked with him in the past and always thought he was solid. He can be a pain in the ass, but he's righteous."

Paul ran his fingers through his hair and took a deep breath. "Let's get some rest and revisit this in the morning. We'll all think more clearly with a little sleep."

"One last thing, Melodie." Cat glanced over at me before turning her attention back to the screen. "I want you to compile a deep background on one Matthew James Pierce. He's spent the last couple of months worming his way into Jason's life, and something about this guy doesn't feel right. I looked into him. He was also Special Forces, and like Mr. Forsythe, his file is also heavily redacted. Is it possible that Forsythe and Pierce are working together?"

My mouth fell open, the pieces coming together. I stood up suddenly, needing to tell them. "Before I left for DC, I called Jason. I told him I was meeting the Ambassador and where I was staying. He could have told Pierce ... why not? It wasn't as if the trip was a secret."

Cat gave me a slight nod of agreement and turned to the Ambassador. "DOD?" she asked, referring to the Department of Defense.

"I'll make a call," Paul said, mentally culling a list of contacts from twenty to six, and then down to one.

Cat looked back at Melodie. "When the documents come in, we need to learn everything there is to know about these two, from where they grew up to what kind of toothpaste they use. Somewhere their paths have crossed; I'm sure of it."

Melodie's eyes had grown wider, but she didn't hesitate. "Yes, ma'am. And I'd like to speak with you and Paul for a few minutes."

Clearly, whatever Melodie had to say wasn't meant for the rest of us. We unknotted ourselves from our seats and drifted toward the double doors while Cat and Paul remained seated. I caught a visual exchange between the two of them and sensed something troubling in the air. I pushed the doors open and glanced back in time to see Paul lean toward Cat. *What's the big secret?* I wondered. *And why aren't they sharing?*

After the room cleared, Melodie spoke. "I found something else. I've been replaying the video of the woman in the terminal when she's talking on the cell phone. I've figured out what she was saying."

"Okay," Paul said expectantly.

Melodie cued the video on the screen. "Watch carefully. Her words are, '*Both of them must be part of Jericho.*' And then she listens for a moment and says, '*Not a problem. See you tonight.*'"

Cat paled, and her jaw twitched slightly. Recovering, she asked, "How certain are you about the wording?"

The answer came without hesitation. "One hundred percent."

"Well," Paul said, "we need to start asking who was on the other end of that phone call and how Sophia would know anything about Jericho. And since she's expecting to meet up with the person, it could be our missing-finger guy, Forsythe. Thank you, Melodie. This was an important catch. Get some sleep and hit it hard in the morning. I'll get the files. You find these people."

Paul waited until Melodie signed off and then held up his hand at Cat, signaling her to stay where she was. He disappeared through the far door of the bubble room and returned with two cups of coffee. Taking a seat directly in front of Cat and sitting almost knee-to-knee with her, as a cop might do with a suspect, he pressed for answers. "You never told me the details of the Jericho mission. Maybe it's time you did."

Chapter 32

Cat sat stiffly, debating how much to reveal to Paul. Jericho had the potential to reap a phenomenal amount of intelligence vital to the security of the United States. There were fewer than a dozen people who had been read in on the mission's broad objectives, and even fewer who knew its operational details. Paul was included in the first group, her colleagues Smith and Jones—and that treasonous fucker Roger—in the latter. Melodie was somewhere in between, because Cat needed someone with eyes and ears open for any mention of Jericho. Technically, she should seek approval from the director before bringing Paul into the inner circle. *To hell with it*, she concluded; *easier to ask forgiveness than permission.*

Cat rested her elbows on the armrests of her chair and leaned forward, her expression taut. "For the past several years, we've had an operative in Iran—inside Mo'talefeh, the Islamic Coalition Party. He's kept an eye on politics, given us insight about the leanings of individual party members, and a heads-up for impending actions by the government and military.

"Most important is that the Mo'talefeh leadership includes two former members of Iran's Atomic Energy

Commission. The operative even has some technical knowledge, courtesy of his father's instruction. His father was a nuclear physicist who helped develop the reactor at Bushehr—prior to the revolution. You've met him."

"The father ... do you mean Reza Badakhshanian?"

"The very same."

Paul digested what Cat was saying, recalling the time he'd spent in Tehran in 1978 and 1979 during the Iranian revolution. After the shah fled the country, the strife and anti-Western sentiment escalated to such a point that the Department of State felt major concern for the safety of American citizens. Accordingly, State requested that Pan Am evacuate the thousands of Americans still living in the country. Paul, whose posting was in Kuwait, had been loaned to the embassy in Tehran during the turmoil.

One afternoon, while processing evacuees at the Hilton hotel, Paul had looked up from his assigned table to see the Badakhshanian family standing before him. He had met the husband and wife previously, and was shocked when they handed over US passports issued under different names. Suspecting CIA involvement and recognizing the inherent danger, he had managed to contain his surprise and process the family normally. The family had flown out of Tehran undetected and resettled in America.

"I don't remember the son's name."

"Jalil."

Paul slumped back in his chair, puffed his cheeks, and exhaled loudly. "*Jalil?* The same Jalil rescued after the explosion in the Seaport earlier this year? *That* Jalil?"

Cat nodded grimly, her lips compressed. "Yes."

"Oh, shit."

"Exactly."

"Is he improving?"

Cat contemplated how to best answer the question, considering that improvement could be measured in so many different ways. Jalil had been kidnapped and held as bait during the planned Boston Harbor attack. After being viciously tortured, he was set up to die in the same explosion that had claimed Smith's life and critically injured Jones.

Roger, who had fully expected Jalil to perish, had promptly swept him away to a psychiatric facility outside of Boston. For weeks afterward, investigators were prevented from interviewing the young man. When permission was finally granted, they found him drugged and unresponsive.

It wasn't until many weeks later that Roger was identified as a traitor. Even then, Cat initially failed to realize how the man had manipulated Jalil's treatment. Roger had manufactured medical records, showing the patient with a diagnosis of schizophrenia and other psychotic disorders. Accordingly, he was placed on a regimen of antipsychotic drugs. Roger, who visited the clinic regularly, supplemented the prescribed medications with drug cocktails of his own making. Predictably, the side effects of the drug interactions had played havoc with Jalil's mind and health.

Too late, Cat had discovered the truth when one of the facility's psychiatrists commented that Jalil's health seemed to have taken a sudden turn for the better. The timing, so soon after Roger's arrest, was too coincidental for her liking. She had enlisted a team of specialists to try to undo the damage. Jalil was steadily improving but still in recovery. Cat blamed herself for not having figured it out sooner.

"The doctors say he's improving. I would tend to agree. But he's damaged."

"When did you last visit him?" Paul asked.

"Just before this meeting. He's coming around, but ... I don't know ... he's there but not there. This afternoon, he mumbled something cryptic, seemingly out of the blue. But one word sure got my heart pumping: *Goreva.* At first I thought I'd misheard, but then he said it again."

Paul's eyes went wide. "As in Natalya Goreva? But she hasn't changed her name yet. How would he know her?"

"But who else could it be? Given what we learned today, we already know she is tied into this somehow."

Paul looked warily at Cat, and asked, "What did Jalil say?"

Cat repeated her conversation with Jalil.

"*What does any of that mean? A boat? Seriously?*" Paul asked sharply, his patience worn thin. "You've said he's damaged. Isn't it more likely that none of what he says is accurate?" He took a breath and shook his head. "That was uncalled for—sorry."

Cat understood his frustration; she had spent hours with Jalil. Aside from uttering a few cryptic phrases, he had heretofore seemed incapable of communicating a coherent thought. Yet the doctors were confident that he would recover ... eventually. With so much intelligence hanging in the balance, it was becoming increasingly difficult to remain patient.

"You're right. Jalil doesn't have all his faculties right now. But he was different today ... more focused. He was so intent on telling me what he thinks he remembers that my heart was breaking. And for him to mention Goreva? This is not just a rambling, Paul. The coincidence would simply be too great."

Paul grimaced. "You're right. So tell me what you're thinking."

"Sophia Capreze may be the key to all of this. When you add Jalil's story to the fact that she's traveled to India, discovered and reverted to her birth name, and used the word Jericho? And then throw in the connection we've found to the Kharoti family? *Everything* points to India. That's where the answers are. I have to get on a plane to Mumbai. As in yesterday."

Paul straightened. "Just like that? By yourself? This isn't the way we agreed to do things. We work as a team."

She held her hand up, palm out, as if to stop him. "I need to work alone on this. Nobody else goes." She began counting on her fingers. "One: more people equals impaired flexibility. Two: more people equals diminished mobility. Three, I don't want to ..."

He interrupted, his eyes kind but solemn. "You don't want to risk losing anyone else. You still feel that you lost Smith and Serita. You didn't. Roger lured them into that godforsaken parking lot and murdered them. Our job is to uncover the others who were involved and bring them to justice. Remember that part? *Our* job?" Cat opened her mouth to speak, but he kept going. "It's not open for discussion, Cat."

Cat knew he was right, but felt the sting of his words and fought to let it go. He'd cut close to the truth ... she felt guilty. Two of her people had died, Jason was in the hospital with a bullet wound to the chest, Lindsey had been kidnapped and almost killed, and she hadn't been able to prevent any of it. Having a team could be a blessing, but in the field things could turn bad in a heartbeat.

They discussed the options, and she ultimately decided to take Arnie and Gabe. Her biggest obstacle in India would be data access, and Gabe's hacking skills were the best she had ever seen. Arnie's expertise with electronics could prove useful ... and he could watch her back. Lindsey, Melodie, and Trent could handle the technical aspects of the investigation stateside.

The decision about whether to travel under false papers or under her own identity was, to Cat, a no-brainer. She was intent upon using one of her old identities, while Paul was adamant that Cat enter India as herself. He reasoned that because she had been posted in Bombay years before, she would be able to mine old sources and be granted access to certain channels of information. She might even be given some latitude if the visit went south. Cat held firm, persuading him that the use of her own name would raise flags, subject her to additional scrutiny, and limit her mobility.

With the matter settled, they turned to the question of which passport to use. One identity stood out from the others, but with a major drawback ... the name would draw attention. The upside was that the mere mention of the name would open doors that would otherwise be off-limits. They discussed alternatives at length, but in the end, her first choice prevailed.

"In the morning," Cat said, "we have to brief the team."

Paul nodded in agreement. "See if you can get your

gear delivered here by morning. I'll get clearance for the team tonight. We will have to tell them everything ... they have a right to know. Are you okay with that?"

Cat winced. "There's never been anything okay about what happened with the Gorevs. Did you get a good look at the picture? Sophia is the spitting image of her mother. It's as if Tanya's ghost has come back to haunt us."

Chapter 33

Monday morning
Fort Bragg, North Carolina

General Carter Haskell glanced at the caller ID on his secure phone and looked at his watch. Seven thirty in the morning. This could only mean trouble.

He had a long and complicated history with Paul Marshfield. While they had known each other for over thirty years and been good friends for most of it, they rarely picked up the phone for a social chat. He briefly considered letting the call go to voice mail but knew that ignoring it would only delay the inevitable. He picked up the receiver.

"Paul? To what do I owe the honor?"

"Carter, how's life at Fort Bragghdad? Still swatting ten-pound mosquitoes?"

Carter Haskell hated the Fort Bragg nickname that had made its way into army parlance during the second Gulf War. He hated it even more than the nickname of *FayetteNam* for the long-suffering town adjoining the base, Fayetteville. And Paul knew it.

"I should hang up now."

"But you won't. You know you're curious."

Carter rolled his eyes and slowly shook his head in mock disgust. Paul knew him too well. "Does this mean that you're going to owe me?"

"It does."

Uh-oh, Carter thought. Paul had some serious skin in the intelligence community. There wasn't much he couldn't get his hands on.

"I need the complete records of two of your own. And I mean *complete*. There's so much black in their files that I'd believe it if you told me they were spray-painted." Paul went on to tell him about Randall Forsythe and Matthew Pierce.

Carter heard the names, and his stomach rolled over. He sat up straighter and took a sip of the lukewarm coffee in his mug. "Sounds like you don't have much to go on."

"You're right ... I don't. But, Carter, I believe these guys are into some nasty business. They're equipped with high-end military hardware, nanoparticle-carrying drones, and we think they're supplying C-4 to the very assholes we're battling against. You remember the Boston Harbor bombing incident last February? Well, we recovered another seven-hundred-plus pounds a couple of days ago, just up the road in Somerville. Identical, military-grade, spiked with DMDNB. This stuff didn't just fall off a truck."

Carter drummed his fingers on the large wooden desk and thought about what Paul was saying. DMDNB is a chemical taggant incorporated into the manufacture of C-4 high explosive. A trained dog will find it in a heartbeat, and airports and the military have systems that can detect the chemical in minute amounts.

In the civilian world, C-4 is incredibly hard to come by. It is somewhat easier to lay your hands on it if you are in the military—particularly if you are in Special Forces. But an operator can't just take it off the shelf ... supply specialists order and distribute all of the weaponry, under the direct supervision of their superior officers, who report to their own superior officers.

Carter was now visualizing an expanding group of uniforms gone bad—or gone blind—and the mental image of a potential scandal bumped up his blood pressure. While he supported the men and women under his command—men and women who had served their country well—he had zero tolerance when they crossed the line for personal profit. But these two men, well ...

"Where are you?"

"Washington area."

"Feel like taking a little drive?"

The silence at the other end told Carter that Paul was surprised by the request. When Paul finally answered, his voice had an edge. "Where?"

"Quantico," Carter replied. "I'm flying up this afternoon. I could leave early and be there by two o'clock. We could have a late lunch and catch up." He knew that the suggestion for a personal meeting would alert Paul to a problem, but Paul would show up. He always did.

Another silence. He could almost see the frown on Paul's forehead as he tried to work out why Carter was stonewalling. He heard the clicking of a keyboard.

Paul responded a few seconds later. "I'll leave at noon; that should put me there by the time you land. Pick you up at Turner?" he asked, referring to Turner Field, the marine corps air facility at Quantico.

Carter agreed and hung up the phone, but it was his

turn to be puzzled. Paul certainly knew how long it took to travel from DC to Quantico—he had driven it enough—so why did he need the computer? *Because he's not in DC,* Carter realized, *and not directly off I-95.* Carter's guess was somewhere west. Rural, unfamiliar roads.

Carter typed a few strokes into the computer and fed his screen to the monitor mounted on the wall. He walked over and stood a few feet away, letting his eyes roam over the image. The map of the Eastern United States was dotted with dozens of tiny icons, each representing a building, home, farm, or lot owned by the federal government. And each had its place in the database, along with blueprints, topography, and other crucial information. Developed for HRT, the Hostage Rescue Team up at Quantico, the database also contained the details of the property's use and purpose, both public and private. Carter had access to the material, as did a few others at Bragg. HRT and Carter's Special Forces people had been known to train together.

Wherever Paul was, it was less than two hours from Quantico. That was a lot of territory, and Paul had resources. But Paul had mentioned that their safe house had been attacked, so he was most likely somewhere that would serve the same purpose, and for multiple people. That narrowed the field. Not that it mattered; Carter would find out soon enough.

He sat down and pulled up the files. He scrolled through several pages of each, and then leaned his elbows on the desk and laced his fingers together. *Randy Forsythe and Matt Pierce,* he thought, *what the hell have you done?* He picked up the phone and punched in a number from memory.

Chapter 34

Monday morning
Orange, Virginia

Fifteen minutes late for breakfast, Paul pushed through the doors in a rush. He was trailed by a striking, elegantly dressed older woman. Her platinum hair was expertly coiffed, with a forelock dangling over her right eye. Her vivid blue-gray eyes—framed by oversize designer glasses—danced around the room, seeming to take in every article and every person present. She walked sprite-ly to the front of the room, secure with the support of a cane in her right hand. A ripple of murmurs signaled that she was well-recognized, the camera bag slung over her shoulder confirming her profession.

"Everyone," Paul called out, "this is someone who needs no introduction. Please join me in welcoming Adele Rutledge." Adele nodded politely.

"Over the years, Adele has provided the CIA with invaluable assistance, both here and abroad. She has also helped train many operatives in the art of photography and deception. Tomorrow, we will dispatch a team to Mumbai and Adele will be on that team. Most of you will return to Boston to locate Randall Forsythe and Sophia Capreze and to pursue leads about the source of the plastic explosives we found in Somerville.

"Our investigation, and the apparent connection to the Kharoti family, has become somewhat more challenging since learning of Sophia Capreze's involvement. They say that the past always comes back to haunt you. In this case, it certainly has."

He nodded to Adele, who acknowledged him with a warm smile before turning to face the group. "First, you must learn to call me Addie." She spoke in a low, raspy voice—payback from her younger days, when newspapers and magazines invariably showed her holding a cigarette. Her speech was subtly accented, hinting at many years of living in France or Switzerland.

"My relationship with the CIA goes back many years, to the days before the world became computerized. Back then, humans gathered intelligence. You used your brains, and you watched and you soaked up every little piece of information you could. Security cameras were rare, and the Internet was still in its formative stages.

"Today, we rely on binary bits of data stored in cyberspace, using computers instead of people to search for the pieces and make sense of the jumble. Today, the NSA vacuums conversations out of thin air and captures more e-mail, texts, and social media posts than any of us could read in a quadrillion lifetimes."

She paused, making eye contact with her audience before continuing, "In many respects, my early years were of a different era. Even so, what we face today is just a continuation of what we faced years ago. Back then we had the USSR and the Cold War; now we have the Russians. Back then we had terrorist groups; today we have terrorist groups ... but on a vastly greater scale. And now, as then, we need humans in the mix to understand what computers cannot—the complexities of human relationships.

"I'm going to India because I understand their culture and can mingle across the social strata. As long as there's a camera hanging around my neck, I can be almost anywhere I choose to be, because—deep down—almost everyone wants their shot at being immortalized.

"I'm sure you've heard it said that to understand the present, one must understand the past, and that is especially true regarding Cat Powell and me. Our story began on a November day in 1979, not long after the embassy takeover in Tehran. I had been in meetings at Langley all morning and would have much preferred to have been outside. It was unseasonably warm—I was wearing only a light jacket—and the sky was a gorgeous deep blue. I remember the day distinctly, because that's when Cat and I were introduced."

PART TWO

Voices from the Past

November, 1979

June and July, 1985

Chapter 35

November 1979
Langley, Virginia

Catherine Ames had just finished yet another interview, this time with one of the boys from the seventh floor asking the questions. *It was getting tiresome*, she thought. How many times and how many ways could one describe the insanity that had existed in Tehran during the revolution? She knew she had been lucky to get out as quickly and easily as she did after the embassy was overrun. Arnie—her boyfriend's cousin and Pan Am's manager at the airport—had been able to secure three tickets on Gulf Air to Bahrain. Otherwise, she would have faced an overland trip through Iran to the Turkish border—a decidedly unpleasant journey considering the tumultuous conditions throughout the country.

She might have been imagining things—the agency did breed paranoia, after all—but her interrogators seemed to be unusually focused on her actions in the months leading up to the final assault on the embassy. They directed their laser-like inquiries toward the names of those she had helped to escape, the methods she'd used, and her thinking behind each. But it had now reached the point where the interview sessions were becoming tiresome and aggravating. If she had to tell the story one more time, she would probably throw a punch at someone.

She was stomping toward the elevator when a voice called her name. *Christ*, she thought. *Give me a fucking break.* She turned around to see the legendary Teddy Younger waving at her. *Really?*

Teddy was in his midfifties, of medium height, with a surprisingly youthful face and shaggy light brown hair. In every other way, he was average and nondescript. But in the world of counterintelligence, Teddy was like a god. His antics, and heroics, had been the topic of many whispered conversations in the cloistered rooms of Langley. If anyone were ever to make a movie about the CIA, Teddy should be asked to write the script.

He caught up to her in three long steps. "Glad I ran into you, Cat. Would you have time for a short lunch?"

The invitation was so unexpected that she merely gaped at him.

"Good," he said. "I know just the spot. I hope you like turkey."

He took her by the elbow and swiftly guided her into the elevator and out the front door before she had time to consider the implications.

Teddy directed her to the silver RX7 in the lot, and tossed a canvas tote behind the seats before driving away from the CIA campus. Five minutes later, he turned into a parking area in Turkey Run State Park. All of the vehicles in the lot, having been driven by normal citizens, were parked nose-in. Teddy reversed the car and parked nose-out. The maneuver was Cautionary Measures 101: give yourself a quick exit. Every time Cat went to the mall, grocery store, or any place where automobiles were present, she took note of the vehicles facing the wrong way. Who owned them? People like Teddy? People like her?

He grabbed the tote and led Cat down a path toward the Potomac. When the dirt track took a jog to the left, he went right, walking toward the river. The woods opened to a twenty-foot rock ledge overlooking the banks of the Potomac, the water sparkling like diamonds under the brilliant sunlight. He sat cross-legged, the crisp autumn leaves crackling beneath him, and gestured for her to do the same. He offered her a sandwich from the bag. "Turkey, for Turkey Run."

As they ate, he explained that he had read all of her reports from Tehran and been impressed. The agency, he said, had a need for talented female agents in the field, particularly in the Middle East. And then he tested her reaction to the idea of a posting in Saudi Arabia. Ordinarily, such discussions took place between agent and handler, rather than agent-to-agent. Cat wondered if he was toying with her, but she played along, raising her eyebrows only slightly and commenting, "I assume you've already set the stage for my fiancé to relocate."

Her fiancé, Tom Powell, was director of Mideast operations for a large engineering and construction firm. They had been living together in Tehran until the embassy hostages were taken. He was currently working out of Dubai while his company considered the best options for relocating the offices. If the agency was asking her to move to Saudi, chances were that they had already rigged the game for Tom to move as well.

An assignment to the largest country on the Arabian Peninsula would be a challenge. Among other limitations, women were forbidden to drive. Typically they were escorted by a male relative, although drivers were sometimes hired. Swimming pools and gyms forbade mixed company. There were specific times when women were allowed—and men were not. As a single woman, conducting agency business in Saudi would be exceptionally difficult. As Tom's wife, however, more opportunities would present themselves. Regardless, there would be occasions when she would have to disguise herself as a male. The irony was that by donning the long, flowing, traditional male garb—the thawb—her task would be made much easier.

"Let's just say that given the number of Saudi projects Tom's company is involved in, having the Middle East director there makes good operational sense."

Cat rolled her eyes. "I might have known. But are you also asking me to push up my wedding?"

Catherine Ames was set to marry Thomas Powell in two months, a week before her best friend would exchange vows with Paul Marshfield. Just three days ago, the two couples had booked—and paid for—a joint honeymoon at the Fijian on Yanuka Island in Fiji.

Teddy grinned. "Wouldn't think of it. It would be in poor taste to start our relationship with such a selfish request. But do make sure that Tom gets your paperwork to the Saudis immediately after you tie the knot."

He offered further advice. "Learn the language while you're there. And learn their customs… it's a different world from Iran. Become familiar with the cultural aspects of the other Gulf states, too. When you return, you'll be ready for the next step."

"What's your interest in this?" she asked him.

He shrugged. "Let's just say that, contrary to my surname, I'm not getting any younger. For years, Mother Langley has been pestering me to pass along some of what I've learned. *Take someone under your wing,* they've told me. But I have trust issues, a terrible temper, and am abysmal with relationships. With that said, you interest me. You have great instincts, and you seem smart as hell.

"Your talents have also come to the attention of certain people upstairs. I might as well tell you that you're being eyed for other projects. Assuming all goes well in Saudi, there may be a very interesting assignment awaiting your return."

He had read her file, of course, but he wanted greater detail. He took notes on the sandwich papers as she described her background, her interests, her dislikes, and her education. While in college, Cat had followed the route expected of her, studying international affairs and refining her linguistic skills. But she had an artistic streak as well, and had spent two summers interning with Corey Talbot, a respected freelance photographer and friend of her father. The work taught her much about the art of photography, the rigors of creating a pictorial documentary, and the adventure of travel abroad. When she told Teddy of the experience, he grinned broadly.

Teddy later told her that the idea of Adele Rutledge was conceived that afternoon, sketched on the paper wrappers of two turkey sandwiches.

Teddy had frequent contact with Cat after that, generally to follow up on reports she had submitted, but occasionally simply to inquire about her well-being. Six months before her posting in Saudi was set to end, Cat was called back to Langley for meetings. In one of the bubble rooms, Teddy explained that their project had been given the green light. They were tasked with manufacturing a prominent female identity—one who could venture abroad, into places both friendly and not, without arousing suspicion. The woman's profession? Photographer.

Typically, operatives blend in, rather than stand out. But another old adage pertaining to spy behavior is that they hide in plain sight. Creating Adele and positioning her in a high-visibility role provided the advantages of having an agent who would be so conspicuous as to be above suspicion and, if caught or detained, would be supported by a massive public outcry. Teddy found the concept brilliant; Cat worried inwardly about her ability to pull it off.

The deception required that Cat change her appearance and assume the life of another for long periods of time. Langley employed an entire department to create disguises and accessories for agents in the field. When in character as Adele, she inserted blue-tinted contacts and donned a wig of edgily styled, short, platinum-blonde hair. The superbly capable staff dressed her in a wardrobe of chic linen and khaki for work and luxurious silks for evening.

Leveraging Cat's knowledge of the profession and her raw talent with a camera, the agency set out to construct her background and transform her into an internationally recognized celebrity. They engaged Marcel Girardot—a renowned French photojournalist—and compensated him handsomely to further refine her skills and become her ongoing advisor.

After two weeks of working side by side with Cat, he appeared one morning with two bottles of Dom Perignon. "You are quite talented, my dear, but so very business-business-business," he said. "You must learn to set free your artiste!" he said, waving his hands. "Your photographs are a performance. Use your mind to look not at what you see, but what you cannot see. You must look behind the smile and the frown to find, instead, the glint in the eye. Look at the parched desert sand and find the seedling. Look at the river's spray as it crashes into the boulder and find the sparkle of reflected sunlight. The artistry of your lens is limited only by the boundaries of your imagination."

With one bottle consumed before lunch and another before midafternoon, Cat found her focus relaxing—shifting away from the obvious and into more nuanced characteristics of the subject. When they developed the film that evening, she realized that—in her alcohol-induced haze—she had produced her finest work to date.

Over the next two months, the master introduced his protégé to those seeking a portrait sitting or a collection created. Claiming health issues, he delegated the work to Adele. Soon, she had assembled a portfolio of headline makers and shakers in their most unguarded moments, as well as a haunting series of Asian peasants at work.

The intensive training session was followed by a well-attended show at a gallery in Manhattan. Adele's star rose. A second show two months later featured an impressive study of ancient temples and artifacts from regions in the Middle East. Adele's name went onto the A-list.

During the ensuing months, the agency compiled a catalog of persons of interest, and Adele made arrangements for photographic expeditions to the subjects' countries of residence. A week spent exploring the scenic treasures of the nation frequently led to invitations to meet and mingle with the local elite, which in turn led to private portraiture sessions.

Adele carried her camera bag into the inner sanctums of some of the world's most powerful figures. Tucked into the jumble of camera bodies, lenses, filters, tripods, and film were a variety of shutter release cables—several of which were equipped with a tiny lens and miniature spool of film. Each press of the trigger snapped a photo not only of the subject, but of other elements in the room. Documents and journals carelessly left in view or in unlocked drawers, personal items, décor, furniture ... all was captured. As well, she found innumerable opportunities for planting listening devices in offices and personal residences.

From revealing ongoing affairs with mistresses to unusual sexual proclivities to impending military actions, Adele's exploits abroad yielded a gold mine of intelligence. Within eighteen months, the results had exceeded expectations to such a degree that the agency made a decision to expand the operation. They founded the Rutledge School of Photography, ostensibly to provide serious artists with on-site experiences under the expert tutelage of Marcel and Adele. The expeditions afforded other opportunities as well, by routinely including a handful of intelligence agents seeking to acquire new skills. As an added bonus, the school made money ... buckets of it.

It was agreed early on that Adele would establish herself

as somewhat of an eccentric. She would occasionally disappear for a week or two, ostensibly to rest and meditate. The school's staff assumed that she was enjoying aromatherapy in an exclusive spa somewhere. In reality, she took on short clandestine assignments—as Cat or some other name from her expanding arsenal of identities. She plied her trade in some of the most dangerous areas on earth—primarily South Asia and the Middle East. Fluent in Arabic and Farsi—and gaining a working knowledge of Pashto and Urdu—she built an admirable resume.

Her real life as Catherine Powell presented its own set of complications. Adele maintained a condo in Manhattan, while Cat lived with Tom on Long Island. In an effort to keep her marriage on solid ground, whenever she was in the States, she spent nearly every night with Tom. Ten minutes after Adele entered her building, her brunette-haired housekeeper emerged and caught the next train from Penn Station to Port Washington. In the morning, she reversed the ride. She became adept at the five-minute character switch, a skill that would serve her well throughout her career.

Under the premise that the longer one lives a lie, the greater the risk that someone will discover the fiction, Cat's active role as Adele was envisioned to last only two or three years. At the appointed time, she would resume her career at an overseas posting. Adele would withdraw from the public eye and adopt a role as a reclusive advisor to the Rutledge School, occasionally emerging from mothballs to retain her celebrity status and, of course, for missions of strategic importance.

Chapter 36

June 1985
Bombay, India

Three years after Adele began lighting up the world stage, a valued operative in Bombay decided to take his breakfast one morning at the Shamiana coffee shop at the Taj Hotel. He ordered the masala dosa—a rice-lentil crepe stuffed with potato, onion, chili, and spices—and was sipping his coffee when he suddenly choked and his body spasmed. His head hit the table, and he slumped to the floor, dragging the tablecloth with him and scattering food and broken dishes for several feet around. He was dead in a matter of moments.

As a declared employee of the US government, Zach Frederick carried identification, and the consulate was notified in short order. Gary Eastman, who worked in the consulate's office of regional affairs, was dispatched immediately. Due to the nature of the dead man's work, Gary was advised to leave no stone unturned in determining the true cause of death.

By the time Eastman arrived, the scene had been thoroughly compromised. Onlookers had rushed to the victim's aid, rolled him over, torn his shirt open, and begun chest compressions in a futile effort to revive the man. Seeing the vomitus on his chin, none had attempted mouth-to-mouth. The table and floor had been cleared of debris and wiped down, the Indian staff admirably performing their job of keeping the restaurant clean and tidy. There was no evidence lying about that might suggest foul play, and if there had been, it was long gone. Transport was called to carry the body to the local morgue, whereupon Eastman demanded permission to accompany the body and observe any procedures that might take place. The attending coroner perfunctorily pronounced death by cardiac arrest and signed over the remains and personal effects.

Eastman, the son of a retired criminal investigator with the San Francisco Police Department, was reasonably educated with regard to forensic protocol. He arranged to have the body—clothes and all—wrapped, bagged, boxed, and iced for air transport. Having just delivered a contingent of general staff for a joint military exercise on the Indian subcontinent, a US Air Force C-20A—the military version of the Gulfstream III—was routed to pick up the remains. The jet, with a range of over four thousand miles, made three refueling stops on its way to the States and the FBI lab at Quantico, Virginia.

The FBI technicians examined Zach Frederick's clothing and personal effects and, finding nothing of note, quickly zeroed in on the small, locally produced tin of saccharine tablets in the pocket of his trousers. Tests confirmed that the tablets were laced with sodium cyanide. The unfortunate CIA man probably would not have detected any subtle difference in the tablets' appearance. Even if he had noticed the very slight variation in color, he would have dismissed it—given that quality control in India was often questionable. Toxicology tests on the body confirmed the presence of the same poison. The agent had been murdered.

Within hours, a team from the consulate entered the agent's residence and found the rooms in disarray. They posted a guard and waited for the arrival of an FBI team. They needn't have bothered. The home had already been thoroughly and expertly searched.

Chapter 37

June 1985
Langley, Virginia

Zach Frederick had kept Langley reasonably well apprised of his contacts and movements. But like so many good operatives, he held some information close. He had sent two reports stating that he was courting someone connected to the Soviet bloc, but hedged when asked the critical question: *who?* Under the premise that murder is most frequently committed by someone close to the deceased, the FBI set about finding someone with motive. They learned that Frederick had no steady female companions, no antagonistic relationships, no coworkers bearing personal grudges, and no ex-wives with murderous intent.

There was also no evidence to suggest that any of his known contacts had the wherewithal to formulate and plant a tin of poisoned sweetener tablets. They considered that he might have planned a meeting at the Taj, which would explain his decision to have breakfast there. On the other hand, the Taj was a popular dining choice for the Western expat community. With other possibilities eliminated, the focus circled back to Soviet involvement—and hit a brick wall. The Soviet consulate employed over sixty people, any of whom might have access to classified information. The FBI team was stymied.

Word of the agent's passing spread quickly through the halls of Langley, with all sources attributing the death to heart failure. He drank too much, he had chain-smoked for years, his job was both dangerous and stressful. He was not an old man, but not young either, and hard lifestyles play havoc with life spans. Cat was saddened to hear the news. Her thoughts loitered on her own choices, and she fleetingly wondered if she would live long enough to retire and enjoy the golden years. And then Teddy Younger called.

Teddy skipped the usual pleasantries. "They're going to send you there."

"Send me where?"

"Bombay."

"I haven't heard that."

"You will. You have developed a certain reputation." He sighed deeply. "It wasn't an accident."

"What do you mean?"

"Zach Frederick was poisoned ... cyanide. The report from Quantico came in this morning."

Cat was stunned. "Any idea who did it?"

"Not exactly, at least not yet. They are playing with the idea that it was the Reds, but no proof."

"Reds? As in the Soviets?"

"As in." Teddy let that sink in before continuing, "You may not know this, but we worked together once. He had an odd habit."

"Don't we all?" she retorted.

"But this habit should interest you."

"I'm listening."

"If you examine his expenditures, you'll find he spent a fair amount on socks."

"Socks?"

"Socks. Because whenever he had an important meet, he would write the meeting place, time, and contact name on the inside of his sock. And not only on one of the socks he was wearing… he always left the same information on a sock in his drawer."

"Did you say he was on drugs?"

Teddy chuckled. "Think about it… socks are always getting lost. Every man I know has a bunch of stray ones just waiting for their mates to reappear. Sounds far-fetched, I know. But I swear to you, Zach did this religiously. He was convinced that if he disappeared, someone would read the socks and find him. Or if he died, the agency would know who did it."

Cat felt her pulse quicken. "You're serious?"

"As a heart attack."

Teddy and Cat drove to Quantico that afternoon and were escorted into the office of the forensics program manager. The man was skeptical, but placed a call and then led them downstairs. An examiner, apparently the recipient of the phone call, met them and pointed to a steel table in the center of the room.

Laid out on the table were all of Zach Frederick's items of clothing, the newspaper he'd been reading at the table, his keys, cigarettes and a matchbook, his wallet, passport, and government ID. For safety reasons, the tin of saccharine tablets was secured in a locked cabinet elsewhere in the lab. Teddy slipped on a pair of the proffered latex gloves, and Cat followed suit.

The two socks were limp and misshapen, having stretched out to accommodate the feet that had worn them. Cat lifted one sock, and Teddy took the other. They turned the socks inside out and held them under a bright light.

"Look here," Teddy said, pointing at the midcalf area of one sock. "You can barely see it."

The manager, the examiner, and Cat all gaped at the barely discernible blue markings on the black knit sock.

The examiner was the first to recover, exclaiming, "Holy shit!" She gently lifted the sock and carried it to another table, placing it under a benchtop magnifier.

They studied the writing, and the examiner wrote the results on the whiteboard.

T Goreva
Taj elev
9:30a 06/14

Cat whirled toward Teddy. "How long does he keep these socks?"

"I don't know. Several days would be my guess. I don't know if he washes them or throws them out. Why?"

"Because he was killed at eight thirty. The meeting on this sock was for after breakfast. Something triggered the poisoning. I want to know who he met with before that."

The manager looked at his watch and shook his head. "Middle of the night over there. How urgent is this?"

Cat and Teddy just stared at him. He picked up the phone and dialed the hotel in Bombay where the FBI team was staying.

Four hours later, they had the answer. One of the wayward socks in the agent's apartment told of a meeting two nights before the murder.

A Gorev
B Candy
6:00p 06/12

As Teddy had predicted, Cat got the call later that evening with an assignment to India. Thirty-six days after Zach Frederick's death, Adele Rutledge announced her intention to quit the limelight and retire to her farm in Vermont ... and Cat Powell was on the Pan Am flight to Bombay.

Chapter 38

July 1985
Bombay, India

From the moment the aircraft door opened at Santa Cruz airport in Bombay, the smell began to seep into the cabin. Pungent sea air, rank mold and algae thriving from the annual monsoon rains, coriander-laced smoke from hot curries, acrid automobile exhaust, rancid meat, rotting vegetation, and the sour reek of human sweat and waste—all wafted into an olfactory assault. The descriptions Cat had heard simply didn't do it justice, she thought.

The warnings about Bombay had been many, but unanimous in that few found it an easy place to live. She had listened to comments from every corner: that the poverty was heartbreaking, that she would want to feed each child begging on the street, that one of the largest slums in the world lay in the middle of the city, that she would find the noise to be a constant irritant, and that the smell was overpowering. Interestingly, most also expressed the sentiment that if she stayed for a year, the city would find a place in her heart.

After shoving her way through the sea of bodies crowding the terminal exit, she spotted the distinctive car in the swarm of vehicles outside. Automobiles in India, as she had learned, were expensive, difficult to acquire, and limited in choice. Nationalization, rigid import restrictions, and the Licence Raj—which imposed limitations on private industry and regulated all aspects of production—made the automobile a precious yet uninspired commodity. The streets of Bombay were choked with two primary types of automobile: the Audi and the Ambassador, both manufactured in India and both reminiscent of cars from the 1940s. Imports were rarely seen, given that the taxes imposed were nearly double the cost of the car itself. A few foreign companies, Tom's included, had chosen to ship in used cars, which still incurred stiff import fees but stood a greater chance of being allowed by customs officials. Tom's car was a 1960-vintage, red Chevrolet—fins on the tail and nearly twice the size of anything else on the road.

Most couples shared a car, with the locally hired driver taking the sahib to and from work and whisking the memsahib to various social events during the day. Quite frequently, such employees—assuming they were reliable—were retained as the Westerners transferred in and out. Tom's assigned driver had been transporting company directors and their spouses for over ten years. The size and weight of the Chevy protected its occupants and could be an intimidating force on the city streets. In short, the red Chevy was a tank. Unfortunately, it was also highly recognizable. The Powells would retain the driver for Tom's transport to work and for social events attended by the couple. But they would depart from tradition in that Cat would purchase and drive her own vehicle: an anonymous white Ambassador.

Arriving late at night, there was little to actually see during the landing and subsequent drive into the city. Only later, flying in and out of the airport during daylight hours, would she see the sprawling shantytown of tarps and cardboard—providing primitive shelter for tens of thousands—that lay at the edge of the runway. Despite all she had been told, nothing could have prepared her for the sight.

As she had been in Tehran and in the three years since, Cat was nonofficial cover—she had no official status as a government employee and no diplomatic immunity. From all official points of view, she was the wife of Tom Powell and just another face in the Western expat community. And like other expat spouses, she had entered on a tourist visa and would submit the forms to receive a multiple-entry visa with the same duration as her husband. Tom had already been in Bombay for two weeks, recently transferred from Saudi Arabia. As his firm's new director of South Asian operations, he would travel extensively—giving Cat the choice of accompanying him or staying behind to conduct her own brand of business.

Tom's company had arranged a flat on the eighteenth floor of an apartment building a few blocks up the hill from the chaotic intersection known as Kemp's Corner. The location was also a mere five-minute drive from the US consulate. The consular building—a grand mansion formerly owned by a maharaja from Gujarat—sat on a two-acre expanse in the Breach Candy district and enjoyed having the Arabian Sea in its backyard. The Powells' flat on the eighteenth floor had a view of the compound from her living room window.

Cat rode up the elevator and rang the doorbell. Tom

greeted her with a huge smile and a beer.

"Kingfisher okay? We're fresh out of Becks."

Cat laughed. "It has to better than the stuff you brewed in Saudi." She sipped the local brew, wrinkling her nose and then grinning. "Although not by much. Yet another hardship to endure. What's on our agenda for today?"

Tom listed the bureaucratic and social events that went hand in hand with their arrival. "And this was delivered to my office today." He lifted a box from the table. "For you."

She nodded, certain of the package contents. Not that it would help if someone added poison to her food, but she was comforted in knowing that she now had a gun.

Chapter 39

Prior to boarding the flight to Bombay, Cat had endeavored to learn as much as she could about India. The country had long been within a hair's breadth of a meltdown. Its status as a nuclear power, shared border with their mortal enemy Pakistan, proximity to China, political and cultural schisms, fractured demographics, sixteen official languages, and more political parties than Campbell's had soup, all contributed to the country being a cauldron of volatility.

When India became a nuclear state in the midseventies, its stature as a player rose exponentially, and it was less susceptible to bullying by the superpowers. The hard freeze of the Cold War had the US government worrying about the Indians falling under the influence of the USSR, from both the strategic and economic standpoints. The Soviets were courting the region, and so were the Americans—albeit not as effectively.

A longtime South Asia analyst had explained that to understand the politics, one needed to consider the geography. The United States was half a globe away, while the hammer and sickle gang was just up the block. The biggest bully in the neighborhood—China—lived next door. The

Indians had to be practical about their choices. The analyst had moved her hands up and down as if measuring weights and said, "Let's see, which is the better option: the geographically distant do-everything-our-way-big-stick-waving Americans, or the enemy-of-our-enemy-is-our-friend-and-sure-you-can-have-some-of-our-MIGs Soviets."

The woman had gone on to advise Cat that the Indians had shown themselves to be very independent-minded, and that they played both sides with relative ease. America, on the other hand, could not stand the thought that India would have anything to do with what Reagan had dubbed "the Evil Empire." Cat became fascinated by the complexity of the Indian political landscape.

The first few days of Cat's introduction to India were spent becoming familiar with life in the city. There were rules for staying healthy—boil the water, filter the water, do not eat raw vegetables or fruit, stay away from dairy products, avoid street vendors—and other eyebrow-raising precautions for survival in the third world.

There were social expectations, as well, such as becoming acquainted with persons of influence in the expat community. On the second morning of her posting to Bombay, she took a taxi to the Taj Mahal Palace Hotel—familiarly called the Taj by the locals—and followed the hallway to the Pan Am office. When living abroad, there were advantages in becoming friendly with the airline's local staff. It had paid off in Tehran, and it had paid off in Saudi. She threw out the name of Arnie Powell, her husband's cousin and the former Pan Am airport manager in Tehran. Brad Doyle, the airline's director for Southern India and Sri Lanka, invited her into his office five minutes later.

As she was leaving, Cat asked for a recommendation for a tour guide ... someone with good knowledge of the city and who would be available for at least a week. Brad and the secretary put their heads together and suggested the secretary's son, a student at Northwestern University and home for the summer. The deal was struck, and they agreed to meet at the Taj at noon on the following day.

As she was leaving the hotel, she stopped by La Patisserie. The pastry shop was reputed to have the finest cakes and cookies in the city. Carrying a box of macaroons and almond crescents, she climbed into one of the cabs at the hotel entry and headed for the consulate.

Cat presented her passport to the guard at the US consulate and was directed to the regional affairs office. Once inside, she asked for Gary Eastman. They had a friend in common, she told the staffer, and she just wanted to relay greetings and drop off some cookies.

Eastman's name conjured up images of East Coast aloof and bore no resemblance to the man. He was more like a cowboy from the old West, she thought—tall, tanned, rough-hewn but gangly, and wearing a silver bolo tie with a large square of turquoise in the center. She was tempted to check his feet for boots, but caught herself.

"Catherine Powell," she said, extending her hand. "Call me Cat."

"Gary Eastman," he offered. "Everyone calls me Gary."

She grinned and handed him the box of cookies. "I come bearing gifts. You dated my friend Annabelle a few years ago. She was my roommate in college." The fabricated story came easily.

Smiling broadly, he picked up the fiction as he led her down the hall. "Wow! There's a name I haven't heard in a while. How is Annabelle? What is she doing these days?

They made small talk until arriving at his office, where he directed her to a seat and closed the door.

"Alias?" he asked in a low voice, using her code name. "Where did you pick up that moniker, anyhow?"

"I have a knack for disguises. Seems like ninety percent of the time I'm someone else ... a regular smorgasbord of assumed identities. A fellow agent once told me I was an alias of myself. It stuck."

"I'm sorry. I would have thought *Maverick* more your style."

Cat laughed. "As in arrogant and hot-tempered?"

"No, as in resourceful and cool under pressure. Your reputation precedes you. I thought you were arriving tomorrow, but I'm glad you're here."

"Thank you. My date stood me up, so I caught an earlier plane." His eyebrows arched, and she winked. "What can I say? I'm always looking for a better offer, so here I am. Let's talk quickly—I don't want to be in here any longer than ten minutes. Who else knows about me?"

"Me, the chief in Delhi, and Ed Freemont. He's here undercover as a consular officer. He's only been in the field for two years, but he's good. The ambassador is in the dark; so is the CG here. Neither one would be happy to be saddled with you."

Cat winced at the reference to the CG, the consul general. "May I be frank?"

His eyes crinkled, and a smile teased at the corners of

his mouth. "From what I've heard, you're going to say what you want to say regardless."

"Well, there is that, she said with a chuckle. "But I've heard mixed reviews about whether or not your CG knows how to keep his mouth shut. What's your take?"

Gary was an astute observer of human behavior. It served him well, not only in his declared position in the regional affairs office, but even more so as the CIA's senior liaison in Bombay.

"He's been known to let things slip after a couple of scotches. Let's just say we're careful."

Cat's eyes narrowed. Loose lips sank ships, as the saying went. She had little tolerance for people in positions of trust who couldn't keep a secret, but the CG could prove to be a useful conduit for misinformation.

Gary seemed to read her thoughts. "And sometimes, of course, people have been known to bait him."

"I'll keep that in mind," she said, giving him a knowing smile before she got down to business. "Zach Frederick had a meeting scheduled two nights before his death, with A Gorev. And he had another scheduled, right after breakfast, with one T Goreva. I have to tell you, that one threw me. Russian isn't my strong suit ... I had no idea Russian surnames adopt feminine-masculine spellings. Anyhow, we are assuming these meetings were with Anatoly Gorev and his wife, Tanya Goreva. His file is a little short on details. What can you tell me about him?"

Agents are required to file reports about every foreign contact. Some follow the procedure religiously; others choose to ignore it. Five months ago, a junior American agent—under official cover as a consular officer in Madras and some eight hundred miles from Bombay—was attending a social gathering at the German consulate there. The agent claimed to have witnessed a small envelope being passed from one of the guests to one of the known resident KGB agents in the city. She had snapped a photo of the guest, learned his name—Anatoly Gorev—and sent a dispatch to Langley.

"He's from Moscow, the son of an army colonel. Studied engineering at Leningrad State University, is married to Tanya Goreva, and they have a daughter ... two years old. He's presently posted here in Bombay as a defense armament advisor. He flies under the radar, but we're pretty certain he's KGB—probably Sixth Directorate."

Cat's eyebrows shot up. "Sorry, I'm not up on my Soviet directorates."

"Industrial security and economic counterintelligence. We've had our eyes on him for a few months, ever since the report from Madras. But even now, we don't have much. He maintains a low profile and is never seen publicly with the other Ruskies. He plays tennis occasionally with the French consul general at the Willingdon Sports Club and has been seen dining there with some of the elite names in the city. What gave it away, however, was the dead drop."

"You found one?"

Gary sighed. "Zach figured out he was stashing microfilm in a changing room by the pool at Breach Candy. He always used the same changing room—no matter what ... even if it meant waiting. There are hooks inside the rooms ... you know, for hanging clothes. In the room he used, however, the hook is hollow."

"That certainly isn't in the file."

"No. We were trying to piece it together." He paused and cocked his head questioningly. "You know how hard it is to spot a transfer? Or find a dead drop?"

Cat nodded. "Very."

"So, what if he was intentionally inept? What if he was just yanking our chain?"

"What would be the point? You said it yourself, he was under the radar. So why expose himself?"

"We were asking the same questions."

Puzzled, Cat frowned. "Tell me about this Breach Candy place."

Shrugging, Gary described the club. "It's a relic of the British colonial era, set up as a trust in the 1930s. Membership is limited to Europeans, with a few temporary corporate memberships available for expats. The main building has the changing rooms, dining rooms, and one partially covered pool for serious swimming. There's also an outdoor pool, which is where most of the crowd hangs out. It's shaped like India ... before they partitioned Pakistan and Bangladesh, anyhow. There's a good-size platform in the middle. If you're looking at an overhead, the diving side—nearest the ocean—would be Pakistan. Fitting, considering how the Pakis have gone off the deep end.

"The outdoor seating is what's really interesting, because it has its own set of unwritten rules. The Eastern bloc sits on the south side; the Westerners congregate on the north side. The Iron Curtain doesn't just divide Europe; it stretches right down the middle of the pool. Nobody ever treads in the other's domain or swims past their side of the platform ... except maybe the French and an occasional Scandinavian."

The crease in Cat's brow deepened. "You've been here for a couple of years, and the Middle East is more my beat, so pardon my ignorance if I get it wrong. But from everything I know, the Soviets abroad are kept on a very tight leash. There's almost always someone watching when they are in public, and very few places where the East and West might even cross paths. Have you considered that he might be trying to establish contact with us?"

Gary blinked. "That would be something."

"Indeed. What was on the microfilm?"

"We don't know. We didn't want to disturb it. We left it there, waiting to see who would pick it up."

"Who did?"

"It's still there. After Zach's death, it went on the back burner."

"Whoa! Five weeks later?"

"I've been debating whether or not to just pick it up."

"Why not? Let's find out what's on the film."

"The thing is, we have no idea who swapped Zach's saccharine with cyanide, or why." Gary ran his hand over his face and pressed his lips together. "What the hell. Nothing ventured, nothing gained. I'll pick it up this evening. You need a membership, by the way. Have your husband submit your names for Breach Candy and the Willingdon Club, to start. In a month, you'll probably want to join the Bombay Yacht Club, too. All of these are social entrées around here ... it's expected."

He handed her a thick booklet, *The Ultimate Visitor's Guide to Bombay*. "Here's your directory. In an emergency, call the number on page 18 and ask for Mr. Sosa. But be warned ... phone and electric service here can be dreadful, particularly on Malabar Hill. They had a fire at a substation a few months back and still haven't recovered. If you're in that area, think of it as a dead zone.

"Your flat overlooks the roof of the consulate. We have a bright pink planter up there. If you see the planter on the wall, the matter is urgent, and we need to meet that day at the prescribed time. If the time has already passed, add seven hours. If the planter is on the table, we'll meet the following day. I'll use the same to confirm I've received your signal. The planters are awkward, but we tried using the umbrellas on the tables, and the staff were always raising and lowering the damn things. Nobody touches the planters."

"Got it. Let's use the far left-corner window of my flat on the eighteenth floor. If I need an urgent meeting, both blinds full-up. Next day, one blind full-up. If I've received your message, blinds half-staff. Otherwise, blinds down."

"That will work. You need to know that we have three safe houses in the city; one is known only to a select few. Nariman Seawalk Apartments, number 303. It's actually privately owned and completely off the books, so don't ever take an asset there. There's a picture mounted above the chest in the landing as you exit the elevator. The top of the frame is spring-loaded. Just push it down hard, and the two sides of the frame come apart ... there's a key inside." Glancing at his watch, he stood. "You're at ten minutes. Take your husband to dinner tonight, seven thirty, at the Golden Dragon in the Taj. We'll connect there."

The forty-four-page guide was seemingly designed for tourists, with each page describing a popular site in the city and ads touting businesses in the immediate area. While innocuous in appearance, the booklet was published by the Malabar-Bombay Press, Ltd.—a business Cat knew to be a CIA front—and would have been more appropriately titled *The Comprehensive Guide to CIA Meeting Places.* Setting meeting locations and times was tricky business, particularly when they needed to vary in both time and location. The booklet solved the problem. Now she would wait for the planter to be moved.

Chapter 40

Following Gary's instructions, Cat and Tom presented themselves at the Golden Dragon promptly at seven thirty. The restaurant, as Cat learned later, was a favorite hangout for the expat crowd—making it an ideal spot for meeting up with friends and associates. And the food was delicious ... and not Indian. Regardless of how much one liked the native cuisine, it grew tiresome. One can only consume so much curry, dal, and spinach paneer.

They were directed to an intimate table against the wall, where they enjoyed a round of drinks, ordered appetizers, and made their selections for the main course. The waiter was just clearing the starter plates when Cat noticed the crowd of a dozen or so boisterous people gathering in the far corner of the room, with Gary Eastman among them.

After coffee, Tom and Cat rose from their chairs and made their way to the entry door. A voice called after them.

"Tom? Tom Powell?"

They turned to see a tall, wiry man approaching from the opposite corner of the restaurant.

"Tom? Ed Freemont. We met in Tehran a few years back ... at one of your rooftop parties."

Tom tried to place the man, but gave up and shook his hand. "Those were interesting times."

"They were insane, actually. Are you visiting, or working here now?"

"Working, I'm afraid, for the next couple of years," he replied and then introduced Cat. "We married shortly after leaving Tehran."

"Congratulations! Would you care to join us for a drink? Get to know a few of the other Americans in town?"

Tom looked at Cat, who glanced at her watch and telegraphed her thoughts.

"That would be excellent. Just for one drink, though. Cat just got in from the States, and she's still adjusting to the time change."

Cat smiled politely and held Tom's forearm as they worked their way back to the noisy table. As introductions were made, chairs were shifted and someone dragged two additional seats into the fray. Cat found herself sitting directly across from Gary Eastman.

Wearing a broad smile, Gary resumed the earlier fiction. "I met Cat this afternoon at the consulate. She was the college roommate of a girl I dated a few years back. How's that for a small world?"

Gary's wife elbowed him and snickered. "A small world is fine, as long as they are continents apart."

He laughed good-naturedly and looked straight at Cat. "You were spot-on correct, you know."

"I was?"

"Yes. Those cookies you brought were delicious ... a real surprise. To think of all the times I've walked right by the pastry shop and never stopped to have a look at what was available."

Playing along, Cat grinned. "I'm glad you enjoyed them." *Well, well, well,* she thought, interpreting Gary's comments. *He's picked up the microfilm. I was right. Our friend Anatoly Gorev wants to play.* She sat back, sipping her drink and allowing the buzz of conversation to float around her ... and waiting for Gary to make the next move.

"Another round?" Gary finally asked.

This was Cat's cue. She nudged Tom as she pushed her chair back and stood. "I think not. I'm all wrung out. Rain check?"

Gary stood as well, leaning over the table to shake her hand and deftly pressing a small pillbox into her palm. "Smart woman. I'm already on my third beer, and it won't be my last. I'll be lucky to make the office tomorrow!"

The merrymakers raised their glasses in salute. "Here, here!"

Cat pasted a smile on her face and gave Gary a nod in acknowledgment.

By the time they got home, Cat was tingling with anticipation. "I'll come to bed later. I have a couple of things to take care of."

Tom was familiar with the routine. When Cat got her hooks into something, the work became all-absorbing. And while running into the group at the Taj seemed innocent on its surface, he knew the signs well. Something was up, and half of the group at the restaurant had been with the consulate. One or more was bound to be CIA ... Eastman, probably. He called out behind her, "You got what you needed?"

"I've got something. Whether it's what I need, well, that remains to be seen."

Cat slipped into the third bedroom of their flat—the space doubling as an office—and locked the door. As the loud click resonated in the tiled space, she felt a moment of regret that this part of her life was walled off from Tom. He was stoic about it, but there were times when she just wanted a sounding board. *Cut the crap*, she thought to herself. *This is what you signed up for. Nobody ever said it would be easy.*

She popped the lid from the pillbox, disgorging a tiny torn note scrawled with the single word *tomorrow*, and a tightly folded photocopy. The document appeared to be a personnel profile for Daniil Barinov—typed in Russian, with handwritten translations into English. Gary must have retrieved and developed the microfilm, and then had this document translated.

A photograph in the upper left corner showed a man with sculpted cheeks, a long, ruler-straight nose, and a chiseled jaw. Some might have considered him classically handsome, but although he was smiling, any warmth evaporated at his eyes. His gaze was as cold and merciless as any she had ever seen—the eyes of a man devoid of humanity. Scrawled at the bottom of the photo was the Cyrillic lettering *убийца* and, beneath it, in English: *assassin*. Cat stared at the picture and felt a chill. In the dozens of photographs Cat had studied before arriving in Bombay, she had never seen this face.

Cat absently twisted her hair and studied the photo. *You're the one, aren't you? You're the one who killed Zach.*

What the hell did he know that made you do it? She realized that she'd been talking aloud and squeezed her eyes shut, trying to clear away the ghosts. She sat back in the chair and kicked her feet up, wondering if the document retrieved from the hidey-hole had been part of the original microfilm, or placed after the murder. If it was there from the start, someone had been trying to raise a warning flag that Gary and his team had missed. Regardless, it seemed that someone was trying to share information with the Americans. Cat was itching to find out if any additional documents were in the film.

Cat picked up the tourist guide. The meeting location and time were determined by first adding the date of the meeting—19—to the number of the month—7, for a total of 26. Dividing by two gave her the time: 13, or 1:00 p.m. She turned to page 26 in the first step of finding the location. The next step was to determine the numeric equivalent of the second letter of the second word, *D*, the fourth letter in the alphabet. She flipped to the fourth page: an article about Crawford Market. The ads at the bottom touted the services of two businesses near the market. Even-numbered days used the ad on the left; odd-numbered days pointed to the one on the right.

The meeting was set for 1:00 p.m. at Chakala Stationers by Crawford Market. If for any reason someone was a no-show or the meeting was aborted, the exercise would be repeated on the following day.

The system had worked well for several years. The number calculations were easy for agents to remember, but without the book it would be impossible to figure out.

Chapter 41

The following morning, Tom's driver dropped Cat at the Taj. The man was pleasant enough, Cat thought, and cautious behind the wheel. In the madness of Bombay traffic—where lane markings were ignored and four lanes became six or seven, and where the use of turn signals and mirrors was unheard of—he was skilled at guiding the car through the melee.

The driver had seemed anxious when she stated that she wouldn't need him for the remainder of the day, and she was instantly suspicious. Was he being paid to inform on her movements? Had Tom insisted that he accompany her? Or was he merely concerned for the well-being of the boss's wife? When he finally bowed his head in submission, Cat realized she was being paranoid—a mental state that went hand in hand with her profession. Regardless, if she was going to be successful here, she would need to understand the Indian culture.

The Pan Am secretary's son, Vijay, proved to be a capable and informative guide. His first order of business was to pull out a map and point out the areas they would be visiting. After a quick tour of the Taj Hotel, commentary on the various restaurants and amenities there, and its stature in the expat community, they caught a cab to drive them around the area known as Colaba.

Originally a series of seven islands, land reclamation had transformed Bombay into a single peninsula by the early 1900s. Colaba, the southernmost section of the city, now occupied two of the former islands and boasted a number of exclusive high-rise apartment buildings. The taxi took them through the Cuffe Parade neighborhood—with its wide seaside promenade and hundreds of small shops—and across the filled-in causeway, down to the green space of the military cantonment at the southern tip of the city. They circled around to the western edge of the peninsula for a view of the thirty-six-story World Trade Center—the tallest building in South Asia—and the elegantly modern Oberoi Hotel on Nariman Point.

They had an early lunch at the Oberoi, with a view of Marine Drive—the waterfront boulevard that curved beside the bay. As they left the restaurant, she asked about shopping, mentioning that she needed to pick up food and supplies. He seemed confused, asking if there was a language barrier with her servants. She winced inwardly at her cultural gaffe—servants were expected in a household of her husband's position—and adopted a worried expression while explaining that they had not yet hired staff. She steered the conversation until he finally mentioned Crawford Market.

As the traffic crawled across the city, she checked her watch and realized that she would have very little time to check the site before the meeting. She considered the implications of having Vijay accompany her—for at least a few minutes—into the market, ultimately deciding that his presence was better cover than without. She would send him on his way as soon as she had established that the area was clear.

With fifteen minutes to spare, they hopped out of the taxi and stepped into the bedlam near the market's main entry. Vendors hawked their goods, shoppers elbowed their way through the pulsing mass of humanity, and there was no escaping the thousands of flies buzzing about. Cat spotted the stationer's store on the other side of the street, but kept her pace brisk and her eyes moving as she walked by. The entire area was unfamiliar and impossibly crowded, making her wish for the eyes and ears of a full support team. She was hanging out there on her own—with a possible assassin in the mix—and the meeting place was in the middle of chaos. She sucked in a deep breath and walked into the market.

Just inside the doors she found a stall offering lemons and limes. She poked and squeezed and sniffed the fruit—keeping her eyes on the shop across the street and its immediate surroundings—while Vijay negotiated the price with the vendor. Cat was absently pulling a handful of rupees out of her pocket when she spied Gary ambling through the crowd. He looked perfectly at ease. His height made him easy to track, and she watched as he stepped into the stationer's shop. Cat shifted her gaze to scan the sea of people behind him. She caught a brief glimpse of another white face. A moving panel truck obscured the view for several seconds. Once it was past, she took several seconds to find the face again, stopped at a tobacco stall some thirty feet behind Gary. Her mouth went dry.

Daniil Barinov, the Soviet from the photo, was buying

a pack of cigarettes. Cat thrust the money at the fruit vendor and dug in her tote for her scarf, which she quickly wrapped around her neck. Barinov lit a cigarette and stepped away from the shop, positioning himself in a recess between two other vendor lean-tos. His head moved slowly and naturally as he surveyed his surroundings. Cat felt her pulse quicken. He was in broad daylight, and it would have been impossible to see into the market's interior, but when he fixed on the market entry, her heart began to pound wildly.

Per their established protocol, Gary would wait at their meeting place for ten minutes and no longer. She quickly visited two other stalls and, purchases in her arms, walked outside into the sunshine with Vijay. She loitered there, in profile to the stationer's shop and the Russian killer, asking Vijay about their itinerary the following day and pumping him with questions about the city and the places they would visit. Out of the corner of her eye, she spied Gary as he exited the shop and turned in Barinov's direction. The assassin casually shifted position, pivoting away as Gary walked by.

Gary had spotted the signal: a scarf tight around her neck if there was danger afoot, draping out of the tote if something felt awry, and not visible if all was clear. If the circumstances were reversed, Gary would have used his glasses or sunglasses: on top of his head, perched on his nose, or tucked into his pocket.

She resisted the temptation to turn and watch the Russian, and instead shook Vijay's hand and said she would catch a taxi home. He seemed grateful; enduring traffic to escort her back to the Taj would have added another hour to his day. She turned to wave for a ride, just in time to see Barinov lower himself into the backseat of a gray Lada sedan with diplomatic plates. In a city of indistinguishable vehicles, the Russian-made car was glaringly different. The man had taken only primitive measures to avoid detection, and was using a car that clearly identified his nationality and conveyed diplomatic immunity. *Poor tradecraft,* she wondered, *or arrogance?*

She returned to her flat, dropped her purchases in the kitchen, and left the building. She took a brisk walk down to Kemp's Corner and found a leather shop offering knockoff designer bags. She browsed for a moment before asking to borrow their phone. She dialed the emergency number from memory and waited. After several rings, a voice mumbled an unintelligible greeting.

"Mr. Sosa, please," she said into the mouthpiece.

The response was incoherent, but a fraction of a minute later, she recognized Gary's voice on the line. "Yes?"

"I missed you at the market today. Any chance we can get together soon?"

"Nariman Seawalk Apartments, number 303. Two hours."

"Perfect."

An hour and a half later, Cat slid out of the taxi. She had changed cabs three times and directed the drivers on a jumbled crisscross of the city streets. She had not seen the gray sedan, nor could she detect any car following her. She was now two blocks from the address Gary had given. She traversed the street and approached the building from the rear, spotting the service entrance in the center. Finding the door ajar, she stepped inside. A uniformed worker turned her way at the sound of the door opening, and she could see the question forming on his lips.

Cat adopted a limp and assumed a pained expression. The worker wiggled his head subserviently and held the interior door as she hobbled toward the elevator. She was beginning to realize that an American or European could get away with a lot in India—the workers were conditioned to quiet acquiescence.

She found the key and let herself into the flat. The furnishings were functional, but Spartan. Uncle Sam hadn't spent any taxpayer money to make the place comfortable. After verifying that she was alone, she took a position against the wall adjoining the hallway ... and waited.

Stiffening when she finally heard the lock click, she was cocked for action when Gary rounded the corner. He jumped visibly when he saw her.

"Christ," he said. "You nearly gave me a coronary." Relaxing, he took a seat. "So tell me what the hell happened today."

"Barinov. He was about thirty feet behind you, and I didn't spot him until you went into the shop. He bought some smokes and just hung around until you came out. Then he jumped into the backseat of a gray Lada."

"A Lada? Not too many of those around here. You're sure he wasn't there by coincidence?"

"Very."

"What's his game? Intimidation?" Gary's voice rose in anger. "If so, I can tell you he's succeeding. I'm pretty goddamn intimidated by the idea of cyanide in my goddamn food. The guy was making a statement that he could get to us at any time and in the most unsuspected way."

Cat tried to keep her expression neutral, but she was puzzled. First, Gary had neglected to pick up the microfilm until she suggested it. Then, his tradecraft at the market had been sloppy, and he had not picked up on Barinov at all. Now, he was becoming nervous and emotional—both traits that could get him or others killed. She had checked him out before coming to Bombay, and he had a good reputation. Something didn't jive.

"But why? Why would he resort to that level of pressure? And is there something else going on with you? Something you haven't shared?" she asked. "From what I've heard, cowering in fear isn't exactly your style."

He became still as a stone. "You're perceptive."

"What is it?" she pushed.

"I had a source inside the Soviet consulate—an Indian girl. She worked as a secretary, but she was observant and smart. You'd be surprised what people leave on their desks or in the trash. Three weeks before Zach was killed, she went to the hospital suffering from stomach pain and severe vomiting and diarrhea. The doctors treated her with antibiotics, but two days later she was dead. They thought she had food poisoning, which is common enough around here. But in retrospect, I'm not so sure.

"Then, day before yesterday, a high-level asset in Moscow dropped out of sight. I recruited him a number of years ago during a posting to London. I've met his family; I liked him. He had a new handler, of course, but I kept an eye on him. Then *poof*, he was gone."

"You think these events are somehow related to

Zach?"

"I don't know. But it's got my attention."

She rolled this new information around in her head. *Could there be a connection?* "We'll need to be more cautious. Barinov isn't taking normal precautions, which either makes him stupid or he believes he's untouchable. Either way, you're right to be worried."

"Maybe we should start hiring tasters."

She laughed in spite of herself. "Great idea. Or go on a starvation diet."

"Very funny."

"What else was on the film?"

"A phone number and a message." He recited the number. "Ask for Mssr. Benoit. Leave a callback number."

"That's it? Anybody could have written it, couldn't they? Gary, this is very thin, and risky."

"I agree that we're way in the dark. It would help if we knew why Zack was meeting them or if he completed the meet. But we haven't found any notes. Doesn't mean he didn't take any ... his flat was searched before we got there. We need to even the odds somehow."

Cat paced the room for several minutes, finally whirling toward him. "I have an idea."

Gary listened intently as she shared her thoughts. He sat silently, bent forward with his forearms resting on his thighs, thinking it over. "You have a set of cojones, Cat; I'll give you that. You think you can pull it off?"

"I don't know yet. I need to know more about him. Where does Gorev live?"

"Malabar Hill, in Malabar Garden Tower on Mount Pleasant Road. Affluent, exclusive, residential. He's on the eighth floor, but I don't know the flat number."

"What kind of car?"

"White Ambassador." He gave her the license number.

"I'll go there tomorrow. Can you arrange a tail for Monday morning? I want to know where Gorev goes and when. I think we should meet here tomorrow night. Can you make that work without being seen?"

"Yes. I'm embarrassed I didn't spot Barinov. I got complacent. Stupid of me."

"Not stupid, Gary. You live someplace long enough, you start to feel comfortable. It happens."

A deep frown creased his features. "How sure are you that he was following me, and not already in place? I doubt our tourist guide system is compromised, but anything is possible."

"It felt like a tail to me, but I can't be certain. What about this place? Who knows about it?"

"You, me, and Ed Freemont. You met him at dinner last night. This flat belongs to an old friend of my mother. She had a textile business and was frequently in India, so she bought the place as an investment years ago. When I took the posting, I thought it might be useful and asked if she still owned it. Turns out, she did, and was happy to offer it to me ... rent free. All the bills go to her, so there's no paper trail pointing to us. We're good, as long as she doesn't drop dead."

"Let's hope she doesn't. If you two are the only ones who know about this place, what the hell do you use it for?"

"In this job I learned early on that you never know when something's going to bite you in the ass. I found it's best to have a stack of passports, a boatload of money, and places to hide."

She looked at Gary in surprise and wondered if they had shared the same mentor.

Chapter 42

At three in the morning, Cat made her way to Malabar Hill, parking her car at the top of Mount Pleasant Road, a quarter mile from Gorev's apartment building. She worked her way around the perimeter, noting the strategically placed closed-circuit television cameras.

The adjoining parking garage was a typical ramp and half-wall structure, surrounded by heavy vegetation to discourage views from outside. The wall was too high above the ground to scale without equipment, but she found a recess—about eighteen inches wide and four inches deep—in the north corner opposite the stairwell. Wedging herself into the space, she pressed her fingers and toes against the lip of the concrete and inched upward. Peering into the first level of the garage, she spotted a camera in the far corner, pointed away from her and toward the stairwell. *Poorly planned*, she thought, with the designers believing that an intruder wouldn't scale the exterior wall.

She took a position behind a car on the first floor of the four-level structure. Cat liked this hour of the morning. There were few people about, and sentries frequently found it difficult to stay awake. The guard here, however, seemed alert, and patrolled frequently and randomly. Sometimes he walked the sloping ramp of the garage, and sometimes he took the stairs. He had been well-trained.

She had a naturally gentle tread and moved silently against the wall, staying out of camera range and grateful that the Indians used plates on both the front and back of their cars. There were three white Ambassadors, but none with the correct number on the plate.

Cat crept back to the point by which she'd entered the garage. Assessing the recess for a climb to the second floor, she realized that she'd never have enough traction to lift herself from her current position. The only option was to go back to the bottom and start over. She breathed a sigh of relief when she found the vehicle on the second floor, knowing that she would never have been able to climb to the remaining two levels.

Several cars on the floor were immaculately polished, but dusty. Similar to Florida, Bombay's climate in the summer was intolerably hot and humid. And similar to Florida, many of the city's elite participated in a mass exodus for the season. She took up position in a corner space, between a dusty car and the wall, and watched Gorev unlock his car at fifteen minutes before six—with the sky lightening but before the sun peeked over the horizon. She noticed, too, that he didn't once glance into the car or around the perimeter. He was on his home turf, confident and unsuspecting. *Good*, she thought. She took note, too, that only a handful of vehicles left the garage between six and seven. *Plenty of time.*

Gorev was also precise, keeping the same schedule each morning for the following two days. Cat assumed the spaces were assigned; he never hesitated or deviated from the spot on the second floor. In her meetings with Gary, she learned that Ed Freemont had followed Gorev from the moment he left the parking garage until he returned at night. The evenings, they discovered, were completely unpredictable, and on two of the three nights, Gorev was accompanied by his wife. Cat opted for a dawn intervention.

On the fourth morning, Cat wore an oversize shirt and tucked the pistol into a holster at the small of her back. Carrying a gun was risky as hell in India, but there was no way she was confronting Gorev without it.

As on the previous nights, she waited for the guard to make his pass, huddling at the front bumper in the shadow of the wheel well. She heard the man walk by, his shoes squeaking against the concrete and the fabric of his cotton trousers rustling against his legs. The footsteps echoed into the distance, and Cat crept to the driver's door.

She used a stiff wire to pop the lock and was inside the vehicle within seconds. After closing and locking the door, she climbed into the backseat and loosened the overhead bulb a fraction. She was hoping that the car itself wasn't bugged. There simply was not enough light to check. Dressed in dark clothing and curled up on the floor directly behind the driver's seat, she was concealed—unless he opened the back door. She shook her head at the thought. *Stop it. He goes straight to the driver's door.*

At precisely fifteen minutes before six, she heard footsteps approaching, and she tensed in anticipation. The key clicked into the lock, the door opened, and the man slid into the driver's seat. The keys jingled as he raised them toward the ignition box.

"Please do not turn around. Drop your keys on the floor and pretend to look for them."

She heard a strangled cry, and his words came out in a high-pitched squeak of fright. "Who are you?"

"Not for you to know. Did you leave me a message?"

"You are American?"

"Answer the question. Did you leave me a message?" *Of course I'm American, you idiot. Nobody else in the world would care about your sorry ass.*

"Yes, yes. I leave message. Call on telephone for Mssr. Benoit. Not attack me in car."

Gorev's English was understandable, Cat thought, but not fluent. She sensed his fright giving way to anger and countered with an angry edge of her own. "What happened with my friend? The one who was killed. Did you meet with him?"

"No, no, no! I saw at pool club. It was party; maybe he follow me. But no talk. Too many people; too dangerous. I tried warn you. I left picture. Man Barinov is killer."

So the photo of the assassin had been placed before the murder. God. "Did he meet with your wife?"

"What? What wife?"

"Your wife. Did he meet with her on the morning he was killed?"

"I do not think this possible. She have ..." He mumbled in Russian, as if trying to find the right words, before finally blurting out, "Hair. At Taj in morning. Always Friday."

Cat mentally translated the broken English: Gorev's wife was having her hair styled on the morning Zach was killed. Suddenly the story made sense. Zach hadn't been going to a scheduled meeting with Gorev at Breach Candy. Instead, he had learned that Gorev would be there and had hoped for an opening to approach him. When that attempt failed, he had discovered the time of Tanya Goreva's hair appointment and intended to use the opportunity to intercept her. Cat was sure of it. It all fit, and explained why Zach had not reported the encounters.

"What do you want?"

"Want? I want go to America. I have wife and baby. I have many secrets. Many value."

She heard the jingling of keys.

"What kind of secrets?"

He didn't answer, and Cat heard the squeak of leather.

Fuck. She pointed the gun at the back of the seat. "Mr. Gorev, I know your real name. I have a gun. If you fuck with me, I *will* shoot you."

"I have film in shoe. I give you."

What? "Please be very careful, Mr. Gorev. Don't do anything stupid."

Gorev grunted, and Cat wrinkled her nose at the sour odor of feet that smelled as if they hadn't seen air in months. He twisted his arm behind his back and dropped a tiny canister of film into the passenger compartment.

"What is this?"

"Places of radar."

Really? "What else?"

"First, you promise safety of my family. We have son in Leningrad with mother of my wife. Three months, I want we go to America."

"Mr. Gorev, we have satellites that can pinpoint your

radar installations. I'd like to help you, but I need more."

"Film has secret radar, and blueprints. Can your satellites show blueprints?"

Cat drew a deep breath. The film would have to be evaluated by the experts at Langley. "Is that all? You have insiders in the Indian nuclear program. Bring me something about their plans."

"I no know nuclear."

"Use your connections. Get me something."

"I give you better. When I am in America, I give you name of CIA man we pay for names of your agents."

An icy chill washed over her. "A mole, Mr. Gorev? Are you saying we have a mole?"

"Yes, I forget American word. A mole."

My God.

Chapter 43

Cat instructed Gorev to leave the parking garage as he would normally, and to make a brief stop after turning out of the drive.

"Just past the place where the taxis are," she instructed him, "stop long enough to let me out." She had picked the space with care after seeing that the road was a few feet wider and that the foliage blocked any view from Gorev's apartment building. It would take only seconds to slip out of the car.

Opening the door as the car rolled to a stop, she said softly, "I'll be in touch, Mr. Gorev. Keep your eyes open."

That night, Cat turned the film over to Gary. "The mole thing was out of the blue," she told him. "I sure as hell didn't expect it. Could Zach have known anything about this?"

Gary paced the floor and rubbed the stubble of his beard with his right hand. "If he did, he didn't share it with me. Of course, mole talk makes one reluctant to share anything with anybody. Christ! Do you think Gorev could be telling the truth?"

"There's the real question. Langley's never going to buy into it with what we have, which is next to nothing. Some nobody Russian named Gorev claims we have a mole? Pffttt. No chance."

"Cat, everyone always *assumed* he's a nobody. There hasn't been anything to indicate otherwise. But if this is real, and that's a big *if*, he's either a player or he's on very good terms with someone who is."

"What do we know about his wife? I've been trying to figure out why Zach would want to meet her. What if the wife is the real source?"

Gary stopped in his tracks and whirled toward her. "You may be onto something. I'll get Langley on it right away. Until we know more, sit tight and I'll signal you."

"Let's hope they have something. In the interim, I'm going to watch our Tanya Goreva. According to her husband, she gets her hair done every Friday. Zach was looking for her at the Taj on a Friday, and they have a salon. I'll start there. Maybe we'll learn something."

"Don't get caught."

"Wouldn't think of it."

Cat felt oddly disconcerted as she looked for a seat in the Shamiana restaurant at the Taj. Two months ago, Zach had been murdered while having breakfast in this same place—while trying to meet up with the same woman Cat was looking for today. *Creepy*, she thought.

She chose a table with a good view of the lobby, certain that Tanya Goreva would use the hotel's main entry. She ordered iced coffee—no sweetener, thank you—and uttapam, a pancake-like dish with tomatoes, onions, cabbage, and chilies. She ate lazily, paid her bill, sipped her coffee, and waited.

At nine twenty-five, Tanya Goreva swept into the lobby, shielded by large sunglasses and her dark hair elegantly hidden by an ivory scarf. Tall and thin, in profile she reminded Cat of Audrey Hepburn in *Breakfast at Tiffany's*. She was in the stylist's chair by nine thirty. Cat was a few minutes tardy for her nine thirty with Shoba, whose chair was two down but from which any conversation could be easily overheard.

Cat caught Tanya's reflection in the mirror and realized that the woman not only had an Audrey Hepburn air about her; she actually resembled the actress. She was quite beautiful. Keeping her own conversation to a bare minimum, Cat listened intently as Tanya related to the stylist that she had recently returned from Moscow. Tanya then asked if the stylist's brother would be at his shop the following afternoon, because she had twenty kilos in her luggage that she wanted to sell.

Stunned by the open admission, Cat was also puzzled, having never heard talk of a Moscow-Bombay drug trade. All became clear when Tanya rose to leave and offered the stylist a small round tin with blue and black markings. Goreva was not a drug smuggler. The instantly recognizable tin contained caviar, which Tanya brought into Bombay to sell on the black market.

Suitably coiffed, Cat found the bank of phones just off the hotel lobby. She called her young guide, asking if he knew of shops that dealt in black market caviar.

"There is only one," he replied. "Nepean Sea Market,

at Kemp's Corner. Many of the Russians sell there."

Upon arriving back at her flat in the afternoon, Cat had peered out the window to find the pink planter positioned on the wall of the consulate's roof. Having begged off dinner with Tom, she was now sitting on the flimsy sofa at the Nariman safe house, listening to Ed Freemont explain the results of his query to Langley. Tanya Goreva was the eldest daughter of a high-ranking member of the KGB. Specifically, he held a rank equivalent to an American two-star general and was assigned to the First Directorate—the department tasked with foreign espionage.

In a rare display of aggravation, Gary slammed his tumbler of scotch down on the table. "And they are just now telling us this? For God's sake!" He stood abruptly, walked to the other side of the room, and leaned against the wall. "I have my own thoughts about how to proceed, but I'd like to hear from you two first."

Ed, equally upset with the bureaucracy that had deprived them of valuable intel, pressed his lips together in frustration. "We have to run surveillance on her. She's probably KGB herself. God knows what she's into. I think ..."

Shaking her head vehemently, Cat interrupted him. "No. Anatoly isn't going to try to defect with their daughter, their son, and the mother-in-law without the full blessing and cooperation of Tanya. It's unthinkable. Assuming that Gorev is committed, they are in this together."

"So what do you recommend?" This came from Gary.

"I'm going to make contact. Tomorrow. Ed, can you

watch my back?"

"It would be a risk," he told her. "They know who I am. If they spot me, they will tie you to me."

"I have a better idea," said Gary. "Smith is in town from Dhaka. He's not known here. Let's put him to use."

"Smith would be good," Ed agreed. "Perfect, in fact."

"Who's Smith?" Cat asked.

The two men just grinned.

Within the hour, the man called Smith joined them at the safe house. Unlike most agents working in the field of clandestine operations, Smith stood out. His head sprouted a thick thatch of strawberry-blond hair, and his nose and cheeks retained a permanent blush. He was renowned for his talent for mimicking accents and for his uncanny knack of inventing diversions on the fly.

Gary pointed out that, as a general rule, the Soviets moved about in twos or threes—the idea being that they would keep a watchful eye on one another, making it more difficult to establish relationships with outsiders or find the means to defect. Whether because of her husband's position or in deference to her status as a KGB general's daughter, Tanya Goreva seemed to be an exception, as previous surveillance reports noted that she was usually alone or in the company of her husband or daughter.

The plan was loose—some might say sloppy—but with the pile of unknowns, any real plan would probably fall apart within seconds anyhow. Nevertheless, the cardinal rule was to prepare for the worst, so they tried to think of every possibility.

The next morning, Smith positioned himself at the east side of the Kemp's Corner intersection, wearing shapeless white cotton pants and a traditional white kurta—a loose-fitting, knee-length shirt with long sleeves and an opening for the head. With a white Nehru hat perched on his head, he looked like a caricature of a Brit gone native. His role today was twofold. As the spotter, he would signal Tanya's arrival—if she came at all—by removing his hat. And if Tanya was accompanied, he would play the decoy.

Cat was a hundred feet away from Smith, meandering among the shops and accompanied by the young man she had hired to be her guide. Smith had voiced his concerns about using a civilian during the operation, but had been outvoted. Cat was confident that having the young man present—and ignorant of the true nature of the quest for caviar—would work to their advantage.

Ed—wearing a long-haired wig, old water buffalo sandals, and wire-rimmed glasses—was sitting on a wall across the street, feigning a hashish-induced haze.

Shortly before eleven o'clock, Tanya Goreva stepped from the left rear door of a taxi. A moment later, the right rear door opened, and out popped the head of Daniil Barinov. Of all the possible complications that could have occurred, this one was completely unexpected. The team would look back on it later and wonder if they should have seen it coming.

Smith considered his next action. If Gary and Ed were correct in their assessment, Barinov was a cold-blooded killer, and it would be dangerous as hell for the team to attempt any contact with Tanya. On the other hand, all Cat needed to do was confirm Tanya's intentions. Fifteen seconds, maybe twenty. No more. Cat had been in the field for several years and was already becoming a legend. She was good, and they might not have another chance. He took off his hat.

Cat caught the signal and aimed for the shop, reaching the entrance ten steps ahead of Tanya. In her peripheral vision, she spotted another passenger in the taxi, and hurriedly pushed the door open. Cat's guide held the door open for Tanya, but remained outside, watching some commotion in the street. The elderly man behind the counter was on the phone, consulting a ledger and speaking in Hindi.

Brushing against Tanya, Cat whispered to her, "Has your husband spoken to you about meeting an American?"

Tanya Goreva's eyes went wide as saucers, and she jerked her eyes at the door in fear. Her companion was still outside. "Who are you?"

"Not yet. Did your husband speak with you?"

"Yes, yes. We go to America, yes?"

"We are working on it, Mrs. Goreva. We need some time to work out the details. I will be in touch. I promise you!"

Tanya Goreva, visibly paler than a moment earlier, nodded slowly. "Thank you."

Cat whirled out of the shop and back toward the street, waving to hail a nearby taxi. She hurried past her guide, murmuring, "I'm sorry. I have to leave. I think I must have eaten something that didn't agree with me." She'd been inside the shop for fifteen seconds. She spotted Smith thirty feet away, standing beside a taxi and gesturing wildly at the Indian driver—while simultaneously arguing almost nose-to-nose with a Caucasian man. Recognizing the profile of Barinov, she casually turned her face away as her heart began to pound. *My God. How much had he seen?*

When Cat arrived at the safe house an hour later, she found Smith with a glass in his hand and a half-empty bottle of scotch on the table. Ed held a bottle of beer, and there were three empties lined up at his elbow.

She pulled the scarf from her head. "Tanya's definitely in, but I didn't have time to learn more. What the hell happened out there?" she asked.

Smith tilted his glass toward Cat. "My guess is that she thinks of Barinov as one of the hired help and expected him to carry the caviar for her. Tanya left the bag in the taxi. Makes you wonder if she has a clue about his profession."

"Are you serious?"

"As a dead sturgeon. It worked out, because it delayed him, and I played the asshole trying to get into the taxi before he was out. But I'll tell you, the man has a short fuse."

"Do you think he spotted me?"

"Not a chance. He was too focused on me."

Ed shook his head. "I think Smith is probably right, but the guy doesn't miss much. He watched your friend climb into a taxi."

Cat's expression dissolved into worry. "What do you mean?"

"Just after Smith commandeered the taxi, Barinov turned toward the shop. I don't know what drew his attention, but he was definitely watching your young guide."

"That can't be good," Smith observed.

Cat tried to calculate the chances. "But there's no way to identify him, right? He was just a kid in a taxi, and there are millions of people in this city."

Ed shrugged his shoulders. "Just saying."

Cat poured herself a drink and sank into the sofa. "Damn it. We can't go anywhere near that kid now."

Chapter 44

While the Gorevs' automobile had worked well for their initial contact, it was simply too dangerous for long-term use. To learn out more about Gorev's habits and movements, Cat wiggled her way into the parking garage for two additional meetings with the Russian. Gorev admitted he was often involved in sessions with the Indian military, but only rarely attended solo. The Soviets kept a close eye on their people, leaving few occasions for the Gorevs to be alone.

As Cat explored the possibilities with Anatoly, he revealed that he and Tanya would often load their daughter into a stroller and walk through the Hanging Gardens and the adjacent Kamala Nehru Park. The two sites offered a variety of opportunities and were ideally located at the top of Malabar Hill, just up from the Gorevs' apartment building. The salon at the Taj hotel, where Tanya spent an hour each Friday, presented other possibilities. Finally, the tiny market near the Soviet consulate—where Anatoly purchased cigarettes every day—could serve as a point of encounter when time was of the essence.

Anatoly carried a briefcase, Tanya carried her compact, lipstick, and a hairbrush in a variety of purses, and they both carried a key chain with a tiny flashlight attached. Cat snapped photos and handed them off to Gary, who sent them to the States in the diplomatic pouch. Within a week, Langley sent back a box of equipment. Packed inside were two flashlights—replicas of those on their key chains—modified to function as cameras, a famous-label designer purse from Italy with a hidden recorder, a hair-brush with a Minox miniature camera concealed in the bristle head, and a duplicate briefcase with a recording device mounted in the base.

Cat and Ed hastily put their heads together to find safer and more suitable methods for exchanging information—signals that could be initiated and recognized by either party in different situations. Recognizing that they would be forced to rely on document drops for their most frequent communication with Gorev, Ed recommended the use of the children's Shoe House in Kamala Nehru Park. When Cat raised her eyebrows, he told her about the two-story structure at the eastern edge of the park.

Modeled after a lace-up boot, the Shoe House paid homage to the old nursery rhyme about the woman who lived in a shoe. In addition to a spiral staircase leading to a balcony overlooking the park, the shoe held a hidden compartment at its base. He explained that the space had been secretly constructed a few years earlier, in anticipation of recruiting a Soviet asset with young children. Hopes had been dashed when an illness in the family prompted their recall to Moscow. Ed had taken the liberty of checking the compartment the previous evening; it was still functional.

Cat risked one more meeting with Gorev, handing him the box of equipment from Langley. She also presented him with what appeared to be an ordinary marker, but which actually used ultraviolet ink.

"Take photos of anything that might be important and carry the film to the Shoe House. You've been there; it's mostly kids inside, so we think it is extremely unlikely that anyone will notice what you're doing. Just stand with your back to the wall and rest your right arm against the side of the doorframe. You'll feel a thumbnail-size bump. Push on it, and at the same time, nudge the wood at the base of the wall with the heel of your shoe. A small drawer will pop open. Drop the film inside and push it closed.

"The walls inside the shoe are covered with graffiti. To the left of the door, just above eye level, you'll see a green infinity sign. When you make a drop, use the pen to draw a small line in the left oval. If it gets full, use the right oval. If you have any reason to think that you may be under suspicion, draw an X. You can't see the writing except under UV light.

"When we leave something in the drawer, our signal to you will be a piece of white tape at the bottom of the fifth iron fence post closest to the shoe. But if you see red tape or if your safety feels threatened in any way, you need to leave immediately. Take a taxi to the Royal Guild apartments on Grant Road, number 203." She handed him a brass key. "Carry this with you at all times. If you go to the apartment, call us as soon as you are inside. Press the round button on the phone; it will dial us automatically."

Cat glanced up at the rearview mirror and tried to read Anatoly's expression. Now that the plans were in motion, he seemed resigned to his fate—almost sad.

"I want promise," he said.

"Yes, we are going to get your son and Tanya's mother."

"No. If I be discover, you must promise. My daughter must go America."

Cat frowned, wondering what had prompted his words. Was he worried that he might be under suspicion? "What is wrong, Anatoly?"

"Nothing wrong. You make promise."

Cat was silent for a moment, concerned. Finally attributing his concern to a case of nerves, she replied, "We will take care of all of you, Anatoly. I promise."

As an incentive to maintain their loyalty, Soviets working abroad were nearly always required to leave one close family member in the homeland. The tactic was very effective in reducing defections to the West. Shortly after Tanya had announced to her parents that Anatoly was being posted to Bombay, Tanya's mother had packed a suitcase for her grandson and hustled him off to Leningrad—the city of their birth. Tanya's father, an upper-level official in the Soviet government, remained in Moscow.

Anatoly Gorev had asked for an extraction within three months. Lifting the Gorevs out of Bombay was one thing, but wresting their son and Tanya's mother from Soviet clutches in the heart of Leningrad was another matter entirely. Langley wanted six months to make the arrangements.

With little choice, the Gorevs reluctantly agreed to the

delay. Anatoly began to mine his consulate for tidbits of information, bringing out snapshots of secret documents carelessly left on desks or discarded as rubbish. Most of the intel was low level and already known to Western intelligence. He and his wife refused to provide the name of the CIA traitor until their family was safe in America.

Headquarters was dubious about the Gorevs knowing the mole's actual identity and generally suspicious of the entire arrangement. How would Tanya be privy to that level of information? Had her father made a slip, or simply decided to confide in her? Either case seemed highly unlikely. Her father would be tried, convicted, and shot before the Gorevs' plane reached its destination. What daughter would sacrifice her father like that? Cat was convinced that Langley's skepticism was the primary reason for the delay in snatching the son from Leningrad. Cat had no such doubts. The Gorevs were telling the truth; she was certain of it.

Tanya was permitted only two visits per year to Leningrad. She was, however, allowed unlimited travel to visit her father in Moscow. She took full advantage of the privilege. While Anatoly may have been the employee of the USSR, it was Tanya who mined the mother lode. On her frequent visits to Moscow, she invaded the study in her father's apartment to look for documents and record his private conversations with the comrades who stopped by occasionally. But when her father requested a pair of custom shoes from India, the CIA operatives in Bombay saw a rare opportunity. Ed intercepted the shoes and implanted a small recording and transmitting device in each heel. Workers in the Kremlin, particularly those in sensitive positions, were regularly wanded for transmitters. The pressure of Anatoly's foot deactivated the transmitter in the heel, preventing detection of the bug when the shoes were being worn. When the shoes were slipped off, the transmitter would dutifully send its recording. Tanya delivered the parcel to her father, and the Americans at Moscow station were given the go-ahead to listen.

Within a matter of weeks after the shoes arrived in Moscow, alarm bells were sounding at a fever pitch on the other side of the Atlantic. On three separate occasions, the bugged shoes had transmitted the voices of the Soviets congratulating themselves for the success of a highly placed source deep within the CIA. The Soviets called him *Kolokol.*

Chapter 45

For the most part, the team in Bombay stayed clear of the Gorevs, using the drop in the Shoe House to exchange information. They had detected no sign of the assassin Barinov since the encounter with the caviar, and Cat wondered if he had been sent elsewhere. Langley distributed the man's profile to its stations worldwide, but there were no reports of a sighting. The situation kept Cat on alert; he could be anywhere.

As the Gorevs approached the four-month mark of cooperating with the Americans, Tanya became increasingly agitated that there were as yet no plans for their extraction. Cat, against her better judgment, booked an appointment at the Taj salon on Friday morning.

Cat had taken great care to avoid the Pan Am offices in the hotel, not wanting to run the risk of running into the secretary or her son. As luck would have it, the young man rounded the corner just as she was approaching the entry to the salon. He was friendly and inquisitive, wanting to know if she was enjoying Bombay and suggesting that there were other sights she might like to see. She politely declined, explaining that she was quite busy helping to redecorate the flats of a few of her husband's colleagues. She wished him well and watched his back as he headed toward the hotel lobby. Foot traffic in the hallway was light and Cat's trained eyes detected nothing amiss, but the encounter left her feeling uneasy.

Watching in the mirror as the scissors snipped away at her hair, Cat kept an ear trained to Tanya's conversation with her own stylist.

"My father very ill," Cat heard her say. "He have cancer of pancreas. Six months doctors said. Now saying only few more weeks."

My God, Cat thought, regretting that the Gorevs had not told her of the situation long ago. Tanya's father was dying, and Cat suddenly understood. He had been encouraging his daughter to flee to the West. That was why Tanya knew his secrets and why she was becoming desperate. If her father died before they escaped to America, she was worried that her deception might somehow come to light or that she and Anatoly might be recalled to Moscow—permanently.

Cat contacted Gary immediately, urging him to support her in recommending an immediate extraction of the Gorev family. Langley must have experienced a change of heart—or they were scared shitless about the mole—because their response was immediate. *Three days,* they replied. *Monday night, 8:00 p.m. Leningrad, 10:30 p.m. Bombay.*

Cat penned a note instructing the Gorevs to be at the Golden Dragon for a late dinner—with their daughter—on Monday. They were to linger in the restaurant until ten twenty-five, and then make their way back to the front of the hotel, where they would be met. They were told to bring nothing with them that they would not ordinarily carry on a night out. Ed slipped the note into the drawer in the Shoe House and wound the white tape around the fence post. When he returned later that night, there was a new star in the right section of the infinity symbol and the note was gone.

On Saturday night, Tom answered a ring on their home phone. The caller asked for Sunita, and apologized on learning that no Sunita lived at the residence. Tom repeated the conversation—word-for-word—to Cat, who exploded out of her chair and raced to the car. *Sunita* was the code Gary and Ed had agreed to use if the Gorevs ever dialed the emergency number. Cursing the entire way, she followed a circuitous route—her training overriding the urgency of the situation. After doubling back and circling around until sure that she wasn't being followed, she pulled onto the road running in front of the Royal Guild apartments.

She hit the brakes a block from the building and, seeing nothing out of the ordinary, squeezed into a parking space. She sprinted up the street and into the building, taking the stairs two at a time to the second floor. Her heart fell as she took in the damage. The front door of the apartment was splintered, as if smashed by a battering ram. Inside, the only sign of the Gorevs was a child's stuffed elephant, smears of fresh blood in the foyer and on the kitchen floor, and a phone whose wires had been ripped from the wall.

Gary, trailed by Ed, pounded up the stairs a few

minutes later. The call had come in at ten fifty-two—dutifully logged, recorded, and forwarded to Gary by a staffer at the consulate—with a panicked Tanya whispering that Barinov had found them. When they listened to the recording later, Cat would hear Tanya's muffled gasp as the entry door was forced open, and the sound of a scream, cut short when the call went dead.

They spent thirty seconds verifying that the apartment was empty before hustling back to the street. On her way out, Cat picked up the toy, the sole remnant of the Gorevs' hopes and dreams, and shoved it into her bag. They stood to the side and watched helplessly as three police cars squealed to a stop in front of the building.

Cat slept little that night, replaying the events of the last few months over and over and desperately wishing for the chance at a do-over. Tom canceled his morning round of golf, cooked breakfast, and offered a shoulder to lean on. While he knew nothing of the night's events, he knew something had taken an enormous toll on his wife. Cat was the strongest person he'd ever known, but this morning she was on the brink.

Cat sipped at a cup of tea, nibbled at the scrambled eggs, and picked up the local morning paper, delaying the mountain of after-action reports she would need to complete in the next few hours. She was scanning the third page when a headline caught her eye: *Mystery Deepens in Mysterious Torture Death*. She found the name in the second paragraph, and the acid roiled violently in her stomach. Her guide, the Pan Am secretary's son, had been found brutally beaten and tortured in the back room of a welding shop the previous day—with a dead cat draped over the body. The owner, upon opening for business Saturday morning, had made the gruesome discovery.

Cat had never told the Gorevs her name, and none of the communiques to Langley mentioned it. Someone had tortured the kid to get the information, and Cat could only interpret the dead animal as a message that she was now a target. *Barinov,* she thought.

Before the day was over, Cat had packed a bag of gear for herself and accompanied Tom to the airport. He purchased a ticket to Dubai on Pan Am, and Cat contacted a private service to protect him day and night. She drove aimlessly around the airport until the familiar white tail with the blue ball lifted off the runway. In the middle of the night, Cat returned to the city, parked her car at Breach Candy, wrapped her head in a Muslim hijab, took a taxi to Colaba, and found a room on the third floor of a cheap hotel catering to not-so-wealthy Asians and Middle Easterners.

The hotel's desk clerk requested her passport, a bureaucratic requirement in certain countries. Some underpaid soul would copy down all the details in a ledger and provide the information to the police, who would look over the list for any suspected ne'er-do-wells. The documents were generally returned within a few hours but were occasionally misplaced—most likely into the palms of someone with a wad of cash. She handed over the forged document from Saudi Arabia, complete with visa and entry stamp. *Thank you, Langley*, she thought. They had not only provided her with three perfect passports, but also the rubber stamps and ink used for the visa, arrival, and departure; all she had to do was fill in the date. She debated calling Gary or Ed, but decided that the less they knew, the better. She was going way off the grid.

Locating a pay phone on the second floor, she dialed a number in Dhaka. It was three in the morning, and the voice was instantly alert. "Speak."

"Do you recall an altercation over a taxi?"

"I do."

"I need help."

There was a long pause, and she heard papers rustling. "The first departure is at eight o'clock, and the flight is four and a half hours. Budget?"

She knew he was weighing the possibility of an upgrade to first class. "Black. Unsanctioned." She would find the funds in some dark account or pay for the flight herself.

"I see. How can I reach you?"

She gave him the name of the hotel and the room number. "Shall I book you in here?"

"I think it would be best to find my own accommodation. Should I assume this is in relation to a certain passenger from that taxi?"

"It is."

"I should be there early afternoon."

"Before you commit, you should know I'm seeking answers. Once I have the information I need, I think a permanent solution would be in order."

"In that case, I'll bring a friend."

"Thank you."

Chapter 46

Having slept little, Cat was already awake when the sun rose. She applied a layer of tinted makeup, slipped on a long-sleeved tank top, wrapped herself in a green and gold sari, wound a scarf around her head and neck, and donned a pair of large sunglasses. She pressed a thin sliver of tape over the top of the door and onto the doorframe and hung the *Do Not Disturb* sign on the door—not that it mattered. In India, the contents of a hotel room were fair game. She had hidden her passports, documents, and the gun above the suspended acoustic tiles in the ceiling of the bathroom. The tiles were old and smoke-stained—and noticeably whiter where they had been shielded by the metal grid. She had been very careful about repositioning the tile exactly so it appeared undisturbed. The passports alone were worth a fortune, but she couldn't carry them; they were as secure as they could be in a place like this.

After leaving the hotel, she walked for several blocks down the Colaba Causeway before flagging a taxi. She flaunted the demeanor of a wealthy Arab woman and ordered the driver to the Breach Candy Club. From Breach Candy, she walked back toward Kemps Corner, strolling from store to store while keeping an eye on a cluster of taxis gathered less than a hundred feet away.

Taxi drivers in Bombay were much like taxi drivers everywhere. Some were dumber than dirt and could not find their way across the street without a map. Others were exceedingly sharp and seemed to know almost everything that happened in the city in which they worked. After observing the knot of drivers for several minutes, she pinpointed one who she hoped fit into the latter group.

Initially dismissive of her request, the man's interest grew in direct proportion to the amount of money Cat offered. They bickered for several minutes before agreeing to a payment of half now, half later. She climbed into the backseat and scribbled the Lada's license number on her palm: *75 CD 18*.

"This car," Cat said calmly, "I need to find it." On its face, the request might have seemed impossible to fulfill. But diplomatic plates are distinctive, and commercial drivers notice them. They are particularly aware of vehicles belonging to the superpowers: the Americans and the Soviets, identifiable by the numeric country code at the left of the plate. The United States was *77*. The USSR was *75*.

The driver didn't disappoint. He demanded more money, and then darted into a nearby shop to use their phone. Five minutes later, he was back. The car's owner lived on Malabar Hill, at an address at the lower end of Ridge Road. Within ten minutes, they were staring at a six-story white apartment building. The Lada occupied a space in the front courtyard. Cat had the driver drop her at the Oberoi Hotel, forfeiting the day's fee, and caught another taxi back to Colaba. Anyone investigating later would remember an Arab woman wearing a sari and a hijab covering her head.

Cat stopped by the front desk to retrieve her passport and then took a seat in the dingy lobby of her hotel, waiting to see if anyone followed her into the building. She waited twenty minutes before boarding the elevator—not spotting Smith, who strolled in just as the doors closed.

Smith headed toward the house phones, his eyes scanning the lobby and taking in the staff and guests alike. His gaze rested momentarily on the black man who had just folded his newspaper and risen from his seat, and who was moving swiftly toward the elevator. Smith veered away from the house phones and instead walked briskly toward the stairwell. Out of sight of the lobby, he took the steps two at a time, reaching the third floor landing a second or two before the black man stepped off the elevator.

Cat was lifting the key to the door latch when she noticed that the tape had been disturbed. She froze, weighing the odds. The chance that someone had tracked her from the airport seemed miniscule; someone from housekeeping was most likely the culprit. Yet she hesitated and took a step back, the key jangling as her hand dropped.

The door flew open, and as quick as a snake strike, the intruder's right hand clenched her throat, and his left gripped her right arm like a vise, wrenching it behind her and upward and doubling her over in agony. The attacker pulled her into the room as her free hand reached back, desperate for oxygen and blindly clawing for the space where his face and eyes should be. She caught a handful of fabric and yanked wildly, ripping the hood from his head. She caught the metallic glint of a knife to her left and thrust her torso violently forward, throwing the man off balance. The surprise movement gave her a microsecond advantage, and she scrambled toward the open door and the freedom of the hallway.

He lunged for her foot and connected. She crashed to the floor, feeling a hot sting, and then agony, as the blade ripped into her leg. She jammed her fingernails into the carpet, frantic for purchase, as he twisted her injured leg and rolled her onto her back—the scream suffocating before it even started, as Barinov slapped a length of tape over her mouth ... and around her wrists ... and around her legs. Her heart roared in her ears, and she knew she was dead.

Chapter 47

Barinov was standing, leering at her in triumph, when Cat registered the muffled *pffft-pffft* of a silenced gun, and a fountain of blood and tissue spouted from Barinov's shoulder and thigh. He collapsed in a messy heap, his limbs splayed awkwardly. And then the tape was pulled from her face, ever so gently, by a huge black hand. When its owner spoke, it was as if an angel was hovering over her. She thought his voice was the sweetest music she had ever heard.

Cat lay on the floor, breathing deeply and trying to calm herself as the adrenaline rush subsided. She started to shake uncontrollably, and the giant man ripped the coverlet from the bed and tucked it around her. He prodded the gash in her leg, and then tore a sheet to fashion a compress. He grabbed Barinov's roll of tape and used it to secure the bandage over the wound. "It's deep," he said quietly. "You need a doctor."

She forced her thoughts away from the pain and turned her head to watch as Smith tended to Barinov. He was using the tape to immobilize the assassin and, as the giant had done, was creating bandages from the sheets. "Don't let him die," she croaked, her throat still burning from the pressure of Barinov's grip. "We need answers."

"He's got diplomatic immunity," Smith countered. "And we have no place to keep him, anyhow."

They were interrupted by an urgent knock on the door. "Front desk, madam. Are you all right?"

Smith pulled Cat to her feet and helped her limp to the door. "One moment," she called.

She shook off the coverlet as Smith licked his thumb and wiped a smear of blood from her cheek. He looked her up and down, and pulled a length of the sari toward her face. "Remember who you are," he reminded her in a whisper.

Cat's head was foggy, and she tried to recall her rôle at the hotel. The thought drifted dreamily until she finally remembered. *Saudi*. She nodded at Smith, who stood at her right hip, gripping her right elbow for support. Leaning so that only her head and left shoulder were visible, she cracked the door and peeked through the narrow opening to find a young man staring at her anxiously. In a flash, she knew that imperious and haughty behavior would only aggravate the situation. *Apologize and be humble*, she commanded herself.

"I am sorry," she said to him. "I tripped over the bedspread, and I fell. I yelled at myself, at my clumsiness. I must have been loud."

The man eyed her with worry, asking, "Shall we call a doctor to examine you?" His suit was shiny and worn and his hair in need of a good cut, but his English was educated and flawless. Her instincts had been correct; he would have been offended and angered by any intemperate behavior.

She was certain that she must appear disheveled, despite

Smith's assurances. She shook her head. "That's very kind of you, but no. I am fine. I was feeling a little sick and tripped on my way to the bathroom. I am not very accustomed to Indian food. I will rest for a little while, and then I will be fine. I regret the trouble."

He stared at her uncertainly before finally bowing his head. "Very well. If you change your mind, we will be happy to summon a doctor."

"Thank you. I appreciate your concern. I will call if I need help.

She closed the door and turned toward Smith, quickly raising her index finger to her lips. She couldn't be sure, but sensed that the employee had remained in the hall, listening. She pressed her ear to the door, finally hearing the muffled sound of footsteps moving away from her room.

Smith's forehead was creased with worry. "He's not happy; I know the type. He's going to go downstairs and think about it, and then he's either going to come back upstairs with a doctor or he's going to call the police. Either way, we can't stay here."

The big man said, "We need to move. I say we call Ed Freemont. He's here in Bombay, right?"

Cat nodded at him. "Yes, why?"

"Because he was a medic during the first Gulf War. He'll know what to do."

He checked himself for blood spatter and seemed satisfied. "Back in a minute." He took the key and let himself out the door.

She limped over to Smith and stared at the unconscious figure on the floor. "Will he make it?"

"Fortune-telling has never been my forte, but he

doesn't look good. God knows I wanted to blow his fucking head off when I saw you on the floor. I went for the arm and the leg only because I knew we needed to question him. He's not spurting so I missed the arteries, but I don't know what the problem is. How are you?"

She jerked her chin toward Barinov. "A whole lot better than him." She touched Smith's arm awkwardly. "You saved my life."

"Jones is the one to thank. I stopped off to pick up a gun, and he came here without me. Good thing, actually. Something must have spooked him, because I saw him head for the elevator just as I was coming into the lobby. I've learned not to question his instincts. I ran for the stairs and happened to get here first."

"Jones? Is that his real name?"

"No idea, but it's the only name I've ever heard. I'm surprised you've never met him, but I suppose it makes sense. You play in different circles. He's mostly Africa, the Caribbean Basin along the northern rim of South America, and Brazil a couple of times. He goes where they send him."

"Where was he yesterday?"

"Addis."

Cat's eyes widened. Addis Ababa, the capital of Ethiopia, was a solid five hours flying time. She stiffened as she heard the door lock turn. Jones rushed in, pushing a laundry bin ahead of him.

"Ed has a truck. He'll be at the hotel loading dock in ten minutes." Jones plastered a strip of tape over Barinov's mouth before hefting him into the basket. They worked together to throw the bloodstained sheets and coverlet on top, adding Cat's belongings and crowning the heap with the clean towels from the bathroom.

Barinov's leg showed no exit wound, but the gunshot to the arm was a through-and-through. They located the bullet and dug it free from the wall under the window. Jones retrieved Cat's passports and gun, while Smith assessed the condition of the room. They were stealing the linens, and the carpet would have to be replaced. He tossed a wad of rupees onto the nightstand to cover the cost of damages and provide a hefty contribution to the staff.

The hallway was empty, and they pushed the cart onto the service elevator without incident. When the ground-floor doors slid open, they came face-to-face with several members of the housekeeping staff. The women, clearly shocked, nevertheless stepped aside and watched in silence as Smith and Jones rolled the cart toward the loading bay.

The small, anonymous, white delivery truck pulled up to the building and Smith raised the loading door. Jones wheeled the cart inside the truck, and Cat hurried after him. "You'll need this," Ed said, handing her a long, black Maglite. "I'll pull over once we're safely away from the hotel." He lowered the door, plunging the truck's interior into darkness.

Cat turned on the flashlight and lay down in the truck bed, elevating her leg by propping it against the side panel. The makeshift bandage appeared to have stemmed the bleeding, but her thigh hurt like hell. She looked over at Jones, taking stock of the man's appearance and realizing that he looked and smelled as if he had not showered for days. "Addis, huh? You got here pretty quickly, considering the flight time."

Jones grinned in amusement. His smile was broad, like

the rest of him, and his white teeth stood in stark contrast to his dark skin. "I was already at the airport in Addis, at the counter checking in for the London flight and a much-needed holiday. Smith tracked me down ... ruined my entire day. The plane to Bombay was getting ready to depart from the next gate. It was as if the fickle finger of fate was beckoning; I switched flights."

"You were in the hotel lobby when I walked in. I saw you on the sofa."

Jones cocked his head and looked at her appraisingly. "I got there before Smith. I watched you. You were good, you know. No one would have taken you for an American."

She frowned. "Small consolation. I slipped up somehow ..."

Jones lifted his hand to stop her. "We'll rehash later. I think we're stopping."

Cat felt the truck backing up, and then the engine cut off. Seconds later, the cargo door rolled open in a flood of light, and the overwhelming odor of fish filled the air.

Looking out, Cat could only see a stand of scruffy vegetation and, beyond, water. "Where are we?"

"Cuffe Parade, down behind Sassoon Docks. Big fish market, hundreds of trucks, a complete riot of activity. I parked down at the end, behind the warehouses. No one's going to pay attention to us."

The men unloaded the laundry cart and hauled Barinov to the floor. Ed knelt over him to check his vitals. A few seconds later, he folded his hands and sat back on his haunches. "This guy's fish food."

Cat pounded her fist on the floor. "What the hell? His wounds weren't that bad."

Ed pointed at the ring on Barinov's right pinkie. "This guy used cyanide on Zach, so he knows something about poison. I heard a tale that some of the Ruskies were issued suicide rings."

Jones pulled a pair of forceps from Ed's medical kit and set about exploring the onyx setting. Twisting the stone to the side revealed a sharp point, similar to a thumbtack. Ed found the puncture wound at the base of Barinov's neck, just above the collarbone.

Cat hammered her fist against the truck bed. "Damn it! This asshole assassinated a CIA agent, abducted the Gorevs, and tortured and murdered a nice Indian kid. And he left me a personal message on that kid's body: a dead cat! As far as I'm concerned, he got what he deserved, but now we're back where we started."

Ed crawled over to Cat and carefully pulled the bandage from her leg. "Well, that's ugly," he commented, examining the wound. "But you should live, unless it gets infected." He pulled a syringe from his kit. "The miracle of antibiotics. Show me your cheek." Cat flipped over, pulled the sari aside, and rolled her underwear down as Smith and Jones looked on appreciatively.

"There's an immensely pleasurable sight," joked Smith.

Cat shot him a fierce glare, wincing as the needle found its target.

Ed treated and stitched the wound and pocketed the bullet he dug out of Barinov's leg. As he worked, the other two men stripped the corpse. They examined Barinov's clothing and probed every orifice of his body, looking for anything the man might have been carrying. They found nothing.

By nightfall, the dock area was deserted, the markets having closed for the day and the boats having set out to sea. Jones hefted Barinov's body from the truck and carried it to the riprap seawall. The entire shoreline was littered with discarded nets and other detritus of the fishing industry, and they used one of the nets to wind around the corpse—along with a number of stones. They dragged the body into the water, anchoring it with more rocks from the scree at the base of the seawall. Ten minutes later, they were all jammed in the cab of the truck and speeding away.

Chapter 48

Ed drove to a small automotive repair shop near Nariman Point. There, they exchanged the truck for Ed's car. Long a front for MI6, the shop cooperatively supplied vehicles, parts, and illegally obtained license plates for both British and American agents operating in the city.

Ed aimed the car north, up Queen's Road and through the interminably busy Churchgate and Chowpatty districts. Cat leaned her head against the window and tried to block out the pain as the men talked.

"It's a foregone conclusion that his people will be looking for him soon," said Smith. "We bought a little time, but someone's going to find that body. The good thing is that there's nothing directly tying him to us, other than we know he was after Cat. The bad thing is that we don't know who he might have told."

Ed rubbed his chin and took a deep breath. "Well, the score's even right now. They eliminated Zach; we eliminated Barinov. I doubt they're going to escalate, and we certainly won't. But with that said, I'm shocked they took action against Zach to begin with."

"They're pulling out all the stops to protect their

mole," Jones offered. "Whoever he is, he's damned important. But it's doubtful they'll retaliate at this point. As far as they know, we milked the Gorevs and Barinov for everything they knew. If we don't make an arrest soon, they'll know their secret is still safe."

Cat frowned as they approached Kemp's Corner. "Where are we going?"

Ed found her eyes in the rearview mirror. "To the consulate. I was headed out to find you when all this started. There has been ... um ... a development. Everybody stay low. No sense in the outside world seeing the four of us together when we drive into the compound."

The guard at the consulate, part of the contract security force, was somewhat accustomed to the unusual goings-on that were a part of life at the US mission. He was, nevertheless, startled by the appearance of three figures crouched inside Ed Freemont's automobile. If Ed were under duress, he would use a verbal code to alert the guard. As it was, he merely stated that his passengers were all American and cleared for entry. The guard fussed, clearly upset by the breach in security protocol, and made the requisite phone call up the chain of command. When the word came down, he reluctantly waved them through, but rested his palm on the stock of his rifle as the car rolled onto the grounds.

"What the hell happened?" he thundered.

Cat told them about seeing the story of the boy's torture and murder in the newspaper—and how she interpreted the dead cat as a direct threat—and that for her own safety she had checked into the hotel under a false identity and placed a call to Smith. She went on to explain that she had tracked Barinov's car to an apartment building on Malabar Hill and returned to the hotel, where Barinov had attacked her. She hung her head, feeling defeated. "Bottom line? People are dead, and we don't know any more than when this fiasco started."

"I wouldn't say that exactly," he replied. "Come with me." He started through the door and turned back, adding gruffly, "I'm thankful you're safe. And I'm glad the bastard's dead."

Gary led them to an interior door near the back of the consular section. "We use this room occasionally for catching a few winks when we're pulling all-nighters." He pushed the door open to reveal a dimly lit room equipped with four cots and two reclining lounge chairs. The only light came from a lamp beside one of the lounges. The woman occupying the chair set down the book she had been reading and placed her index finger to her lips. "Finally asleep," she whispered.

Cat's eyes swung over the furnishings, coming to rest on a bed against the opposite wall. She tiptoed across the room and found herself staring at the sweet and innocent face of a young girl, no more than two years old. The child had thick, curly, dark hair and the cherubic face of a Raphael painting. A gasp escaped her throat as the realization struck. This was the Gorevs' daughter.

After herding them back to the office, Gary handed Cat an envelope. "Tanya Gorev left her daughter with a couple on the first floor of the Royal Guild apartments.

They had never met, but she told them some story about being in danger. Good Samaritans that they were, they agreed. The deal was that if she didn't return within two days, they were to bring the girl to the consulate."

The letter was hastily scrawled and written in broken English, telling how Tanya and Anatoly had spotted Barinov in the park and feared for their lives. Regardless of the outcome, she told of wanting their daughter to live in the West, in America, and that the American spy-woman had promised to get them there. She also begged for her son, although she must have known in her heart that any hope for extraction had now evaporated. And, in her final plea for the safety of her children, she had given up the name of the mole: *Amos*.

Chapter 49

Monday morning
Orange, Virginia

Adele stretched her neck and reached for a glass of water. Looking around the room, I concluded that I wasn't the only person mesmerized by the tale; she had the rapt attention of the entire group. Her performance was as good as anything I had ever seen on Broadway—and perhaps better for its real-life drama.

I had not recognized the face or the voice or the mannerisms ... had not initially recognized that Adele and Cat were the same person. Even after she had spoken of meeting with Teddy, and how Adele had come to be, I was a step behind in putting the pieces together. It seemed that every time I thought I had reached a point of knowing my sister well, there was yet another twist to make me realize that I did not. Her life was a constellation of secrets.

She took a few sips from the glass, laced her fingers together, and let her eyes drift upward, as if searching for what to say next. When she continued, her expression was grave and her voice pained.

"The agency investigated the name Tanya gave us, *Amos*, but got nowhere. Our operatives and assets continued to be exposed. The loss, both in terms of life and intelligence, was staggering. It wasn't until 1994 that the FBI uncovered Aldrich Ames, nine years after the Gorevs told us about the mole who was code-named Kolokol. Tragically, Tanya—with her limited English—had misspelled the name, giving us *Amos* instead of *Ames*. Nobody connected the dots." She glanced away for a moment, a flash of anguish clouding her face.

"I never did learn what happened to the Gorevs or their son. Were they tortured? Executed? Sent to Siberia? I can only speculate. I was told later that Tanya's father died in December 1985, not long after she disappeared. My only consolation was that her daughter was safe. It took some doing, but we brought the little girl to the States, changed her name to Sophia, and arranged for her adoption by Nick and Maria Capreze. I kept my eye on her for a few years, but she was in a loving home and thriving, and I felt the secrets of her past were locked up tight. I stopped checking up on her.

"When Sophia's name came up last night, I was shocked. The Caprezes never knew her real name, so I'm very much interested in how she might have learned it."

Trent cleared his throat, and we turned our attention to the monitor. He was haggard and unshaven, suggesting that he had been up all night digging for answers. "Now that you've shared her history, we can float a few ideas. Her chances of being recognized in India during her internship—by someone who had known her mother twenty years earlier—seems pretty remote. She did some travel in connection with her modeling, but again, what are the odds? She was not a supermodel; she didn't have a huge endorsement contract that would have given her worldwide exposure. Would a Russian have spotted her in a fashion magazine and connected the dots to her mother? Not likely.

"We could go around and around with complicated theories, but let's apply Occam's razor, instead, which suggests that the simplest explanation is usually correct. There are dozens of former KGB who immigrated to New York. She is a lawyer in New York who has provided legal services for the Russian mob. Isn't it more likely that, during the course of her work, she ran into someone who knew her mother ... someone who noticed her resemblance to Tanya Goreva?"

Digesting the possibility, Cat nodded slowly. "I agree that your theory is the one that makes the most sense. But it still leaves an unanswered question: what prompted her to apply for a name change? That did not happen because of a resemblance. She would have required proof."

"Whoa!" Gabe said excitedly. "She must have had her DNA tested!"

"Exactly," Adele agreed, cocking her head and crossing her arms across her chest. "And whom did they use for comparison?"

"My God," Paul gasped, the answer hitting him like a sledgehammer. "One of the Gorevs is still alive."

PART THREE

The Seeds We Sow

July, present day

Monday through Monday

Chapter 50

Monday afternoon
Quantico, Virginia

At 1:45 p.m., Paul pulled the door open and stepped into Base Operations at the Marine Corps Air Facility Quantico. Despite having been officially renamed back in 1941, it was still known colloquially as Turner Field—its original name. Old habits die hard. He glanced up at the flight board and focused on the row where some airplane—labeled as a C-20—was marked as having arrived four minutes ago.

He walked over to the long window and recognized the gray Gulfstream IV parked on the visiting aircraft ramp. Why the military thought it necessary to rename every damn aircraft was beyond him. *Call a spade a spade, and call a Gulfstream a Gulfstream*, he thought. He closed his eyes and told himself to calm down. He was irritated at having to drive down to Quantico, and even more irritated because he could sense that this meeting was going to turn his day upside down.

He eyed a group of uniforms walking fast across the ramp and easily found Carter Haskell among them—his long stride outpacing the others. They exchanged a warm handshake, and Paul tilted his head toward the parking lot. Thirty minutes later they set the Subway bag on a picnic table near the visitor center at Prince William Forest Park.

"Turkey and ham, right?" Paul asked, extending the sub to Carter. "And water?"

Carter took a drink of water and started unwrapping the sandwich. "Thanks for coming. It's a long drive for fast food."

"It was a slow day anyhow."

"Liar."

Paul bit into his sub and chewed for a minute. "So how are you going to ruin my day?"

Carter put the sandwich down. "The C-4. It came from a shipment to Bragg."

Paul choked. "What?"

"Five thousand pounds, plus five thousand feet of det cord."

Paul was stunned. "You have got to be kidding!

Carter shook his head disgustedly. "Nine months ago. Somebody pulled in some favors because there hasn't been even a sniff from the press. FBI has the lead, and CID is working it, too. But the investigation has been spinning its wheels for a while now."

CID was the US Army's criminal investigation arm. Frowning, Paul said, "What the hell happened?"

"Hijacking over near Greensboro. The driver stopped at a truck stop and was overpowered climbing back into the cab. The truck was civilian ... long-term government contract. The company had been running shipments for over a year, used the same driver most of the time, and both were clean as a whistle—then this. The feebs looked at the driver ...

did everything but stick a camera up his ass. He wasn't involved. Last I heard he was still having nightmares."

"Are you telling me they left him alive?"

"Go figure. They taped him up in a ball and left him and the truck behind—with a shitload of other weaponry—and vanished."

"Vanished? No art? Prints? DNA?"

"Nada. These guys were smart. The driver never saw them, never heard them because they never talked. Not once. They wore gloves. And at the end, they sprayed bleach on everything, so no DNA. All we know is that they had two pickups or vans and at least three people—one to take down the driver and two to drive the vehicles. The FBI pulled in camera footage from everywhere looking for two vans or trucks traveling together.

"My aide—who is a very smart guy—thinks they split up the cargo to handle the load. Twenty-five hundred pounds in two vehicles is easier to manage—and disguise—than five thousand pounds in one van. And he believes they would have taken separate routes."

Paul rubbed his chin. "That makes sense. They knew the driver would hear two vehicles, and that's what everyone would be looking for. But they didn't take the whole load, and they didn't kill the driver. Why?" Something tickled at the back of his brain, but he couldn't put a finger on it. "So just the C-4? Nothing else?"

Carter sucked in a deep breath. "Two Stinger launchers ... and twenty missiles."

"My God! What in the hell were they doing on an unguarded truck?" Stingers were widely used, shoulder-fired surface-to-air missiles that had gained notoriety in the eighties—when the CIA supplied hundreds of them to the mujahideen during the Soviet-Afghanistan war. While the United States had ultimately recovered some of the unused weapons, others had made their way into other countries, notably Iran. They were particularly good at taking down aircraft. Aim, fire, boom. Paul was horrified at the thought of such weapons on the loose.

"They shouldn't have been there. The army had been conducting some comparison tests on new warheads. When the tests were concluded, some major decided it would be more expedient to put them on the truck to Bragg rather than go to the expense of a full-blown convoy. Needless to say, he's been transferred and has a letter of reprimand in his file."

"They should court-martial him, find him guilty of utter stupidity, and send him to Leavenworth."

"Can't say I disagree."

"So, Forsythe and Pierce. What can you tell me?"

Carter grunted. "I would like to think you're barking up the wrong tree. Unfortunately, I think it fits better than anything the feebs have come up with. We all know that there had to be insider information, either on our side or the trucking company. They looked long and hard at the people in Requisitions and Supply—anyone with even tenuous knowledge of these shipments—and found nothing. If you're right, and Forsythe and Pierce are involved, it's going to give the army a black eye the size of Montana. And it could destroy my career."

Paul grunted. When something goes wrong in the military, the guy in charge is going to take a hit. If Special Forces personnel were involved, Carter might not survive the backlash, and that would be a shame. He considered Carter to be one of the best.

Carter wasn't finished. "When they investigated the attempted harbor bombing up in Boston, it was determined that the lot numbers on the explosives were part of that same stolen shipment. That accounted for 160 bricks, with 3,840 still missing. Every damn day I've been waiting for some catastrophe, either from the C-4 or some lunatic with a rocket.

"I got a call from CID right after your call. The seven hundred pounds of C-4 you found in Somerville? Well, that was also part of the shipment."

Paul was beginning to feel sick. *Five thousand pounds, and missiles,* he thought. *Holy God.* He rewrapped the sandwich and threw it in the bag. "I've lost my appetite."

"There's more. My aide—like I said, a very smart guy—got to wondering, *What if they are spreading this stuff around, a few bricks here and a few bricks there? Set off a few pounds of C-4 in a handful of grocery stores or theaters, and you'd have a national panic.* He thinks the guy in Somerville may have been a distributor, not a bomber."

Rubbing his neck, Paul tried to process this new information and imagined a few dozen people on the loose, each with a few bricks of C-4. "I need those files."

"I'll arrange it. Secure online, no hard copy," Carter replied. "Who else needs access?"

Paul gave him the names of his two NSA people, Melodie and Trent.

"These boys have been into some serious shit over the years. If any of it gets out, I'll be looking for you personally. I'll give you twenty-four hours. After that, you'll be locked out automatically." He bowed his head. "And at that point, I'll have to tell CID."

"Why not turn it over to them right now?"

Carter looked up at the trees, their leaves shimmering in the sunlight. "Because Randy Forsythe is my nephew… my sister's kid. Just promise me that you'll do your best to keep him alive."

Chapter 51

Monday evening
Orange, Virginia

The drive back to Montpelier gave Paul time to reflect on the meeting with the general and the likelihood of Randall Forsythe's involvement. Although there was currently no direct evidence tying the soldier to the C-4, Paul believed there was a high probability of his participation; there were simply too many coincidences. And the man's actions—including the attempted mugging of Lindsey in February, his attempt to follow the team to the safe house, and his association with Sophia Goreva—pointed unwaveringly to his involvement.

Paul made three calls, first to Melodie and Trent, then to Adrian, and finally to Cat. The mission of Cat's team, he told them, was to nail down the India connection. The mission of the remainder of the team was to find Randall Forsythe and Matthew Pierce. They would devote all of their resources to pinpointing the soldiers' whereabouts and, if the men were found, travel to their last known location.

Cat listened quietly as Paul told her about the afternoon's meeting at Quantico, sharing what he had not told the others: the general's relation to Randall Forsythe.

When he finished, she said, "We have to find Forsythe before General Haskell makes that call. Once CID is in the loop, our chances of finding him alive are considerably diminished."

"You're going down the same dark alley as the general. What's CID going to do? Assassinate him?"

"I think you're misinterpreting the source of the concern," she said. "I don't think it's CID personnel he's worried about. Remember, Paul, we're thinking this is a weapons-for-drugs deal. So far, I still like that script. But if we're right, Forsythe and Pierce are in the middle of a chess game with some very nasty players. People who buy drugs to distribute and people who buy explosives to blow up humanity are not going to sit idly by while these two soldiers spill their guts. If this goes to CID, word *will* leak, and those two will have targets on their chests faster than you can say *fire in the hole.*"

Paul arched his eyebrows. He could always count on Cat to see the dark side of a situation and, consequently, pose the worst-case scenario. He had always respected CID; the idea of a leak there was disappointing. He wondered when moral fiber had ended up on the endangered species list.

"You know what's bothering me?" she asked.

"I can guess. The truck driver? And Lindsey?"

What had started as a tiny twinge had grown into a full-blown itch. Anyone who sold explosives to terrorists and drugs to the street had lost his moral compass. Those circles swirled with violence and death. People had attacked the safe house ferociously; they had shot Jason. If Pierce and

Forsythe were actually at the hub of the mayhem, why had they allowed the truck driver to live?

"What are we missing?" she asked.

Paul straightened, his brain toying with an idea. "Cat, this scheme isn't the work of just two men; it's bigger. What if there are two factions?"

It was Cat's turn to be surprised. "Then we have a bigger problem. We don't know who is on which side."

Chapter 52

Tuesday morning
Orange, Virginia

With little to go on—other than a supposition that Forsythe was staying somewhere on Boston's North Shore—the team's focus shifted to Sophia Capreze. With her history of slipping away from New York for weekend getaways to Boston, they agreed that she was their most likely hope of finding Randall Forsythe.

The Manhattan landscape is saturated with cameras, many of which regularly upload their video streams to the cloud for storage. In today's world, governmental entities, small businesses, and large corporations have learned the value of maintaining images for potential later review. The team had no trouble following Sophia's digital trail.

When the cameras outside her midtown condo yielded no results from this morning, they retrieved the video from the previous day. They found her right away. On Monday morning, Sophia had exited her building and taken a taxi to her law firm on Park Avenue. Emerging thirty minutes later with a wheeled suitcase, she had flagged another cab. Video footage followed the cab to the Midtown tunnel, through the tunnel beneath the Hudson River, and onto the Brooklyn-Queens Expressway, finally merging into the Grand Central Parkway toward LaGuardia airport. They pegged her entering the Delta terminal at 10:19 a.m., passing through security at 10:34 a.m., and boarding the plane at gate C-32 at 10:43 a.m. At 12:23 p.m., she had walked off the jet bridge at gate A-6 at Logan.

A white SUV met Capreze in front of the terminal and was picked up by cameras as it followed the exit lanes out of the airport and onto Route 1A north. A camera at the Wonderland T station picked it up a few minutes later, still headed northeast. Taking a chance, Gabe burrowed into the network at the Swampscott Police Department and into their video storage in the cloud. A few minutes later, he found the SUV, continuing to the northeast ... toward Marblehead.

Trent asked Lindsey and Gabe about possible camera locations. They looked at each other, initially baffled—Marblehead was a quiet town. They suggested the police and fire stations, two schools, and a bank in the middle of town.

It took ten minutes to tunnel into the police station's video feed, and another five to access the images on the cloud, but there was no evidence of the SUV. The fire station had no feed, and the schools' cameras were aimed toward the school grounds rather than the street. Accessing the bank took longer, but was profitable—the SUV passed in front of the camera, moving in the direction of downtown and the harbor.

While they had narrowed the target area, finding the precise destination of the vehicle was another challenge entirely. The images were already over a day old, and the car could be anywhere by now. But at least they had a place to start.

Questions lingered about the integrity of the remaining safe houses in the Boston area, although none appeared to have been compromised. The assessment was that the Foxborough location had been identified by the detection of nanoparticles on their vehicles, and that the others remained secure. Regardless, none were close to Marblehead. Jazz began scouring the web for a suitable rental.

The pain and trauma of my accident were taking their toll, and I lost patience with the idea of finding another place to stay. "I want to go home," I stated flatly. "And if I took an apartment elsewhere in town, can you imagine the questions it would raise?"

Paul exchanged a look with Cat, but conceded the point. "We can make that work, but only if someone else is with you." He looked over at Jazz, the question written on his face.

"I'm good with that," Jazz answered.

I was ready to volunteer Adrian for the assignment, instead, until I realized it would force Jazz and Jones into an awkward arrangement. "As for Jones and Adrian, why not use Jason's place on Gregory Street?" I offered. "I have a key."

Paul was on his third cup of coffee when his BlackBerry dinged. The encrypted message contained two links—each to a document on a secure server at DIA, the Defense Intelligence Agency. The links were valid for twenty-four hours, after which access would be denied. The files, one labeled POI-1 and the other labeled POI-2, were several hundred pages each. Melodie took the Forsythe file and Trent the Pierce file.

Chapter 53

Tuesday night
Washington Dulles International Airport, Virginia

As she approached the gate, Adele scanned the throng of waiting passengers. She spotted Arnie, leaning casually against a pillar. Her eyes slid over him, deliberately avoiding any acknowledgment, and she presented her boarding pass at the podium.

Her celebrity status had greased the wheels for the same-day issuance of an Indian visa. Preferring not to advertise any association between the travelers, Paul called in a favor and arranged an expedited visa for a close friend of the family, Arnold Powell.

Adele would disembark at Heathrow, while Arnie—seated in business class on the same flight—would catch a connecting flight to Mumbai and make preparations for her arrival a day later. Gabe had flown to New York and spent Tuesday waiting in the interminably long queue for his visa. He would board a flight that night from New York, on Qatar Airways through Doha.

She presented her boarding pass for the Virgin Atlantic Airbus 340 to London and wished—not for the first time—that she had a gun. There would be weapons waiting in Mumbai, but she was uncomfortable without the Walther PPK nestled against her body. There were simply too many lunatics loose in the world—any of whom could be flying today. Security in America today—airport or otherwise—simply could not deter the committed mayhem enthusiast.

Shrugging off her unease, she settled into seat 2A—in the snooze zone at the front of the first-class cabin. She stowed the computer tote and overnighter and checked her phone again for messages. None had been received.

Adele had placed a call to an old friend at Vauxhall Cross, inquiring if there had been any recent tickles regarding one Anatoly Gorev or his daughter, Natalya, or her adoptive name, Sophia Capreze. Vauxhall Cross was the headquarters of the British SIS, the Secret Intelligence Service. Commonly referred to by its old name—MI6—the SIS kept files on all manner of persons of interest. They maintained particularly good notes on former agents of the Soviet Union who had disappeared without a trace. The Americans often subscribed to the preponderance-of-evidence way of thinking, and Langley had tossed Anatoly Gorev's file in the Most-Likely-Dead archive. The Brits, on the other hand, adopted a more cautious approach and generally demanded incontrovertible proof of an agent's demise before closing the file.

Adele had other questions, too, and suggested that the discussion would be better suited to a face-to-face encounter somewhere away from SIS headquarters. With that in mind, she had booked a suite for one night at the Connaught, an iconic hotel in London's Mayfair district—just around the corner from the US embassy.

The phone vibrated and blinked an incoming message. Relieved to see the sender's name, she opened the secure e-mail and smiled as she read the message.

> Addie, it will be lovely to catch up. A driver will be waiting at Heathrow.

She glanced up as the flight attendant approached.

"Ms. Rutledge? May I offer you something to drink before we go?"

"Sparkling water with lime, please. No ice. And no dinner this evening," Adele replied. "And I would like a blanket and pillow, please."

"Certainly, Ms. Rutledge. Straightaway."

Adele pressed the phone's mirror app, adjusted the lighting, and peered at her reflection. A familiar yet unfamiliar face stared back. The smartly cut wig of short white hair—with a waved forelock and the sides swept back from her face—gave her a regal appearance. The designer dress implied wealth, as did her first-class ticket. The blue-tinted contacts concealed her hazel eyes, the cheek pads reshaped the contours of her face, the padding around her torso added bulk to her figure, and the oversize designer eyeglasses contributed to the facial misdirection. The cane, which she typically held in her right hand, completed the transformation from Catherine "Cat" Powell to Adele "Addie" Rutledge.

The act of passing the cane through the machine at the TSA checkpoint had caused her blood pressure to tick upward. Despite assurances from its craftsman that the cane's hidden assets would go undetected, and despite a number of previously successful forays through airport security, there was always a chance that something could go wrong—and she had no explanation that would satisfy the bureaucrats.

The design of the cane's titanium shaft had originally been conceived by a master sword maker, who had passed the craft down to his son—a man Cat encountered in Hokkaido, Japan, while shadowing a suspected terrorist. The craftsman's idea was that a bit of intricate artistry could effectively disguise the cane's true purpose. Similar to a Japanese puzzle box, a series of movements would cause the prop to disassemble, revealing a number of tools for offensive and defensive use. The son had updated the design to account for modern security measures. Cat patted its handle affectionately and slid it under the seat.

She was aware that her use of the Adele identity presented some risk, but was balanced by greater access and flexibility than other options. Paul's recommendation that she meet with the team—as Adele—had been brilliant. Up until the moment when she had revealed that Cat and Adele were one and the same, she had managed to deceive them all—even Lindsey had been duped. It had been an effective test, demonstrating that she could still play the part. What amazed Cat most was how easily they had all transitioned to thinking of her as Adele. Cat had been vanquished to obscurity—repackaged and relabeled as Adele.

Three minutes before departure, her phone vibrated. Trent. "What's up?"

"We've intercepted a transmission. It doesn't make mention of a specific city, but there are keywords that correspond to messages we've seen in the past. Just afterward, the chatter meter spiked and is still running high. Something big is about to go down, and everything we have suggests London. You're headed there, right?"

Adele felt her pulse quicken. "Any idea of the target?"

"There's a phrase that includes the word Benjamin. It could refer to Big Ben. If so, we'd be talking about the Westminster district. Lots of high-profile targets there ... the palace, House of Commons, Westminster Abbey, the tube station."

"My flight's leaving. You'll have to drive the bus." She rattled off a number. "Call and ask for *Jumper.* If there's no answer, keep calling. Send texts. Tell him you're calling for Addie, and give him everything you have. Right now."

She hung up, her heart now racing, and tried to sip the water. It tasted like acid. She willed the phone to flash a message saying that Trent had been successful, but the screen stayed black. Reluctantly, she switched the phone to airplane mode when she heard the muffled thump of the aircraft door closing.

After takeoff, she connected to the plane's Wi-Fi system and accessed her e-mail. Nothing. After a half hour of furiously checking her inbox, she gave up. The rational part of her brain told her that there was nothing to be accomplished from thirty-nine thousand feet and that Trent was fully capable of getting the job done. Besides, she would need to be sharp for the day ahead. Adele adjusted the seat to its lay-flat position and reached for the bottle of little pink sleeping pills that she carried religiously when traveling. As the captain announced a fast flight time of six hours and twenty minutes, she mentally adjusted for five hours of rest. Earplugs and eyeshades in place, she lay back and closed her eyes.

Exhausted and medicated, sleep should have come easily. Instead, Adele shifted and squirmed and—from a lifetime and an ocean away—thought of the Gorevs and suicide bombers in Westminster.

Chapter 54

Wednesday morning
Heathrow Airport, London, England

Adele felt the plane shift to a nose-down attitude and pulled up her eyeshades. A few of the flyers had opened the window shades, and the sun was streaming into the cabin. She grabbed her phone and reconnected to Wi-Fi. Trent had sent only two e-mails, one advising that he had passed the warning to Jumper, and the other to let her know that nothing unusual had happened ... yet.

Listening to the arrival announcements, she groaned to herself when the pilot announced that the plane would pull into gate 22 at Terminal 3 ... a twenty-to-thirty-minute hike to baggage claim and customs. Walking with a cane placed unaccustomed strain on her joints and muscles, and was the only truly annoying aspect of her role as Adele. Some well-meaning airline staffer might summon a wheelchair, thereby ensuring that she would have to engage in pleasant chitchat with the handler. On the other hand, hobbling the entire distance would draw the attention of passersby. She sighed and wished that someone would just beam her into the city.

The moving sidewalk helped. She clung to the handrail as the able-bodied masses—rushing to make their connections or to be the first in line through passport control—strode swiftly past the standees on the right, and zigzagged aggressively around those clinging stubbornly to the left. Aside from being jostled by swinging shoulder-carried bags and the roll-aboard that took a path over her foot, she made it to the arrivals hall unscathed.

Passport control was a swift process, the official polite as he inquired about the nature of her visit to the United Kingdom. She had seen the spark of recognition when he examined her passport, and the knowing nod as he took in the well-worn camera bag slung over her shoulder. He asked a few perfunctory questions about where she was staying and the length of her visit before waving her through. "I hope the weather cooperates for you," he said. She thanked him, marveling at the cool reserve of the British. An American might have invited her for dinner and asked if she could take pictures at his daughter's wedding.

One of the advantages of being a photographer was that the profession afforded some degree of anonymity, even at her stature. Although Adele's name and work were widely known, her face was much less recognized. She was a woman behind the camera ... not in front of it. As passengers milled about, waiting for the baggage to come tumbling out on the carousel, she was surprised when one woman asked for an autograph. Several others caught wind of the name, and within a few seconds, a line had formed. Adele signed several notebooks, paper napkins, T-shirts, and even a pair of blue jeans before managing to extricate herself and retrieve her luggage.

With nothing to declare, she breezed through customs and exited into the chaos of the terminal's public meeting area. It took only a moment to spot the person holding the sign for *Ms. Rutledge*. The grim-faced young man scooped up her bags and led her outside to the waiting black BMW. He opened the door for her on the passenger side, then walked around the car. Sliding into the driver's seat, he extended his hand to her. "Adam Moxley, Ms. Rutledge. Welcome to London.

"We're having a bit of a situation this morning. Ten minutes ago, we had four simultaneous bombings on the Tube: Green Park, Earl's Court, King's Cross, and Westminster."

Chapter 55

Wednesday morning
London, England

The M4, the main artery from Heathrow into the city, was at a standstill. Adam steered southeast, in the direction of Wimbledon, before veering north into the city. Much of the city was locked down, and Adam had suggested joining her friend for breakfast in Waterloo, which was to the south of the Thames River. The bombings had all taken place on the other side. The usual one-hour drive took over two.

Adele found Jeffrey Albright perched atop a stool at the back of the café. The place was packed, and tiny—more a place for coffee and a light snack rather than a traditional breakfast. But the aroma of fresh pastries and the sight of a cappuccino, whimsically stenciled with delicate swirls of frothy milk, sent her salivary glands into overdrive.

On any other day, they would have chatted amiably—about the weather, American politics, or the effects of greenhouse gases—before getting down to business. Today, there was no thought of such drivel. The latest count was 123 dead and over 500 injured. Bile rose in Adele's throat as she listened to the news. She bit off chunks of a croissant to help settle her churning stomach and intently watched Jeffrey's face as he checked his messages. He rarely let his face give anything away, but whatever was on his phone had upset him. He ordered two more coffees in takeaway cups, pointed his chin upward, and wrinkled his nose as if catching a whiff of a foul odor. "Let's take a stroll, shall we?"

Jeffrey Albright, code name Jumper, was not a tall man—the top of his shiny bald head barely reached the tip of Cat's nose. He had acquired his moniker after an incident in Beirut, where he and Cat had first crossed paths.

After an explosive-laden truck had squirted ahead of a planned street ambush, Jeffrey had dropped from a second-floor apartment balcony onto the truck's cab as it passed below. Hanging onto the hood near the windshield, he had somehow managed to fire a round into the shoulder of the surprised driver. With one arm incapacitated, the driver was forced to use his good arm to hold the wheel. When the passenger leaned into the console, Cat—from her hidey-hole half a block away—pointed the M16 near the top of the truck's windshield and let rip two three-round bursts. The bullets stitched from left to right across the passenger's torso and the driver's head, reducing flesh and bone to pulp before either man could reach the detonator.

Jeffrey's nickname was earned not so much from the initial jump as from his desperate leap—to a truck passing in the opposite direction—before the dead men's vehicle crashed head-on into the wall of a building. Jeffrey had always been athletic and energetic, and wore his age well. Today, however, Adele thought Jumper just looked tired—tired of worrying, tired of the hate, tired of the killing.

They trudged slowly up the street—the speed of their

pace hampered by the crowds packing the sidewalks. Adele was comfortable with Jeffrey—they had shared secrets before. He was one of the few who knew of her dual identity, and she had found him to be unfailingly discreet. Five minutes later, they reached the park known as the Waterloo Millennium Green and sat on an isolated bench.

"So Adele is no longer retired?" he asked.

"Adele has a hankering for a photo shoot in Mumbai."

"Nasty place, that. Stay away from the water—if the stuff out of the tap doesn't kill you, a swim in the ocean might."

"Not to worry. I've seen the raw sewage floating on the water at Marve. Went windsurfing in it once, actually… thought it was algae."

"Ouch. Well, you survived it. That's what counts. Now, what's this about Anatoly Gorev?"

Adele told him about the attack on the safe house outside of Boston and about the cache of high explosive that had been discovered in Rajeev Malik's apartment. Jeffrey knew most of it, the Brits and Americans being generally cooperative about sharing such information. But he raised his eyebrows in surprise when she filled in the details about tracing the Conrad27 e-mail to India.

"Our working theory is that it's a drugs-for-weapons deal. How else does Rajeev Malik get his hands on military-grade high explosive?"

Jeffrey caught on quickly. "From some disenfranchised former soldier who served in Afghanistan? Of course. And your soldier is connected with someone in India—that someone having a pipeline to Afghanistan."

"That's about the sum of it. The wrinkle is Sophia

Capreze, aka Natalya Goreva."

"Anatoly's daughter?"

"One and the same. SIS was always fastidious about monitoring KGB. I need to know what happened to Anatoly and his wife." Adele told him about the girl's prospective name change from Capreze to Goreva.

Jeffrey was awestruck. "So you really did it? Bundled the girl off to America in the middle of the night?"

"Not the middle of the night, exactly, but yes. It's what the parents wanted."

"We always thought the woman was daft."

It was Adele's turn to be surprised. "The woman?"

"Tanya Goreva. For years, she was on a campaign to find her daughter."

"Tanya is alive?"

He cocked his head. "You didn't know?"

Adele stared at him in disbelief. "I never heard a word of this. I heard a whisper that Tanya's father had passed away and that Anatoly was presumed dead. Period."

"Anatoly died at a prison camp in Siberia in the winter of 1990, just a year before the breakup of the Soviet Union. Apparently Tanya's father successfully pleaded his daughter's case because she was released shortly before he died; there's no other plausible explanation for letting her go. We lost track of her for some time. We believe she returned to St. Petersburg, or Leningrad as they called it at the time, but the details on that are a bit hazy. We do know that in 1995, she returned to Mumbai. It was shortly afterward that she began making claims about someone absconding with her daughter. Everyone denied it, of course."

Adele's lips flattened into a straight line, and anger

sparked in her eyes. "They denied it because they were afraid of what they might find if they looked under that rock. So they buried the inquiry and never looked into it. In fairness, they might have been hard-pressed to even come up with the right questions to ask. There were only six people who knew about the daughter going to the US, and all six of us believed the Gorevs were dead. We had promised ... *I* had promised ... to get the girl to America. We went to extraordinary measures to do so, and no one was the wiser. We've kept it secret for all these years."

"What a cock-up."

"In the end, maybe. But I don't have a single regret about what we did for that little girl. There was no way I was sending her back to Moscow, particularly not after their assassin took out one of ours and tried to do the same to me."

"Point taken. But Tanya went off the rails when no one could produce her daughter. She was spouting a lot of anti-Western rhetoric. We were targets of her ire as well, when we politely refused to intercede with you Yanks. To be frank, we all thought she was quite insane."

"Where is she now?"

"Still in Mumbai, as of three days ago. One of ours spotted her lunching at the Willingdon."

"Nice club, but she must have been a guest. My understanding is that new membership has been closed for years. It's like the family silver that's passed down from generation to generation—outsiders only get to handle the flatware on special occasions. Any idea who she was with?"

"I do, actually." He pulled his phone from his jacket's inside pocket and thumbed the screen. "We captured him in full color."

Adele leaned over to look at the image on the screen and gasped involuntarily. Two men appeared in the photo, both of whom she recognized. On the left was Farshad Kharoti, the son of the old man whose Internet account was associated with Conrad27. On the right was Aashif Ahmedani—the old man's nephew. The woman in the middle was indisputably Tanya Goreva—still strikingly beautiful.

As she studied the photograph, a realization dawned. "Tanya may be in this photo, but that's not why you took the picture. You were watching the two men."

Jeffrey's eyebrows rose perceptibly. "You were always quite sharp," he said, closing the phone.

Adele abruptly grabbed his forearm. "What aren't you telling me?" Her mind was spinning and, before he had an opportunity to respond, made her own guess. "You've connected them to the Tube explosions this morning. Did they use C-4?"

"Initial reports say yes, it was C-4. We'll run chemical analysis to confirm. I assume that your people have done the same with the product in Boston. Are they from the same source? We'll know soon enough." He shrugged and pulled a package from his pocket, shook two pills into his palm, tossed them in his mouth, and offered the package to Adele.

"Heartburn?" she asked, waving the tablets away. "You drink too much coffee. You should be a good Brit and go back to tea."

He smiled wanly. "Too many mornings like this one, and tea is for pansies."

"You know that I'm going to ask you for your file on the Gorevs and the Kharotis."

"And you know that I will tell you that I will run it by the chief. We cannot just lift up our skirts and bare all, you know. We have to show some propriety ... or at least embellish the act with the illusion of foreplay."

"Please don't ask me to put my tongue in your ear."

He smiled at that—he, a faithful husband of almost forty years and the father of three. "As tempting as that diversion might be, we will have to settle for dinner. Adam will arrange the details; he still knows the social scene. I've lost touch." He stood, his expression sober. "You still have not asked about Westminster or how they did it. We deployed personnel all around Parliament and the palace ... a smaller force at the Underground. I'm not sure it would have mattered how we spread them out, but I thank you for the alert."

She grimaced, having hoped that he would volunteer details about the bombing without being asked. Suddenly she understood that she would not like the answer about how the bombings took place. "What did they use?"

He looked up and down the street at the throngs of Londoners caught up in the tragedy—ordinary people desperate to contact their loved ones, emergency personnel dealing with the aftermath, others just trying to free themselves from the gridlock, all shell-shocked. "Wheelchairs. The stations all had step-free access. The bastards rolled right in."

Chapter 56

Wednesday night
Mumbai, India

The planes carrying Arnie and Gabe, one from London and the other from Doha, arrived at Chhatrapati Shivaji International Airport in Mumbai a little under three hours apart. Each man hailed a taxi, rode into the city, and checked into the Taj Mahal Palace Hotel.

The hotel had guaranteed a large suite for Adele, who was scheduled to arrive the following night, while the reservations for Arnie and Gabe relegated them to smaller rooms. Like the travel bookings, all of the hotel reservations had been confirmed separately, giving no indication of an association among the parties. The challenge, Arnie knew, would be to secure rooms on the same floor without announcing that the three were working together. The vigilant employees would catch on soon enough, but the longer their relationship could hover beneath the radar, the better.

Arnie had, over the years, performed a number of odd jobs for various American intelligence agencies—including the installation of highly sophisticated spyware on the computers at several renowned scientific research facilities.

He had brought an arsenal of software with him, but bringing certain electronic hardware into India would surely have raised questions if he had been stopped by customs officers. He would have to purchase the equipment they would need. He compiled a lengthy list, and then showered and stretched out on the bed.

At eight o'clock the following morning, Arnie made his way down to the Shamiana coffee shop for a light breakfast. Reaching for a packet of sugar substitute, he remembered Zach—poisoned by the Russian, Barinov. He put the packet back in the bowl and opted to take his coffee bitter.

Gabe—his face drawn and haggard—appeared ten minutes later and took a seat a few tables away from Arnie. After a few moments, he stood—a newspaper tucked under his arm—and wandered over to browse the offerings of the sumptuous buffet. Arnie followed in short order, filling his plate and ultimately picking up the newspaper that Gabe dropped between the bains-marie filled with dosas and uttapams. Arnie returned to his table and unfolded the newspaper, whereupon a small square note dropped into his lap. *Case of Delhi Belly*, the note said. *Here's the list of what I need.* Gabe had written five items.

Arnie glanced up to see Gabe moving at a half-run across the lobby—toward the restrooms—and cursed under his breath. They had planned to meet at nine thirty, out of sight of hotel watchers and staff, at the Grant Road station. From there, it was a short walk to Lamington Road—Mumbai's equivalent to Tokyo's famed Akihabara district—with stalls upon stalls of vendors selling everything an electronics aficionado might want.

He took a few sips of coffee and left his food mostly untouched before signaling for the bill and heading back upstairs. Approaching his room, Arnie noticed a man emerging from a door across the hall. The man was Caucasian, powerfully built, and he was looking directly at Arnie. "Mr. Powell," the man said—stating, not asking. "I'd like a moment of your time." The accent was clearly British. Arnie noticed the slight bump in the man's jacket and tensed, his brain debating fight or flight. The man saw the hesitation in Arnie's eyes and quickly added, "I am here at the request of Her Majesty's government." Arnie stepped into the room.

Chapter 57

Wednesday night
London, England

Adele woke in the unfamiliar bed and, as she had done so many times before, took a moment to orient herself. Which country? Which city? Her thoughts skipped back to the morning's meeting with Jeffrey. *London.* The bedside clock read seven o'clock, and she was thankful for the little dot indicating *PM*. How many times had she called the front desk to find out if it was morning or night?

Adam Moxley had dropped Jeffrey at SIS headquarters before escorting Adele to the hotel. With much of the center city cordoned off by roadblocks, he had flashed his credentials and gained passage. They made plans to meet at eight that evening, at a pub in Mayfair not far from the hotel. "If Jeffrey and I can break away sooner, we'll ring you," he had told her.

Once in her room, she had enabled her mobile's voice encryption and dialed Paul. He tied Melodie and Trent into the call, and she told them about Tanya Goreva's return to Mumbai and Tanya's association with the Kharotis. She finished by asking them to dig up every speck of information available on both the Gorevs and the Kharoti clan, including their circle of friends and extended family.

Paul had been skeptical, questioning the capabilities of the Kharoti group. Adele had to concede the point—the Kharotis hadn't even been a blip on American radar until two days ago. She remained convinced, however, that the men were worth investigating. The Brits had been mindful of the men's whereabouts. In her book, that said something.

Trent—who had some experience in obtaining data from India—had warned them that the country was still heavily reliant on paper records in some sectors. He had suggested asking the Indians for help. Worried that any request through official channels could make authorities curious about the subject of the inquiry—and draw undue attention to those making the request—Adele had cautioned them against contacting anyone in the Indian government. *Never mind that such inquiries have a way of finding the ears of the quarry*, she had thought.

Adele also asked them to compile a list of government offices where one might go to paper records. Once the team arrived in Mumbai, she had every intention of turning Gabe loose to work his magic—electronic and otherwise. After disconnecting from the call, she had conducted some research of her own—looking for a hook that would get her into a meeting with Ghadir Kharoti. Finally succumbing to the temptation of the king-size bed, she had slept.

Adele found the pub easily, situated on a side street a short walk from the hotel. It was dark, cozy, and boasted an extensive selection of lagers and ales—as should any proper

British pub. The menu, chalked on a large board above the bar, listed traditional pub grub, as well as several other interesting offerings.

She ventured farther inside and craned her neck, looking for Jeffrey or Adam. The barkeep, a tall, silver-haired, heavyset man in his late sixties, came out from behind the expansive bar and strode directly toward her.

"I have your table, just over there," he said, pointing toward the back wall of the building. She followed his gesture and spotted three small tables, with a *Reserved* sign perched on each.

Before she could comment, he added, "The other two tables will be empty while you are here. They should provide an appropriate buffer for your conversation." He noticed her blink in surprise. "I worked with your friend for thirty years ... retired a year ago and bought this place. He told me to expect you."

He escorted her to the table and suggested an ale, offering a swallow from a tasting glass. She took a sip and smiled appreciatively at the nicely hopped brew and found herself wondering about the affordability of a pub in Mayfair.

The answer came ten minutes later, when Adam appeared with the hand of an older woman resting lightly on his arm. It took a few seconds for Adele to recognize Sheila Moxley, the two-time Oscar-winning actress. *Adam's mother,* she thought. *And father*, she realized when Adam called out to say hello to his dad behind the bar. *No worries about affordability there.*

Adam greeted Adele with a laugh. "I will introduce you later, but it could prove awkward when she wants to book you for a session." He looked over his shoulder at the bodies hovering around his mother. “Mum will keep the clientele entertained. We should be private enough back here.” He passed an electronic tablet across the table. “I will send you the complete file, but these are the highlights.”

Adele sped through the document, absorbing the salient points. The SIS had compiled a significant amount of information on the family’s history. She read it again in detail, glancing up only to acknowledge Jeffrey’s arrival.

The elder Mr. Kharoti had been, in fact, previously married. Wife number one died of an aneurism a few months after the wedding, with no record of any offspring. She was an only child, so no nieces or nephews to be found on that side of the family. He did, however, have three sisters, all of whom found their names changed by marriage. The eldest had two sons, one of whom was murdered by Sikh extremists back in 1983. The other, a software executive, was well-respected and reputedly squeaky clean. The middle sister was a widow with no children and seemed unremarkable.

The youngest sister, however, was the attention-getter. She had married a man living in Mumbai at the time, but whose family roots were in Pakistan. They had three children—two boys and a girl—all of whom visited Mumbai frequently while growing up, but were educated in the urban area of Islamabad. Both boys later attended school at the Pakistan Military Academy, located less than three miles from the infamous compound where Usama bin Laden had been cornered and eliminated.

The sister’s elder son had been shot and killed in 1999 during a border skirmish with India. The document’s author had inserted his own acid-laced remarks about the incident: “Daddy, who was by then a rising star in the ranks of the Pakistani army, thought it would be a good learning experience for his son to accompany him to the conflict area.”

The daughter, while in Mumbai for a visit in 2003, was raped, beaten, and left for dead in a hotel room by an American tourist. The girl never recovered, was shunned by her family for having accepted the young man’s invitation to his room, and eventually fell under the custodial care of the Indian government. She was currently in a public long-term care facility on the outskirts of Mumbai.

Their only remaining child was Aashif Ahmedani—the nephew staying with Mr. Kharoti in Mumbai.

Adam and Jeffrey sat quietly while Adele read, waiting for her reaction to the document. Finally returning the tablet to Adam, she reached for her beer and took a long sip before speaking. “How much tragedy can one family bear? The Indians and Americans have wreaked destruction on that family. I’d call that motive,” she said. “Wouldn’t you?”

“Indeed, I would,” agreed Jeffrey, “which explains why we’ve had eyes on Ahmedani for quite some time. We suspect that he has ties to Lashkar-e-Taiba ... and that he may have been involved with the Mumbai bombings back in 2008. We have no substantive proof, of course. What we don’t know is the extent to which Mr. Kharoti and his son are implicated.

“Then I guess I have my work cut out for me,” Adele observed.

Adam frowned. “You are doing this alone?”

Wondering how much they already knew, Adele decided there was little point in withholding her plans. “I have helpers. They should have arrived in Mumbai by now."

Jeffrey cleared his throat and glanced first at Adam and then at Adele. "We were wondering if you might like a bit of assistance in that effort."

Adele blinked at the unexpected offer. "From one of your operatives?"

"In a manner of speaking."

Adele looked quizzically at the two men. "Meaning?"

Adam grinned, answering, "My mother."

Thinking she had misunderstood, Adele cupped her ear. "Sorry, what did you say?"

"Mum's public resume omits a few of the more interesting roles she has played over the years in the service of Her Majesty's government."

Adele lifted an eyebrow and waited.

Jeffrey leaned forward and spoke in a low voice. "Even if you do manage to ensnare Mr. Kharoti, it doesn't get you close to the son and nephew. Agreeing to a sit-down for a magazine article is one thing, but it is quite another to suggest a film project to which Dame Sheila Moxley is committed. The entire world loves a movie star, and Sheila is a magnet. Even the two young men will find the opportunity to meet her irresistible."

"I assume you have a publicity plan?"

"A well-placed blurb or two in the press and a few tweets on Twitter should spark initial interest. From there, enthusiasm will gather its own inertia. To interest Mr. Kharoti, specifically, we are thinking of having the gala hosted by the DHC," he suggested, referring to the British Deputy High Commission. "Our people would work up a guest list of all the right people, including some of the Bollywood crowd and, of course, Mr. Kharoti. I can guarantee that he will attend. When you approach him about a personal interview, he will crawl over himself to set the time."

"And mum always travels with an entourage," Adam said. "They have been known to create extraordinary diversions when necessary."

Adele quickly considered the possibilities. "Diversions that might allow enough time to, say, upload a bit of malware to an untended phone?"

Adam smiled wickedly. "Exactly."

"I love the digital world," she said with a grin.

The two men stood and made their way to the bar, leaving Adele alone to contemplate this new turn of events. Their offer was tempting, but she was somewhat aggravated that the actress might already know of the mission. She wasn't going to commit until talking with Sheila and taking a measure of the woman. Noticing that the crowd was beginning to thin, she checked her watch and was surprised to discover that she had been in the pub for over three hours.

As if on cue, Sheila extricated herself from the remaining hangers-on and wandered to Adele's table. The two women smiled politely at one another—wary but curious.

Sheila quickly broke the ice. "I can imagine that you might be annoyed at the thought of a prima donna actress usurping your mission. The saving grace is that while I've had a turn or two on the dance floor, I have no wish to be in charge. I would be delighted to accompany you."

Surprising herself, Adele took an instant liking to the actress. *This could work*, she thought.

The following morning, Sheila Moxley's private car slid to a stop in front of the Connaught, where the liveried doorman ushered Adele to the backseat while the porter attended to her luggage. Sheila sat erect, holding a crystal flute in one hand and a bottle of Dom Perignon in the other. "A little bubbly to celebrate our adventure?"

Adele hesitated for a split second before accepting the glass. "Why the hell not?"

The text came in when they were halfway to the airport.

> Press arranged. Seat 5K.
> Watch yourself.

By the time they reached Heathrow, the two women had polished off the champagne, fine-tuned the parts each would play, and were giggling like schoolgirls. In character, Sheila tripped while stepping out of the car, even grabbing the sleeve of a businessman awaiting his own ride. Adele chuckled to herself, amazed at the actress's ability to wrap herself in the role. Adele thought of herself as an expert in the game, but recognized that she had met her equal.

The gaiety extended into the British Airways flight, where the actress and the photographer—seated beside each other in 5E and 5F—dropped the privacy panel between the seats and swapped stories. They regaled the crew with naughty tales of unnamed rich and famous—tantalizingly leaving the true identities to the imagination of the listener. The entire conversation was duly recorded by the man in seat 5K, who was the victim of a booking mix-up on his scheduled flight on Turkish Airlines—

thirteen hours with a stop in Istanbul. He had been ready to raise a ruckus when, by some miracle, he had been handed a first-class boarding card on the nine-hour nonstop on British Airways.

Already delighted by his good fortune, he became positively ecstatic when he discovered that two celebrities were seated just beside him. He considered himself a journalist—despite his affiliation with a tawdry rag tattling about all things Bollywood—and was soon drafting the story that would appear in the next day's edition.

Chapter 58

Early Friday morning
Mumbai, India

With the time change, it was just after midnight when Adele and Sheila emerged from the airbridge and into the turmoil of the terminal. Like every public area of Mumbai, the building teemed with people competing for space. The only thing missing, thought Adele, was the constant blare of taxi horns. The building itself was new since the days when she had worked South Asia, its grand opening just over a decade ago. But it had already begun to show signs of aging. As her husband Tom was fond of saying, everything in Mumbai is instant-old. It didn't matter. Aside from the Goreva incident, she had found the city enthralling.

The air still held its exotic flavor, and she felt transported back in time, the old excitement returning. India had never been a simple place and, having emerged as a technological powerhouse, was even more complex today. One did not have to look far to find all manner of intrigue in the teeming metropolis.

Adam is so right, she thought, marveling at the number of people staring, pointing, and asking for autographs from the famous actress. *Sheila is a magnet.*

While Adam had stated that Sheila traveled with an entourage, Adele was taken aback by the number of staff hovering around her. The group had been seated in business class, materializing only after making their way to baggage claim and finding Sheila in the throng. Sheila introduced them as her personal assistant, hairdresser, makeup artist, trainer, and fulfillment technician.

"Fulfillment technician?" Adele asked.

"If we need a fresh lime soda, a newspaper, or any type of errand, he will fulfill the request." She laughed at the expression on Adele's face. "Trust me," she said, "the others have very specific jobs to do, and I am not going to waste their time running errands. It's worth it."

Adele's initial thought was that the idea was absurd, although she could see Sheila's point. What was really bothering her, she decided, was that Sheila had summoned all these people with a late-night phone call and expected them to show up a few hours later for a trip to India. *I hope she pays them extraordinarily well,* she thought.

Watching her, Sheila suspected what was going through Adele's mind. "I am not an ogre," she said quietly. "Barbara Raynor, my assistant, has been with me for almost thirty years and is more friend than employee. Honestly, I would be lost without her. She normally travels with me in the front, but I had to forfeit her seat so the nosy magazine writer would get the scoop on our visit. The others are very well-compensated and will have a week off when our little adventure is done. Plus, they've come with me to India a few times before and seem to enjoy it."

Glancing over at the group, Adele noticed the assistant

directing the baggage retrieval. Barbara Raynor was a striking woman, tall, with closely cropped diamond-white hair and creamy skin that only the English seem to inherit. *Must be the lack of sun and all those dreary, foggy days,* Adele thought. And with a typical British stiff upper lip, she carried herself perfectly erect despite having suffered through the nine-hour flight.

Adele tried to picture the woman in her youth, imagining her as a redhead—a fitting attribute, considering the fire with which she suddenly lit into one of the Indian porters for his rough treatment of Adele's equipment cases. She chuckled to herself, and then stared in amazement as Barbara spoke a few phrases in Hindi and demonstrated the proper handling.

Sheila cupped her hand over Adele's ear and whispered, "And did I mention she speaks Hindi? For this trip, a very desirable skill, I should think."

Adele's eyebrows lifted ever so slightly, and then she smiled. "Indeed."

They were met outside customs by the security officer from the British consulate, leaving Adele to wonder if the courtesy was commonly extended to celebrities from the Empire or whether it was the women's mission that merited the special attention. The man led them to his car, inviting Barbara only after Sheila demanded that she be included. The remaining entourage was shuffled into two ordinary cars for hire.

The gala, the officer informed them, was set for that evening—barely eighteen hours hence. Three hundred hastily printed invitations had been addressed by two women with impeccable handwriting and had been hand-delivered that afternoon by a dozen young men who performed odd jobs for the staff. The consulate was all abuzz about the event, the man added, as they had not hosted a celebrity of Sheila's stature for quite some time. Sheila and Adele scanned the guest list, relieved to see the names of Mr. Ghadir Kharoti and his son, Mr. Farshad Kharoti, each with a checkmark confirming his intention to attend.

Approaching the Taj Mahal Palace Hotel, Adele observed that the roads and buildings had changed little since her posting—the only major transformation being the renaming of the city from Bombay to Mumbai. The promenade along Colaba Causeway stretched south, caressing the water's edge for almost a quarter-mile, beginning at the massive arched monument known as the Gateway of India. The entire area around the structure was, even at this time of night, choked with a sea of humanity.

She turned her head away from the monument and stared at the magnificent hotel directly across the street. The building was an architectural and cultural treasure of another era. Its design was legendary, with a large central dome encircled by small turrets, additional large turrets at each corner of the building, the façade interlaced with stone, intricate woodwork, myriad arches, and an abundance of balconies overlooking the sea.

The grand old hotel stood majestically and stoically, despite the insults that terrorism had thrown its way. Confirming what she had read in the reports, the building's perimeter was now fortified by a double row of barricades. She shook her head sadly at the sight, a grim reminder of the events in 2008 that had shocked the world and left the city reeling. A coordinated attack by Pakistani terrorists had lasted four days and targeted specific locations frequented by foreigners. To this day, reports varied on the number of casualties. Adele's sources confirmed 166 victims deceased and more than 300 injured. Both the Taj and Oberoi Hotels had suffered heavy damage, and Adele could vividly recall newscasts showing thick smoke billowing from the Taj.

After the disaster, Israeli and American experts were enlisted to help beef up security, and the hotels had adopted many of the recommendations. A fellow intelligence officer had, however, recently reported that civic authorities were levying sizable monetary penalties against the hotels because some of the fortifications occupied public space, blocking vehicular and pedestrian traffic. *Complacency always sets in, and it doesn't even take that long*, she thought.

Barbara was first out of the car, rushing ahead to attend to the check-in details, providing the security man with an opportunity to speak privately. "After consulting with our home office and your Ambassador Marshfield, we have positioned a former SAS man in a room on your floor. He has already introduced himself to your men Arnold Powell and Gabriel Winters. I would suggest that you meet with him in short order so that you will recognize him and so he can share anything he may have learned thus far. Please keep in mind that we have deployed him as a precaution and to provide support as needed. All care will be taken to ensure he works in coordination with your team, Ms. Rutledge. We would ask only that you do not reveal his identity to Ms. Moxley's personal staff."

Adele wondered if there was some hidden meaning behind his request to keep the staff out of the loop. "Why?" she asked.

"Foremost, because they are not as practiced at deception as the two of you. We are aware that Ms. Raynor has been with Ms. Moxley for many years, but quite frankly, those years of training mean that she instantly recognizes and greets familiar faces. And while the others are very good at following directions, we would still be more comfortable if our man was allowed to remain unknown."

"And just to be clear, you are not entertaining suspicions about any of Sheila's people?"

His eyes narrowed, and he gave her an appraising look. "I have heard that about you. You are suspicious of everyone."

"A cynicism of the trade, I'm afraid. But it's kept me alive more times than you know."

His face relaxed visibly. "No suspicions. Just a preference to protect our own, you know."

"I understand, but we are going to make an exception for Ms. Raynor. As you said, she has been with Ms. Moxley for many years. And tonight, she will be integral to the success of our operation. We are relying on her to engage with our targets and keep them distracted while we compromise their communications. This is not negotiable."

The man was used to issuing orders, not having them thrown back in his face, and his surprise at being challenged was evident. He opened his mouth to speak, but on seeing Adele's hard stare, changed his mind. The woman was not only a legend; she had friends in powerful places. "As you wish," he conceded. "I will let him know of the change in plans."

"I appreciate that; thank you." She stretched one leg out of the car and turned back to face him. "We will take good care of your man, I promise."

Lips drawn in a thin line, he nodded. "Good luck tonight."

"You're not joining us?"

"Not inside, no. I will be outside, watching. I am reaching the point where I rather detest these gatherings. Despite all the precautions ..."

She did not let him finish. "We are in this together, and I won't let you down. Go have a good sleep. We're going to get these people."

Chapter 59

Adele walked out onto the balcony and looked out over the harbor and the imposing Gateway of India, orienting her room in the context of the building's exterior. She closed the floor-to-ceiling curtains and turned back to face the living room of the sumptuous suite. She spotted the package resting atop the credenza, addressed to her from the Maharashtra Personal Marketing and Consulting Group. She tore the wrapping from the box and examined the contents before picking up the phone and asking Sheila and Barbara to join her.

The twin Sig-Sauer 9 mm compact pistols were small enough that the women could easily carry them in a purse—or even in the pocket of loose-fitting pants or a jacket—but Sheila balked when she saw them. "I must tell you that I have reservations," she said. "At one time, my marksmanship was excellent, but it has been years since I've fired a gun, and they are no longer familiar to me. We cannot afford to arouse any suspicion, and I think I would be nervous about a gun in my pocket."

Conceding the point, Adele nevertheless insisted on giving Sheila a refresher in using the pistol. She also asked that Sheila carry one of the spare magazines ... just in case.

Running Sheila through the paces, Adele was impressed. Sheila's form was still very good, and she handled the weapon deftly and comfortably. Whoever had trained her had done a superb job of it.

Adele heard the soft taps on the door—single knock, single knock, double knock—and opened the door to admit Arnie and Gabe, followed by a man they introduced as Cam. *The SAS man*, she thought.

"Good," she said. "I was just about to show off my cane. It will pass through airport security without so much as a blink, so even if bringing a gun along is out of the question, I still have a weapon. You should all know how it works." She showed them how to twist and turn and pull on the intricately conceived device, revealing a stiletto, a tactical folding knife with finger holes, a throwing knife, a heavy Bowie knife, and a push dagger.

The men gaped at the display of weaponry, while Sheila smiled appreciatively. "Clever, my dear, and quite beautifully crafted," she said. "Barbara has a similar weapon mounted in her office."

"Really?" Adele now noticed that Barbara seemed riveted by the cane. "Would you like to try it?"

"It is quite beautiful ... in so many ways. I would love to try to open it, if it's not a bother."

Adele handed the cane to her and watched admiringly as the woman manipulated the cane and withdrew the first stiletto. "Very good! The artist who crafted my cane makes only two or three a year. How did you acquire yours?"

"My father was in Burma when the Japanese advanced on Rangoon during World War II. He told me that his best friend had been killed by a Japanese officer using a weapon hidden in a cane. He shot the soldier and brought the cane home as a souvenir. I will admit that it took us quite a long time to learn all its secrets."

Turning toward Arnie, Adele asked, "What will you need from us tonight?"

Arnie rubbed his hand over the scruff of his three-day-old beard. "Our best starting tactic is to clone their phones. I went on a little shopping excursion this morning, with the help of our British friends here. Assuming Kharoti and his son have not changed out their phones since their last surveillance, we should have all of the gear we need."

"The older man uses a low-end InFocus phone and uses it rarely," Cam offered. "The son and the nephew are a little more hip ... they are each carrying a Lara Iris ... it's a brand made in India. We have multiple videos of them punching in a four-digit number when picking up the phones, so we have assumed they are password-protected."

Adele looked at him appraisingly. "You took the photographs ... the lunch with Tanya Goreva at the Willingdon." The statement carried no hint of a question.

Cam nodded. "I did. We have been watching them for some time, but the home office never gave us approval to take any action."

"Let's hope we get our chance tonight. I've been thinking about how we can get the Kharotis to part with their phones, and I've come up with the idea of offering a portrait sitting to a few of the guests. We could include the Kharotis in the mix. If they are wearing jackets, we could pose them in shirtsleeves. If they have their phones in a shirt or pants pocket, I can say that the phone's outline disturbs the photo composition. Either way, I think it's doable. How much time will you need?"

Arnie scrunched up his face. "For the old man's phone, two or three minutes. For the son, Farshad? More like ten or fifteen. I'll clone the phones, and Gabe has a special app that he'll inject, courtesy of our friends at Fort Meade. Once installed, it will turn the device into a microphone capable of picking up conversations within a few feet. As long as the device is connected to Wi-Fi or is in range of a cell tower, any sound it picks up will stream to one of our servers."

"What about the nephew, Aashif Ahmedani?" Sheila asked.

Cam shook his head. "He keeps a much lower profile and rarely socializes. We thought it would feel a bit off if he were included in the invitation. But if we can't get access to Aashif's phone, your microphone may be the next best thing. The two of them spend almost all of their free time together."

"I have a bad feeling about Aashif. When Farshad goes to work, what does Aashif do for the remainder of the day? That's the part that worries me. Am I the only one who is having difficulty understanding why someone suspected of being involved with LeT is living openly in Mumbai?"

"We have attempted to follow him on numerous occasions, but we are stretched for resources. We do know he often goes to the Jama Masjid—the mosque up by Crawford Market—but we always seem to lose him in the crowd."

Adele turned to look at Arnie and Gabe. "Did you receive the package from the dip pouch?" she asked, referring to the protected bags and crates that are routinely shipped by governments to their diplomatic missions abroad.

"I wondered what you had in mind for the pixie dust."

Arnie grinned.

Looking over at Cam and Sheila, Adele explained. "Our technicians have supplied us with a small device that sprays nanoparticles ... and a trio of tiny drones to track them. It's Friday, so the timing is perfect. If he is truly among the faithful, he will go to the mosque for the Salāt al-Jum`ah—the Friday noon prayer." She swiveled back to Cam. "How does he travel? Does he have a driver?"

"No driver. Taxi, almost exclusively."

They devised a plan to pinpoint and spray Aashif before he entered the mosque. Arnie's swarthy skin and his dark, gray-streaked hair—and the fact that he had never crossed paths with the target—made him the obvious choice to deliver the spray. Gabe would stay in the hotel. From the shelter of the balcony overlooking the sea, he would launch and man the drone.

"What is the status of Tanya Goreva?"

"The crazy Russian woman?" asked Cam.

Adele was surprised that Jeffrey had not shared the content of their discussion in London. "Crazy or not, I have reason to believe that she may be playing an active role here in Mumbai."

Cam's eyes went wide. "In what capacity?"

Recalling Jalil's cryptic statements of being on a container ship traversing the Arabian Sea from Iran to Mumbai, she stitched together a minimal accounting of his story and watched the team's faces and posture carefully as she spoke. "I have information that she may have traveled from Iran to Mumbai a few months ago—by freighter. Her exact intentions are, at this point, unknown, but I am quite certain this was not a vacation cruise."

The mention of Iran was an attention-getter. "We'll find her," said Cam.

"Success with the phones tonight is vital. The visuals of Aashif are critical, too, but I'll be happier when we have audio, too. For tonight, we'll plan for the photography session, but everyone should be prepared for the unexpected. Code words, everyone! *Cinnamon* means we need a distraction. *Iceberg* means abort. If we have to pull the plug, make sure those phones get back to their owners without delay. And the last, *God save the Queen,* will indicate that I intend to lift a phone myself. If that happens, we will all have to improvise. I can't stress how important it will be for you to be on your toes."

Gabe spoke up. "I have to tell you that I was sick as a dog all day. I took some meds, but ..."

"It's India. It happens," said Sheila. "Keep dosing yourself, and hopefully it will pass. If you have a problem tonight, we will manage it."

Adele nodded her agreement. "And the Brits have booked the ballroom downstairs for tonight, so your room is only a staircase away." She turned to Sheila. "You've done this more than I. The invitations went out for seven thirty. What time should we be there?"

"Again, it's India. The first guests will likely not arrive until at least eight. Let's be down there at six. I'll arrange to get a diagram of the room layout so we can review it in advance."

"Good. Let's meet here then, at two, to review our plan and attend to any last-minute details. That will give Cam and Arnie time to visit the mosque and for the rest of us to get some sleep. I'll order lunch."

Chapter 60

Friday morning
Mumbai, India

The skies leaked a steady drizzle, depositing even more moisture onto the already sodden earth. A month into India's monsoon season, the effects were already evident. Mold and algae clung to exterior surfaces, making roads and walkways slick and transforming walls from gleaming white to stained streaks of green and black.

They sat in a white Hyundai, less than 150 feet from the front door of the Kharoti bungalow on Malabar Hill, waiting for Aashif Ahmedani to make an appearance. Each wore a miniature wireless earpiece that communicated—via the Bluetooth pack strapped under their shirts—with an encrypted two-way radio.

Shortly after eleven, the front door opened, and an elderly male servant stepped out to the street. Two minutes later, a black taxi with a distinctive yellow roof pulled up to the entry. The servant held the car door open for Aashif as he left the house and slid into the backseat. Cam started the engine and slipped into the stream of traffic while Arnie typed the text to Gabe. On our way.

Gabe stiffened when the text came in. The drone was ready, but he was not sure that he was. Aside from manipulating the controls for electronic games, he had no experience at handling a device like this. He had readied the machine, but feeling unsure of himself, checked the GPS coordinates for the third time. He opened the window and turned on the power. The highly sophisticated little machine flapped its wings, ascended to a height of five hundred feet, and maintained the elevation as it navigated in the direction of the mosque. At a speed of approximately ten miles per hour, the little bird they called *Cheep One* should be at its destination in fourteen minutes.

Four cars behind the taxi, Cam jockeyed for position as they proceeded down the hill and in the direction of Chowpatty Beach. By the time they veered onto Marine Drive, he was in the lead by two cars. He split off at the flyover, heading east toward Crawford Market. Within a few blocks, the mosque came into view, and traffic slowed to a mind-numbing crawl. He glanced at the rearview mirror and verified that Aashif's taxi was still behind him.

"He's going to bail."

"You think so? The weather is crappy. I'll bet he stays in the car all the way to the entrance."

"No, he's opening the door. Get moving."

Arnie jumped out of the car and opened the umbrella against the rain. The communications gear was advertised as water-resistant, but he knew from experience that electronics and water are a bad combination. "Still behind me?" he asked.

"Cutting across the road. White shirt, yellow backpack, green umbrella. Green as in the flag of Pakistan. Subtle, isn't he?"

"Got him. Moving to intercept."

Arnie was tall and muscular, but surprisingly nimble. He quick-stepped into a position at Aashif's five o'clock and dropped the umbrella slightly to block the view of any observers. Raising his left arm, he swept his hand in a counterclockwise arc a mere three feet from the Pakistani's body. The fine, nearly invisible mist blossomed out of the canister, drifting onto Aashif's head and upper torso, and then down to his trousers and shoes.

"Breaking away," he whispered, continuing to walk at the same speed and angle. "Pick me up."

Cam watched Aashif continue onward—into the mosque and oblivious to the contamination—and sent the text: All that glitters is not gold.

The bird was flying a circular pattern above the mosque, its onboard photodetector sampling the spectrum of light below and waiting for the first observation of a very specific wavelength. The stream of nanoparticles from Arnie's canister flashed beneath its viewer, activating the video stream back to base. Sensitive to ultraviolet light and coated with a mixture of binder and luminescent additive, the silicon nanoparticles absorbed the ultraviolet light and reemitted it in a shifted wavelength per the properties of the coating's additive—making the spray specifically visible to the drone per its programmed acquisition instructions.

Unless instructed otherwise, the drone would remain focused on the object or person displaying the greatest nanoparticle concentration. It thus followed Aashif across the street and to the mosque's entry, where it lost track of the target. It hovered there, awaiting another wash of light or another command.

When Aashif reemerged after the noon prayer, the little machine with the bird's-eye view reacquired the blaze of nanoparticles and followed them across the street to a taxi, to an elbow resting on the taxi door's open window, and then north toward the suburbs—in the opposite direction from the hotel.

Gabe frowned and glanced over at *Cheep Two* and *Cheep Three*, resting silently on the breakfast table, and calculated the deployment. The drone's battery life was three and one-half hours when fully charged, but the recommended maximum time aloft was three hours. *Cheep One* had already been airborne for fifty minutes and was a little over two miles north of the hotel. He would allow the little bird to travel for another fifty-five minutes, assuming it continued its current route of travel. After that, he concluded, he would be forced to command the bird to return. To maintain continuous surveillance on Aashif, the second drone would need to be in position before recalling *Cheep One*. He hesitated only a moment before launching *Cheep Two*.

At half past noon, having driven to the Bandra-Kurla Complex in the northern suburbs of the city, Arnie and

Cam walked into the security office at the British Deputy High Commission and requested a linkup with Adam Moxley at Vauxhall Cross. Despite the early hour in London, the call was patched through immediately. Fifteen minutes later, they left the building with answers to the questions they had asked, including the last-known address for Tanya Goreva.

Tanya's address was in a crowded block of small shops and low-rises just north of Crawford Market. Cam eased the car into a tight vacant space two blocks away, and they set off in search of her flat. They located the building—whose street-facing ground floor consisted of a hodgepodge of tiny shops selling party goods, mobile phones, cigarettes and sundries, leather goods, and clothing—and found the main entry around the corner. The open archway led to a courtyard cluttered with discarded household items. On the far side, another open archway revealed the stairwell.

They climbed to the third floor, where a tangle of children played in the hall. The youngsters eyed them curiously as they knocked on the door to Tanya's flat. One boy—Arnie guessed him to be about six—chattered at them in Hindi. Hopelessly lost, Arnie gave up trying to interpret the child's jabber and shrugged. The noise must have alerted the child's caretaker, because a woman's head emerged from a nearby door.

"Excuse me," Cam said. "We are looking for Memsahib Goreva."

The stream of English seemed to surprise the woman, who searched for a reply. "No Memsahib."

"When will she be back?"

The woman seemed flustered and finally called over

her shoulder to someone behind her, whereupon a teenager stepped into the hallway. His head bobbed as he spoke. "Memsahib is not here."

Cam tried again. "When will she be back?"

The boy spoke in the lilting singsong English of the subcontinent. "It will be one week, or it will be two weeks. I cannot be sure. You see, she has packed a suitcase."

"Did she say where she was going?"

"I think she must be taking the airplane. She had the green suitcase."

"Green suitcase?"

"When Memsahib goes on short trip, she is taking the red bag. When she goes on long trip, she is taking the green bag."

"Where is the airplane taking her?"

The boy beamed. "She is meeting her daughter."

Arnie's heart did a flip. "Where is she meeting her daughter?"

The boy frowned. "This I do not know."

"When did she leave?"

"Yesterday."

The taxi carrying Ghadir Kharoti's nephew crawled forward for a little over seven miles—hopelessly mired in the daytime Mumbai traffic—and finally approached the Dharavi neighborhood forty-five minutes after departing the mosque. Gabe now fully understood why the technicians had warned him that the drones were typically confined to a two-mile radius ... a car traveling at any normal rate of speed would quickly outdistance the little birds.

Cheep One recorded Aashif climbing out of the taxi. It then followed him as he proceeded on foot—into the warren of flimsy, metal-roofed shacks that comprised one of Asia's largest slums.

Gabe fully intended to recall *Cheep One* when *Cheep Two*—trailing fifteen minutes behind and fifty feet lower than its companion—arrived on the scene. *Cheep Two* was thirty seconds out when Aashif ducked into one of the shanties. From the multicolored leather sheets tacked around the doorway, Gabe inferred that the shop produced leather goods—one of the small-scale industries that had sprung up in Dharavi over the years. Maybe, he thought, he could have the fresh drone hover above, and use *Cheep One* to take a peek inside the hut.

Having read a number of articles and white papers about Mumbai during his flight over, Gabe had gleaned a bit of knowledge about the notorious neighborhood. Estimates put the population of Dharavi at somewhere between seven hundred thousand and over a million inhabitants—all crammed into a space of about 550 acres. To put it in perspective, Dharavi occupies a space that is about 65 percent of the size of New York City's Central Park. Manhattan's population density is estimated at 111 people per acre. Using the lower figure of seven hundred thousand souls in Dharavi, its population density is 1,273 people per acre.

The area was packed with people, vehicles, small industries, and flimsy residences. While many of the shacks had access to electricity, running water and sanitary facilities were rare. Some reports estimated a ratio of one toilet for every fourteen hundred residents, the end result being that many used the nearby Mithi River instead. The river was also used as the dumping ground for sludge, industrial and household waste, and pollutants of every stripe.

Gabe decided to take the chance. He circled *Cheep One* lower and lower, waiting for a moment when the alley was comparatively free of human activity. Finally seeing an opening, he sent the little bird diving down to the front of the shop. The bird hovered for only a few seconds at the doorway, streaming the video of an empty room, before ascending to the window on the second floor. Gabe could see men sitting on the floor of the room, crowded like sardines in a can. The imagery was good, and he held the drone in place. One second, two, three, four ...

A man suddenly sprang to his feet, pointing at the window. Gabe, miles away, was startled by the motion and actually jumped in fear, as if the man were looking directly at him. He commanded the drone to a higher elevation, and the bird shot upward and over the rooftop, the man now leaning out of the opening and gesturing wildly. *Cheep Two*, unnoticed and hovering directly above, captured his face in full color, as well as the faces of two others who joined him at the window.

Gabe issued the command for *Cheep One* to return to the hotel and wiped the sweat from his forehead. He moved *Cheep Two* to a lower position, hovering just above a nearby rooftop.

He watched as a stream of men poured out of the shop, all shouting frantically and rushing in different directions. *Cheep Two* captured them all, sending their faces back to Gabe. Aashif bolted through the door—another man trailing close behind—and *Cheep Two* followed, locked on to the glow of the clinging nanoparticles. The men strode quickly through the web of pathways and back to 60 Feet Road, which bisected the settlement, and raced toward a passing taxi.

Gabe, wondering why the men had panicked and fled, eventually realized that they feared a drone-targeted missile strike. *Prior experience?* Gabe wondered. *Cheep Two* attempted to trail Aashif, but traffic was moving, and the little bird could not keep pace with the taxi. He called Adele. She calculated the time difference to the United States and blew out a frustrated sigh on realizing it was only four in the morning on the East Coast.

"Send everything to Melodie and Trent," she told him. "But the answer is going to take a while."

Chapter 61

Friday night
Mumbai, India

Adele and Sheila, with Sheila's entourage in tow, pushed open the doors of the ballroom two hours before the function's start time. Expecting to find the room empty, they were surprised to find a number of staff from the British Deputy High Commission already present. If the Brits had any inkling about the true purpose of the evening's gala, they gave no indication as they introduced themselves. To any observer, their sole purpose was to ensure that their guests, both ordinary and extraordinary, were well attended to.

Adele, eyeing the stage at the far end of the room, preemptively claimed the space as a makeshift studio. To Sheila, she whispered, "It's perfect. We can hold their belongings backstage. We'll just need my equipment delivered and that back room for Arnie and Gabe to work."

"This is why I have a fulfillment technician," she said with a wink. She called the young man over and issued the instructions.

He nodded rapidly, turned on his heel, and left in search of the event coordinator. He returned a few minutes later, a key dangling from his fingers. "This is the key to a small dressing room behind the stage," he said. "And Ms. Rutledge's cases will be delivered shortly."

Adele leaned into Sheila's ear. "Any idea where I can get one of those for myself?"

Giggling, Sheila said, "He is good, isn't he? A shame that he's so young, or I'd have him fulfilling other needs as well.

Arnie, a backpack slung over his shoulder, walked onto the stage and watched as Adele finished assembling the fabric drapes, studio strobes, softboxes, diffusers, reflectors, and other pieces of lighting equipment.

He spoke softly. "Gabe is on his way. Where are we setting up?"

She shook his hand, as if in greeting, and pressed the key into his palm. "There's a dressing room behind the stage."

He noticed the troubled look in her eyes. "We came here to do a job. We'll get it done."

"I hope you're right."

Joined by the British Deputy High Commissioner and his wife, Sheila and Adele stood near the middle of the ballroom and greeted arriving guests. From the list of invitees, they had chosen several likely candidates for abbreviated portrait sittings. Ideally, Adele would already have a subject on stage and another waiting in the wings when Ghadir Kharoti and his son appeared. By having the subterfuge already in progress, there would be little reason for him to be alarmed when they invited him to sit for a photograph. Her team was ready—all they needed were the players in the show: a few selected guests and the Kharoti men.

Recognizing the name as the DHC introduced a prominent Mumbai industrialist, Sheila launched into a pitch about her upcoming documentary and explained that Adele was shooting a few stills in preparation. Adele looked him up and down, as if measuring his suitability for the camera, and then asked if he might consider posing. Interviews, she explained, would follow later, once they had drafted a storyboard. He beamed with pleasure, as most people would when presented with an opportunity to be photographed by Adele. She led him up the steps behind the stage, where Barbara relieved him of his jacket and tie, and then onto the stage proper. When he commented on the baby grand that stood stage right, she seated him at the keyboard, adjusted the lighting, framed him in her lens, and began shooting. She promised to deliver the mounted and framed result within a week.

Adele photographed the subjects in the order that Barbara presented them. The industrialist was followed by a banker, who was followed by the principal of an IT outsourcing company. Sheila had been shaking hands with the IT man when she spotted Ghadir Kharoti and his son fewer than ten feet away, waiting their turn in the reception line. While the IT man was not on their list of preferred interviewees, fate and his position in the line elevated his status. Sheila repeated her spiel, invited the man to become a subject of Adele's lens, and asked her fulfillment technician to escort him backstage.

Mr. Kharoti, having overheard the conversation, was surprised and flattered to be included. He did not really understand what he and the IT man had in common, but shrugged the thought away. Westerners often had unusual ideas that translated to great cinema.

Unlike the industrialist and the banker, the IT man wore a traditional long-sleeved white kurta, intricately embroidered around its neckline and deep front placket. Barbara saw the Kharotis approaching and noticed that they, too, wore kurtas. She smiled inwardly, realizing that the IT man would be the apparatus by which the Kharotis would learn that wallets, keys, and mobile phones were inappropriate accessories for a photo session with Adele.

Adele shook the banker's hand and turned to greet the IT man. As she introduced herself, Barbara caught her eye. Without any hesitation, Adele commented on his attire and stated that she was pleased that at least some of the subjects were wearing traditional Indian clothing. As she spoke, she nodded to the Kharotis, effectively including them in her comments. "I want you to feel comfortable and relaxed … to just be natural. Often, the most outstanding shot is one in which the subject—you—is caught off guard. My goal is to capture that singular moment.

"Also, a photograph is defined by light and shadow, and we don't want anything that distracts the eye. The contents of your pockets are such a distraction. You might not notice a bulge, but the camera will. So please leave your keys, wallets, phones, coins, et cetera with Barbara. She will lock your possessions in the dressing room, where they will be quite safe."

Much like someone going through airport security, the

IT man obediently emptied his pockets, placing everything into the small basket that Barbara held. The Kharotis looked on, absorbing the activity. Adele could detect no indication of alarm on the faces of the man and his son.

With the Kharotis waiting in the wings, Adele now had to balance the timing. If she took too long with the IT man, the Kharotis might grow impatient. If the time spent with him was too short, the men would wonder why she was taking longer with their session. Sheila, still in the receiving line, would take care not to send the next subject until the Kharotis were walking offstage.

Ghadir and Farshad Kharoti followed the lead of the IT man and placed their possessions in the basket for Barbara to mind. Adele adopted a casual stance, observing as the men surrendered their phones. Her breath caught as she saw that both phones were the same make, manufactured in India. She stole a glance at Barbara, who didn't seem to notice the discrepancy, and quickly ran her eyes over the young man's body. *There,* she thought. *Back pocket.* While some people need two phones—one for business and the other for personal use—the young man did not. And he was hiding the Lava phone from his father. She had little doubt now that Farshad Kharoti was engaged in a business he would have done well to avoid. Ushering the men onto the stage, she exclaimed, "God save the Queen! The two of you together will make for a smashing portrait."

Adele's voice carried above the chatter in the ballroom and was heard by both Sheila and Barbara. The code phrase propelled both into action—with Barbara rushing forward to brush a wayward lock of hair from Farshad's forehead and flick an invisible speck off his shirt. Adele simultaneously gave Farshad a delicate nudge, while in the same instant lifting the phone from his pocket and dropping it down the front of her blouse. She moved him into a position by the cello, placing one hand on the neck of the instrument and the other on the shoulder of his much shorter father. As long as his hands were raised and she kept him distracted, he would not be able to pat his backside. Her hope was that he would never realize the phone was missing.

Turning back to Barbara, she untucked a section of her silk shirt from her pants and let the phone drop into the basket. Barbara scurried away, and Adele turned back to the business of photographing the Kharoti men.

She engaged them in pleasant conversation, asking questions about their business and life in Mumbai, while continually repositioning their stance and rearranging their hands—with Farshad's always well away from his hips. After what seemed an interminable length of time, Barbara reappeared from behind the curtain, gave a brief nod, and twisted her wrist to display the phone in her hand. Adele subtly beckoned her over, palmed the phone, and moved behind the men for yet another pose. She pretended to brush some lint from the older man's shoulder and then smoothed a nonexistent wrinkle from the younger man's shirt. As she groomed Farshad, she tucked the phone back into his pocket. Her move was so delicate, so obscure, that only an expert would have recognized what she had done. Five minutes later, she escorted them backstage.

As they reclaimed their possessions, Adele inquired about the possibility of a full interview—in the setting of their home—to discuss their views on India's economic future.

Ghadir Kharoti's smile widened. "I would be delighted to share my views. We have come a long way, and my dealings with exports to America have given me much to consider. Unfortunately, I am departing tonight. We are opening a new store in Boston on Sunday."

Adele swallowed her astonishment, fighting back the urge to scream. "New store?" she repeated, keeping her voice level.

"It is part of a new center in the Seaport, near the Museum of Contemporary Art. The grand opening is Sunday. There are quite a few Mumbaites flying over, and a number of dignitaries from Boston will attend. I am sorry that you will not be there to record the event for your movie."

"I am sorry as well," she said, managing to remain outwardly calm. "Is your son accompanying you?"

"Yes, we are traveling together. It will be good for him to spend more time in your country." His expression seemed to darken as he looked over at his son. "There are influences here that could lead him astray. But these things are not your concern; I apologize." His face brightened. "Thank you for this evening. I look forward to the interview."

"As do I," she said, passing him a business card with her mobile number. "I will be in touch."

He shook her hand, beckoned to his son, and left the stage.

Chapter 62

Adele signaled to Sheila to send up the next guest selected for a photo session and took the dressing-room key from Barbara. She flung the door open and leaned back against it as it closed. "Tell me you were successful," she said urgently.

Arnie and Gabe simply stared; it was unusual to see her rattled.

Arnie blurted, "We were successful. What happened?"

"Contact Melodie. I want someone listening to those phones round-the-clock, starting immediately. And find out everything you can about an event in Boston this Sunday ... a new cultural center opening in the Seaport. If I'm right, that's their next target."

Gabe sat up, suddenly alert, and thumbed his phone. "On it."

"I have to get back out there and finish this charade. Gather any info you can, and we'll meet afterward." She shook her head as if to clear it, checked her appearance in one of the full-length mirrors, ran her fingers through her hair, and left the dressing room.

Sheila, caught in the receiving line, tried to read Adele's body language. Something was off. While Adele was certainly involved in the photo session, making small talk and snapping photo after photo, it was evident that she was preoccupied. Sheila was considering calling a halt to further sessions when Adele caught her eye and drew a finger across her throat. Sheila mentally ran through the list of those scheduled for a photo and counted two who were waiting. She surreptitiously showed two fingers to Adele, who dipped her chin in acknowledgment.

As the final guests in the line moved away to join the party, Sheila shook the hand of the DHC and his wife and offered her thanks for their efforts in staging the gala on such short notice. She could see the question in his eyes and, smiling warmly, said, "The evening has been of great value, and the people we have met tonight will be instrumental in the success of our venture."

He regarded her for a moment, reading between the lines, and replied, "The pleasure was ours." He then leaned toward her and said quietly, "Happy hunting."

Adele admitted Cam, closed the door to her suite, and threw the dead bolt. She urged him ahead, into the living area, and pivoted toward Gabe and Arnie, who were huddled together over a laptop. "What do we know?" she asked.

"First, Trent is working on the faces from the drone. We should have more in a few hours," Gabe replied.

"Second, during the party I ran the bird over to the Kharoti mansion to see if I could spot the nephew. No dice. No activity in the house at all.

"Third, conversation between father and son is what you would expect after meeting you and Sheila. They were both excited, almost giddy, at having their photos taken. Neither has made any phone calls on any of the three phones tonight." He turned to face Arnie. "Tell her what you found on the Lava."

Looking at Adele, Arnie knew that she wasn't going to like his report. He blew out a frustrated breath. "Farshad's phone is a prepaid, registered to one Leetje Koning, a philosophy student from Amsterdam. In the wake of the Mumbai attacks, India started demanding ID with the purchase of a prepaid, but there is a hefty black market ... a tourist buys a phone, uses it while they are visiting, and then sells it on the street before they leave ... as this young woman apparently did.

"The phone's log shows a series of calls—both outgoing and incoming—to a single number. That number is also a prepaid; Gabe's working on it now. Farshad doesn't keep any contact information, images, or anything else of note on that phone. And he has disabled the phone's location tracking."

"He's careful."

"Yes, he is."

"Whoa!" The exclamation came from Gabe, who had continued to work the keyboard of the laptop. "I think we can assume that the lone number on Farshad's phone log belongs to the nephew, because the phone associated with that number bounced off cell towers in Malabar Hill this morning and continued on a path consistent with his excursion to Dharavi. After that, there are pings wandering west, again consistent with the nephew's last known position from the drone.

"I was able to hack into the phone account and pull all the call records for that number. At nearly the same time as the nephew left the Kharoti house to go to the mosque, a call was made. On a hunch, I pulled cell tower info for *that* number. When the nephew's phone left Dharavi in the taxi and traveled to Juhu, this second phone took the same path. I think we can assume that this second phone belongs to the man who got into the taxi with Aashif.

"Both of those phones then went to the airport."

Adele's eyes widened, and her back straightened. "The airport? Let me make sure I have this right. Tanya Goreva left yesterday, Aashif—and the man he met with—went to the airport today, and the Kharotis are leaving tomorrow."

"Yes," breathed Arnie.

She pressed her fingers to her temples. "And what do we know about this event in Boston?"

"It's a big deal," Gabe said. "In addition to several prominent citizens from Mumbai, the mayor of Boston, the governor of Massachusetts, and a number of civic leaders from the commonwealth are planning to attend. Plus, it's open to the general public. They're opening up fifty thousand square feet of retail and restaurant space, along with a cultural awareness exposition, an interactive technology museum, and some sort of programming contest. Whoever comes out on top wins a scholarship to MIT, so you can count on some big dogs to show up for that."

Adele continued to massage her temples. "And we have, so far, found about eight hundred pounds of C-4 in Boston. Put that with the hundred pounds or so that was used in the London bombings, and that leaves over four thousand pounds unaccounted for." Noticing the shocked expressions on the faces of the Brits in the group, she was reminded that they were unaware that two tons of high explosive were in the wind.

"There was a hijacking several months ago. Bricks of C-4 from that theft were used in an attempted bombing in Boston Harbor in February. We also found a sizable cache in a Boston suburb last week, and explosives from that same shipment were used in the London bombings two days ago. We only recently learned that they were all connected."

She ran her eyes over the group. "Right now, is there anything that points to a target other than this cultural center?" In turn, they shook their heads. "Let's get Paul on the line. Right now."

Chapter 63

The connection was so clear that Paul could have been across the room instead of halfway across the world.

"Paul, we have a credible threat." Cat described what they had learned about the cultural center in Boston, the nephew's secret meeting in Dharavi, and Tanya Goreva's departure from Mumbai. "I'm not sure yet how it all ties together, but all of these events are related."

"Where is the nephew?" he asked.

Gabe and Arnie shrugged.

"Unknown at this moment. His phone is still a virgin," she responded, meaning that they had been unable to compromise Aashif's mobile. "We don't have the equipment or personnel to operate the drones round the clock. We have to wait for a call, or pull the call and tower records, or wait to capture their verbal communication on the microphone software we uploaded to the Kharoti phones."

"And the person he met in Dharavi?"

"We sent the art to Melodie and Trent ... "

"I was just going to call you," interrupted Melodie. "Trent ran facial recognition on the images from the drone. He's identified two who are known supporters of LeT. The man who got into the taxi with Aashif, however, is of greater interest. His name is Zahid Kashani, and he is ..."

"Pakistani," interrupted Adele.

"Well, this is where it gets interesting. He's in possession of a Pakistani passport under that name, but we actually got two hits under facial recognition."

"Two?"

"Yep. The other name is Farid Mahdavi. He's ..."

"Iranian."

"Iranian father, but the mother was Pakistani," Melodie corrected. "We have paper on this guy. The file is thin, but there has obviously been some interest."

"What's his story?"

"His mother was killed in one of the protest marches in Tehran, just after the shah fled the country. His father worked in their nuclear program and was killed on Iran Air 655."

"My God!" Adele breathed, and then turned to Gabe. "One of our cruisers launched surface-to-air missiles at a civilian airliner—Iran Air 655—back in 1988. Everyone on board was killed. The debate rages on to this day, but I believe it was one of our darkest moments." She ran her hands through her hair and told Melodie to continue.

Melodie cleared her throat and said, "Farid—or Zahid—was sent to live with relatives in Pakistan but, in the last few years, has spent increasing amounts of time in Tehran. He is believed to have a connection to their Intelligence Ministry, but it's not clear in what capacity."

Adele's eyes narrowed. "And what is the certainty of these two being the same man?"

"Trent says ninety-three percent."

Adele sat down and drew a long breath. "And he uses two passports because there are places to which he cannot easily travel under his Pakistani passport, such as India, and places he cannot travel under his Iranian passport, such as the United States. Tell me that's not the case."

Melodie drew a long breath. "He was in the US in February. He took a flight out of Boston four days after the attempted harbor attack."

Adele clenched her hand into a fist and tapped her lips. "He was working with Roger. He was running the operation."

"It's not airtight, but the circumstances are pretty compelling."

"It gets worse, Paul. This is the guy we saw in Dharavi with the nephew, Aashif. They went to the airport together."

"I'll spread the word. I've triggered an alarm and forwarded what we have to the appropriate parties. Those parties have called a meeting with Homeland in the morning."

She knew that the parties were the three intelligence directors who had instigated the formation of her current unit. The Department of Homeland Security, on the other hand, knew nothing of the unit or its activities. "They'll want to know the source of the information."

"And our people are very creative. You're covered."

"And Aashif and this Farid guy got on an airplane twelve hours ago. They're headed for Boston; I can feel it. We need to find them."

"And I agree, which is why I want you back on the first available flight."

Chapter 64

Friday night
Marblehead, Massachusetts

Dancer took a bottle of water from the fridge and made his way back to the second bedroom that Jason used as an office. Squid had kept an eye on the house in the days following Jason's shooting, but the slate-gray home had stood quiet and empty. Ultimately, with the shipment due any day now, the temptation of convenience had been too great. While the temporary apartment in Beverly served its purpose, it was a twenty-minute drive from Marblehead. Squid had opted for the practicality of staying in the house, and Dancer had joined him. Squid, having frequently stayed with Jason overnight, had become a familiar face, and the nosy neighbors seemed to pay him no mind. No one seemed to realize that Jason had not made an appearance in several days.

He was just finishing the e-mail when he heard a key turn in the lock. *What the hell?* Jason was in the hospital and would be there for a least one more week. And if Squid was right, Lindsey had not been to the house a single time in the last several months. His mind raced. He had last seen Lindsey two days ago, walking out of the hospital with a cast on her arm and accompanied by the guy they now knew to be an FBI agent. Dancer had tried to follow, but lost their car in the heavy traffic of the District. If she was back, this could be his opportunity to finish the job.

He blanked the screen and stepped into the hall, heading for the living room, running the scenario and considering the best way to play his reaction. Startled, he thought, as anyone would be, at least until he knew who was entering the house unannounced. Rounding the corner, he did not have to feign his surprise. Two men were stepping over the threshold, the one in front dark-skinned and as big as a house, his bulk shielding the other from view. "Hello?" he said, feigning a nervous smile and allowing the question to hang in the air.

The black man was the first to react, his eyes registering first, surprise, and then recognition. In an instant he was reaching under his jacket for the gun and moving sideways, shouting something to his companion.

Dancer dove back into the hall, his shoulder bouncing off the wall, and hit the first bedroom running, slamming and locking the door in one fluid motion. He shoved the dresser against the door as reinforcement and then picked up the heavy desk chair and swung it at the window. The glass shattered, spilling to the lawn below. He tucked his head into his shoulder and followed the glass out, headfirst.

Adrian was behind Jones and facing sideways, holding the door, when he heard the voice. He felt the big man tense, and a fraction of a second later, Jones went tearing down the hall, yelling at Adrian to cover the outside.

Dancer hit the ground in a roll, springing upright as the momentum of the fall propelled his legs around. He sped into the yard next door and vaulted the fence just as Adrian rounded the corner of the house. Dancer was two blocks away before he remembered the laptop. *Fuck,* he thought.

Adrian had caught a glimpse of the man's back as he went over the fence, but nothing more, and knew that a foot chase would have been futile, particularly at night. *That guy is fast*, he thought as he walked back into the house. He found Jones in the bedroom, eying the damage.

"That answers one thing," commented Jones.

"What?" Adrian asked.

"The question of what happened to the guy who was in the car with Lindsey. He looks different, but there was something about his eyes. I recognized him."

A cloud of anger spread across Adrian's face. "That was him? I never saw his face, but gauging by the fact that he came out to the living room instead of bolting right away, I'd say that he didn't expect to be recognized at all. What the hell was he doing here?"

Jones backed out of the room, and Adrian trailed him down the hall. They stepped into the office and stopped, eyes fixed on the laptop computer atop the desk. Adrian walked over and touched the mouse pad, optimistically thinking how sweet it would be if this machine had all the answers. The password screen popped up.

"We secured Jason's laptop before he went to the safe house. This one belongs to someone else."

Jones leaned over the side of the desk and scooped the padded bag from the floor. Fingering the tag on the handle, he said, "Matthew J. Pierce. So the guy who rabbited and Jason's friend Mr. Pierce have been staying here ... or at least using the place."

Adrian pulled out his phone and dialed Melodie. "I've got a laptop here that could belong to Matthew Pierce, but it's password-protected. Can you give me something to try?"

Melodie was silent for a few seconds, thinking. "Social Security number," she said, and gave it to him.

He typed the nine digits and hit the *Enter* key. "No go," he said, looking at the failed login. "Anything else?"

She thought about Matthew Pierce, his life reduced to the content of the file. He had been a member of an elite unit, involved in dozens of operations in the Middle East, Eastern Europe, and Africa. By all accounts, the man was a hero ... and a patriot. Even the psych eval painted a picture of a well-balanced and intensely loyal man who had, on multiple occasions, put his life on the line for his country and his fellow soldiers. The army was his entire life, until he had been caught up in a reduction in force eighteen months ago. She called out his detachment designation, "1-S-F-O-D-Delta."

"Delta Force?" Jones said, his eyes wide. "Shit. What is he doing mixed up in this?"

Adrian knew that Melodie's talents as an analyst were second to none, but he was still surprised when the password was accepted. "We're in!" he exclaimed.

"Bingo," she replied, the smile radiating through her voice. "You still have the flash drive, right?"

"Got it right here."

"Okay. Plug it in and count to fifteen, then take it out.

I'll let you know what we find."

"Mind if I poke around for a few minutes?"

"Not at all. You won't even know we're there."

Adrian had just clicked on the laptop's file manager when the thought hit him. *Lindsey.* A cold shiver of dread slipped down his spine. He pulled out his phone, hit the tiny photo of her face, and waited for the ring. He pulled on Jones's sleeve. "Call Jazz. They need to get out of the house. And let's get a couple of cops over here to keep this place locked down."

"Too late," Jones said, looking out the window at the red and blue strobes lighting the night. "They're already here."

Chapter 65

Dancer walked briskly up the narrow street, wondering how the black man had recognized him. He ripped the SIM card from his cell and broke it into pieces. As he tossed the fragments into the gutter, he cursed again. He had acted hastily, forgetting to warn Squid before destroying the phone's chip. Now he needed a working phone. He took a circuitous route through town, sticking to one-way streets that would make him more difficult to locate. Twenty minutes later, he walked into the Starbucks and ordered a flat white. He took a seat against the wall, near the manager's office and with a view to the outside.

There were few people in the store, and he quickly realized that lifting an untended laptop or phone without being noticed would be next to impossible. He stood to leave just as a young woman picked up her coffee and turned to go. Dancer held the door and watched as she walked toward the green Toyota, its lights blinking as she punched her key fob. He noticed the yacht club sticker on the windshield and decided to risk it, taking eight long strides and opening the passenger door just as she was inserting the key into the ignition. She turned toward him, surprise and then shock written on her otherwise pretty face. A frightened squeak escaped when she saw the gun.

"Oh God, please ..."

"Start the car and keep your hands on the steering wheel. Do you understand?"

The woman nodded, tears pooling in her eyes.

"Pull out of the lot. Where do you live?"

He could see the lie forming on her lips and reached for the wallet she had laid on the console. He read the address on her license. "Is there anyone else at your home?"

She shook her head. "No. Please ..."

He wondered for a moment if she had kids. That would be a problem, but the car seemed devoid of the usual detritus that accompanied a family. "Do you have children?"

"No," she stammered, tears now streaming freely down her face. "I live alone."

"Good," he said. "Just drive home and don't screw up."

She drove away from the center of town, toward the border with Swampscott, and pulled into a short drive beside a small Cape house.

He pointed the gun at her chest, thankful that it was nighttime and that the small lot wasn't brightly lit. "Pick up your coffee and get out of the car. I want you to turn around and smile at me, and then we're going into the house. Do exactly as I say, and you won't get hurt."

She did as she was told, although he could see the quiver in her lower lip. As she walked up the steps to the front door, he noticed for the first time that she was wearing exercise clothing, as if she'd come fresh from the gym or a yoga class. She was trim and fit, her legs and arms tanned and muscled. When she put the key in the door's lock, he saw the gentle swell of her breasts and felt himself harden. He pushed the door open, taking her elbow and guiding her forcefully inside before kicking the door closed. He grabbed her wrist, and she tried to pull away.

"Don't make this any harder on yourself," he said. "Where is your electrical tape?" He saw the panic in her face then, and he slapped her—hard. "Where is it?"

Sobbing, she pointed toward the small kitchen. "In the drawer!"

He pulled her arm up behind her back and shoved her forward and, as she opened her mouth to scream, pinned her against the refrigerator. "Shut up and don't fucking move." He pressed his weight against her and pulled the drawer open with his free hand. Finding the tape, he used his teeth to rip off a long strip. He bound her hands and used more tape to secure a kitchen towel over her mouth. When he withdrew a knife from the block on the counter, he saw the hope dim in her eyes. He smiled and then dragged her up the stairs to the bedroom.

Chapter 66

Matt Pierce turned onto Gregory Street and hit the brakes. A block and a half away, two patrol cars blocked the street, their emergency lights flashing. He could see clusters of people standing on the sidewalk, wondering what was going on. Matt wondered, too. Jason's house was lit up like Gillette Stadium on game night. He willed himself to breathe, and slowly turned left at the next corner. He drove cautiously through town, his thoughts racing, and finally pulled into a parking area on Village Street.

He thumbed through his phone. No missed calls, no texts. Whatever had happened with that maniac Dancer, there had apparently been no time to call or send a warning text. He pulled up a Facebook page that was generally spot-on at reporting Marblehead's newsworthy material in a timely fashion, but found nothing. *Dammit,* he thought. *This could ruin everything.* Months of preparation, and the entire operation could fall apart ... all because of Dancer.

He had never trusted the guy. Even Sophia, who spent a good deal of her time defending psychotic Russian mobsters, found her nerves fraying when Dancer was nearby. Tin Man had brought Dancer into the group, insisting that his skills were a necessity for the operation to have any chance of success. From Matt's point of view, Dancer's only talent was a penchant for inventing terrible ways of taking human life. On multiple occasions over the last few months, Dancer had pointed out innocent passersby, referred to them as "witnesses," and described the manner in which he would like to interrogate them using torture and mutilation. And then he would smile.

Matt and Sandbox believed that Dancer's warped psychosis was, in their opinion, a detriment to the mission. Their assignment was not about a lust for vengeance or sadistic pleasure—this was about protecting the homeland from those who would threaten it—and they had no confidence in his commitment. They had spoken to Tin Man, who had promised to address the issue. But Dancer's behavior was so disturbing that, after taking great pains to let the truck driver live after hijacking the explosives, Sandbox had climbed into Dancer's van instead of riding with Squid. They were afraid that Dancer would circle back around to eliminate "the witness."

Christ. Witnesses. He picked up the phone and dialed Sandbox. "There are cops at the house," he said when Sandbox answered. "And there's nothing from Dancer. He's either gone dark, or they have him in custody. Or he's dead."

"Did you call Tin Man?"

"Not yet."

"Good. I'm just crossing into town from Salem. Where are you?"

"The parking lot at Village Plaza. I can't leave the car here, though. I'll find a space on the street. Pick me up around the corner, on Village Street."

Five minutes later, Squid stepped to the curb as the big black SUV made the left turn. He climbed into the car and pointed. "Pull over up there. Let's talk."

Behind the wheel, Randall Forsythe looked over at his best friend. "What's your gut telling you?"

"I left him at the house two hours ago. He had no reason to leave unless something spooked him. Still, he should have called. My worry is that Jason's friends are back in town. Maybe one of them dropped by, and things went to shit. Regardless, if the girl is back, it's trouble. He wanted to kill her down in DC. I have a feeling he might try again."

"Piece of crap. He's going to jeopardize the operation. What all did you leave at the house?"

"Clothes, computer, toothbrush. There are plenty of prints and DNA, if that's what you're asking, but someone would have to have some serious juice to pull our records. I changed the password on the computer yesterday ... used our old unit designation. I had Dancer memorize it, but it's not something that a cop is going to guess. Doesn't matter, anyhow. I don't keep any operational details on that machine; everything's encrypted and tucked away on the cloud."

"Unless Dancer screwed up."

"Always a possibility."

"Which way?"

"Move over. I'll drive." Matt took the wheel and steered the car through the narrow roads and up the hill onto Abbot Street, toward Lindsey Carlisle's house.

Chapter 67

Squid pulled to the curb and cut the engine—two houses down from Lindsey Carlisle's home. A lone lamp, along with the winks of light from a television, illuminated the crack between the curtains in a ground-level room. Otherwise, the house was dark.

"Options?" asked Sandbox.

"We can't sit here very long; we'll attract attention. This is a small town; people notice strangers and cars they don't know."

"Maybe we should encourage her to get out of the house for the evening… give ourselves a chance to track him down."

"How do you want to play it?"

"Report a fire?"

"That could work."

A big SUV came around the corner in front of them, its headlight beams on bright and causing them to squint against the light. A fraction of a second later, another pulled up behind. Squid swiveled to look over his left shoulder and came face-to-face with the muzzle of a gun.

"FBI! Put your hands on the wheel, asshole!" roared Jazz. When the driver hesitated, she yelled, "Don't even think about it."

Sandbox grabbed the door handle, ready to leap out of the passenger side, and found himself staring at Lindsey. She had a gun leveled at his chest, but the hand that held it was shaking."

"Wait a minute," he shouted, and then flung the door open, striking the girl and sending her stumbling backward. He rolled out of the car and sprang to his feet, pulling his own gun from his waistband and moving fast. He slapped the gun out of the girl's grasp and flung his forearm around her neck, pulling her backward and using her as a shield. *Fuck*, he thought. *It's all going to shit. Time to put the cards on the table.*

"You can't win this," Sandbox yelled. "NCSC is onto you. It's only a matter of time. They want to hang you, and if you kill me, they won't think twice about taking you out."

Adrian, having shoved the SUV into park and jumped out of the vehicle, had circled to the side of the man holding Lindsey just in time to hear him speak. Adrian blinked, confused. What the hell was the man talking about? *NCSC? The National Counterintelligence and Security Center?* From the darkness, he yelled, "Mr. Forsythe, I am Special Agent Adrian Santori from the FBI. Let the woman go, and we'll talk."

"There's nothing to talk about. You think that badge protects you? We know what you've done."

"Mr. Forsythe, I don't want to have to shoot you, but I swear to God that if you don't drop your gun and release the woman, I won't give a damn that General Haskell asked us to keep you alive. I *will* put a bullet through your brain."

Sandbox stiffened at the mention of his uncle, the

general. The general knew about the operation, knew what he was doing. They had told him that the general had signed off on the mission. Why would he have told these guys anything? "Nice try," he called back. "My uncle is a good soldier ... a patriot. He would never have anything to do with the likes of you."

Adrian was now thoroughly confused. *What in the hell is going on here?* He glanced at Jazz, who continued to be focused on the form of Matthew Pierce sitting rigidly behind the wheel. Quickly scanning the street, he spotted the dark shadow creeping up behind Forsythe.

"Mr. Forsythe, drop the gun so we can talk this out. You are a hero to your country. You don't want to hurt this innocent woman." He could see Lindsey's eyes, wide with fear ... but there was a set to her mouth, and he saw her arm wriggle free from the sling ... *Oh no!*

Lindsey twisted her torso down and around, swinging her arm up and smashing the heavy cast solidly into Randall Forsythe's nose and forehead. Forsythe's gun hand moved reflexively, and he pulled the trigger as he staggered backward, straight into the massive hulk of Jones. Jones ripped the gun away and wrenched his arms back, driving Forsythe to his knees. Forsythe was strong and a master of close combat, and he started to spring up, arching his body away, when Jones raised his massive arm and swung the butt of the gun into his temple.

"No!" Adrian screamed, running over to the heap on the ground that was Lindsey Carlisle. He pulled out his phone and dialed 9-1-1, yelling at the operator and frantically trying to check Lindsey's body, every semblance of calm lost.

Lights had popped on in the houses lining the street, people peering out their windows or venturing to step outside their doorways. Jazz, still pointing her gun at the frozen figure of Matthew Pierce, yelled into the night. "This is the FBI. For your safety, please stay inside and lock your doors until the situation is under control. Please! Right now!"

Wanting to make sure the crowd was obeying her commands, she let her eyes drift away from Pierce for just an instant. It was enough. He thrust the door open and dove out of the car, rolling solidly into Jazz's legs and knocking her to the ground. She had managed to hold onto the gun, but she was out of position. He leveled a kick at her arm, and the gun clattered to the street.

A split second later, Matt was on the run. His legs pumped furiously as he charged straight into the knot of curious onlookers, knowing that the feebs would never shoot into a crowd of bystanders. He kept moving, low and fast, behind walls and cars and trees, and then he was clear. He heard the wail of sirens and slowed his pace, to all appearances just someone taking a stroll on a pleasant summer night.

Lindsey had landed facedown, and Adrian could see a pool of blood spreading beneath her. He rolled her over and carefully began searching for the wound. The lack of light hampered visibility, and at first he thought she had taken a shot to her chest, because of the blood saturating the front of her shirt. He finally discovered the oozing hole in her upper arm and knew the bullet had found a major vein. He yanked off his belt and wound it around her upper arm, tightening the loop until it seemed that the blood flow had slowed.

Her eyes fluttered open, and she groaned. “You’re okay,” he murmured. “You’re going to be fine.” He stood, intending to help Jazz, when Jones called out, telling him to stay with Lindsey. He knelt, cradling her head in his lap, and did his best to reassure and soothe her.

Matt worked his way down the hill, and then back in a wide circle. He slipped silently behind the dark brown house and eased to the ground, belly-crawling down the sloping lawn toward the boulder near the corner of the lot. His position and the pulsing emergency lights from the police cruisers and ambulances afforded a clear view of the chaos on the street.

He spotted Randy on a stretcher—unmoving and eyes closed—with an attendant checking his vital signs. Randy’s arms were hidden beneath his body, and Matt knew that he was handcuffed behind his back. It wasn’t until the attendant wrapped the bandage around his head that Matt realized his friend was still alive. He almost laughed then, wondering if Randy was awake and the cuffs were already open ... and what his next move would be.

Not twenty feet away, Lindsey Carlisle lay on the ground, with two EMTs working feverishly and FBI Special Agent Santori kneeling beside her. Their voices were surprisingly audible.

“I nailed him,” Lindsey said.

“You certainly did.”

“I think I may have rebroken my arm. I hit him hard.”

"We'll get it fixed."

"Did he shoot me? I can't feel my other arm."

"Yes, but you're going to be fine."

"Look, ma, no arms." She tried to laugh, but the effort dissolved into a sob.

Matt noticed the belt wrapped tight just above her armpit, and he could make out the *T* someone had scrawled on her forehead. *Tourniquet. Shit*, he thought.

Chapter 68

The Marblehead Police had resisted Adrian's request that they lock down Jason's home on Gregory Street. They had finally agreed, grudgingly, to place a patrolman at the scene until Adrian and Jones returned. Adrian had downplayed the danger posed by the man who had jumped through the window—spinning the tale of a computer geek who had run afoul of the FBI's cyber division.

But now the local cops were steamed. One of their citizens had almost been murdered on one of their pretty little streets, and cooperation among agencies was quickly fading as it became apparent that Adrian wasn't sharing all he knew.

"One down," Adrian said to Jones and Jazz. They were standing at the edge of the sidewalk, away from the crowds that had gathered on both ends of the street. "I really thought the man from Jason's house would show up here. I didn't expect these other two."

Jazz put her hand on her hip. "He could still show up, you know. You said he's on foot, and I'll bet you that thing with Lindsey in DC probably didn't sit well. Now that he knows we're in town, he could be out for some payback.

Jones and I should hang around for a while, just in case."

Nodding, Jones agreed. "What have we got to lose?"

Adrian winced. "A lot, actually. Okay, do it. I'll make nice with the locals. They're going to impound Pierce's car; I'll convince them that ours aren't directly involved. Jazz, take one of our SUVs and find someplace else to park it. Damn thing is like a big neon sign screaming *Feds*. And both of you, be careful."

Dancer was driving down Pleasant Street, just passing Village Plaza, when two big black SUVs and three cop cars—light bars ablaze—pulled out a block ahead and turned his way. He pulled the green Toyota to the right curb and waited for the little parade to pass. He turned his head to watch, cursing out loud when he recognized the SUV trailing the lead patrol car. From the sticker on its front bumper, *Your mind is your best weapon*, he knew the vehicle belonged to Sandbox. The windows of the second SUV were darkly tinted, but he could guess who was in it: the same men who had entered Jason's house.

He unraveled the sequence of events quickly enough. Sandbox and Squid had been searching for him. They were fully aware that he wanted to eliminate the girl—the bitch had almost killed him—and they assumed he would show up there. Well, they were right about one thing: he was going to show up. But where was Squid?

He parked the car behind the movie theater, locked the doors, and walked up the hill to Abbot Street.

The house was easy enough to locate, with one lighted room downstairs, a cluster of neighbors lingering on the sidewalk, and the police photographer capturing every detail. He kept walking, on the opposite side of the street, nodding a polite greeting to the bystanders, while noticing the latex glove on the grass and the irregular circle of disinfectant that had been poured over a blood spill.

He wondered about the victim—or victims if Sandbox and Squid had been involved. Part of him hoped it was the girl, although the thought agitated him. He wanted her for himself. His thoughts turned back to Squid and Sandbox, and he waged an inner battle about whether or not to be concerned with their fate. He finally shrugged off any concern about Sandbox. While Sophia would take exception if something had happened to her man, Squid was the more important component. The operation would be crippled without him. Dancer bit back his worry; he would know soon enough.

Returning forty-five minutes later, he found the neighborhood quiet and empty of police. The sole light in the house was still on, leading him to wonder if it was on a timer or if the girl was actually inside. He slipped into the backyard, stepped onto the deck, and quietly made his way to the back door. He pulled the two picks from the seams of his wallet and smiled as the lock easily succumbed to his touch.

He stepped into the kitchen and stood perfectly still. He listened to the house talk, its windows chattering as the trees waved their branches over the glass and its wooden frame emitting the occasional groan. Leaving the back door ajar, he crept silently across the hardwood floor. Three steps into the room, he heard it: a sound not made by the house, but rather by someone in it. He was not alone. He waited, completely still, thinking about the girl.

The rollover in Virginia had been an eye-opener, and he would not underestimate her again. He now knew that she had received at least some rudimentary training—most likely from Jason—and was observant and resourceful. He found the thought of wrestling with her tantalizing. Involuntarily, he started breathing a little faster.

The only light in the room emanated from the digital clock of the microwave ... not enough to see clearly but enough to detect the mass of the appliances and cupboards. His senses were heightened, his eyes now fully adjusted to the dark, and he thought he detected a shadow passing over the wall in the adjoining hallway. He rose on the balls of his feet, preparing to pounce, when he heard the unmistakable metallic *clack* of a round being chambered. He tried to absorb the curious realization that the sound had come from behind him.

"FBI," the voice thundered. "Raise your arms out to the side! Right now!"

A second voice, this one female and from somewhere in front of him, yelled, "Do it, asshole!"

He sprang into action instantly. In one fluid sequence he pirouetted back toward the door, threw it open, powered across the deck, and leaped mightily onto the lawn. He seemed to float midair for a moment, as if in a ballet, his legs split in a classic grand jeté.

Jazz lifted her weapon but did not fire, the beauty of the leap so visually stunning. In her hesitation, the man disappeared into the night.

"What the hell was that?" she howled in frustration. "Fucking *Swan Lake*?"

Jones flipped the light switch and found the roll of paper towels. He tore off a sheet and wiped the perspiration from his forehead. He had been standing in the tiny pantry at the back of the kitchen, covering the back door, when the man had broken in.

He shook his head in wonder. "You know, Adrian said that guy was fast, but I've never seen anyone take such an incredible jump. It was like watching Mikhail Baryshnikov."

"Incredible or not, we just got our butts handed to us. What now?"

"The hospital. I don't think ballet boy will be coming back anytime soon, so let's go see how heroic that other asshole is feeling now."

Convinced that Dancer would eventually make an appearance at Lindsey Carlisle's house, Matt had waited. He had watched the police cruisers and the ambulance depart, observed as the photographer painstakingly documented every possible item of evidence, and seen the crowd of gawkers gradually wander back to their homes. After years of working in Special Forces, he had learned the value of patience. This time, he was rewarded by the shadow flitting across the side of the house and into the backyard.

He inched around the boulder and over the dewy lawn to the retaining wall and lowered himself to the sidewalk. He stepped noiselessly across the street and, as Dancer had done, crept low along the side of the house. He was just peering around the back corner when he heard the crash. It took a second for his brain to process that Dancer had flown out of the house and across the yard in one of his amazing leaps.

Matt eyed Dancer's direction of travel and hustled back to the street. He hit the sidewalk at a good clip and headed down the hill on what he calculated to be a reasonable intercept path. Sure enough, he spotted Dancer a few minutes later, fast-stepping in the direction of the theater.

He was almost caught up when Dancer pressed the fob in his hand and the lights of a green Toyota winked in response.

Making no effort to cover the sound of his approach, he trotted over to the car as Dancer turned around to face him. "Where did you get the ride?" he asked. This wasn't just a vehicle stolen from the street; Dancer had keys.

Dancer eyed him calmly. "Borrowed it from a friend."

Matt opened the passenger door and peered inside. *Not a guy's car*, he thought. He opened the glove box, pulled out the registration, read the name Dianne Talbot, and felt the hairs rise on the back of his neck. "Fuck! What the hell did you do?"

Dancer gave Matt a feral grin and climbed into the car.

Chapter 69

Saturday morning
Marblehead, Massachusetts

Matt Pierce stood at the Boston Yacht Club's dock on the west side of Marblehead Harbor, waiting to board the first launch of the morning. He cast an anxious glance at Dancer, who had been behaving like some hopped-up meth head all night. The weirdo seemed calmer now, although his eyes still held the hint of a wild animal.

Matt had commanded Dancer to pop the trunk of the green car—sure that Dianne Talbot's corpse was inside—and found it empty. Dancer had insisted that the woman was a friend who had gone out of town for a few days, although Matt found that hard to swallow. Dancer hadn't spent enough time in Marblehead to establish any sort of relationship with anyone. Still, they had returned to Dianne's house and spent the night there—Matt in the downstairs guest room and Dancer in the master bedroom on the second floor—before leaving the house just before dawn.

They parked the car on Washington Street and walked down to the town landing for an early breakfast at the

Driftwood—an omelet for Matt and French toast for Dancer—before heading up the hill to the BYC. Matt's uneasiness had spiked when Dancer insisted that they walk instead of drive, claiming that parking would be impossible to find near the yacht club. It made no sense. With parking on the street limited to two hours, it wouldn't be long before the police ticketed the car ... and then they would tow it. Dancer had shrugged it off, and Matt had not pressed the issue further. He had bigger questions to consider, not the least of which was whether or not Sandbox had revealed anything about the operation.

The sixty-foot Manhattan Sunseeker had been moored near the harbor entrance since early May. One of Sophia's clients, ancient and feeble and richer than God, had been so taken with her that he had offered the use of his yacht whenever she liked. Sophia had never taken him up on the proposition—until last September, when she asked if she might borrow the boat for the following summer. The old man had readily agreed, provided that she find a suitable captain. Matt, an accomplished yachtsman, fit the bill.

The geezer had gone a step further, insisting that they moor the boat in Marblehead, rather than Beverly, and applied to the Marblehead harbormaster for a temporary mooring. After waiting anxiously through the fall and winter, the confirmation had finally come through in April. They left Long Island at the beginning of May, cruising first to Newport and then on to Marblehead.

While the mooring was inconvenient to their leased apartment in Beverly, it was certainly closer to Jason's apartment, and Matt began to spend more time there. Proximity to Jason, however, also meant proximity to Lindsey and the potential of a surprise encounter. But Lindsey had not stopped by, and indeed had spent little time socializing with Jason over the last few weeks. And they were no closer to Cat Powell than they had been months ago. Although, he now realized, they might have an opportunity if Lindsey's injuries drew the spy to her bedside. He pushed the notion aside. *First things first.*

Matt and Dancer thanked the launch driver and hauled themselves onto the sleek yacht, the *St. Petersburg's Penance*. Matt had never been told the meaning behind the boat's name, but he could guess. The old man was a Russian mobster.

Matt conducted a check of the yacht's exterior and interior before moving up to the cockpit and starting the twin Volvo Penta engines. The props spun up, and he set them to idle before signaling Dancer to release the mooring ropes. Easing out of the harbor, he set the navigation system to take them to a spot near Georges Island, one of the thirty-four spots of land in the national recreation area known as the Boston Harbor Islands.

The ride to Boston took just over an hour. At a few minutes after ten, he motored up to the Georges Island dock, where Sophia Capreze and Tanya Goreva stood waving.

With Dancer right behind her, Sophia climbed up to the cockpit, her face a mask of distaste. She leaned over to Matt and hissed in his ear, "Get him away from me!"

Matt pointed at Dancer. "Get the ropes and let's get off this dock."

Dancer's face reddened. "I'm not your deck bitch."

Keeping his tone even, Matt turned to face him. "Unless you know how to run this boat, you'll do exactly what I tell you to do. Now, go tend the ropes."

Dancer thrust him a defiant look, standing his ground for a good fifteen seconds before backing away.

"God, I detest that man," Sophia said.

"He's not my favorite person, either."

"Where's Randy?"

This was the moment Matt dreaded. "The police have him, Sophia."

Her eyes flew open. "What?"

"That FBI guy and some black guy showed up at Jason's last night. Dancer bolted, but without his phone. Randy had gone out, and when he got back, saw all the cops. He called me, and we went looking for Dancer. We thought he might try to find the Carlisle woman, so we drove to her house. We got jumped. The whole thing went to shit, and I managed to get out; Randy didn't. I'm sorry, but there was nothing I could have done."

Matt knew her to have a temper and expected a volatile reaction. Instead, she said, "It's not your fault. I know that you would do anything for Randy, as he would do anything for you. It's that asshole Dancer who caused the problem."

"To be fair, Sophia, those guys just barged into the house and Dancer ran. Can't blame him."

"He should have taken his phone."

Matt pressed his lips together. There would be no reasoning with Sophia on this issue. "We can't focus on that. We've got a job to do."

Sophia looked out over the water, her eyes moist. "Then let's go."

Matt motored across the water to Peddocks Island, dropping anchor just offshore.

"Is he on time?"

"Yes. Everything is set. He's on an airplane now and has a few things to take care of once he lands. He'll catch the ferry at three o'clock and should be here by four forty-five."

"Let's get settled. We need to look natural, like we're out for a day in the sun. You and your mother should slather on some sunscreen and make yourselves comfortable on the bathing deck. I'll make sure Dancer doesn't bother you."

"If he does, my mother will probably carve his spleen out. She's very protective."

Matt wondered how she had invented the foundation for that remark, but resisted the temptation to respond. From everything he had learned from Randy, Tanya Goreva had not done a very good job of protecting her two-year-old daughter all those years ago.

Chapter 70

Saturday night
Boston, Massachusetts

Adele exited the Boeing Triple Seven and joined the other tired passengers funneling into the immigration and customs checkpoints at Boston's Logan International Airport. She had received the text from Melodie at four minutes after ten, within seconds of the plane touching down on the runway: Govt Center. Everyone. Transport waiting at the curb.

The message itself was not so worrisome; rather, it was the timing: ten o'clock on a Saturday night.

Leaving the customs area, she pointed the group toward two waiting Suburbans, grabbed her overnight tote, and strode to the restroom. Cat Powell emerged three minutes later, dressed in jeans and a black sweater, with the wig and cane tucked into her bag.

As she climbed into the second Suburban, she wondered what had transpired during their grueling eighteen-hour journey from Mumbai to London to Boston. She had checked her e-mail frequently during the flight, found it empty each time, and wondered at the anomaly. Now, the lack of communication and the diversion to Government

Center bore ominous undertones.

With the drivers disinclined to participate even in the most pedestrian of conversations, the behemoth vehicles sped through the Sumner Tunnel and into the city, finally disgorging their human cargo into the underground parking garage of One Center Plaza. When the men wordlessly ushered them to the elevators, she bit back the urge to say *Six, please, FBI Boston Field Office* and instead leaned tiredly against the glossy panels at the back of the car.

She knew something was wrong the instant the doors slid open. Paul and Adrian, their faces grim, were waiting. *It's bad*, she thought. *This is why my e-mail has been so eerily quiet.*

The question popped out unbidden. "Tom?" As one they shook their heads, and before either could speak, the other name escaped her lips. "Lindsey?" The calmness of the question belied the wave of fear threatening to consume her.

Adrian nodded and took her elbow, drawing her away from the group. "She's at Mass General. She's going to be fine, but she will be there for a few days."

"What happened?" she asked, keeping her voice level.

"She was shot during a confrontation with Randall Forsythe and Matthew Pierce."

Her eyes narrowed to slits. "Confrontation? We brought her on as an analyst. She was never supposed to be operational ... that was our agreement!"

Deciding to save the details for another time, he gave her the briefest of summaries. "It wasn't like that. She saw a situation and thought she could help. She grabbed the spare weapon from Jazz's pack."

She took a deep breath and looked up at the ceiling. "How bad is it?"

"The bullet hit the brachial vein. The doctors say it's likely she'll suffer muscle and nerve damage, although it's too soon to quantify the extent."

"Who's with her?"

Paul smiled. "Tom."

Adrian added, "Your husband is taking very good care of her."

"Thank you for calling him. I'm feeling somewhat reassured. Just promise me that you will keep me informed."

"That's a promise."

"So fill me in. What is happening?"

They led her into the crowded conference room, where Leo Farrell, the Special Agent in Charge of the Boston office, was huddled with Jeffrey and Adam from MI6, and a man in military uniform she recognized as General Haskell.

Sheila, Barbara, and Cam pressed against her, finding seats as Paul called the group to attention.

"Last night, our team got into a confrontation with two operators originally from Delta Force. These men are part of the group that we believe to have been involved in the North Carolina hijacking a number of months ago, in which a significant amount of C-4, as well as a quantity of Stinger missiles, were stolen."

A low rumble of surprise echoed through the room. Most knew of the missing C-4, but few knew about the other weaponry.

Paul paused a moment to let the emotions settle before continuing. "One of those men is presently at MGH—Massachusetts General Hospital for those of you who aren't from Boston. We are waiting for him to regain consciousness." The screen behind him lit up with the file photo of Randall Forsythe.

"When Forsythe wakes up, General Haskell," Paul said, tipping his head toward the two-star, "is here to help convince the soldier to talk."

Paul flipped to the next image, a photo of Matthew Pierce.

"This is the man who escaped. We are in the dark about his current whereabouts. Take a good look at his face, because we have reason to believe that these men are part of a plot against a new facility being opened tomorrow in the Seaport district. A number of high-profile guests are scheduled to attend, including the governor, the mayor of Boston, and a delegation of foreign dignitaries and businesspeople.

"Our British friends," he said, acknowledging Jeffrey and Adam, "have been trying to get a bead on Farid Mahdavi and Tanya Goreva. Once the Indians learned that Mahdavi has some connections to Pakistan, they became considerably more cooperative. They finally sent word that Mahdavi boarded an Emirates flight for Dubai yesterday afternoon.

"Once we knew his destination, we used a bit of influence to determine that Mahdavi completed government formalities and entered the country legally on his Iranian passport. Our second request, for information on his Pakistani alter ego, took a little longer."

He displayed the two file photos that had been used in the facial recognition match, and followed them with the image taken by the drone.

"We now know that Mahdavi, using the name Zahid Kashani, boarded an Emirates flight to New York and landed at nine this morning. We believe that he is orchestrating the plot, and Melodie and Trent are working now to learn his whereabouts."

"He is coming here," Cat stated flatly. The sound of her voice startled her; she had meant it as a thought to herself.

"I believe you are most likely correct, but ..."

The speakerphone crackled to life as Melodie interrupted. "Cat *is* right. He went over to JetBlue, arrived Logan at eleven thirty, and hopped into a cab. Jones tracked down the driver, who says he dropped Mahdavi at Davis Square in Somerville."

Adrian whistled. "That's the area where we found the C-4 in the apartment."

"Interesting," Cat observed. "Let's come back to that. What about Tanya Goreva?"

Paul rested his arm on the table and leaned forward. "Tanya Goreva was more of a challenge. While Gabe was flying over the Arabian Sea, he managed to access the security camera system at Mumbai's airport. He finally found her, checking in for a nonstop on United Airlines to Newark Thursday night. She arrived at five twenty yesterday morning."

"She has a US visa?" Adrian asked.

"She does, issued by the consulate in St. Petersburg, sponsored by her daughter, Ms. Cabreze."

"Despite the fact that she is the wife of a former KGB agent?"

Paul nodded patiently. "She's not the first. We have issued visas to many former KGB personnel, and their families, since the breakup of the Soviet Union. Melodie, did you find Tanya?"

"Yes. We have video from Newark. She took the monorail from the airport to the rail station and boarded a train headed north at ten twenty yesterday morning. We then have her on camera arriving at Boston's South Station at three fifteen yesterday afternoon."

"And from there?"

"Unfortunately, the exterior camera at the exit she used wasn't working. We're still looking for other sightings, but that's all we know as of now."

"So, they are both here already," Cat observed. "There are a couple of things bothering me. First, and maybe not the most important but it's nipping at my brain ... why would Mahdavi go to Somerville? Is he planning to collect the C-4 we found at Rajeev Malik's apartment? Surely he would have tried to contact Malik and would be concerned that there's no response. A smart person would avoid the place like the plague, and I think this guy is *very* smart. So why go there? Is there another sleeper? Is it feasible that the armaments from the North Carolina truck hijacking have ended up in Somerville?"

Adrian considered the state cop who had first appeared with the bomb squad in Somerville and later when the safe house in Foxborough had been attacked. The coincidence and the man's hostility had bothered him at the time, but he had not given it much thought since. There was also the matter of the Somerville police captain who seemed to bear some ill will toward the Statie. Why? He rubbed the back of his neck and said, "That's a good question. We'll look into it," and then entered a reminder into his phone.

Cat gave him a thumbs-up and continued, "The most critical question, however, is why would Matt Pierce and Randall Forsythe stay in Marblehead and use Jason's house? Jason was in the hospital; Lindsey and Gabe were not in town. There has to be a reason. What's the attraction?"

"They needed a temporary place to stay," offered Jones.

"I agree, but why?"

Arnie spoke up. "The harbor. That's the attraction. And the boats. "

Cat felt the gears drop into place. "They have a boat. Somehow their plan involves a damn boat. Get the Marblehead cops on the line and send them pictures of Forsythe and Pierce. I want those faces in front of the harbormaster and every launch driver who's been on duty in the last two months. Someone has seen them ... and their boat."

Jazz contacted the Marblehead Police, who contacted the harbormaster and the commodores of the town's five yacht clubs, who in turn did an admirable job of rousting their employees to complete a late-night task.

In years past, they would have scurried to find a sizable room, such as the cafeteria at the middle school. But in today's world of mobile devices, all could be accomplished in a simple text with two attachments. The assignment was simple: look at the attached photos. If the recipient had seen either of the faces, the Marblehead Police were to be contacted immediately.

The response was almost instantaneous. Patti Wegman

reported that she had taken two men out to the *St. Petersburg Penance* on the first run of the morning, but that she could only match one of them to the photos. She picked out Matt Pierce and described the other as five-ten or -eleven, light brown hair, gray eyes, weirdly graceful, and very jumpy. She had wondered if he was a drug addict.

When asked to clarify her "weirdly graceful" comment, she replied that it was the odd way he had jumped from the launch to the yacht … like a ballet jump.

Both the harbormaster and the commodore of the BYC confirmed that the boat was no longer tethered to its assigned mooring.

Young Patti helpfully added that the Finches and the Morriseys were also on the launch, so maybe they could offer more details.

The Morriseys stated that they had waited for another couple to join them, and so had not seen the big yacht leave the harbor. The Finches, on the other hand, were positive that the boat had steered a course south, toward Boston. They had watched it make the cut around Marblehead Neck and had marveled at its speed.

Adrian drummed his fingers on the table, weighing the best course of action. A general safety marine broadcast ran the risk of being heard by the very people they were trying to intercept, so he opted to make three personal calls to the US Coast Guard, the harbormaster of the Boston Police Harbor Unit, and the general manager of Boston Harbor Cruises. The latter held particular promise, as their fleet of over twenty vessels covered the entire Boston waterfront and many of the harbor islands. By the time the sun came up, a full-scale search would be underway.

As Adrian was wrapping up his last call, the phone buzzed with an incoming message. He checked the screen and then stood, mouthing to the others, "Forsythe's awake."

Chapter 71

Early Sunday morning
Boston, Massachusetts

General Carter Haskell peeked through the window into the hospital room where Randy Forsythe lay hooked to the tubes and electronics of modern medicine. The anomaly for this world-renowned institution of patient care was that both the hands and the legs of the patient were restrained. Forsythe seemed to be asleep, his face turned to the wall, but the general suspected that the man was fully awake and alert.

As they waited for the physician to finish his examination, Adrian Santori faced the highly decorated soldier. "I appreciate that you came, General. Ambassador Marshfield speaks highly of you, and we could certainly use your influence with Mr. Forsythe."

"Paul filled me in somewhat. I will talk with Randy and try to get him to cooperate, but I still don't fully comprehend what's going on."

"Nor do we, General. As we were trying to talk him down from a hostage situation last night, I mentioned your name ... something to the effect that I would shoot him despite your hope that we could keep him alive. His response was that you knew about his mission and that you would never have anything to do with the likes of me."

The general's face wrinkled into an expression of bewilderment. "What? What is he talking about?"

"That's what we need to find out. As you know, we have a credible threat against interests here in Boston, and we have proof that he is somehow involved. If he refuses to talk, there are a number of protocols that could be invoked, one of which is turning him over to Homeland. But I have an uneasy feeling that we're missing some crucial element. We need your help getting him to open up."

Carter Haskell shook his head slowly. "Randy isn't a terrorist ... it's always been his mission in life to wipe them off the face of the earth. It makes no sense."

"Then get him to tell us what he knows."

The door swung open, and the physician shut the door behind him, blocking their access. "This man was unconscious for almost twenty-four hours, which by our definition constitutes serious head trauma. He seems coherent at the moment, so I will allow you to see him, but he may well show confusion and loss of memory. Please keep your visit to fifteen minutes. If he shows any signs of delirium or seizure, or any abnormal symptoms for that matter, call for medical assistance immediately."

"Thank you, Doctor," Paul said. "I appreciate that you care about this one patient, but we have no time to wait for him to improve. I can assure you that if his condition deteriorates or becomes abnormal in any regard, we will call for help. But we cannot restrict our time to fifteen minutes given the urgency with which we need to proceed, because I'm sure that you can also appreciate our wish to avoid a flood of new patients requiring your care."

Startled, the doctor took a moment to absorb the implications of Paul's words and started to speak. "If he ..."

"Yes, we will call for help," Paul interrupted. "You have my word."

The doctor nodded and stepped away from the door, watching as the four serious-looking men and two women filed into the tiny room. Jones, trailing the pack, shut the door behind him and leaned against it, his broad back blocking the view from the hall.

Forsythe was propped up in bed, his eyes opening slowly at the sound of company. His face registered surprise on seeing the general, and his eyes opened fully when he recognized the Ambassador, but he quickly tamped his expression down to an impassive stare.

"Randy," the general said, "I don't know exactly what these people think you've done, but I do know that you are a patriot and would never intentionally bring harm to your country. You need to tell them whatever it is that's going on."

Forsythe was still groggy from his encounter with the big black man, but an icicle of dread pierced his consciousness as he heard the general's words. What was the general trying to tell him? He tried to muster his senses. "General Haskell, you know this is a classified operation. I cannot discuss mission-specific details without permission to do so. Are you ordering me to reveal this information?"

"Son, I am not aware of any classified mission involving you or your friend Pierce that has my name attached to it. So if you are somehow under the misconception that I have approved of your *mission*, you are mistaken. Now unless you have explicit orders from someone above my pay grade, and I find that exceedingly unlikely, you had damn well better start talking, right damn now!"

"Operation Jericho, sir!" Forsythe blurted.

General Haskell was perplexed. "Son, I have no idea what you're talking about." Wondering if the head injury was indeed causing delirium, he turned a questioning look to Paul Marshfield.

But Paul Marshfield's face had turned the color of ash. "Operation Jericho?" he managed to ask.

Forsythe angled his head toward the ambassador and said bitterly, "You have been trying to undermine us every step of the way."

Paul squinted at him in disbelief. "Mr. Forsythe, Operation Jericho is one of our most highly prized and classified operations. There are fewer than a dozen people on the planet who know of the program, and I can assure you that you and the general are not among them. So that begs the question of exactly what you think it is and where you got your information."

The realization hit Randall Forsythe like a stun grenade. He balled his hands into fists and broke out in a profuse sweat. He squeezed his eyes shut, seeing it now. The stranger had displayed his credentials, and he knew *everything*. He knew of Randy's exploits, his work with Delta Force, and his relationship to the general. He had even revealed the truth about Sophia's past. But when Randy thought back on the oddities—the curious assignments he and Matt had been given, the obscure communications, the involvement of that psycho Dancer—in the stark light of day, it all looked *off*. After the RIF, he had been at a loss—

desperate to get back in the game—and he had wanted to believe, had taken the man at his word. Now he just wanted to scream.

"He told us that Jericho was a black op you were running, with one of your people smuggling a dirty bomb, by ship, from Iran into India. He said your idea was to spark a major confrontation, with India on one side and Pakistan and Iran on the other. Tanya's job was to follow the operative, and she did ... onto a ship bound for Mumbai. When the boat docked, our job was to capture the man and wring out everything he knew."

Sickened, Paul recalled Jalil's rambling statements to Cat about being on a boat with a beautiful woman. "Mr. Forsythe, who told you this fairy tale?"

"I've never seen him in person; we met over Skype, and he kept the upper part of his face out of the viewer. I don't even know his real name," he said softly, opening his eyes. "He calls himself *Tin Man*."

Chapter 72

Randall Forsythe explained, "Tin Man enlisted Matt and me to be part of an undercover team. Sophia got into it a little later, helping us out with surveillance. Tin Man is a good friend of a guy whose son works at an ammunition plant; that's how he found out about the truck shipments. He told us that some of the loads weren't kosher. So, one of our first assignments was to intercept an illegal load of explosives. It was two and a half tons of C-4, along with some Stingers. We followed the instructions and delivered them to a warehouse in Somerville."

"And the logic for not having a full team of ATF and FBI to do the takedown?" Adrian asked.

"He said it was because they needed to keep it under wraps while a more thorough investigation took place. He said there was more of this going on, and they still didn't have enough to indict the ringleader. If there had been a regular squad, it would have become public, and whoever was at the top would just disappear. But by using us, it would just look like a rogue theft."

Incredulous, Jones asked, "And you believed this?"

Forsythe hung his head. "Mostly, because we felt like we were making a contribution. Matt and I did wonder if drugs might somehow be involved, but we didn't find anything to support that. And considering our mission, it didn't seem terribly important."

They questioned him further about the munitions, but Forsythe seemed to have no additional knowledge, claiming that everything had been left at the warehouse. He added that, with a map, he could probably find the building.

Adrian leaned forward, closer to Forsythe. "Let's talk about Lindsey. I'm assuming it was one of your team that took her from the Marriott down in DC?"

"Dancer. He doesn't really have anything to do with Matt and me; he's tight with Tin Man. I never heard his real name, just Dancer. All I can tell you is that he's a psychopath."

"Dancer?"

"It's like he studied ballet, or something like that. He does these bizarre leaps and shit."

Jazz and Jones looked at one another, and Jazz's right eyebrow lifted ever so slightly.

Adrian kept his eyes fixed on Randall Forsythe. "Why go after Lindsey?"

According to Forsythe, the person called Tin Man had proof that Lindsey's sister, Cat Powell, was one of the planners of Jericho. The sister, however, was so deep underground that no one knew how to find her. They thought Lindsey might know of her whereabouts, and had bugged her house and office. Matt had even been assigned to worm his way into Jason's life simply so they could use Jason as a conduit of information from Lindsey.

"And how was this Dancer person going to get this information?"

"Like I said, he is a psycho. I think he takes pleasure in torturing women, although he certainly enjoyed himself with that operative that Tanya brought to us."

Disgusted, Adrian slammed his fist on the bed. "And so when this guy missed his chance in DC, you decided to do a raid down in Foxborough? What were you going to do? Kill the rest of us?"

Randy's head jerked upward as if startled, looking at Adrian with wide eyes. "No! No! I swear to you, I had no idea what was going to happen down there. Tin Man said he had a tip from a credible source that the Powell woman was going to be there. They were going to arrest her."

"And yet everyone escaped, except Jason. Were you the sniper who shot him?"

"Sniper? What the hell are you talking about? Jason was caught in the crossfire!"

"No, Mr. Forsythe, he most certainly was not. Someone wanted him dead, because a sniper shot him while we were sitting in a truck having a face-to-face conversation with the State Police. Was it you? Or was it Matthew Pierce?"

"No! What? No way! We weren't even there!"

Paul listened to the soldier explain that they had been instructed to take the boat out after leaving the airport that morning. He was beginning to believe the man. How had this decorated veteran, who was certainly no dummy, been so thoroughly duped? *You believe what you need to believe*, he thought sadly.

"Tell us about the boat, Mr. Forsythe. What are they planning?"

Randy's eyes focused on the source of the question,

seeing her for the first time. "You ... you ..." he stuttered.

"Yes, I'm the one you've been looking for," Cat said. "But enough about that. Tell us about the boat."

Matt, he explained, was a sailor. He had grown up on the water, was sometimes more comfortable in the ocean than on land, so his friends had nicknamed him *Squid*. And he knew everything there was to know about boats. The plan was to pilot the big yacht from Marblehead into Boston, where they would pick up Sophia and her mother, Tanya Goreva, as well as another associate of Tin Man. On Sunday, they would help take down the financiers behind Cat Powell's organization.

"You said Tanya Goreva—with one of our operatives—was on a ship that docked in Mumbai. How is she involved?"

"Involved? She had some experiences in her past and wanted to help. She's dealt with some real monsters in her past and knows how to handle a gun. Or at least that's what she told us. She also said she wanted to help her daughter."

Cat shook her head and pressed her fingers to her temples. "Mr. Forsythe, do you have any idea what's on that yacht?"

"What do you mean?"

"Did you ever do a thorough search of that boat?"

"I don't understand. Are you telling me there *are* drugs on the boat?"

Cat tilted her head and stared at him, waiting to see if the pieces would snap into place. She watched the soldier's facial expressions, uncertain, questioning, puzzled, and finally, comprehending.

"This isn't about drugs at all, is it? This is about the

explosives and the missiles, isn't it?"

Continuing to hold his eyes, Cat let him work it out. "What do you think, Mr. Forsythe?"

"We would never ... oh my God! Matt and Sophia! They have nothing to do with this! Do you think these other people are going to try to ... that they're planning ..." He gave a low, mournful groan. "This isn't possible."

"Mr. Forsythe, this is very possible. We are doing our best to find them. When we do, we may need your help."

General Haskell stood, his face dark with barely contained anger. "I'm going to make a call. I'll have a SEAL team here in ninety minutes. I think you're going to need all the help you can get."

Chapter 73

Sunday morning
Boston Harbor, Massachusetts

Farid Mahdavi stood on the hydraulic swim platform at the yacht's stern and let his eyes adjust to the 3:00 a.m. darkness. Despite the absence of a moon, the glow from the city refracted through the thin cloud cover and cast a glow over the sea. Abeam, the outline of Peddocks Island formed a black hole against the shimmering water.

He pulled the paper from the tube and unrolled it, and then studied the thin adhesive decal before determining the correct position. He removed the backing first from the left lower corner, pressed it lightly against the surface, and then did the same with the upper right. Dissatisfied, he tried again.

With the boat rolling in the choppy seas, he was rocking back and forth and having trouble leveling the rectangular sheet. The decal was bright white, the exact shade of the transom, and should cover the existing paint. The length of the boat's name, *St. Petersburg's Penance*, complicated the effort because no trace of the original could be allowed to peek from above or below the new. Slowly and ever so methodically, he peeled the backing from the remainder of the decal and pressed the adhesive firmly into place.

He stood back, inspecting his work and frowning contemptuously at the new name: *Rasputin's Revenge*. He tossed the backing paper into the ocean, climbed back up to the main deck, and crept forward to the pulpit. Hooking an arm on the rail, he leaned over the port side of the bow and applied the new decal for the logo, and repeated the maneuver for the starboard side. Nauseated from the unrelenting motion, he once again leaned over the side and vomited into the churning water.

Wiping his mouth with his sleeve, he cast his gaze toward the city lights and smiled before turning and tiptoeing back to his berth. The yacht's new name and the logo would stand a cursory inspection, and even a computer check of the documentation. They might eventually discover that the real *Rasputin* was presently docked at a marina on the south shore of Long Island. By then, however, it would be too late.

As the sun erupted over the horizon, Matt Pierce stepped out of the forward cabin and moved into the galley. He set the coffee to brew and looked out over the water, eyeing the clouds gathering to the southwest, and then poured a mug of java and carried it over to the main helm console. Sinking into the soft leather seat, he called up the marine forecast. Hot today, with squalls predicted midafternoon.

He had been uneasy since picking up the third passenger from the dock at Peddocks Island the previous afternoon. The man had introduced himself as an Indian from Hyderabad, but Matt wasn't buying it. While he wasn't fluent, he'd spent enough time in Pakistan to recognize Punjabi when it was spoken, and he had overheard part of the man's phone conversation last night.

Something was off, and the little voice in his head—the one that had kept him alive all these years—was screaming like a banshee. While the others were occupied, he had decided to do a search of the yacht. The Stingers weren't difficult to find—it's not that easy to hide a five-foot-long case, much less two of them. With the yacht's proximity to Logan Airport, he could only imagine what mayhem might be planned for the day.

He picked up his mug and walked across the deck to the pulpit, studying the two boats anchored nearby. Both were still, their occupants probably enjoying the last minutes of quiet before the harbor became a beehive of activity.

He was turning back to the helm when he noticed a splotch of rusty-brown near the starboard rail. He moved closer and leaned out over the rail, where the stain ran across the bow and down to the waterline. Someone had been sick last night. He was pulling back when the oddity registered. He stuck his head back over the water and blinked. The logo had been changed. And on closer inspection, he could see the edges of the decal. *What the hell?*

He threw the remainder of his coffee over the rail, a plan forming in his head. He would see this mission through, but he had to get Sophia and her mother off the boat first.

Chapter 74

Sunday morning
Boston, Massachusetts

By 9:30 a.m., Adrian had reports of five Sunseekers spotted within the harbor and its immediate vicinity. The team pored over the images taken by the harbor police and the captains from the water taxis and ferries, but none matched the name or logo of the boat in question. The *St. Petersburg Penance* had vanished.

"They are here," Cat said forcefully. "It's not that they have gone someplace else ... we just haven't found them." She held the coffee mug in both hands, stroking it. "I've been thinking ... if I steal a car, the first thing I'm going to do is to change the license plate. If I were stealing a boat ..."

"You'd change the name! Check the images again. Do any of them look like they've been tampered with in any way?"

It was Arnie who, having a sharp eye for detail, figured it out. "Look at the logo on this boat," he said, pointing to a photo of a yacht with a pair of skis painted on the bow. "Gabe found this photo of *Rasputin's Revenge*, from Lido Beach, which is out of Long Island in New York.

"This yacht's logo has the skis standing vertically, with

the tips at the top. This morning's picture of the yacht in the harbor has the ski tails at the top and the tips at the bottom. It's probably a decal that someone stuck on the bow, but they screwed up," Arnie said, pointing at the image. "They slapped it on upside-down."

The photo had been taken off Peddocks Island at nine twelve that morning. Other images showed the boat to be at anchor, with the helm unmanned. The supposition was that all of the yacht's occupants were belowdecks.

Cat took a sip of coffee and clicked her nails against the ceramic mug. "We need to shut down Logan Airport."

Paul frowned but did not argue. He beckoned Leo Farrell into the conference room, where Cat made a case for shutting down one of the nation's busiest airports. By the time she was finished, Farrell's skin was noticeably paler.

"I'll leave it to you to figure out how to phrase the request in a publicly acceptable manner." Cat left Farrell to make up some bullshit story and sidled over to Paul and the general, beckoning Jazz and Jones to join them.

"Once Logan is set," she said softly, "I want Mr. Forsythe to make a call to Mr. Pierce."

Paul frowned. "Is that wise? He knows Forsythe was injured ... that he's in custody. Even if he takes the call, he'll be suspicious."

"Forsythe and Pierce have been tight for a long time, under the most unforgiving circumstances. They have given up a great deal for this country, and while they may have been stupid when falling for this scam, I believe we have a better chance of taking that boat cleanly if we have them on our side. General, what's the status of that SEAL team? Can they board that yacht in the next ten minutes?"

"They're already in place ... air and water," replied the general, "roughly equidistant to the five yachts you found. Eight minutes will do it."

Cat looked first at Adrian, who rubbed his hand roughly over the scruff of his beard before nodding, and then at Jones and Jazz, who locked eyes and held a wordless conversation. Jazz turned back to Paul and said, "We agree." The general picked up the phone.

Chapter 75

Ghadir Kharoti and his son Farshad took an early breakfast in the sunny Café Fleuri at the Langham Hotel downtown, indulging in the lavish spread. Farshad sat patiently with the older man until the check was delivered, and then asked permission to spend a couple of hours walking around the city.

Kharoti's pen lingered on the tip line as he worked through the implications of his son's request. He had taken Farshad on trips before, but never once had the young man asked to venture out into a new city by himself. Finally, he raised his eyes and stared at his son. "This is all? You wish only to sightsee?"

Farshad's eyes darted to the right before responding. "I would like to see Boston."

The elder Kharoti felt his stomach tumble; something was not right. "My son, you must speak the truth. I cannot bear it when I think of what might happen if you continue to listen to the poison of your cousin. I fear that you are falling under his spell. I have brought you here in hopes that you will awaken and see the corruption and falsehood of his words.

"Farshad, you must tell me the purpose of your wish to

walk around the city."

The young man hung his head and stared at the table, unwilling to meet his father's eyes.

"Farshad, you are my son, and I fear that I am losing you. I can help you if you will let me. Can you not see that your cousin has lost his way? We can visit a mosque here in Boston this week; I have already reached out to the imam, and he would welcome a conversation with you."

The young man raised his head languidly and shrugged his shoulders. "Aashif says that the imams here are not true to Allah. They have been corrupted by the false teachings of the West."

The older man shook his head in disgust. "Aashif spews lies and hate. This is not the way of Islam. You can see for yourself... you will meet this imam today at the opening of the cultural center."

The young man sat up suddenly, surprised. "The imam will be there today?"

Ghadir Kharoti felt a stab of hot fear pierce his abdomen. "Farshad? Has Aashif planned something to happen at the opening? Has he sent someone here?"

Farshad jutted his chin out arrogantly. "Aashif is here himself."

The older man could hardly breathe. "What have you done?" He reached for the phone as Farshad pulled a jacket from his suitcase and walked swiftly to the door. "Farshad! You must stay here! You must talk to the authorities!"

Farshad opened the door and stepped into the hall, pulling the door closed behind him and ignoring his father's cries. He never looked back.

His fingers trembling, Ghadir Kharoti called the front

desk and asked for hotel security. Explaining that he believed his son might try to attack the new cultural center in the Seaport, he provided a brief description and then hurried to the elevator.

The Langham's director of security, a decorated former policeman and army veteran, did not hesitate to act, racing to the elevators while directing his men to cover the stairwells. Ten seconds too late, he rounded the corner to reception and missed seeing Farshad Kharoti push through the revolving glass door to the street.

When several minutes passed with no sign of the young man in question, and out of an abundance of caution, he thought of calling 9-1-1 to report the threat. Instead, he held the phone in his hand and, after the briefest pause, thumbed through his contacts and found the number for a man with whom he played tennis on occasion ... an agent at the FBI's local field office.

SAC Leo Farrell hurriedly ushered the agent into the conference room. "Everyone needs to hear this. Put him on," he ordered.

The agent held his phone out and pressed the button to activate the speaker.

"This is Frank Moffett, head of security at the Langham," the agent said. "One of their guests is insisting that his son could be involved in some sort of extremist action today."

Adrian was at the phone in three strides. "Mr. Moffett,

what is the guest's name?"

"Mr. Ghadir Kharoti," came the voice over the speaker. "I have him secluded in one of our offices. Would you like to speak with him?"

Adrian cast a glance at the SAC and let his eyes drift to Cat, who was forcefully mouthing, "Bring him here!"

His eyes moist, Ghadir Kharoti sat in the leather chair, wringing his hands and wondering if he had done the right thing. He had traveled to the United States many times, but he had never had any occasion to deal with America's police or security forces. He was torn between the need to protect his son and the need to warn innocent people of the potential for harm. He desperately needed advice, and from someone with clout.

He rocked forward and back, worry and fear clutching his heart, and had a sudden inspiration: the photographer woman, Adele Rutledge. She had been in all manner of situations and knew people in high places. Maybe she could point him in the right direction. He found her card, still in his wallet where he had tucked it after the gala, and dialed.

Cat felt the phone vibrate and glanced at the screen. *A call from India?* The number seemed familiar but she rarely answered those that were not in her contact list. Her finger hovered over the button to ignore the call when, like a thunderclap, the memory clicked. "Quiet!" she hissed to the room's occupants, and then, into the phone, "Hello?"

Those in the conference room stared in amazement as

they listened to the one-sided conversation.

"Mr. Kharoti! I'm delighted to hear from you! But I thought you were traveling to Boston?" Pause. "What do you mean?" She listened for a long time. "Mr. Kharoti, I have a friend who is with the FBI. I can ask him for help." Pause. "I can't imagine how difficult this must be for you. Let me call my friend now; I'll put you on hold."

She muted the call and looked across the room. Finding Adrian, she said, "He's reaching out for help. Since he already called security, my guess is that he wants to land on the right side of this, but he's desperate to save his son, too. Let's find out what he knows."

Adrian swung his head toward Farrell, whose face was pinched with concern. "I agree. We're running out of time and manpower. Let's skip the formalities and get him over here."

"Do it," Farrell said.

Cat rejoined the call and told Kharoti that someone from the hotel would take him to the FBI offices. Adrian relayed the instructions to the hotel's director of security and was signing off when he read the scribbled note that Cat held in front of his face. "And we'll need remote access to your security recordings from this morning."

Cat turned her attention to Gabe. "Get with Melodie and Trent and the hotel people and find out where Aashif went."

Gabe shook his head. "Takes too long. I've got his cell phone, and it's broadcasting."

"You're kidding! He didn't change out the SIM card?"

"Not yet. Looking at the towers he's hitting, I'm reasonably confident that he's on the Red Line."

Her brows knitted in frustration. "Somerville again." She looked over to Adrian. "We have to notify the Somerville cops."

Adrian turned to Leo Farrell. "Do we have someone we can send over there?"

Leo rubbed the back of his neck. "I've concentrated our people at the cultural center. We don't have anyone close enough to get there quickly."

Picking up the phone, Adrian dialed the chief of the Somerville police. His voice was grave as he described the situation. "We're sending you the photo. We need this man, but first we have to know where he's going. Once you've established his destination, evacuate the area and take him down. This man likely has access to explosives; don't make any assumptions. Think suicide bomber."

Chapter 76

Sunday morning
Somerville, Massachusetts

Farshad Kharoti looked at his watch and sprinted up the steps of the T station at Davis Square. He was ninety minutes late, and his cousin would be furious—if Aashif was even still there. He emerged at the entry facing Davis Square and checked Google Maps. He turned left, toward the Somerville Community Path, and started to jog. His clothing and leather dress shoes were out of place among the runners, walkers, and bicyclists using the trail, and his unusual appearance caught the eye of the officer in the unmarked patrol car parked on the corner of Grove Street.

When the photo and the BOLO—an urgent notice sent out alerting police to Be On the LookOut—popped up a few seconds later on the unmarked's console, a shot of adrenaline coursed through the officer's system. As he picked up the radio's handset, he could still see the man's head bobbing along the path. The officer reported his position and the suspect's direction of travel on the path.

Knowing that the man could be lost within moments in the tangle of narrow streets, the officer made the decision to follow on foot. He called in his intent, and then locked the car and ran in pursuit of the suspect.

Within five minutes, a motorcycle, a bicycle, and two patrol cars were coordinating a search pattern that ran eastward along the roughly parallel Highland and Morrison Avenues, looking for the jogger.

Twelve blocks east, Tin Man heard the report and recognized the young man in the photo. Tin Man was already in his car, driving west and listening to the ongoing progress reports. Regardless of how much he had learned, or not learned, from his cousin, the kid had now become a potential witness—and a problem. One block east of his destination, Tin Man pulled into a vacant spot and hurried around the corner to the green house with the brown trim. He slowed his pace and stepped up to the porch, looking behind him and sweeping his gaze over the other houses nearby. Satisfied that no one was watching, he unlocked the door for the ground floor of the two-family home.

He pushed the door open and quickly made sure that he was alone before returning to the front hall. The knock came moments later. He wrapped his hand in the tail of his shirt and pulled the door open to admit the heavily perspiring Indian.

The panting young man stepped inside and, following Tin Man's gesture, moved into the small living room before resting his hands on his thighs and trying to catch his breath. He had looked up, swiveling his head to survey the room, when the first bullet from the silenced gun caught him in the throat. He had just enough time to realize something was dreadfully wrong when the second bullet struck him in the forehead, just above his right eye.

Tin Man slipped out the side door and pushed his way through the shrubs to the narrow walkway between the houses. He was twenty feet from his car when he spotted the cruiser at the end of the block, moving slowly in his direction. He slowly twisted away, facing the backyard, and bent over as he pretended to scrape pet droppings from his shoe. As soon as the patrol car was past, he climbed back in his car, worked his way back east, and returned home.

Secure in his own home, Tin Man thought about the green house. He was certain that there was no way by which he could be connected to the building. The place was owned by a company registered in the Caymans, which was known for its discreet banking practices. Even if the authorities managed to uncover the company's origins, they would find a shell company within a shell company, all having been neatly and untraceably established by Roger Pulaski, formerly of the CIA.

Tin Man shook his head at the thought of his friend languishing away in a federal lockup. There had been no communication between the two since the catastrophic events in February, when the former intelligence officer had attempted—and failed—to frame Cat Powell in a quest for revenge decades in the making. The first few weeks after Roger's arrest had crawled by, with every hour spent imagining that he would be next. Instead, Roger had kept his mouth shut.

While Roger's goals may have been noble, albeit

misguided, Tin Man's were much simpler. He wanted a new life and the money to enjoy it. He had already purchased a large villa in Croatia, and after today he would have enough cash to live like a king for the rest of his life. The Russian woman might even join him there, although he wasn't going to bet the farm on it; she had her own agenda. He looked around the living room of the home he had occupied for thirty years and wondered briefly if there was anything he would miss from his old life. *No*, he thought; he'd been screwed over in life and career and love, and he just didn't give a damn about any of it.

The officer who had given chase to Farshad stood on the sidewalk, carefully scanning every house and every window on the street, convinced that the suspect was somewhere in this block. Running a hundred yards behind the jogger, he had seen the man turn onto this street. But when he turned the corner himself, the man was nowhere to be seen. He had run to the next corner, but found the road and sidewalks empty. The man was here, in one of the dozen or so houses lining this block; he could feel it.

Thirty minutes later, as the cops were conducting a door-to-door search, one of them knocked on the door of the green house. Receiving no response, he walked around the ground floor and peeked in the windows, which is how he spotted the newly deceased Farshad Kharoti.

The notification went out immediately to the FBI, who recommended both an evacuation of the area and a search for explosives.

Having spent face time with the FBI when the cache

of C-4 was found in Rajeev Malik's apartment, Captain Samms of the Somerville police was the obvious choice to lead the local investigation into the murder of the Indian national. He accepted the callout and was on the scene within an hour after the shooting.

Sergeant Wayne Wilson, of the Massachusetts State Police, was also afforded a call and arrived at the house shortly after Samms. His dog took no time at all in locating the explosive-laden vest that was hanging in the laundry room closet. It would take longer to ascertain that the residue throughout the house indicated that a large amount of C-4 had once been stored there.

Jazz, refusing to wait for the house to be cleared, pulled the video camera and transmitter out of her trunk and followed Wilson into the house. She activated the satellite connection and spoke into the headpiece. "Are you receiving?"

"Yes," came the reply. "Loud and clear."

She hustled to the laundry room, where the dog had first alerted, and panned the camera over the scene. "What am I missing here? Why would anyone leave an explosives vest in plain view?"

"I suspect its intended wearer was Farshad," answered Cat. "What else is in the house?"

Jazz moved from room to room, capturing it all on camera. The house was sparsely furnished and the appliances older but hardly used. The refrigerator was completely empty. The only curiosity was the sewing machine in the back bedroom, along with a few scraps each of green, orange, and white fabric and several spools of matching thread.

"Someone's been sewing," said Cat.

"But sewing what?" Jazz picked up one of the fabric scraps and tried to stretch it. "This is ballistic nylon, the kind you use in luggage."

"Part of Kharoti's business is luggage, but it's pretty high-end. I don't see him selling bright green and orange suitcases. What you're seeing are the colors of the Indian flag.

"Maybe someone was making flags, but that seems odd."

"You're right. We'll get word out about the nylon colors. Maybe someone will make a connection. Unless you see anything else, head over to the cultural center. We can use your eyes and ears there. Paul and I have a stop to make at MGH. Everyone else is on the way."

Chapter 77

Sunday morning
Boston, Massachusetts

Aashif Ahmedani had agreed to pay the regular bus driver $50,000 for calling in sick today. He had stood nearby, the cash in a cardboard box, as the man explained to his supervisor that he was down with the flu but could send his brother instead. The supervisor, young and eager to please those who held the purse strings, had been desperate to find a driver for the elite private school at the last minute on a Sunday morning. He had finally agreed to the arrangement, pending receipt of the brother's credentials via e-mail. Fifteen minutes later, the forged documents had been received, the supervisor had authorized the replacement, and the original driver lay dead on the floor of his small garage.

Now Aashif was climbing into the yellow school bus in the school's parking lot, joining the group of three chaperones and twenty excited six-year-olds—all first-grade students at the exclusive Back Bay institution. The children were scheduled to perform a short program at the cultural center's opening today and had been practicing for two weeks. Their parents were delighted, eager for their children to have such an experience at this early age.

He opened the two big cardboard boxes and handed each child a gift that he claimed to be from the cultural center. The small nylon backpacks were available in a choice of green, orange, and white—matching the colors of the flag of India—and were emblazoned with the new center's logo on the flap. And each contained a small bag from a local deli, with a turkey sandwich, an apple, and a chocolate chip cookie inside.

The backpacks were sturdy, padded, and well-made. They were also heavier than one would expect a child to carry, but no one seemed to notice. Aashif had designed the backpacks himself, using techniques learned from the luggage side of his uncle's business, and Tin Man had found a seamstress to construct them. He had made a few adjustments to his uncle's manufacturing specifications by leaving one seam at the front and one at the back unfinished. Last night, he had placed the padding in each pocket—along with a thinly rolled sheet of C-4 and a small, remotely activated blasting cap—before stitching the seams closed.

He slid into the driver's seat, checked his mirrors, cheerfully wished everyone a day of fun, put on his hat, and started the bus.

Chapter 78

The meeting room was on the second floor of the cultural center, overlooking the water. When designed, it had been envisioned as a place where people of all cultures could meet and share and learn. At the moment, however, the room held Cat's team, the British team, police commanders, a number of their subordinates, the team from the Boston field office of the FBI, and a team from ATF—the Bureau of Alcohol, Tobacco, Firearms and Explosives.

With Cat, Paul, and Farrell still at One Center Plaza, Adrian was on his own. But he had been thoroughly briefed about what *not* to say. C-4 was bad enough, but the mention of the word *Stinger* would really set the locals' hair on fire. He stood before the group and tried to think of some way to present what he knew while keeping the diverse groups on the same page. He took a deep breath and dove in. "We have reason to suspect that an attack may be planned at this site today. We have pled our case to both the Indian delegation and to the state and community leaders who will be attending this afternoon's ceremonies. Despite our urgings, they are refusing to postpone the ceremony."

The men and women in front of him faced the same idiocy day in and day out. If you canceled an event and had no damage or arrests to show for it afterward, there was hell to pay. If you let the event go on as scheduled and something terrible happened, there was hell to pay. It was a no-win situation.

He passed out three pictures. "The people in the photos are Aashif Ahmedani, Farid Mahdavi, and Tanya Goreva. The men are originally from Pakistan and are known supporters of LeT. The woman is Russian, and may have been KGB. All of these people are highly skilled and extremely dangerous. We know there is at least one other man involved and there could be others. We do not have any additional photographs. We suspect that they will try to detonate explosive devices in, or near, the center. Our job will be to cut these monsters off at the knees before they can do harm to anyone here.

"Let me be clear about the nature of these explosives. We believe that this group is in possession of a significant quantity of military-grade C-4. We do not know how much they plan to use today, or how. The explosives were stolen from a government shipment several months ago, and several agencies have been working ever since to track them down. The information we have is raw and still developing.

"We believe, but cannot yet confirm, that they may also have a vessel in the harbor. Another team is working on that as we speak.

"Based on information uncovered this morning, the C-4 may be wrapped or packaged in containers utilizing ballistic nylon in the colors of the Indian flag: green, orange, and white. Keep your eyes open. Also, there are undercover people among us, and you may not recognize them in the crowd. Our code word today is *Pyramid*."

Adrian looked out at the grim-faced audience and could not find an inspirational closure. "That's it. Let's go find these assholes."

Chapter 79

Sunday morning
Peddocks Island, Boston Harbor, Massachusetts

Matt had just started the engines and was hoisting the anchor when he felt his phone vibrate. He stared at the phone's caller ID and rapidly worked through the possibilities: Randy was either in the hospital or jail, or perhaps he had escaped, or one of the cops was on the other end of the line. *Answer or not?* he wondered. And he took the call. "Hello?"

"Matt, it's Randy. You've got to listen to me. I think those Stingers are on the yacht!"

"I know. I found them early this morning. I have ..."

"You've got to get away from the airport! Dancer and Sophia's mother want to bring down a passenger jet!"

"They can't ... Sophia's mother? What do you mean?"

"They think she's part of this."

"That makes it harder. Dancer's on board, and there's another man we picked up last night."

"Matt, this is Paul Marshfield. You'll have company in less than ten minutes. The man who joined you last night ... is he Pakistani?"

"I think so. He was speaking Punjabi on the phone.

The whole thing was starting to feel wrong. Listen ... about the Stingers ..."

Matt heard feet beating against the steps to the main deck and closed the phone, tucking it into his windbreaker.

"What are you doing?" the foreigner screamed. "We are not to leave our position until this afternoon!"

"We have plenty of time. I'm heading over to Spectacle Island. Sophia was a bit nauseous this morning, and someone got sick over the rail last night. It will be best for everyone to walk around on land for an hour or two."

"Stop the boat!"

Matt looked over his shoulder and found the man pointing a gun at his back. "Whoa, buddy! We're not altering the plan; we're just taking a short break."

"I said, stop the boat!" the man screamed, his voice going up an octave and spittle flying from his mouth.

Matt shoved the throttle into reverse, throwing the man backward. The gun flew from his hand and skittered across the deck. Matt jammed the throttle into idle and then leaped for the weapon, but the man was closer. The shot tore up the deck at Matt's feet, spitting splinters at his bare legs.

"If you kill me, you'll have no one to drive the boat. You'll be screwed."

"And perhaps I will tie your friend's girlfriend to the front of this boat and send it full speed into a very large ship. Turn the engines off and go below. When we are ready, you can drive the boat from that other seat with a wheel."

While it was evident that the man had never spent much time on the water, he had managed to grasp that this yacht could be manned from the flybridge or from the helm on the main deck. Matt tried to think of some clever ruse that would enable him to stay up top, but came up empty.

He switched off the engines, looking out over the water as he did so. The Pakistani's shouting had caught the attention of a number of nearby boaters, most of whom were now retreating from the area while keeping an eye on the drama taking place on the *Penance*. He held his hands up and went down the stairs leading to the main deck.

The foreigner pointed his gun at the helm, motioning for Matt to sit, and called back over his shoulder, "Dmitry! Come up here! Bring Sophia!"

Dmitry? Pierce thought. *Is that Dancer's name?* He remained standing, trying to adopt a relaxed and unthreatening posture by leaning back against the console. If he sat down, he knew it would slow down his ability to react.

Sophia and her mother, Tanya, emerged from the lower deck cabins, with Dancer holding a knife at Sophia's throat. Matt had been to hell and back on many of his missions, with men trusting each other with their lives, but this was his best friend's girlfriend ... the girl Randy wanted to marry.

Matt caught Sophia's eyes and held them. *I will get you out of this. Trust me.* Sophia lifted her chin defiantly, the message clear: *I trust you.* He shifted his gaze to Sophia's mother and was startled to see that she did not seem at all upset about the knife at her daughter's throat. Calm, clear-eyed, posture-perfect, and her eyes were hard.

"Mr. Pierce," she said in her heavily accented English, "you have tried to change our plan. This you cannot do. Farid and I have planned this event for a very long time.

Farid will make sure you do not interfere."

The Pakistani inclined his head in a tiny acknowledgment and leveled the gun at Matt's chest.

A look of consternation spread across Sophia's face as she tried to absorb her mother's words. "Farid? Who is he? What are you doing?" she asked in confusion.

"Dmitry, go below and bring the package," Tanya ordered. And then, turning to her daughter, she said, "You will see. The Americans will pay for destroying our family."

Sophia's expression morphed from confusion to horror. "What do you mean? What are you going to do?" she said fearfully. "I don't understand."

"Americans. They think they can do whatever they want. I will show them that there is a price to pay."

Trying to reason with her, Matt said, "Tanya, whatever has happened, you have to let it go. You have discovered your daughter! If there are issues, we can all sit down and talk them out. You and Sophia can enjoy your lives and move forward!"

Her words were venomous. "You think that this is something to just forgive and forget? This is not possible. Look what they did to my Sophia! Look what they have done to my Dmitry! They destroyed my family."

Matt tried to make sense of what she was saying. "Dmitry?"

"They have ruined my son," she said plaintively.

Sophia's mouth opened in shock. "Dancer ... Dmitry ... he is my brother? No! I don't believe it!"

Softening her tone, Tanya reached out to touch Sophia's cheek. "You are both my children. You will learn to love him as the brother he is!"

Her lips twisting in contempt, Sophia slapped her mother's hand away. "He is not my brother. He is a monster. I was so happy to find you ... to learn of my past." Tears began to well in her eyes, and she brushed them away with the back of her hand. "But now I am realizing that I don't know you at all ... and I wonder if I even want to."

Matt chanced a glance at the Pakistani, who was alternating his focus between Matt and the two women. Matt leaned slightly forward, shifting his weight to his toes, and was ready to pounce when Dancer flew up the steps and set the long case on the deck. Tanya bent over, popped the case open, and was awkwardly lifting the launcher when the man with the gun reached to take it away from her.

Seizing the opportunity, Matt sprang forward—two hundred and fifteen pounds of death and destruction. The Pakistani, seeing the motion from the corner of his eye, fired blindly and missed. Matt slammed into Tanya, knocking her down and sending her ricocheting into Sophia. In one fluid motion he rolled to the right and drove his foot into Farid's knee, bending the joint in a direction it was never designed to go. Matt never saw Dancer lift the launcher and swing it at his head. Sophia was crawling toward Matt when the sonorous whine of an engine and the rhythmic beat of a helicopter's blades cut through the cabin.

Farid stood weakly on one leg, his other knee ruined. "Give it to me!" he screamed, reaching for the launcher and swinging it up to his shoulder. He slammed the battery into place, raised the sight assembly, hobbled over to the stairs leading to the flybridge, and worked the safety and actuator device to activate the weapon.

Sophia heard several loud thumps as the team of SEALs fast-roped onto the yacht. "Put the weapon down!" a voice shouted. "Put the weapon down right now! Put it down!"

For years Farid had dreamed of watching a US airliner explode and fall into the sea, raining fire and debris and pieces of American men, women, and children over the water. He had cheered raucously upon learning that Pan Am's flight 103 had exploded over Lockerbie, Scotland. But even that event had never assuaged him; he had always wanted to be the one to pull the trigger. As he lifted his arms to point the missile at the helicopter hovering overhead, he thought of his father. When the bullets slammed into his body, he slumped forward and, just before dying, was sure that he felt his father's embrace.

Matt regained consciousness in time to see two SEALs wrestling anxiously with the Stinger. "Take your time; they're harmless," he said. "I disabled them."

Chapter 80

Sunday afternoon
Boston, Massachusetts

Jazz had reservations about including Barbara on the team at the cultural center. While she was smart, observant, and committed, she had no real operational experience. The size of the center and the limited number of personnel available, however, meant overlooking such deficiencies. She pulled Adele's cane from her duffel and handed it to Barbara. "Cat told me to give this to you. You probably won't need it, but I want you to at least have something to protect yourself. It's quite heavy ... you could probably swing it at someone's legs and immobilize them temporarily."

Their assigned area was adjacent to the large vehicle drop-off area, down from the main entry at the front of the building. There were several shops already open behind them, their colorful banners adding a festive touch. Jazz and Barbara had searched the shops after the meeting, and were now concentrating on the increasing crowd.

Fifty feet away, the yellow school bus pulled to the curb, and its door swung open. Almost instantaneously, a gaggle of children poured out of the bus, their chaperones close behind and trying to maintain order. The driver helped one youngster down the steps, lifting her on to the sidewalk and patting her backpack as he urged her forward, and his hat slid off his head and into the street.

The children, Jazz thought, were adorable... all dressed in school uniform, giggling, and carrying brightly colored kids' backpacks. Realizing what she was seeing, her eyes popped open, and she turned halfway toward Barbara, who was staring at the driver and twisting the cane. Jazz pressed the button on her radio and spoke into the microphone on her collar. "I have a positive sighting at the southwest corner, at the bus drop-off. There are little kids involved. They're all wearing backpacks."

As the driver turned to climb back on the bus, Barbara took off, running full speed toward the bus, a lone knife in her left hand.

Jazz ran toward the children holding up her badge and screaming at the chaperones, "Take the backpacks off the kids! Tell them to run inside! Now!" She reached the first little girl and twisted the backpack from her torso, sending the child sprawling. "Run!" she shouted at the girl as she grabbed the second child and did the same, adding, "Hold your friend's hand! Run!"

The chaperones froze for an instant and then grew wild-eyed, screaming and yanking at backpack straps and instinctively knowing that the orderliness of the fire drill they so often practiced in school would do them no good here.

The driver turned around, surprised to see the children scattering, leaving chaos in their wake. He shook his head at the disarray—they were supposed to be together—

and reached into his pocket. He sensed the motion before he saw the blur of a woman raising her arms high and swinging down. In that first instant, he did not realize what had happened, the brain synapses not yet registering that the heavy blade had nearly severed his right hand just above the wrist. As the neurons finally fired and he started to scream in pain, Barbara slashed him again, this time fully amputating his left hand.

"They are just children, you filthy animal!" she shouted at him as he lay writhing in agony. "Just children!"

Jazz shooed the last child toward the building and realized that she had never considered that the bombs might be on a timer or other trigger. She yelled at the knot of cops nearby to cordon off a large area, shouting the code word *Pyramid,* and then approached the bus. Barbara was standing above Aashif, still screaming at him.

Wrapping her arm around Barbara, Jazz guided her away from the blood and the hate. "You saved those kids," she said softly. "Their families will remember forever what you did."

Barbara's face clouded, and the first tears sprang from her eyes as the reality of what she had done hit her. "I was so angry; they were only children! When he reached in his pocket, I was sure he was going to set off the bombs. But I didn't really know, did I? He could have been reaching for his keys. Was it him? Tell me it was him!"

"It was him, Barbara. I can tell you right now that he wasn't reaching for his keys," Jazz said softly. "You saved all of us."

"Is he dead?"

"I think so. The EMTs aren't allowed to touch him

until the area is secure. When the bomb squad gets here, we'll know for sure."

Two hours later, after the backpacks were secured and their blasting caps removed, the bomb squad approached the body of Aashif Ahmedani. In his right pocket, they found the cigarette-lighter-size device that was the remote trigger.

Chapter 81

Sunday night
Boston, Massachusetts

Cat made coffee while Adrian pored over the documents for the two-family house in Somerville, the house where Farshad Kharoti had died. Linking ownership to an actual person was presenting a mammoth challenge.

"They're shell companies," Cat said. "This is Roger's work, I just know it. He knew about the Gorevs. He knew about my connection to Iran. He set this whole thing in motion."

"Probably so, but he had help. He has someone on the outside, and that person is Tin Man. We just need to figure out who he is."

"And judging from the estimated time of death, you think someone should have seen Farshad's killer?"

"I do. Whoever killed Farshad, they were in that house at nearly the same time that the officer turned onto the street."

"So this person presumably went out the back or side doors, unless they dug a tunnel."

"Precisely. But there are exactly two cameras in the

entire neighborhood, and we haven't found anything."

"Wait ... cameras ... the cops were covering the area pretty well. Do they always have their dashcams on? One of them might have caught something and didn't realize it."

Adrian jumped up, took her face in his hands, and kissed the top of her head. "Brilliant, Cat! Dashcams!"

Half an hour later, Melodie and Trent had tunneled into the server housing the Somerville Police dashcam recordings.

"These cars came from all over the city. We're really only interested in this one neighborhood. Let's try a half hour before time of death until an hour after."

"What are we looking for?"

"It was Sunday morning. People are inside, having breakfast, playing with their kids. Let's get an image of anyone who doesn't fit that profile, and we'll mark them on the map."

"What about cars?" Cat asked. "A car that leaves the area within an hour after TOD?"

"That too," Adrian said.

It was nearly midnight when Trent said, "Hmm."

"What?" asked Adrian.

"This is from cruiser 243, one block east of the murder scene, just around the corner, as a matter of fact."

The image quality was less than desirable, and Adrian stared at it for a long time. "It's a bad angle, but that looks like Frank Samms. He's bending over, though. Anything of him standing?"

"Yes, but it's too far away. The face just looks like a blob of pixels."

"Back up. Try the middle of the block."

"Okay."

"What is that?"

"What?"

"That car. Is that a Chevy Impala? Can you get the plate?"

Trent had the answers in five minutes. "That's a 2013 Chevy Impala, and it's registered to the Somerville Police Department. Assigned driver of record? Frank Samms."

Adrian's expression soured. "He's got a perfect record. And he's respected; I could tell that from the way his men reacted to him when we found that first cache of C-4. How did someone like him get mixed up in this?"

Cat patted him on the shoulder. "They say that you can never know what's going to twist someone. I'm sorry."

"I've got more," Melodie said. "There are three small warehouses registered to that same shell company. And look who is standing in front of one of them on Facebook! He uses it for charity bashes for local kids with life-threatening illnesses."

Adrian hung his head. "I'll never understand it."

"No," agreed Cat. "No one ever does."

"Let's get an evidence team together and get this guy off the streets."

Chapter 82

Monday afternoon
Boston, Massachusetts

Cat sat across the table from Tanya Goreva and stared at the beautiful face. She still carried herself like Audrey Hepburn, but the spark had gone out of her eyes.

"You stole my daughter," Tanya said with a slur.

After talking with Sophia earlier in the day, Cat was not surprised at the statement. Tanya had woven quite a tale for her daughter, managing to convince her that the Americans had stolen her as a toddler and used her as a bargaining chip to obtain secrets from the Soviets.

According to Sophia, Tanya would never have known what happened to her daughter if not for a visit several years ago from a man she knew only as Roger. He had described an American criminal enterprise run by the CIA—an organization that specialized in kidnapping children for secrets and money—with Cat at the helm.

Cat had called her husband, Tom, and asked him to bring a document that she kept in the garage ... in the false bottom of her toolbox. The pages were brittle and yellowed with age and, after Sophia read them, tearstained. Had

Tanya snapped at some point? Or had Roger showed her some forged document that told a different story? Sophia could not say.

Now Cat held the papers out to Tanya, allowing her to read, but not touch. The woman's eyes misted over as she translated the words to Russian. "My husband wrote this."

"Tanya, it is your handwriting."

She seemed perplexed. "He must have forced me."

"But you told me you wanted to come to America. You begged me to arrange it."

"Anatoly wanted to come here. For a time he made me want to go, and I thought it would be a good thing for us. But what is a place without roots in the earth? But then in St. Petersburg, they kept me from my son. Both of my children, taken from me."

"I'm very sorry, Tanya. We were trying to do the right thing."

"The right thing? You ask us to spy, and you call that right? If we had never met you, my family would be whole."

Cat gently lowered the papers, understanding that no amount of truth would heal the woman's pain. Tanya had wrapped herself in a cocoon of her own version of the past. Cat sat for a few more minutes, waiting to see if Tanya would say more, but the woman stayed mute. Finally, Cat stood. "I hope you will find a way to heal, Tanya. I really do." She turned and knocked at the door, signaled for the guard, and stepped out into the hall.

Adrian and Cat met outside One Center Plaza, and they walked across the street and down the wide steps toward Faneuil Hall.

He passed his phone to her. "Did you see these?"

Children Targeted in Failed Seaport Attack
–by Elaine Lieberman

Twenty first-graders from the prestigious Boston Founders School in Back Bay were rescued in the Seaport today after explosive devices were discovered sewn into their backpacks. An unidentified man, believed to be the driver of the bus, was also critically injured during the evacuation. Details of his injuries have not been made available. The children were to take part in the grand opening of the new Indo-American cultural center at the Seaport. Events at the center were canceled following the discovery and all venues closed.

The bombs were detected by an alert ATF agent, who noticed unusual bulges in the children's backpacks. None of the students were seriously injured in the incident. Two children suffered minor scrapes and bruises and were taken to Mass General, where they were treated and released.

With the rise in terrorism abroad and the continuing threat of violence against Americans, the presence of police and federal agents has become common at large functions throughout the country. The governor praised their efforts, stating, "If not for the gallant efforts of our law enforcement community, we would have experienced an unspeakable tragedy."

The mayor of Boston decried the plot, calling it "barbaric."

The governor and the mayor have scheduled a joint news conference on Monday.

Harbor Training Exercise Terrifies Boaters and Travelers
–by Elaine Lieberman

A military exercise in Boston Harbor yesterday sent airline travelers and boaters alike scurrying when onlookers reported suspicious activity on a vessel near Peddocks Island.

According to authorities, the exercise was planned to test preparedness in responding to a potential incident of terrorism. It has long been held by authorities that coastal cities are vulnerable to attack by water. The exercise, which included the participation of a Special Forces team, involved the interception of a large yacht.

Witnesses had reported that one of the yacht's occupants was in possession of what appeared to be a shoulder-fired missile. General Carter Haskell, in town to observe the exercise, gave assurances that the "missile" was a disabled device and that the public was never in any danger. "We conduct these exercises to gauge our ability to circumvent an attack while operating in an urban environment. While we have state-of-the-art training centers, we can never simulate the human element. These exercises help us be better prepared to protect our citizens."

Local officials were quick to condemn the exercise. Senator Oscar Sheffield complained that "scaring the pants off several thousand people isn't an exercise; it's lunacy." An inquiry is underway.

Cat rolled her eyes. "Elaine Lieberman is actually a decent reporter. She might keep digging ... there are a lot of unanswered questions in these stories."

"This wasn't my idea. I'd rather paste the entire story on the front page of the *Globe*, but there would be a lot of fallout. But I don't think Ms. Lieberman is going to ever find out what really happened on that yacht. And she'll never learn about Barbara Raynor or her role in taking down Aashif Ahmedani. There was so much chaos with the kids that no one even saw her. Speaking of, did you manage to retrieve your cane?"

"Jazz was smart ... she scooped up all the pieces, thank God. It might have been a little difficult to explain otherwise. What's the status on Samms?"

"We sent a team to his place early this morning. He's gone, and so is his car. We're looking through airline and credit card records, but I think he's bolted. On a good note, we found the rest of the C-4 in one of his buildings."

"I'm relieved to hear that a couple tons of high explosive are no longer sitting around waiting for someone's next fun trick," she said acidly. "Samms is twisted, like Roger. They were friends, you know, lifelong friends ... went to school together until Roger's family moved away. But Samms was never a star like Roger. By all accounts he was a decent person, but he had big dreams and could never get ahead. He was turned down at the FBI and CIA, and a few years ago applied for a job with the State Police, on their bomb squad. They gave the position to Wilson, instead. That, I guess, explains the animosity."

"So he made a conscious decision to trade his morality because he couldn't afford a McMansion or a new Ferrari? You know, if he had been there this morning, there's a part of me that would have liked to put a bullet in his brain. I think of Roger, living like a fat cat in a federal lockup, yet still managing to wield his power. Samms would be the same."

"But you wouldn't have done it."

Adrian stopped and turned toward her. "His actions almost cost Lindsey her life, and a lot of other people too, so there is a part of me ... but no. I still believe in the law."

"I'm glad," she said. "Otherwise it's just too costly."

Epilogue

Saturday morning
Boston, Massachusetts

I am an early riser, but when I glanced at the clock by the bedside and saw that it was only five thirty, I groaned. Another hour of sleep would have been just the ticket, before the flock of nurses descended on me for their morning routine of bloodletting and torture. I turned my head and found Adrian staring at me from the chair beside the bed.

"Hey, sleepyhead!" he said.

"Hey, yourself. What are you doing here?"

"Taking you home. And to add to the pleasure, Jason's being released as well. They'll bring him down here when he's ready to go."

I smiled at the thought. After a week of being imprisoned in the hospital, I was ready for parole. I couldn't even imagine Jason's relief to be getting out. I glanced over at Adrian and noticed that he seemed less than cheerful. He seemed off ... pensive. "What's the matter?"

He leaned back in the chair, resting his head on his right hand. "We've found Frank Samms. He's in Croatia."

"Croatia?"

"No extradition treaty with the US. Pretty affordable, too, by US standards ... although I'm quite sure he'll lose his pension."

"No way to bring him back?"

"Nope."

"After what he did? Unbelievable. I really do think I could kill him and never look back."

"I've had those same thoughts, but ..."

"I know ... lest we devolve into monsters ourselves. What's happening with Pierce and Forsythe, and Sophia?"

Adrian stretched his legs out and held my eyes. "We're not going to charge them. They were completely duped by Samms. They thought they were working for the government."

"Good," I said, feeling relieved. "Pierce is really some kind of hero." We had learned that Matthew Pierce had sabotaged both launchers shortly after the hijacking, long before they were stowed on the yacht. Regardless of what Pierce had been told about their mission, he had been uncomfortable with two live Stingers being in the possession of anyone other than the US Army. "It's just too bad you didn't know he'd disarmed them."

He shook his head absently, his eyes focused on some distant spot on the horizon. "You know, I listened to the tape from when we called him, and he tried to tell us a couple of times, but then he hung up because he didn't want Farid to know he'd been on the phone. He was already working out his own way of saving the day."

I laid my head back against the pillow. I knew he was going to talk about Tanya and Dancer, and I didn't want to hear any of it. I didn't care.

"Lindsey?"

"Just tell me they're still locked up."

"And never getting out."

Matt Pierce had asked Adrian to check on Dianne Talbot. Adrian had accompanied the Marblehead Police to her home, where they had discovered her brutalized body stuffed in the closet of her upstairs bedroom. I might never get over my encounter with the man they called Dancer. If I hadn't grabbed the wheel of that car, I might have been another victim, just like Dianne. *What if?*

"He's insane, Lindsey. So is his mother."

"The devil and her spawn."

He took a deep breath. "Yes, but she never recovered from giving away her daughter. And the Soviets had taken her son, too. I think that losing both children drove her mad."

"It doesn't excuse *him*. And he got a fucking free ticket to America." I had learned that, once upon a time, Dmitry Gorev, the man everyone called Dancer, had been a principal at the Mariinsky Ballet, the company I've always called the Kirov. He had immigrated to the United States eight years ago and spent six years with the American Ballet Theatre, when he left under a cloud ... apparently he had been a little too rough with some of their female dancers.

"We've learned a little more. It seems that the people he stayed with in St. Petersburg abused him severely, both the husband and the wife. I guess he never told anyone, but Lindsey, he has scars in places you cannot imagine."

I followed his gaze and looked out the window, my eyes settling on an anonymous building in the Boston cityscape. "I'm sorry for what they went through. Maybe someday I'll be able to forgive, but that's going to be a long time in coming. Right now, I think they should both rot in hell.

September
Zagreb, Croatia

Marie-Françoise Bourget stepped out of the terminal at Zagreb International Airport and reveled in the brilliant blue sky of the warm September afternoon. She found the rental car easily enough, a small, white Renault with GPS. After tossing her bags into the back, she took a moment to stretch her back and survey her surroundings. While there was no reason to suggest that anyone would be following her, she had learned long ago that one can never be too careful.

Satisfied, she slid behind the wheel and plugged in the destination. She put on her sunglasses and settled in for the three-hour drive south to Pjescana Uvala, a village just south of Pula. The small boutique hotel she had chosen was charming and perfect for a week's vacation, with its reputedly exquisite and comfortable rooms and its panoramic view overlooking the Adriatic Sea.

For three days, she immersed herself in the local history and visited various restaurants and shops. She took a short drive each morning and each evening, enjoying the scenery, and always passing the Villa Ljubka that sat on the hill just opposite the hotel. In the late afternoon, she took long walks that invariably wandered by the Villa Ljubka's walled garden. And she watched the villa's lone occupant from a distance, learning his habits, while she went about the business of playing tourist.

On the fourth day, she ate lunch in the quaint café, enjoying the fresh oysters and crisp white wine. The tall, weathered man looked her way, but Marie-Françoise did not seem to notice, burying her nose in her book. On the fifth day, she took her morning coffee at an outdoor café, her back to the door, and again the man looked her way. This time, however, he introduced himself and suggested that they might enjoy a cup of coffee together. She invited him to have a seat, and they chatted amiably—she about her many excursions to exotic locations and he about the challenges faced by an American living in Croatia. Marie-Françoise's English was somewhat fluent though her accent heavy, but he seemed to understand her. She, on the other hand, seemed to have trouble understanding his colloquial Americanisms.

On the sixth day, she left the hotel for her afternoon walk, as was her custom. On this day, however, the Mercedes stopped, and the tall gentleman offered her a ride, which she shyly accepted, as well as an invitation to dinner, which she accepted as well.

They sipped the local wine and dined on squid and scampi, and gnocchi and spinach, and when he invited her back to his villa, she accepted yet again. They strolled into the garden and near the pool, and he took her hand and drew her close. He reached to unzip her dress, but she reached back and slid the zipper herself, letting the top of the dress fall to her waist. "Take off your clothes," she whispered, and he rushed to comply. She reached for the top of the dress, slipping the syringe from its pocket on the zipper, and then wrapped her arms around his neck.

When he felt the sharp jab of the needle, his eyes widened in shock. He tried to slap her hand away, but his fingers fluttered and his legs started to give way, the paralytic working quickly. "Too late," she whispered in his ear in perfect English. "It's already in your system." She held him under his arms and lowered him to the ground.

"There are consequences when you sell your soul for money. Did you actually think that you could try to kill all those innocent people and help murder two of my team, and then just walk away? Your past will always come back to bite you, Mr. Samms. And your payback is hell."

Frank Samms lay on the decking beside the pool, unable to move, unable to respond.

Cat Powell rolled him into the water, zipped her dress, and walked back to the hotel. When she checked out the next morning, the staff inquired about her stay.

"It was ... cleansing," she said.

Acknowledgments

While writing a novel is generally a solitary pursuit, authors often reach out to those who have skills and knowledge we do not possess. I am grateful to all those who were kind enough to take the time to answer, explain, and instruct. Any errors or inaccuracies are solely mine.

Scott, who I sometimes think knows the characters as well as I do, makes a concerted effort to keep me on the path of plausibility—although I am sure I stretch those boundaries—and we have shared a few good laughs over the leaps in my imagination. To MM, there are moments when I am relieved that you have failed at retirement. The world should be grateful, too. Sallie Pecora-Saipe, longtime buddy and fellow traveler, you astound me with your ability to recall the minutiae of our time in Bombay.

Chris Cinkoske, former special ops USAF, is a great teacher and is always available for a trip to the gun range or to discuss the best weapon for a particular situation. John Lindahl, avid sailor, patiently fills the many gaps in my knowledge of vessels that travel on the water rather than above it. Dr. Kerry Reynolds from MGH unfailingly provides great insight into medical procedures and terminology, and offers alternatives when I need the story to move in a particular direction. Software architect Aram Hovhannisyan and I spent many an evening on Skype, amusing ourselves with the dialogue of my Russian characters.

Thank you to Delta Captain Benjamin Pierce, who happened to turn in my direction as I was working on a passage dealing with aviation. Seizing the moment, I cornered the poor guy. He graciously took a seat and gave the question serious thought, ultimately preventing me from making an embarrassing mistake.

My fantastic, eagle-eyed editor Cheri Madison continues to keep me out of trouble by finding the flaws in both my prose and my logic.

Thank you, as well, to other early readers of the book: Karen Thrasher, Susan Mayer, Cindy Pritchard, Susan Reynolds, Brian Reynolds, Morgan Pecora-Saipe, and Fawn Choate. And a special fist bump to Candy Provines and Joanne Swift for a fine time in Napa and the SF peninsula.

To my family and friends, you have been a life raft of love and support over the past year. During a time of great personal loss, you helped me persevere.

And to my readers, thank you for your continued support and kindness. I enjoy hearing from you and am happy to respond to your questions and comments. Please visit me on Facebook, or at LMReynolds.com, where you can also send a photo of you and the book for posting on the site. Happy reading!

About the Author

IT consultant and Pan Am veteran LM Reynolds pens suspense thrillers born of an ongoing interest in international intrigue. Often inspired by actual incidents, her yarns tell of long-held secrets and their influence on the present. Her award-winning novel *Spies in Our Midst* employed the harrowing setting of the Iranian revolution. Its sequel, *Spies We Know*, is centered in India. When not exploring the globe, she lives in Florida.

Author photograph by Brooke Vande Zande

LMReynolds.com
Facebook.com/LM.Reynolds.author
@LMReynoldsBooks

Made in the USA
Middletown, DE
10 July 2016